my LiTTLe PONY

Twilight's Kingdom

Publis
Printed
IDW Pub

Special thanks to Meghan McCarthy, Eliza Hart, Ed Lane,
Beth Artale, Heather Hopkins, and Michael Kelly.

ISBN: 978-1-68405-064-2
20 19 18 17   1 2 3 4
www.IDWPUBLISHING.com

IDW

Licensed By:
Hasbro

Ted Adams, CEO & Publisher
Greg Goldstein, President & COO
Robbie Robbins, EVP/Sr. Graphic Artist
Chris Ryall, Chief Creative Officer
David Hedgecock, Editor-in-Chief
Laurie Windrow, Senior Vice President of Sales & Marketing
Matthew Ruzicka, CPA, Chief Financial Officer
Lorelei Bunjes, VP of Digital Services
Jerry Bennington, VP of New Product Development

my LiTTLE PONY

Twilight's Kingdom

Written by
Meghan McCarthy

Adaptation by
Justin Eisinger

Edits by
Alonzo Simon

Lettering and Design by
Gilberto Lazcano

Production Assistance by
Amauri Osorio

MEET THE PONIES

Twilight Sparkle

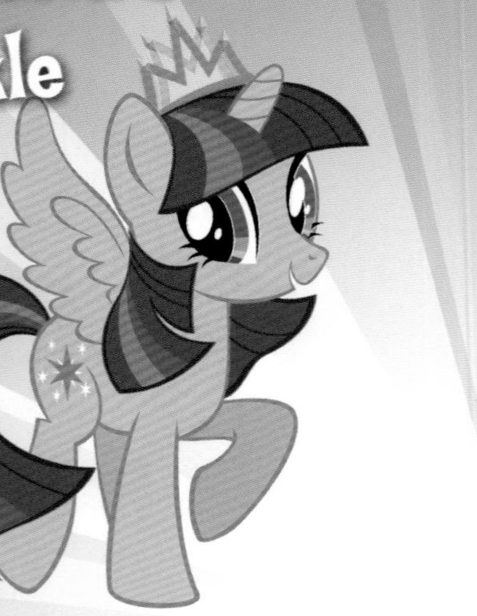

TWILIGHT SPARKLE TRIES TO FIND THE ANSWER TO EVERY QUESTION! WHETHER STUDYING A BOOK OR SPENDING TIME WITH PONY FRIENDS, SHE ALWAYS LEARNS SOMETHING NEW!

Spike

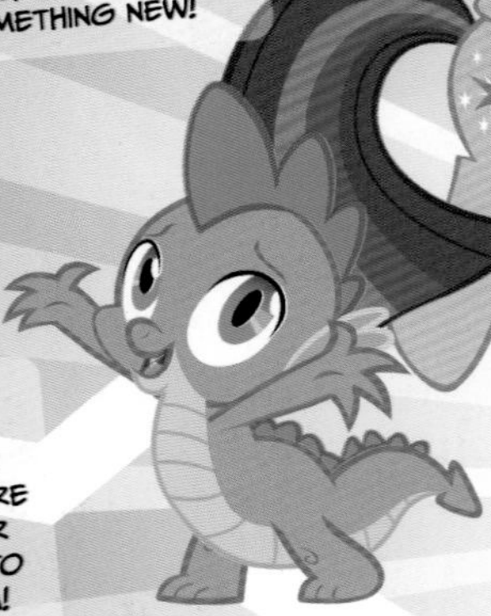

SPIKE IS TWILIGHT SPARKLE'S BEST FRIEND AND NUMBER ONE ASSISTANT. HIS FIRE BREATH CAN DELIVER SCROLLS DIRECTLY TO PRINCESS CELESTIA!

Applejack

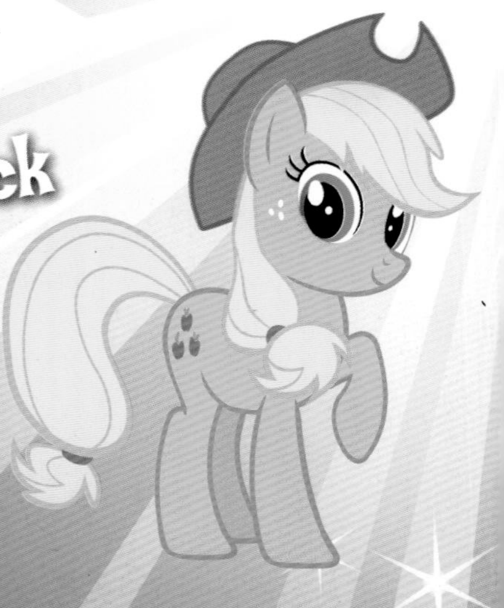

APPLEJACK IS HONEST, FRIENDLY, AND SWEET TO THE CORE! SHE LOVES TO BE OUTSIDE, AND HER PONY FRIENDS KNOW THEY CAN ALWAYS COUNT ON HER.

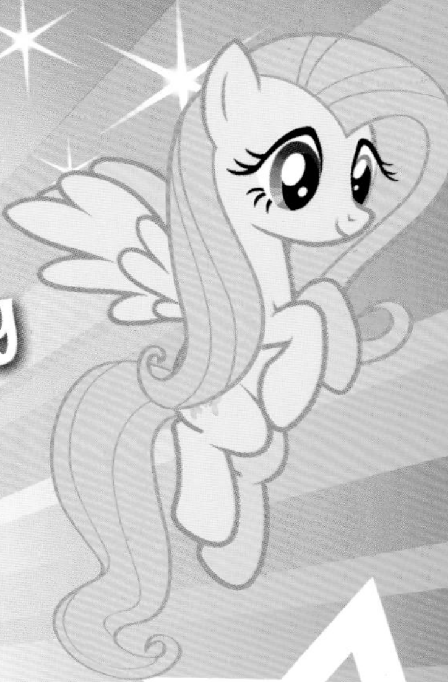

Fluttershy

FLUTTERSHY IS A KIND AND GENTLE PONY WITH A BIG HEART. SHE LIKES TO TAKE CARE OF OTHERS, ESPECIALLY HER LITTLE ANIMAL FRIENDS.

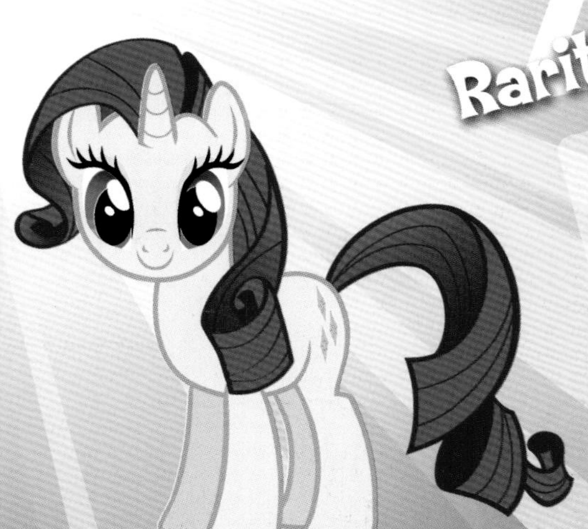

Rarity

RARITY KNOWS HOW TO ADD SPARKLE TO ANY OUTFIT! SHE LOVES TO GIVE HER PONY FRIENDS ADVICE ON THE LATEST PONY FASHIONS AND HAIRSTYLES.

Pinkie Pie

PINKIE PIE KEEPS HER PONY FRIENDS LAUGHING AND SMILING ALL DAY! CHEERFUL AND PLAYFUL, SHE ALWAYS LOOKS ON THE BRIGHT SIDE.

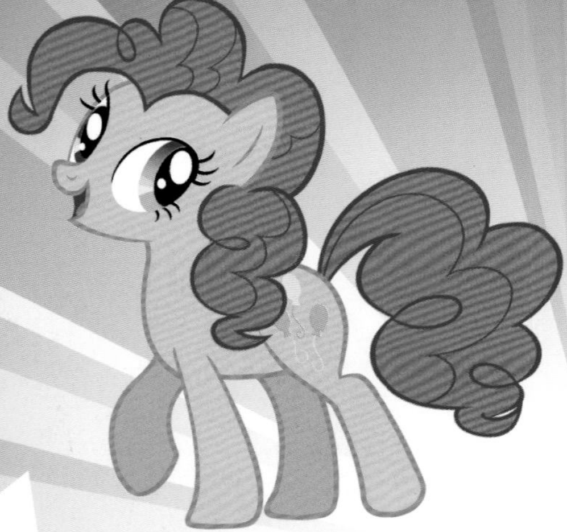

Rainbow Dash

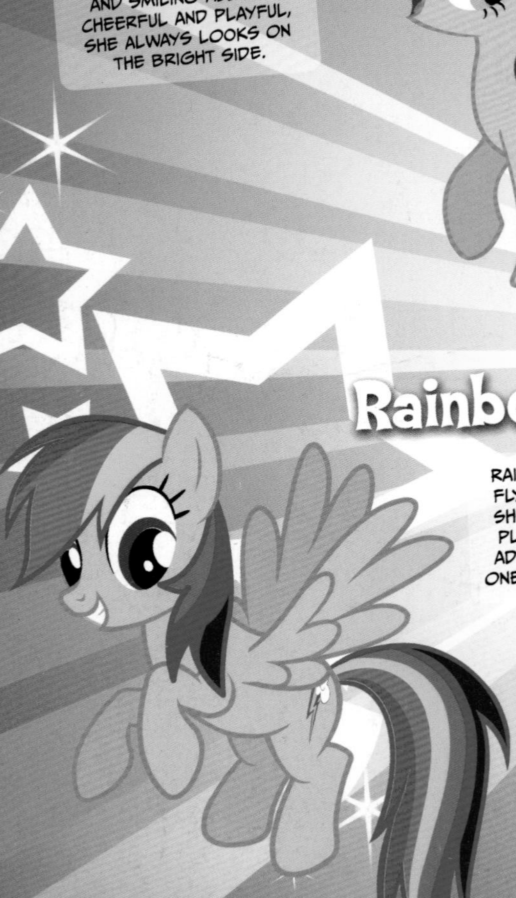

RAINBOW DASH LOVES TO FLY AS FAST AS SHE CAN! SHE IS ALWAYS READY TO PLAY A GAME, GO ON AN ADVENTURE, OR HELP OUT ONE OF HER PONY FRIENDS.

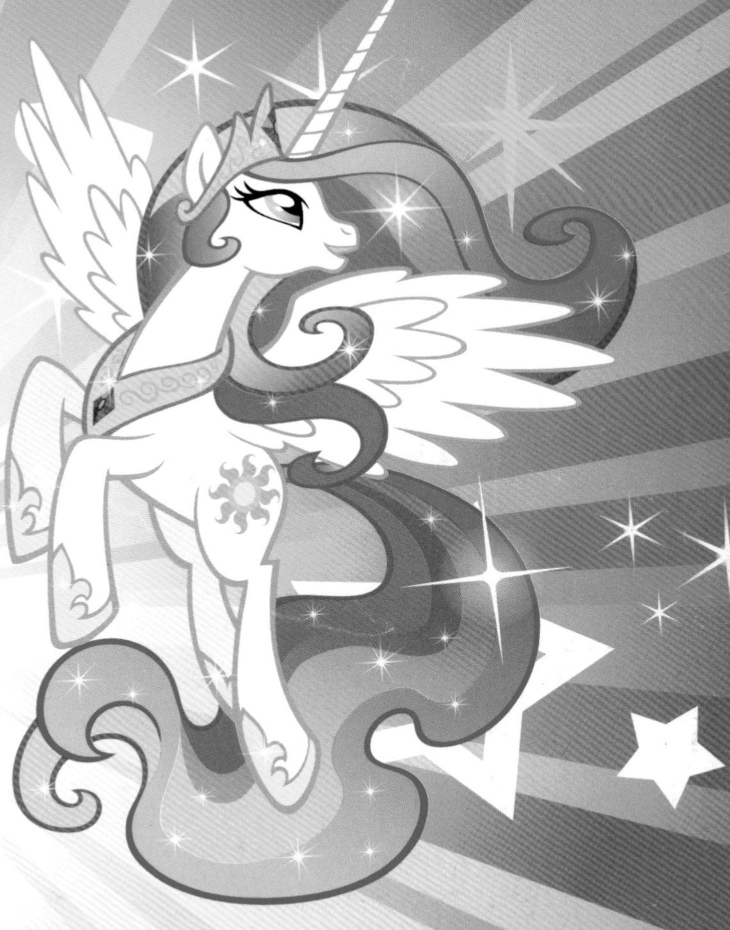

Princess Celestia

PRINCESS CELESTIA IS A MAGICAL AND BEAUTIFUL PONY WHO RULES THE LAND OF EQUESTRIA. ALL OF THE PONIES IN PONYVILLE LOOK UP TO HER!

Twilight's Kingdom

LIFE HAS RETURNED TO NORMAL AT CRYSTAL EMPIRE CASTLE...

...AND FRIENDS RETURN TO VISIT.

SEEMS LIKE ONLY YESTERDAY I WAS SAVING THIS PLACE FROM BEING TOTALLY DESTROYED.

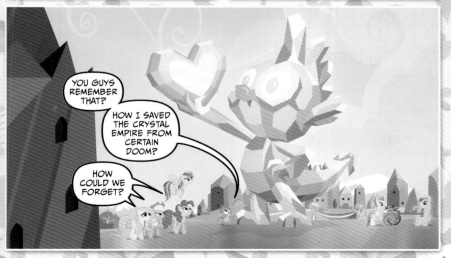

YOU GUYS REMEMBER THAT?

HOW I SAVED THE CRYSTAL EMPIRE FROM CERTAIN DOOM?

HOW COULD WE FORGET?

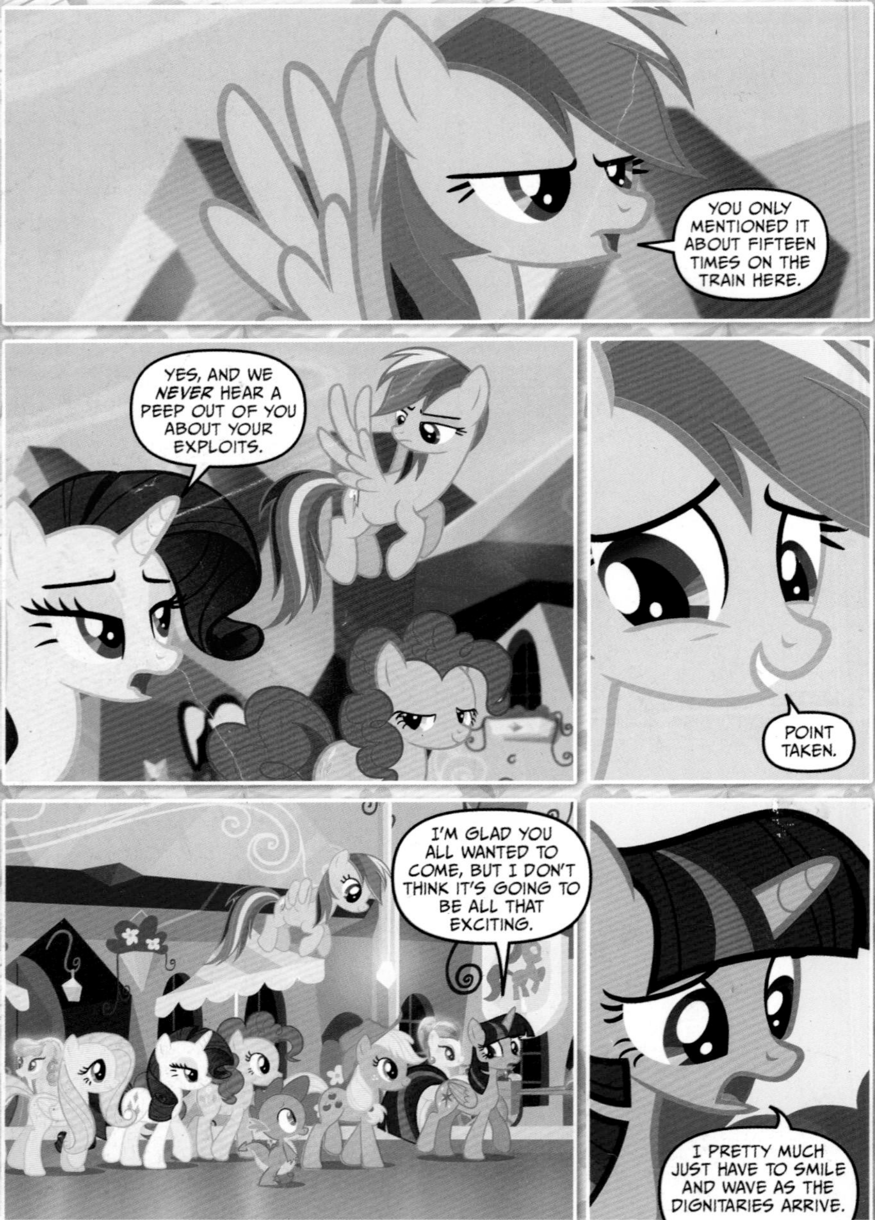
YOU ONLY MENTIONED IT ABOUT FIFTEEN TIMES ON THE TRAIN HERE.
YES, AND WE *NEVER* HEAR A PEEP OUT OF YOU ABOUT YOUR EXPLOITS.
POINT TAKEN.
I'M GLAD YOU ALL WANTED TO COME, BUT I DON'T THINK IT'S GOING TO BE ALL THAT EXCITING.
I PRETTY MUCH JUST HAVE TO SMILE AND WAVE AS THE DIGNITARIES ARRIVE.

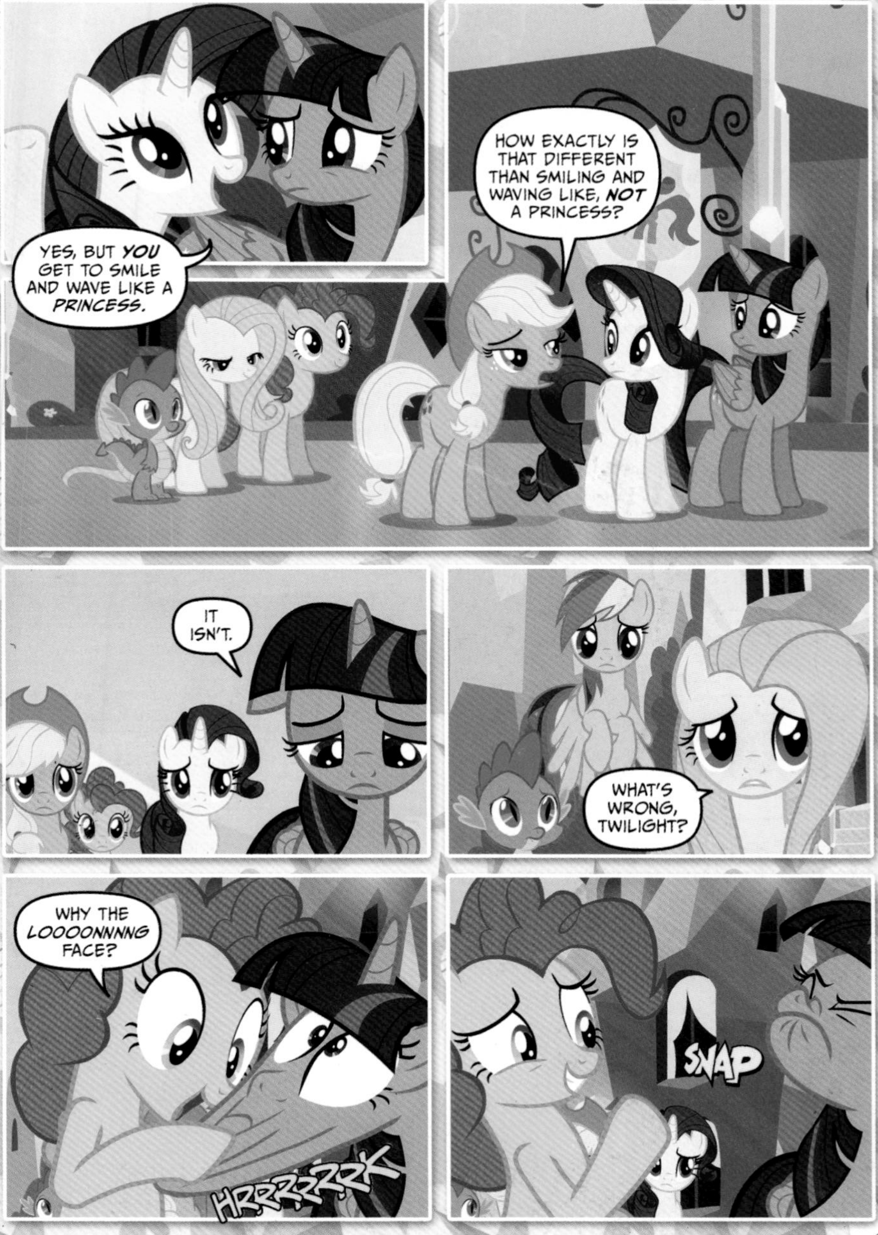
YES, BUT *YOU* GET TO SMILE AND WAVE LIKE A *PRINCESS.*
HOW EXACTLY IS THAT DIFFERENT THAN SMILING AND WAVING LIKE, ***NOT*** A PRINCESS?
IT ISN'T.
WHAT'S WRONG, TWILIGHT?
WHY THE *LOOOONNNNG* FACE?
HRRRRRRK
SNAP

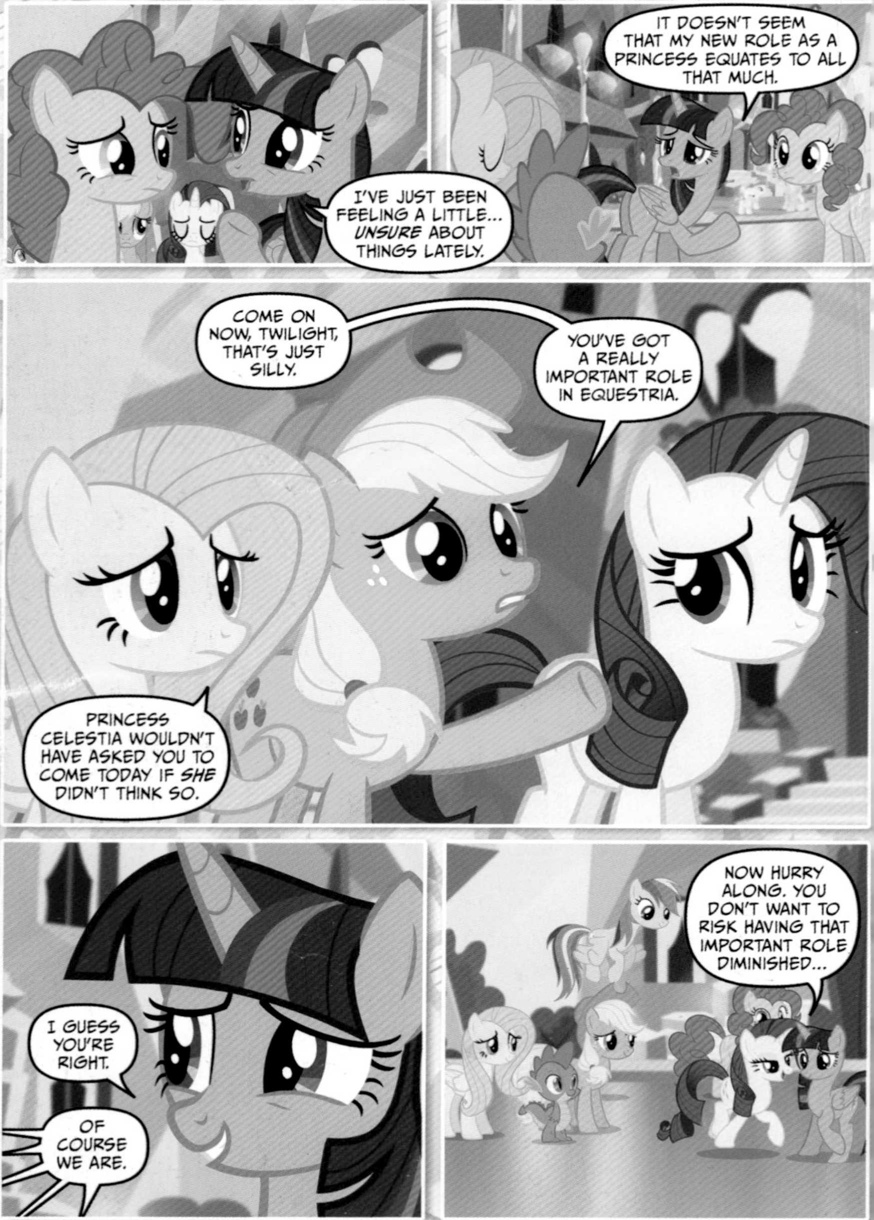
I'VE JUST BEEN FEELING A LITTLE... *UNSURE* ABOUT THINGS LATELY.
IT DOESN'T SEEM THAT MY NEW ROLE AS A PRINCESS EQUATES TO ALL THAT MUCH.
COME ON NOW, TWILIGHT, THAT'S JUST SILLY.
YOU'VE GOT A REALLY IMPORTANT ROLE IN EQUESTRIA.
PRINCESS CELESTIA WOULDN'T HAVE ASKED YOU TO COME TODAY IF *SHE* DIDN'T THINK SO.
I GUESS YOU'RE RIGHT.
OF COURSE WE ARE.
NOW HURRY ALONG. YOU DON'T WANT TO RISK HAVING THAT IMPORTANT ROLE DIMINISHED...

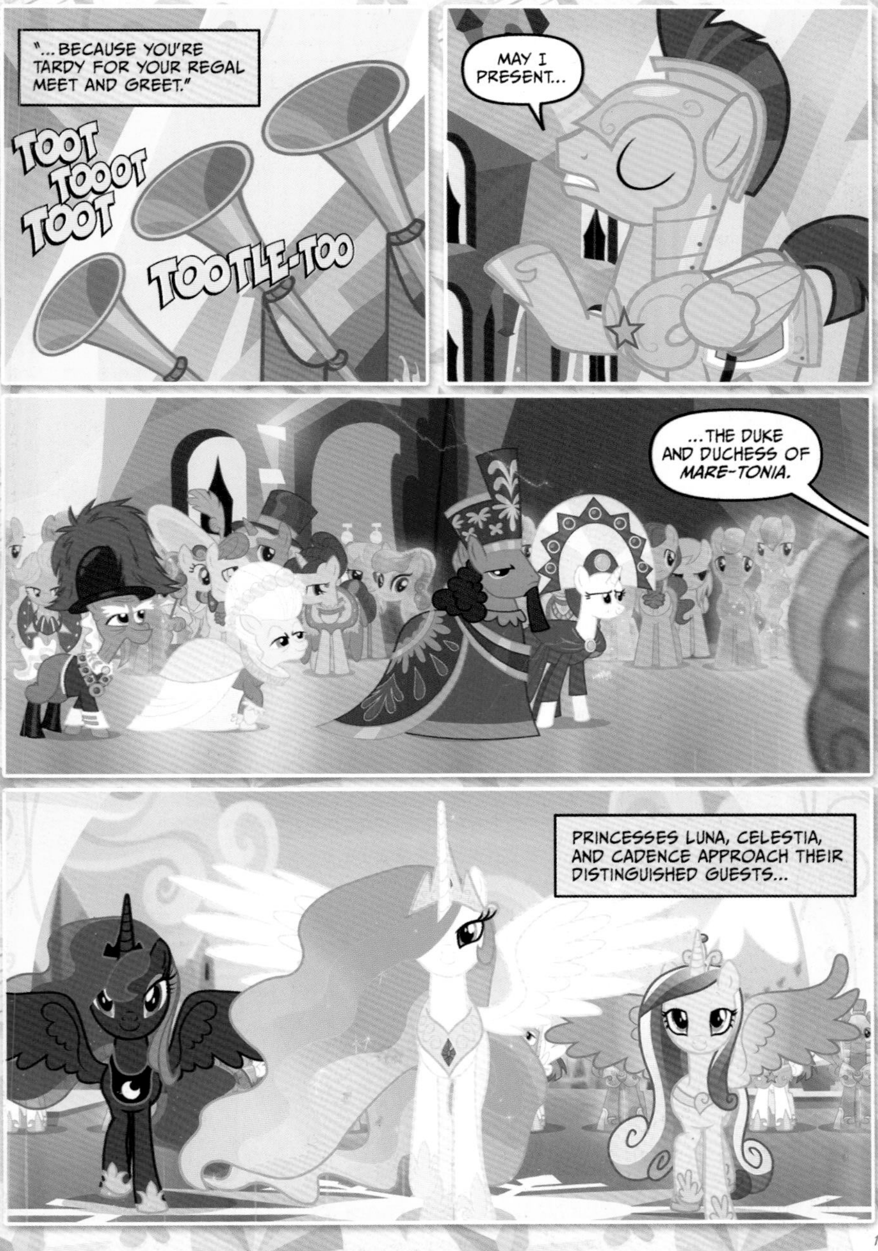

"...BECAUSE YOU'RE TARDY FOR YOUR REGAL MEET AND GREET."
TOOT TOOOT TOOT
TOOTLE-TOO
MAY I PRESENT...
...THE DUKE AND DUCHESS OF *MARE-TONIA.*
PRINCESSES LUNA, CELESTIA, AND CADENCE APPROACH THEIR DISTINGUISHED GUESTS...

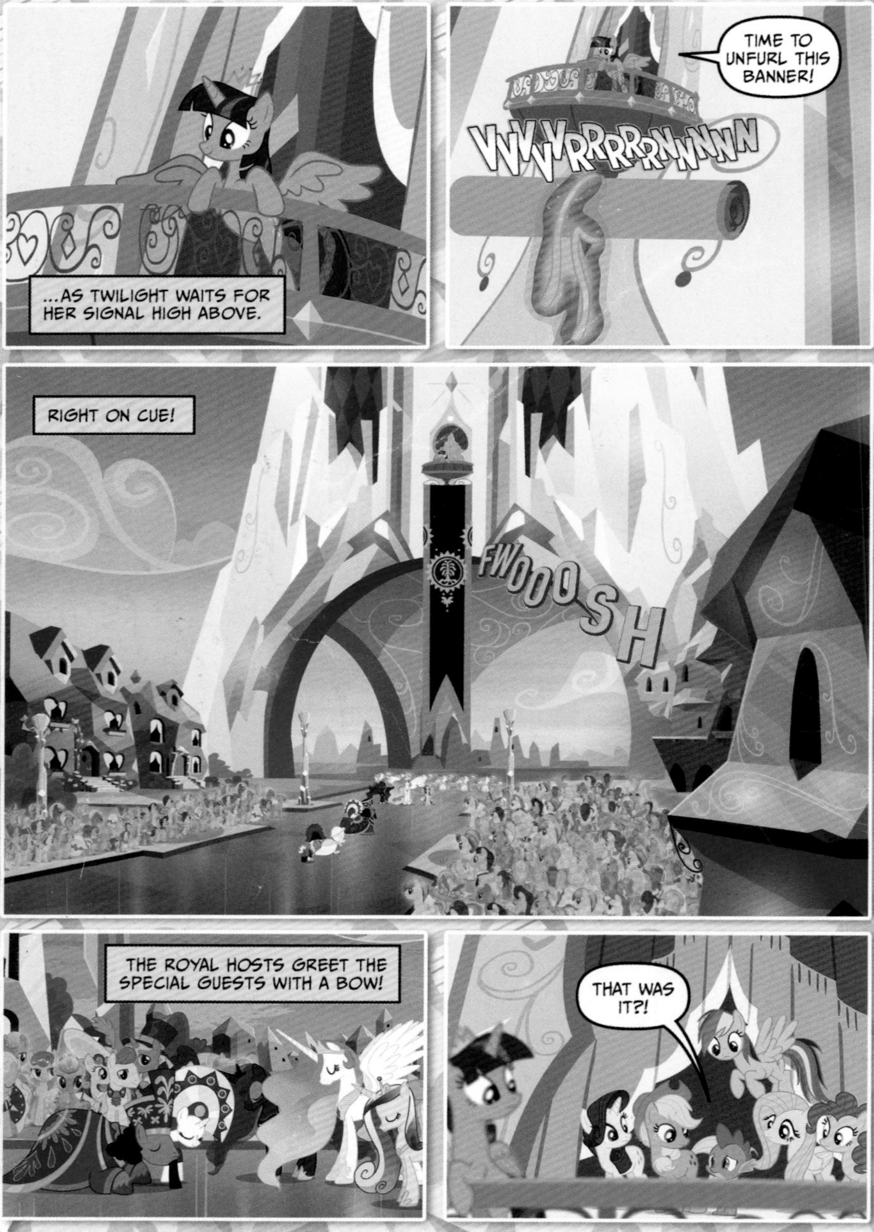
...AS TWILIGHT WAITS FOR HER SIGNAL HIGH ABOVE.
TIME TO UNFURL THIS BANNER!
VVVVVRRRRRNNNNN
RIGHT ON CUE!
FWOOOOSH
THE ROYAL HOSTS GREET THE SPECIAL GUESTS WITH A BOW!
THAT WAS IT?!

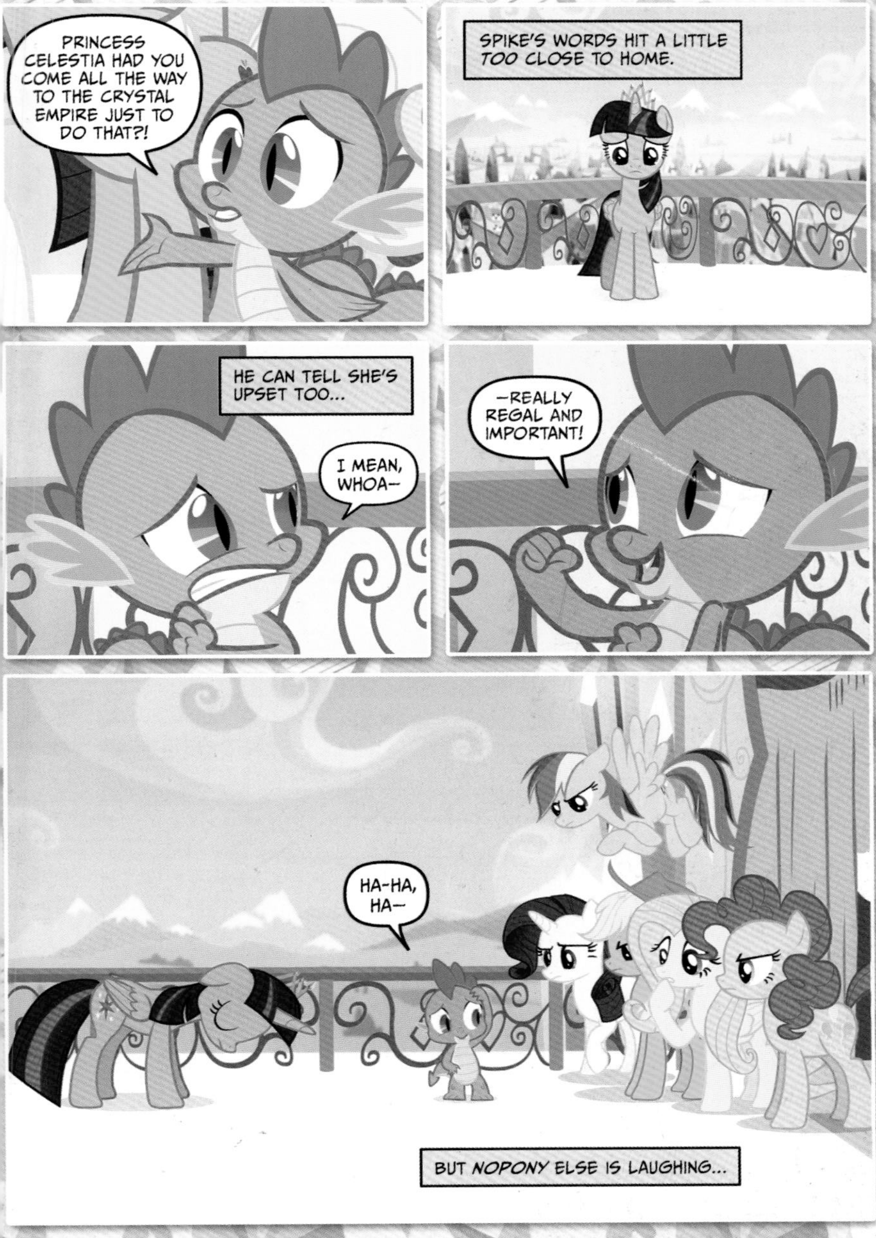
PRINCESS CELESTIA HAD YOU COME ALL THE WAY TO THE CRYSTAL EMPIRE JUST TO DO THAT?!
SPIKE'S WORDS HIT A LITTLE *TOO* CLOSE TO HOME.
HE CAN TELL SHE'S UPSET TOO...
I MEAN, WHOA—
—REALLY REGAL AND IMPORTANT!
HA-HA, HA—
BUT *NOPONY* ELSE IS LAUGHING...

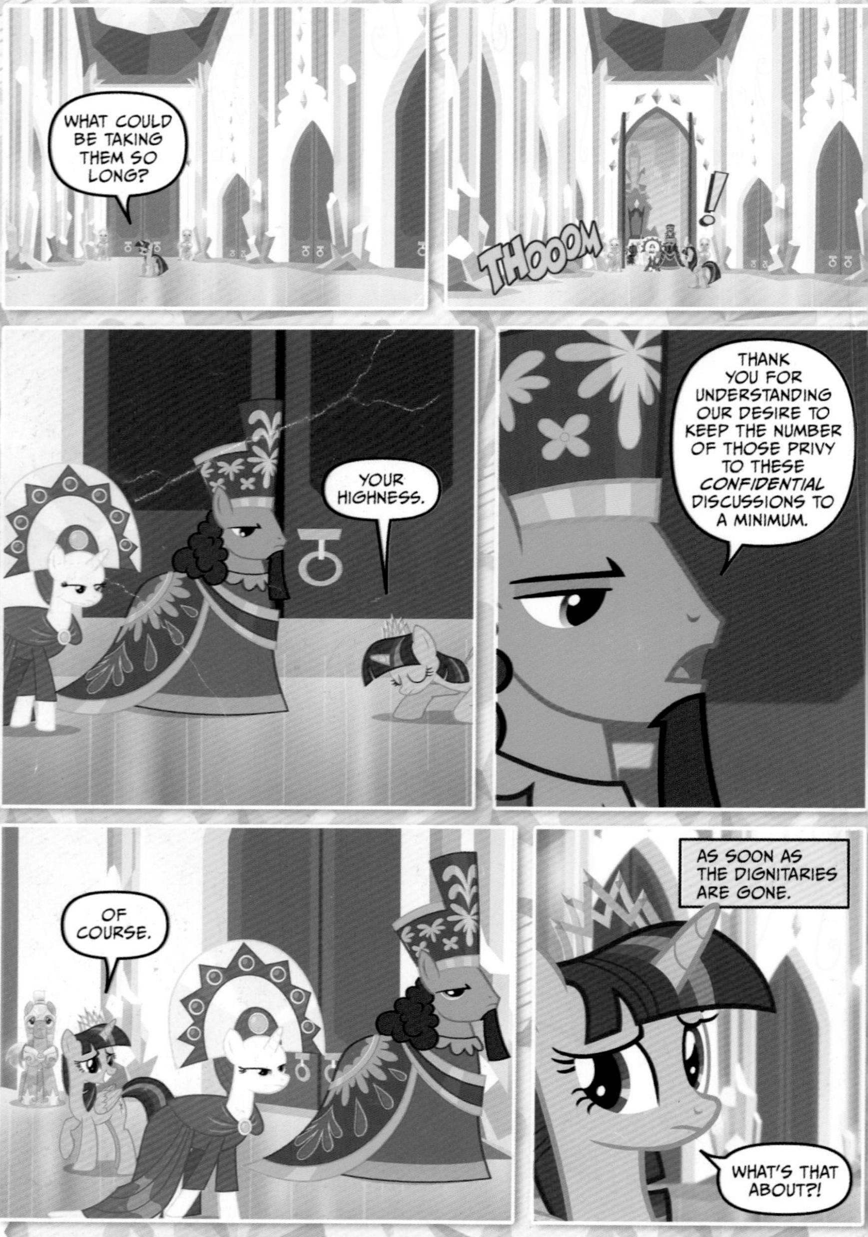
WHAT COULD BE TAKING THEM SO LONG?
THOOOM
!
YOUR HIGHNESS.
THANK YOU FOR UNDERSTANDING OUR DESIRE TO KEEP THE NUMBER OF THOSE PRIVY TO THESE *CONFIDENTIAL* DISCUSSIONS TO A MINIMUM.
OF COURSE.
AS SOON AS THE DIGNITARIES ARE GONE.
WHAT'S THAT ABOUT?!

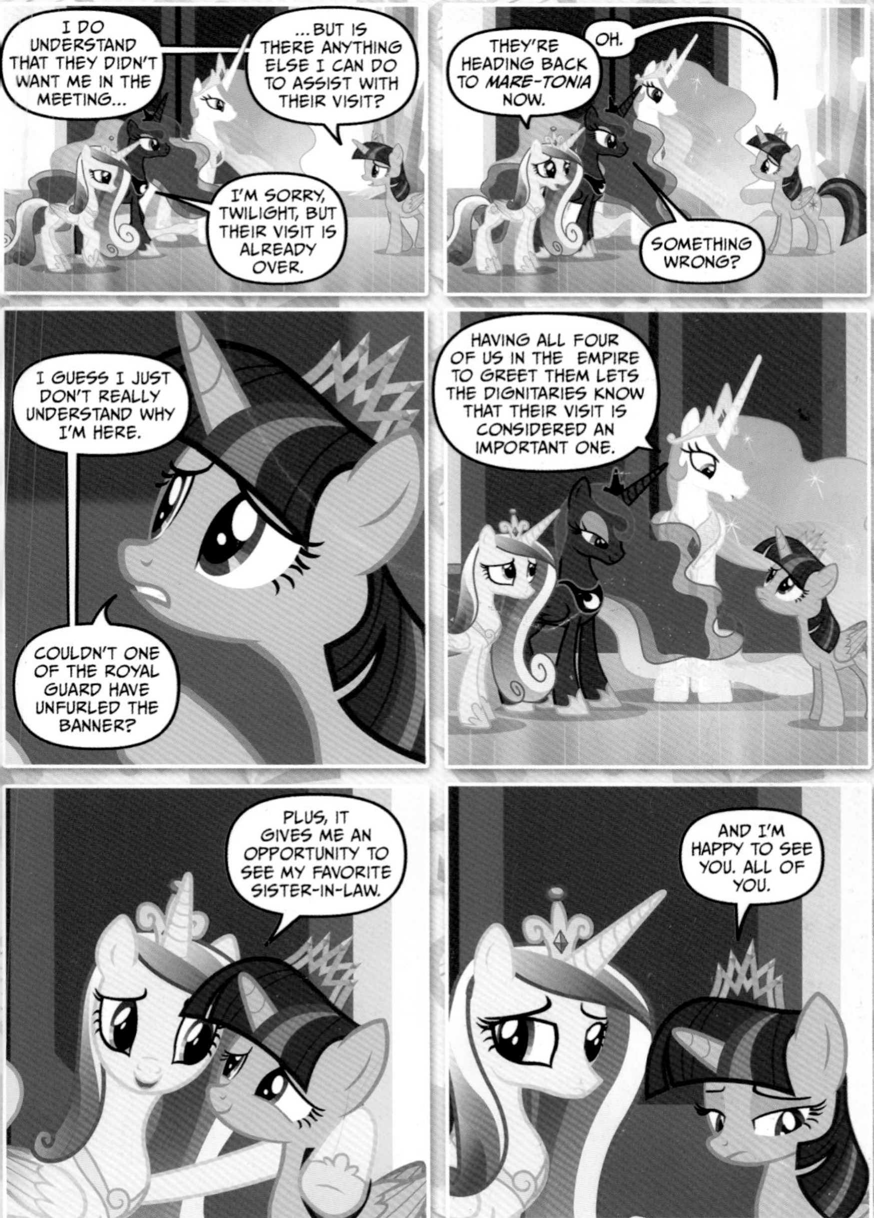
I DO UNDERSTAND THAT THEY DIDN'T WANT ME IN THE MEETING...
...BUT IS THERE ANYTHING ELSE I CAN DO TO ASSIST WITH THEIR VISIT?
I'M SORRY, TWILIGHT, BUT THEIR VISIT IS ALREADY OVER.
THEY'RE HEADING BACK TO *MARE-TONIA* NOW.
OH.
SOMETHING WRONG?
I GUESS I JUST DON'T REALLY UNDERSTAND WHY I'M HERE.
COULDN'T ONE OF THE ROYAL GUARD HAVE UNFURLED THE BANNER?
HAVING ALL FOUR OF US IN THE EMPIRE TO GREET THEM LETS THE DIGNITARIES KNOW THAT THEIR VISIT IS CONSIDERED AN IMPORTANT ONE.
PLUS, IT GIVES ME AN OPPORTUNITY TO SEE MY FAVORITE SISTER-IN-LAW.
AND I'M HAPPY TO SEE YOU. ALL OF YOU.

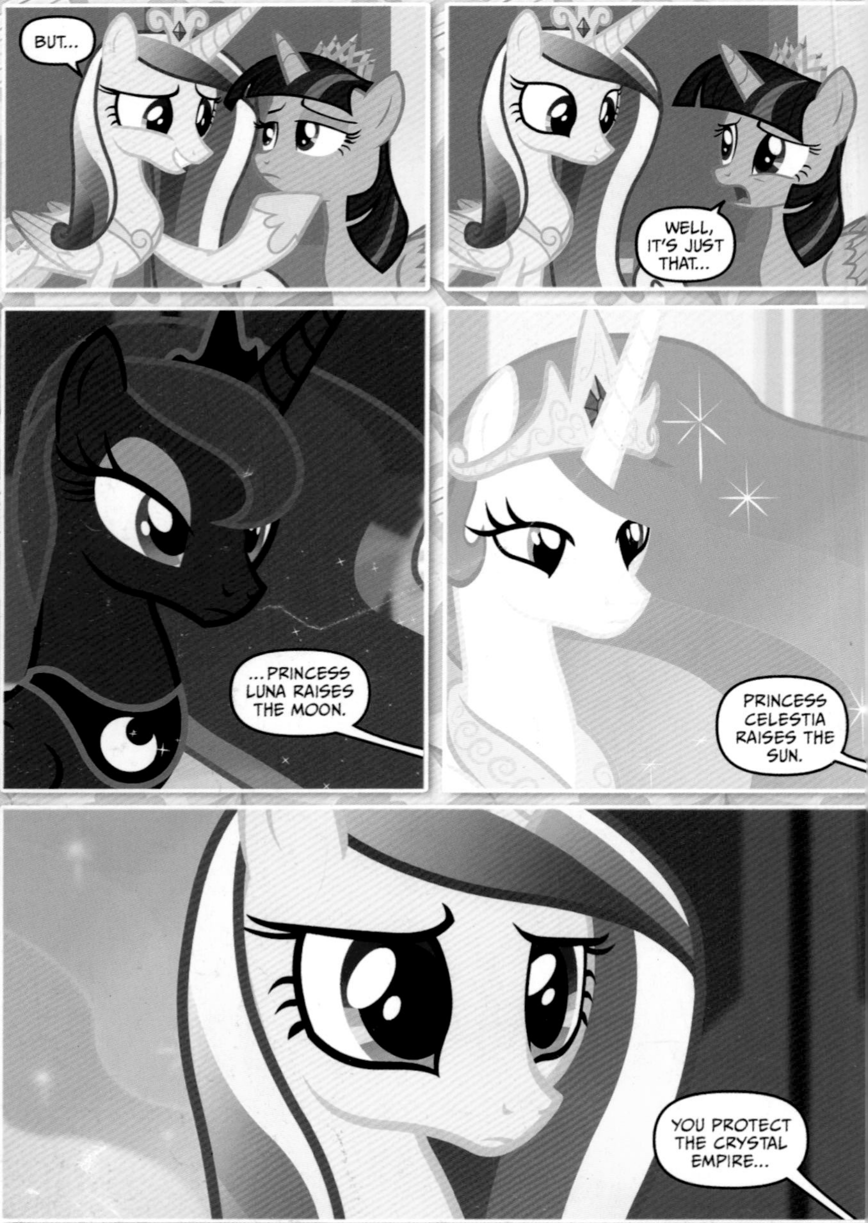
BUT...
WELL, IT'S JUST THAT...
...PRINCESS LUNA RAISES THE MOON.
PRINCESS CELESTIA RAISES THE SUN.
YOU PROTECT THE CRYSTAL EMPIRE...

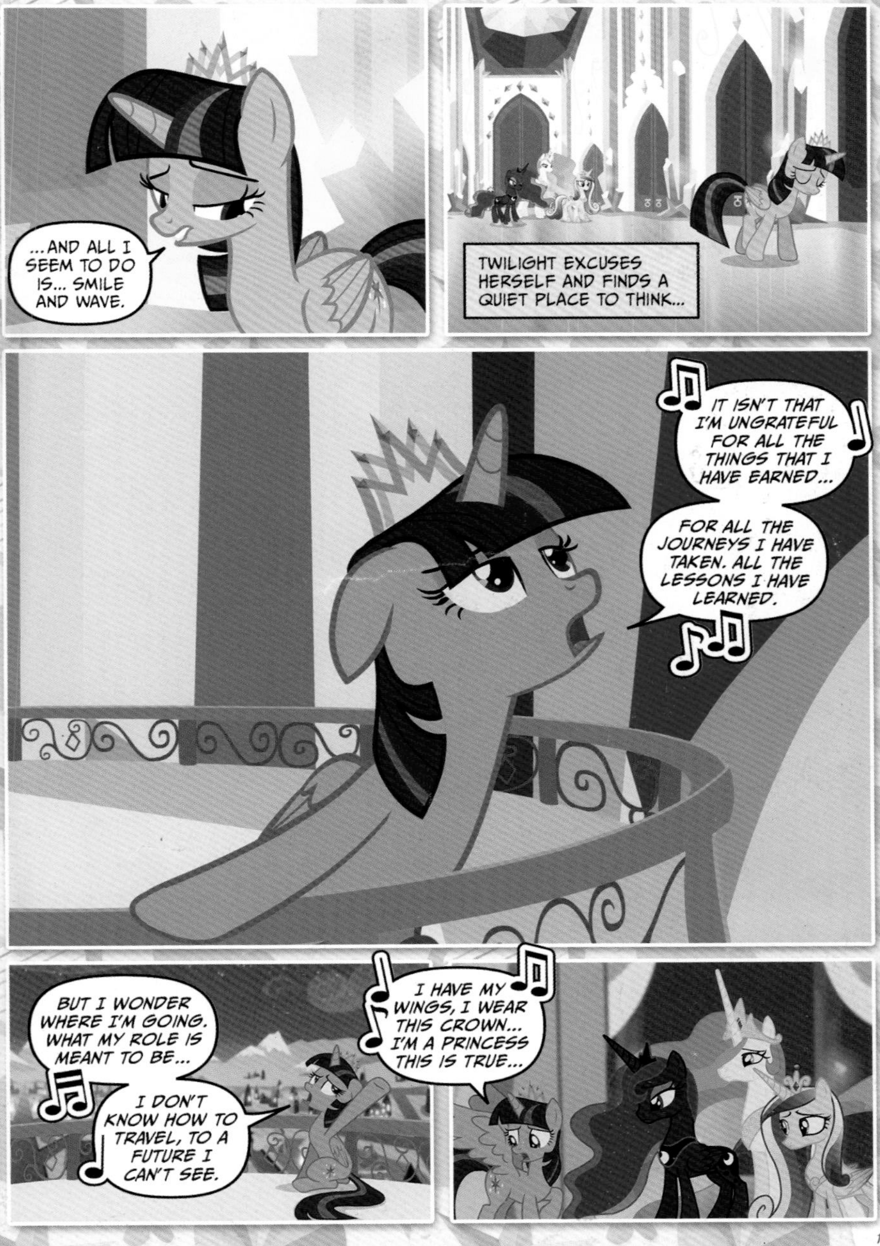
...AND ALL I SEEM TO DO IS... SMILE AND WAVE.
TWILIGHT EXCUSES HERSELF AND FINDS A QUIET PLACE TO THINK...
IT ISN'T THAT I'M UNGRATEFUL FOR ALL THE THINGS THAT I HAVE EARNED...
FOR ALL THE JOURNEYS I HAVE TAKEN. ALL THE LESSONS I HAVE LEARNED.
BUT I WONDER WHERE I'M GOING. WHAT MY ROLE IS MEANT TO BE...
I DON'T KNOW HOW TO TRAVEL, TO A FUTURE I CAN'T SEE.
I HAVE MY WINGS, I WEAR THIS CROWN... I'M A PRINCESS THIS IS TRUE...

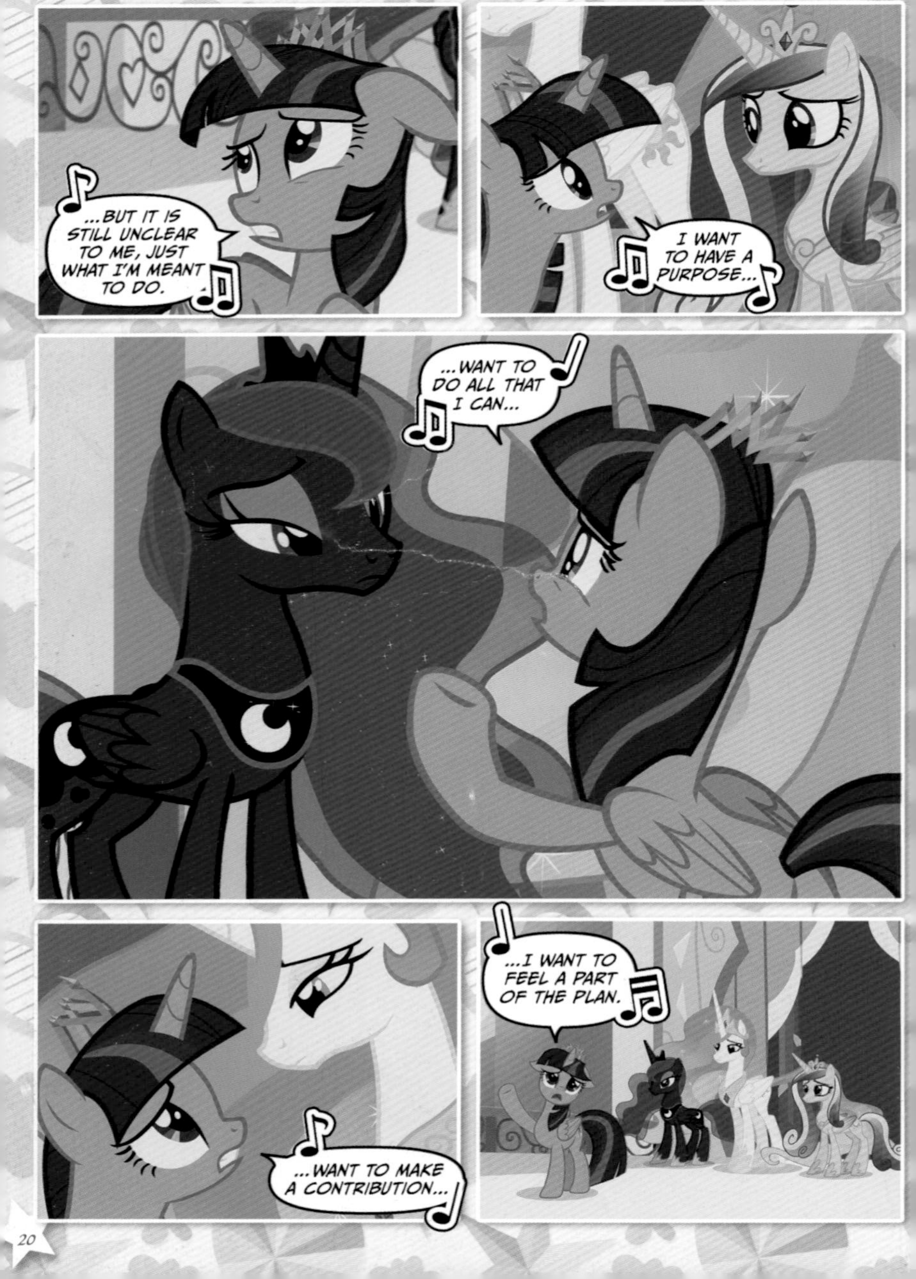

...BUT IT IS STILL UNCLEAR TO ME, JUST WHAT I'M MEANT TO DO.
I WANT TO HAVE A PURPOSE...
...WANT TO DO ALL THAT I CAN...
...WANT TO MAKE A CONTRIBUTION...
...I WANT TO FEEL A PART OF THE PLAN.

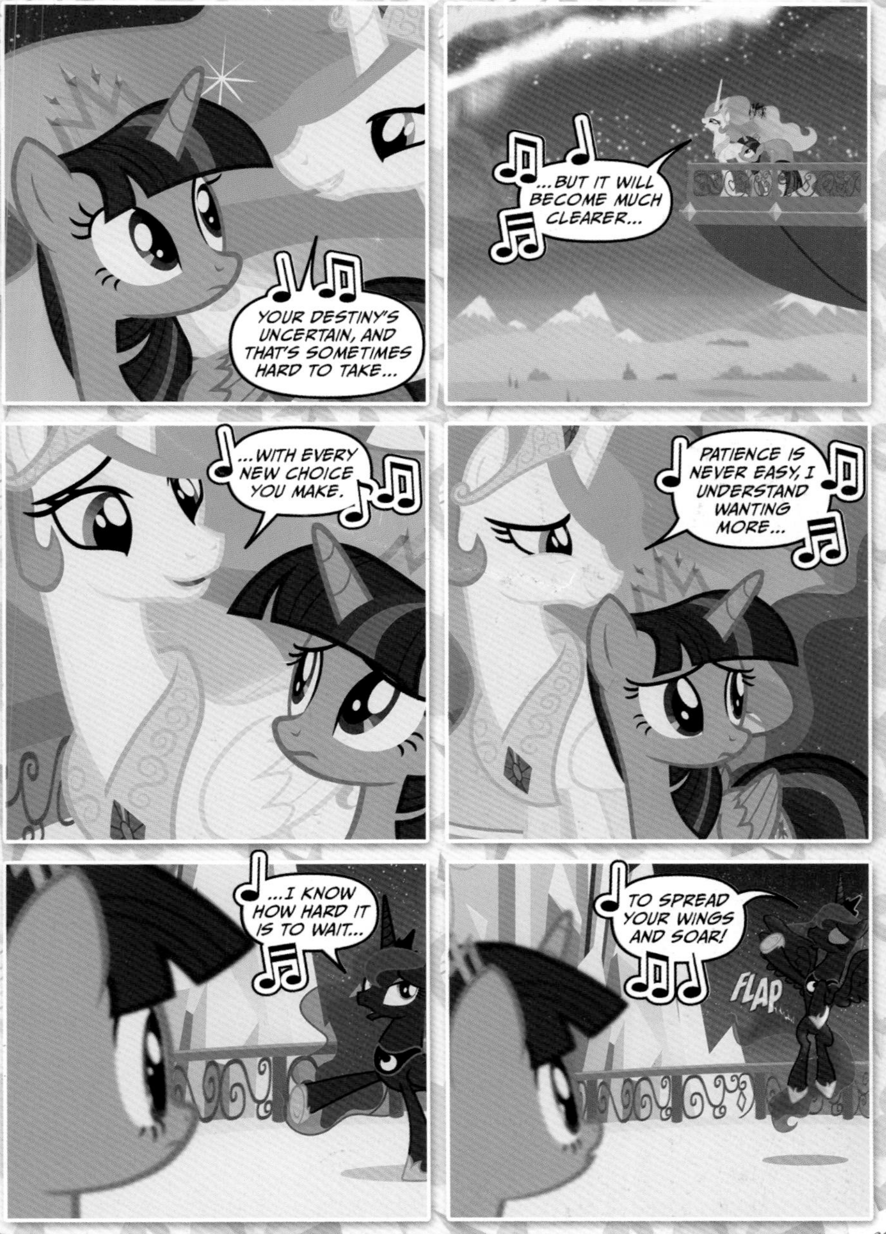
YOUR DESTINY'S UNCERTAIN, AND THAT'S SOMETIMES HARD TO TAKE...
...BUT IT WILL BECOME MUCH CLEARER...
...WITH EVERY NEW CHOICE YOU MAKE.
PATIENCE IS NEVER EASY, I UNDERSTAND WANTING MORE...
...I KNOW HOW HARD IT IS TO WAIT...
TO SPREAD YOUR WINGS AND SOAR!
FLAP

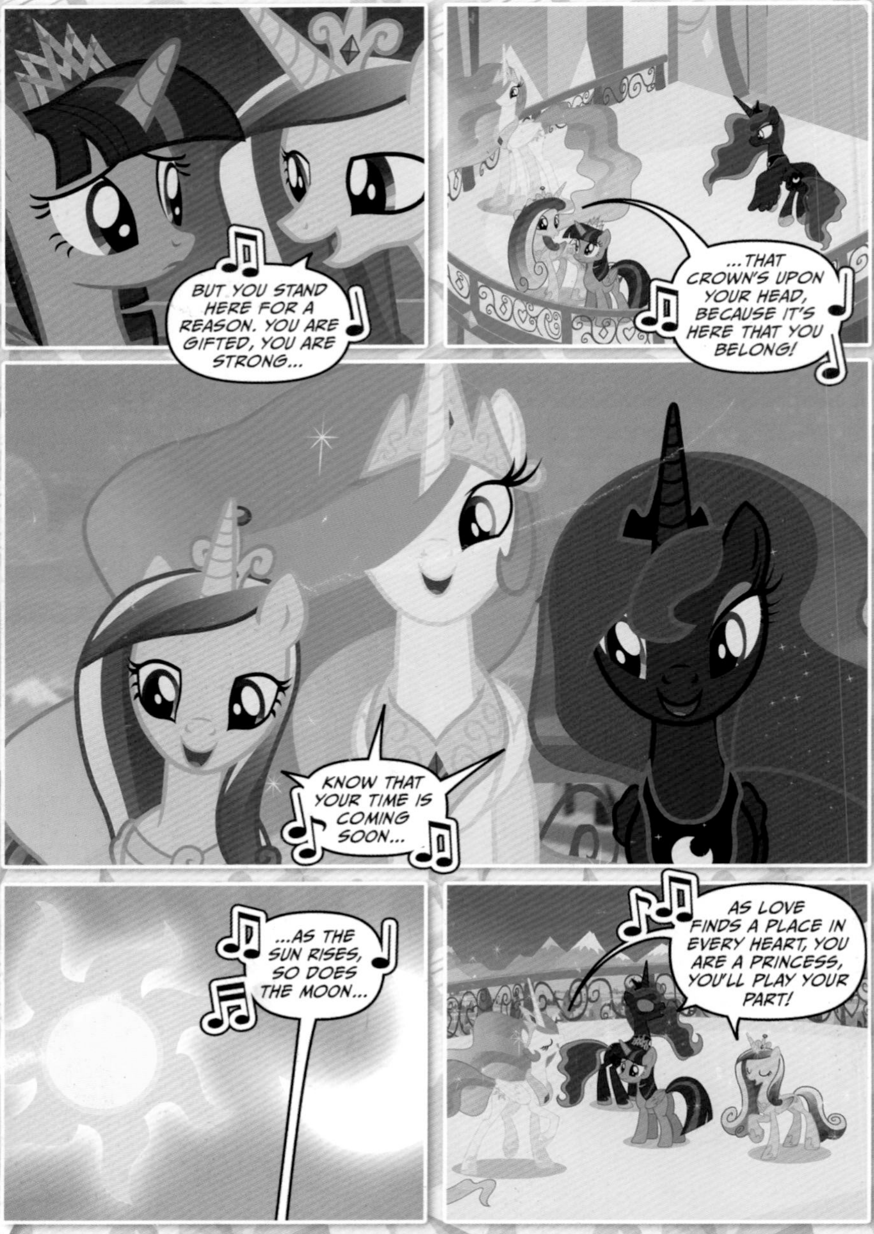
BUT YOU STAND HERE FOR A REASON. YOU ARE GIFTED, YOU ARE STRONG...
...THAT CROWN'S UPON YOUR HEAD, BECAUSE IT'S HERE THAT YOU BELONG!
KNOW THAT YOUR TIME IS COMING SOON...
...AS THE SUN RISES, SO DOES THE MOON...
AS LOVE FINDS A PLACE IN EVERY HEART, YOU ARE A PRINCESS, YOU'LL PLAY YOUR PART!

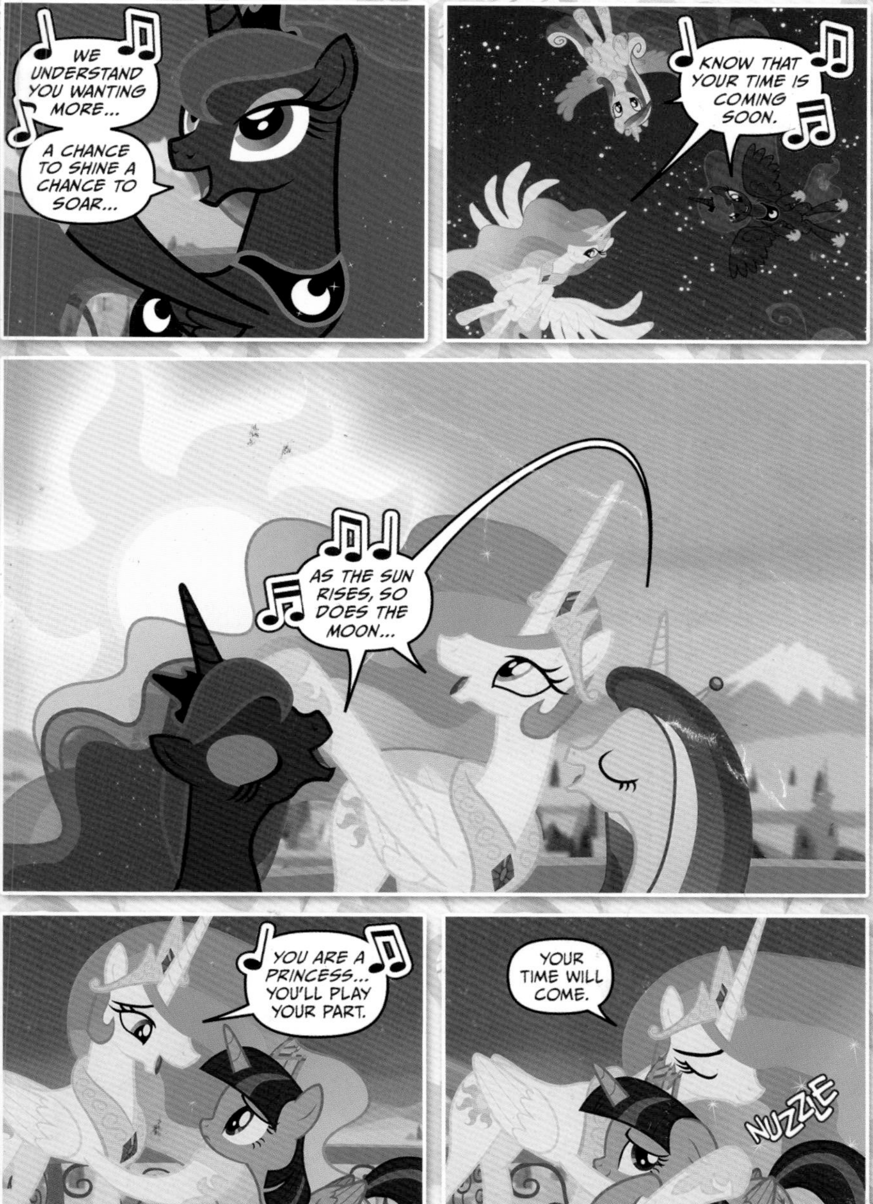

WE UNDERSTAND YOU WANTING MORE...
A CHANCE TO SHINE A CHANCE TO SOAR...
KNOW THAT YOUR TIME IS COMING SOON.
AS THE SUN RISES, SO DOES THE MOON...
YOU ARE A PRINCESS... YOU'LL PLAY YOUR PART.
YOUR TIME WILL COME.
NUZZLE

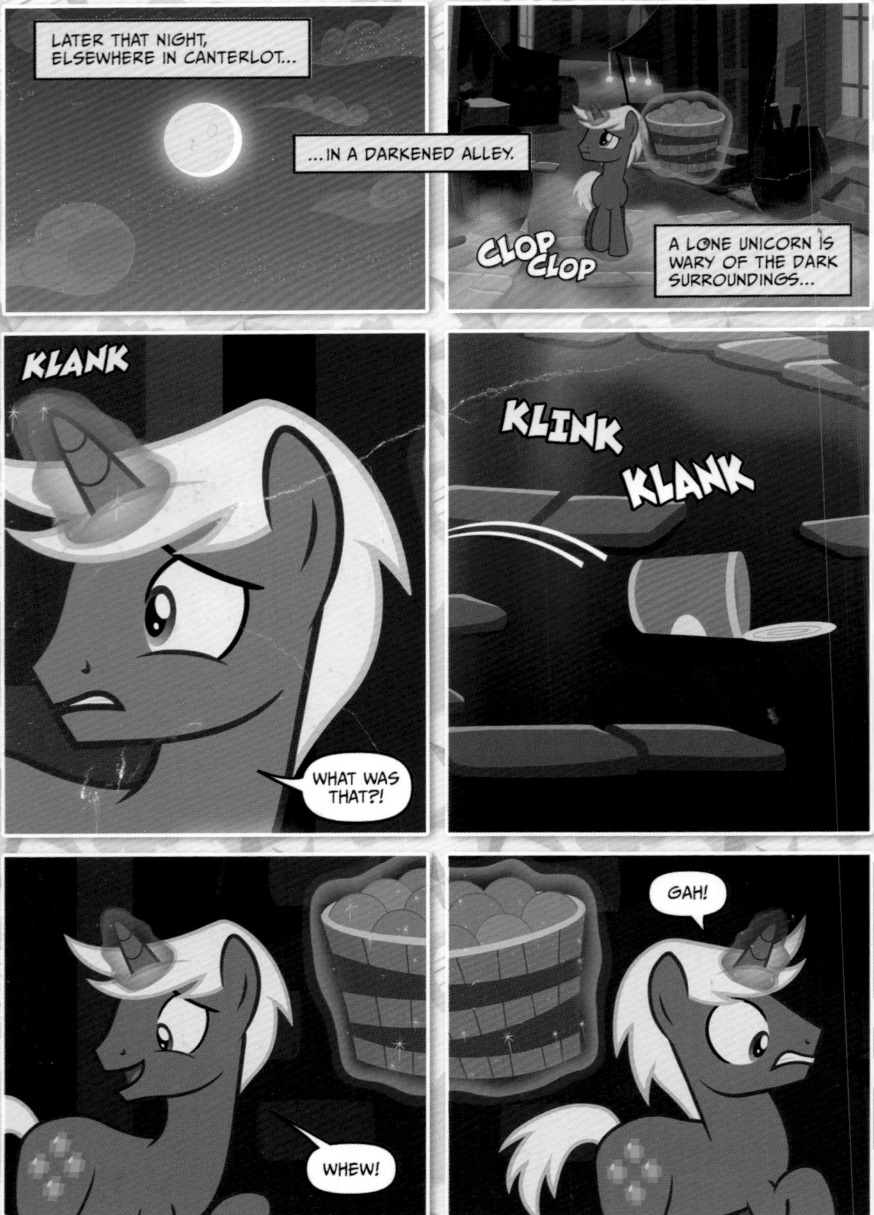
LATER THAT NIGHT, ELSEWHERE IN CANTERLOT...
...IN A DARKENED ALLEY.
CLOP CLOP
A LONE UNICORN IS WARY OF THE DARK SURROUNDINGS...
KLANK
WHAT WAS THAT?!
KLINK
KLANK
WHEW!
GAH!

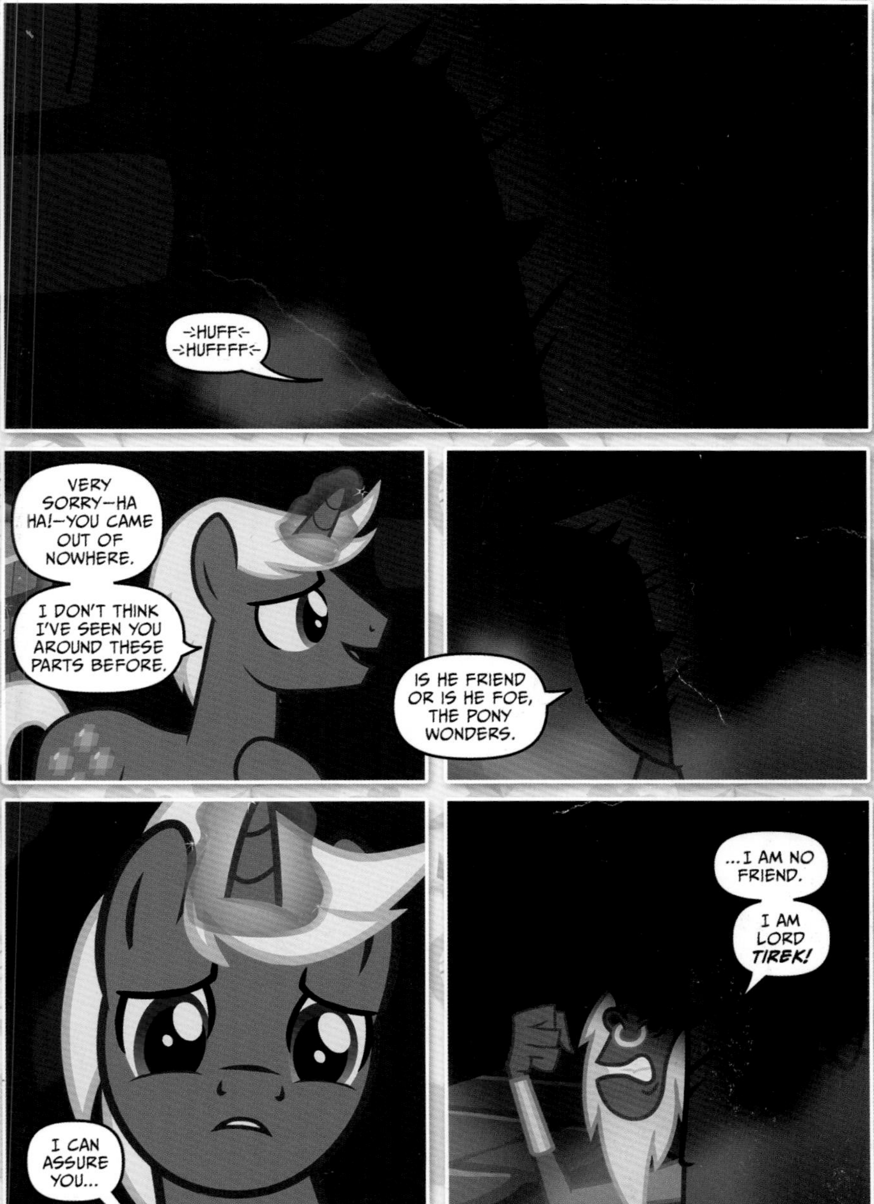

-HUFF- -HUFFFFF-
VERY SORRY—HA HA!—YOU CAME OUT OF NOWHERE.
I DON'T THINK I'VE SEEN YOU AROUND THESE PARTS BEFORE.
IS HE FRIEND OR IS HE FOE, THE PONY WONDERS.
I CAN ASSURE YOU...
...I AM NO FRIEND.
I AM LORD TIREK!

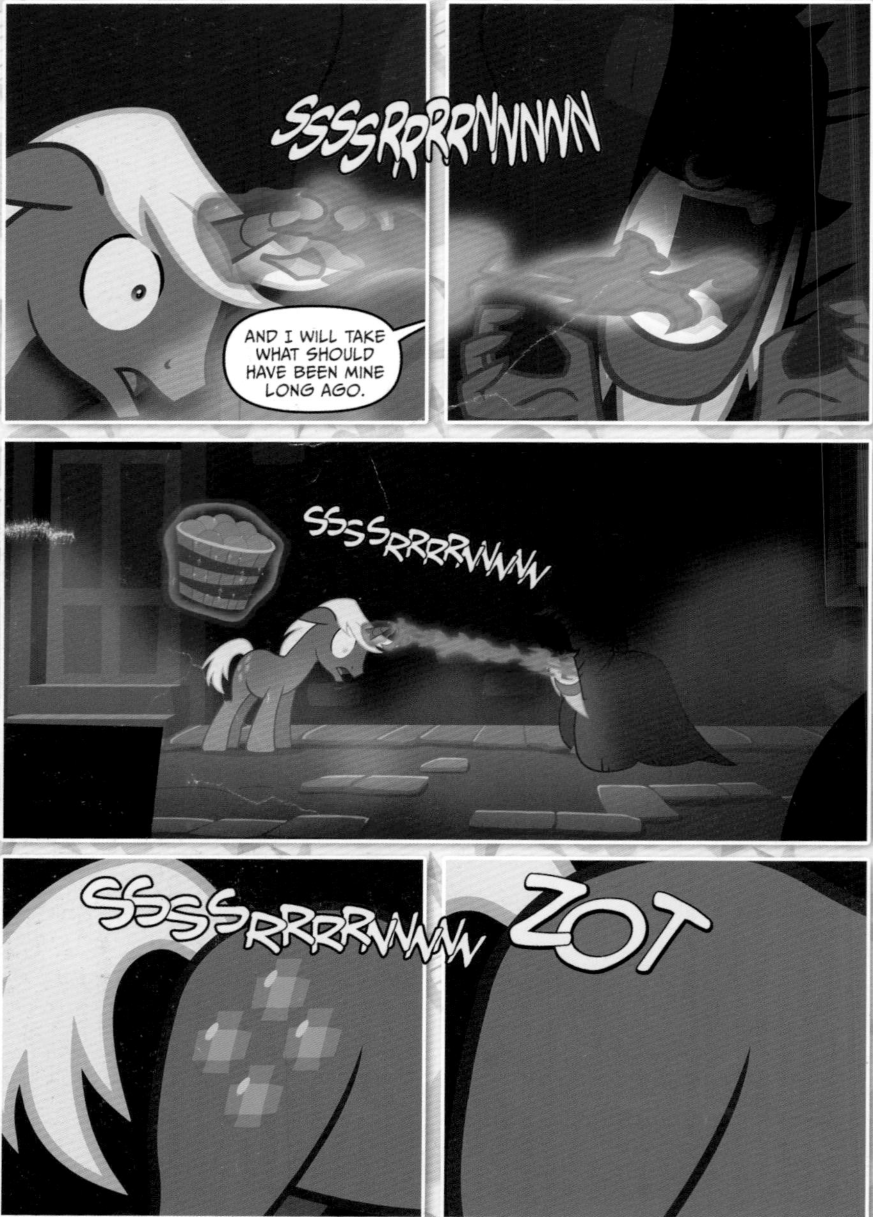
SSSSRRRRNNNNN
AND I WILL TAKE WHAT SHOULD HAVE BEEN MINE LONG AGO.
SSSSRRRRNNNNN
SSSSSRRRRNNNNN
ZOT

THUMP

AS THE CUTIE MARKS FADE...

WHAM

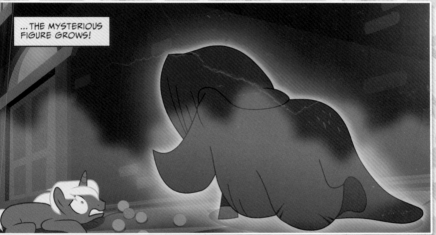

...THE MYSTERIOUS FIGURE GROWS!

BWHA WHA WHA!

BWHA WHA WHA HA

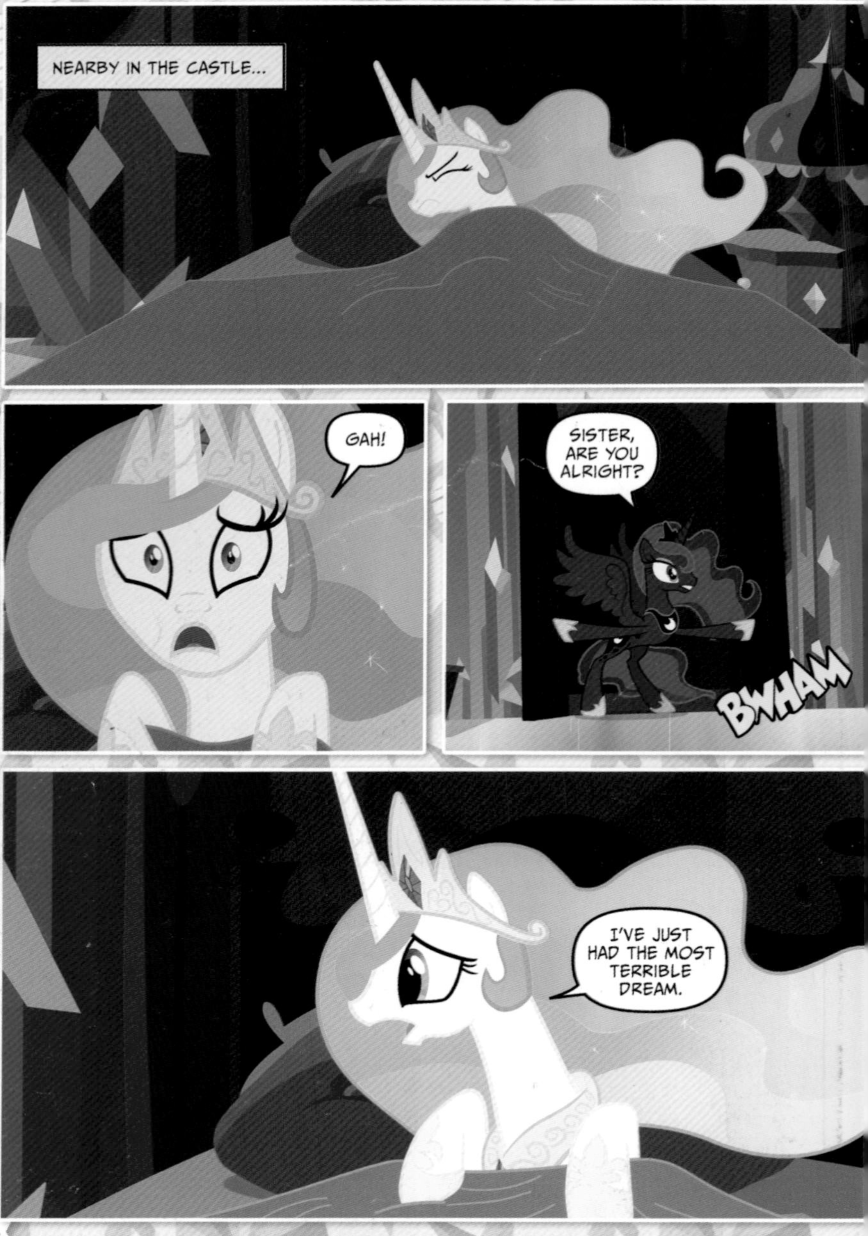
NEARBY IN THE CASTLE...
GAH!
SISTER, ARE YOU ALRIGHT?
BWHAM
I'VE JUST HAD THE MOST TERRIBLE DREAM.

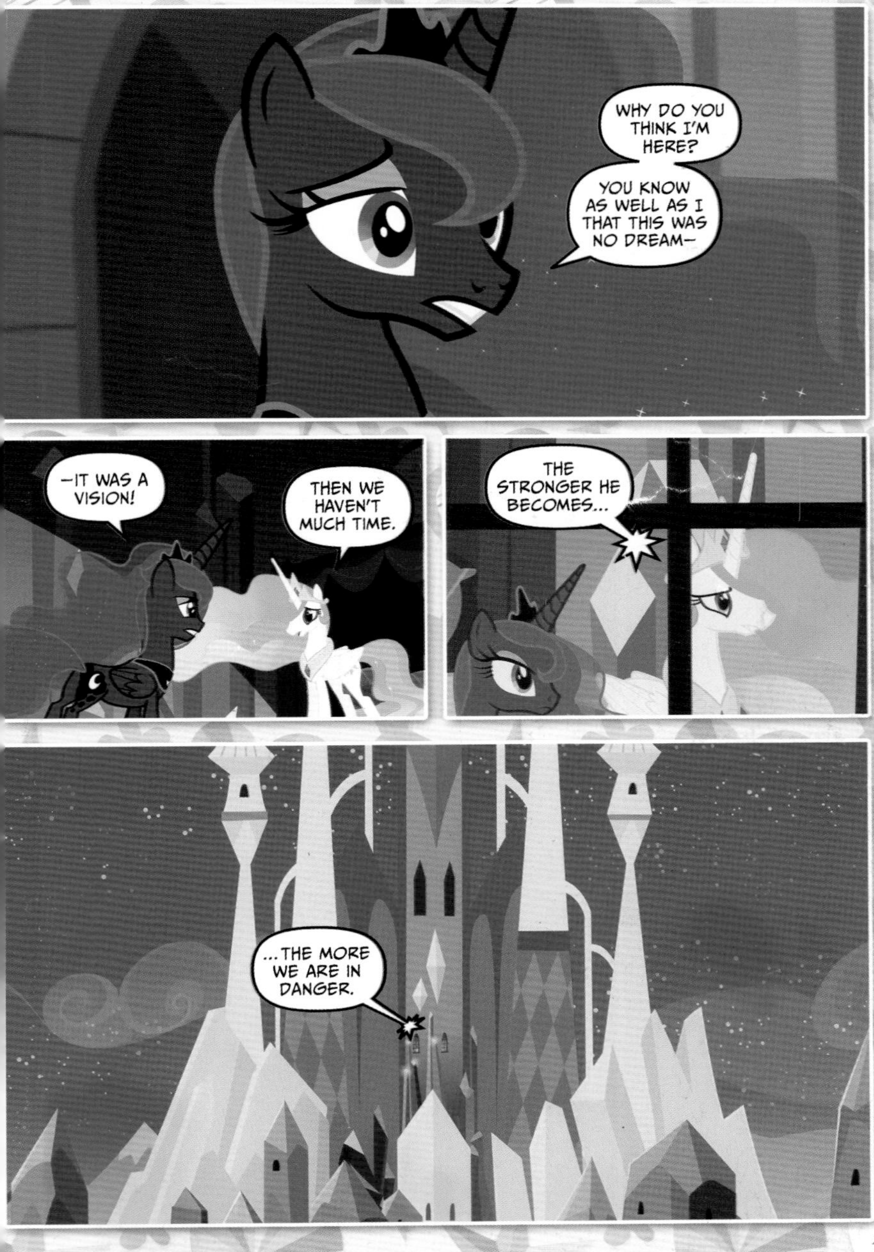
WHY DO YOU THINK I'M HERE?
YOU KNOW AS WELL AS I THAT THIS WAS NO DREAM–
–IT WAS A VISION!
THEN WE HAVEN'T MUCH TIME.
THE STRONGER HE BECOMES...
...THE MORE WE ARE IN DANGER.

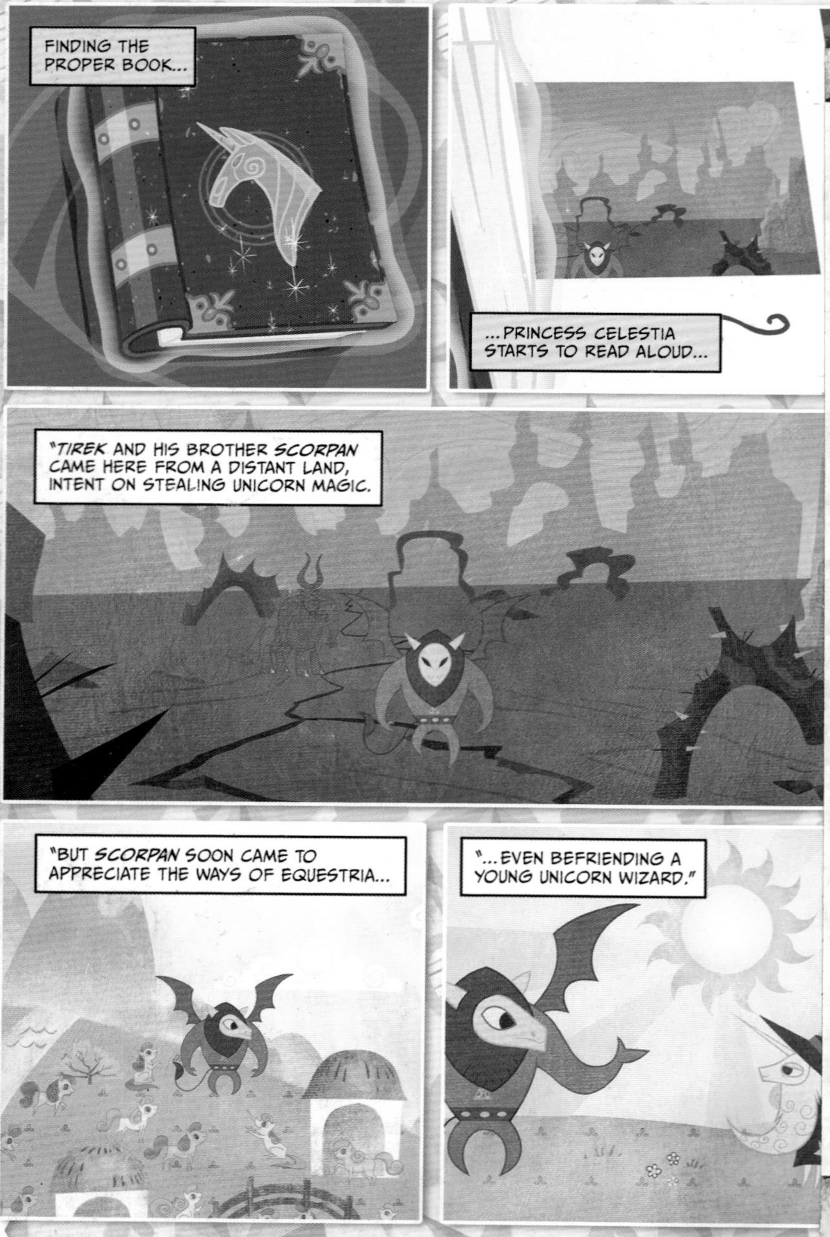
FINDING THE PROPER BOOK...
...PRINCESS CELESTIA STARTS TO READ ALOUD...
"TIREK AND HIS BROTHER SCORPAN CAME HERE FROM A DISTANT LAND, INTENT ON STEALING UNICORN MAGIC.
"BUT SCORPAN SOON CAME TO APPRECIATE THE WAYS OF EQUESTRIA...
"...EVEN BEFRIENDING A YOUNG UNICORN WIZARD."

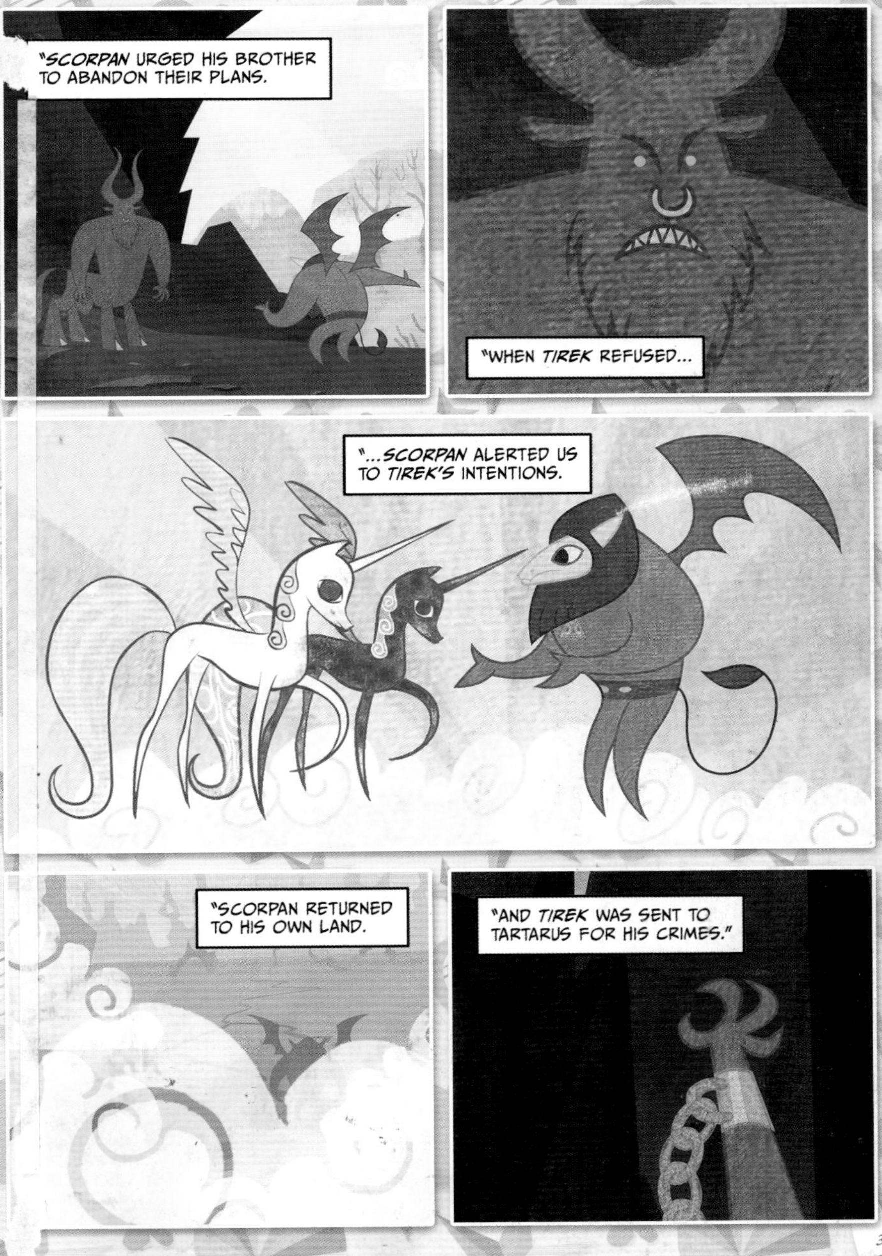
"SCORPAN URGED HIS BROTHER TO ABANDON THEIR PLANS.
"WHEN TIREK REFUSED...
"...SCORPAN ALERTED US TO TIREK'S INTENTIONS.
"SCORPAN RETURNED TO HIS OWN LAND.
"AND TIREK WAS SENT TO TARTARUS FOR HIS CRIMES."

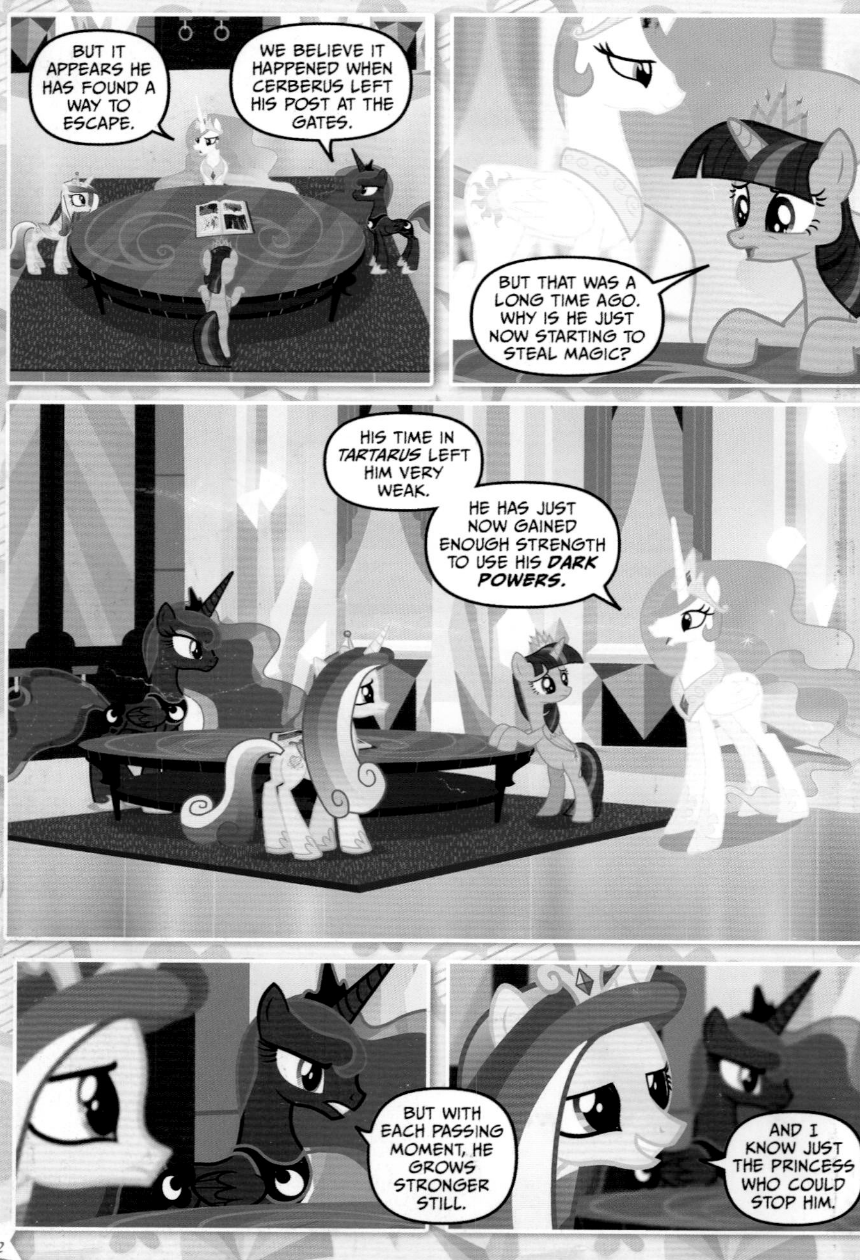
BUT IT APPEARS HE HAS FOUND A WAY TO ESCAPE.
WE BELIEVE IT HAPPENED WHEN CERBERUS LEFT HIS POST AT THE GATES.
BUT THAT WAS A LONG TIME AGO. WHY IS HE JUST NOW STARTING TO STEAL MAGIC?
HIS TIME IN *TARTARUS* LEFT HIM VERY WEAK.
HE HAS JUST NOW GAINED ENOUGH STRENGTH TO USE HIS ***DARK POWERS.***
BUT WITH EACH PASSING MOMENT, HE GROWS STRONGER STILL.
AND I KNOW JUST THE PRINCESS WHO COULD STOP HIM.

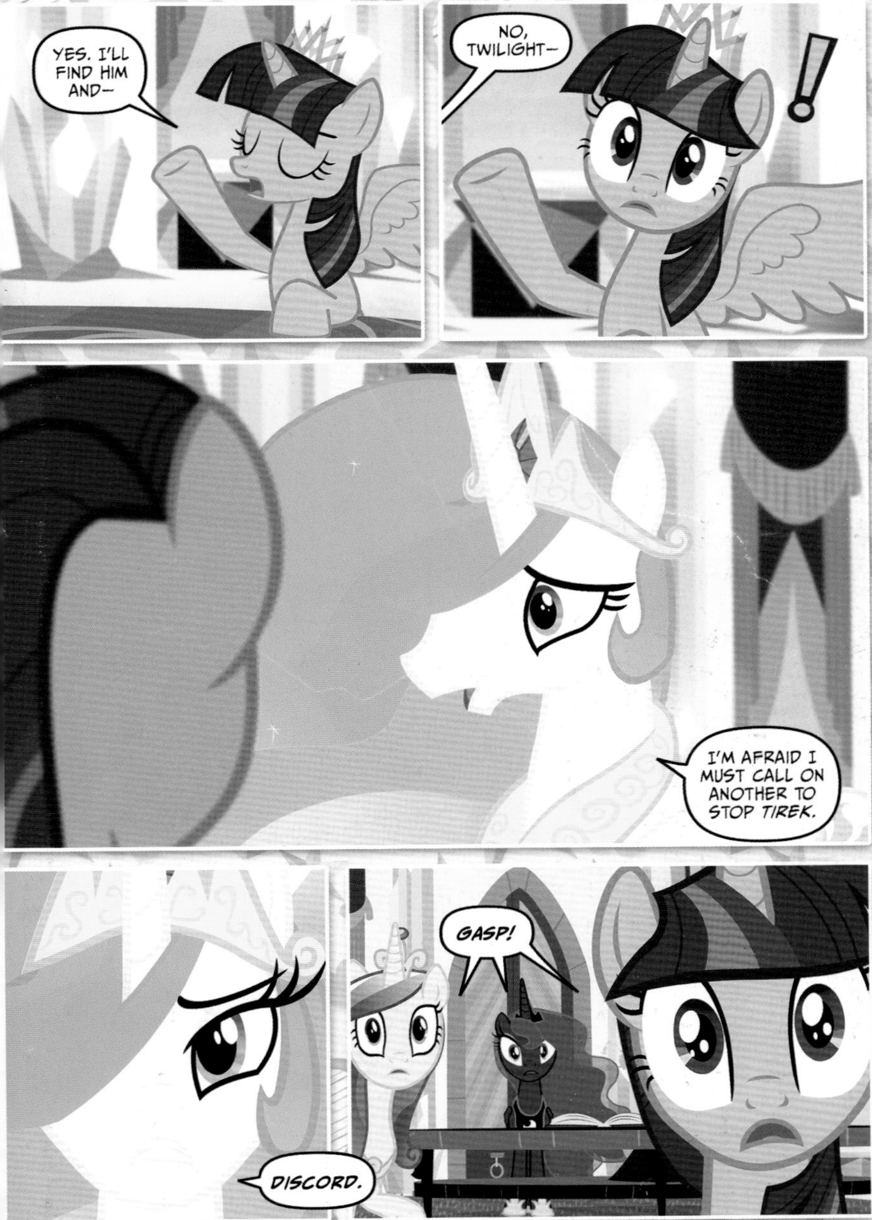

YES. I'LL FIND HIM AND—
NO, TWILIGHT—
!
I'M AFRAID I MUST CALL ON ANOTHER TO STOP *TIREK.*
DISCORD.
GASP!

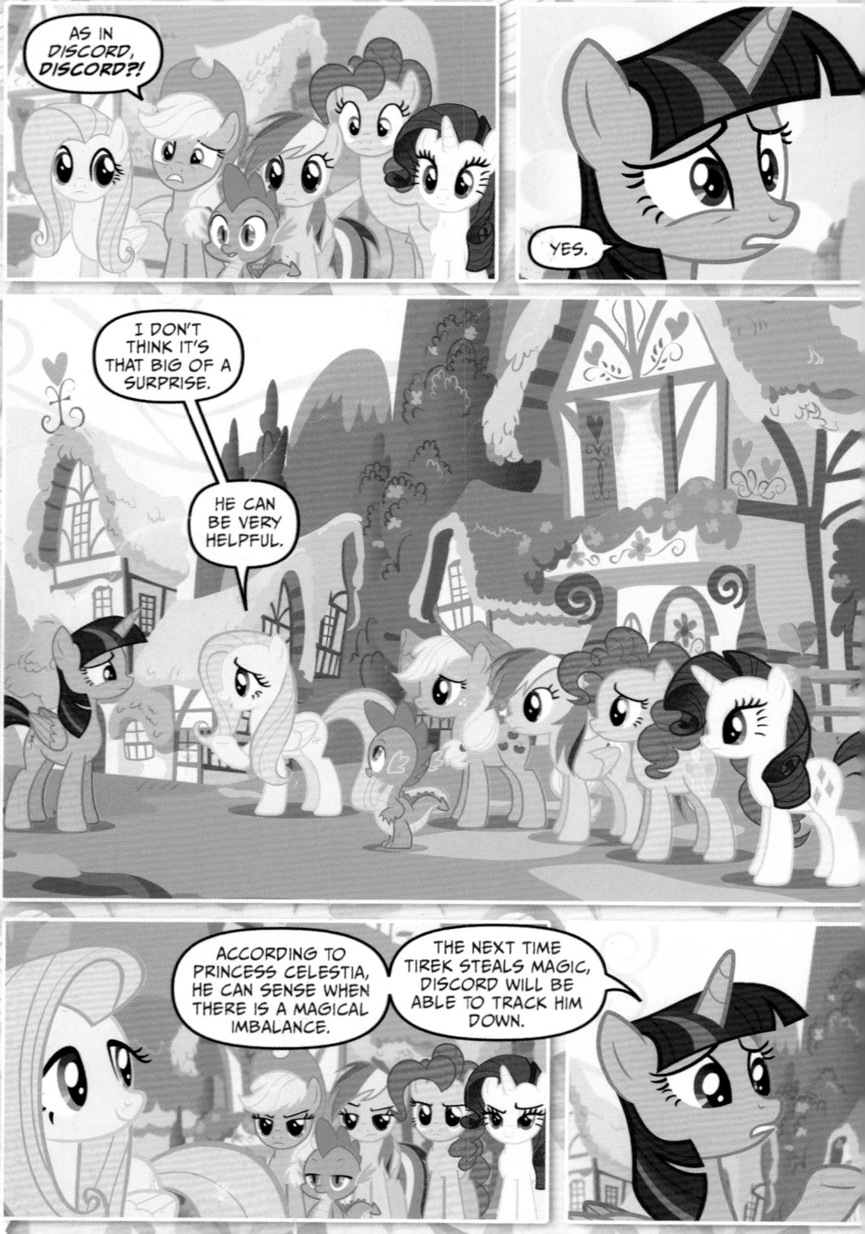
AS IN DISCORD, DISCORD?!
YES.
I DON'T THINK IT'S THAT BIG OF A SURPRISE.
HE CAN BE VERY HELPFUL.
ACCORDING TO PRINCESS CELESTIA, HE CAN SENSE WHEN THERE IS A MAGICAL IMBALANCE.
THE NEXT TIME TIREK STEALS MAGIC, DISCORD WILL BE ABLE TO TRACK HIM DOWN.

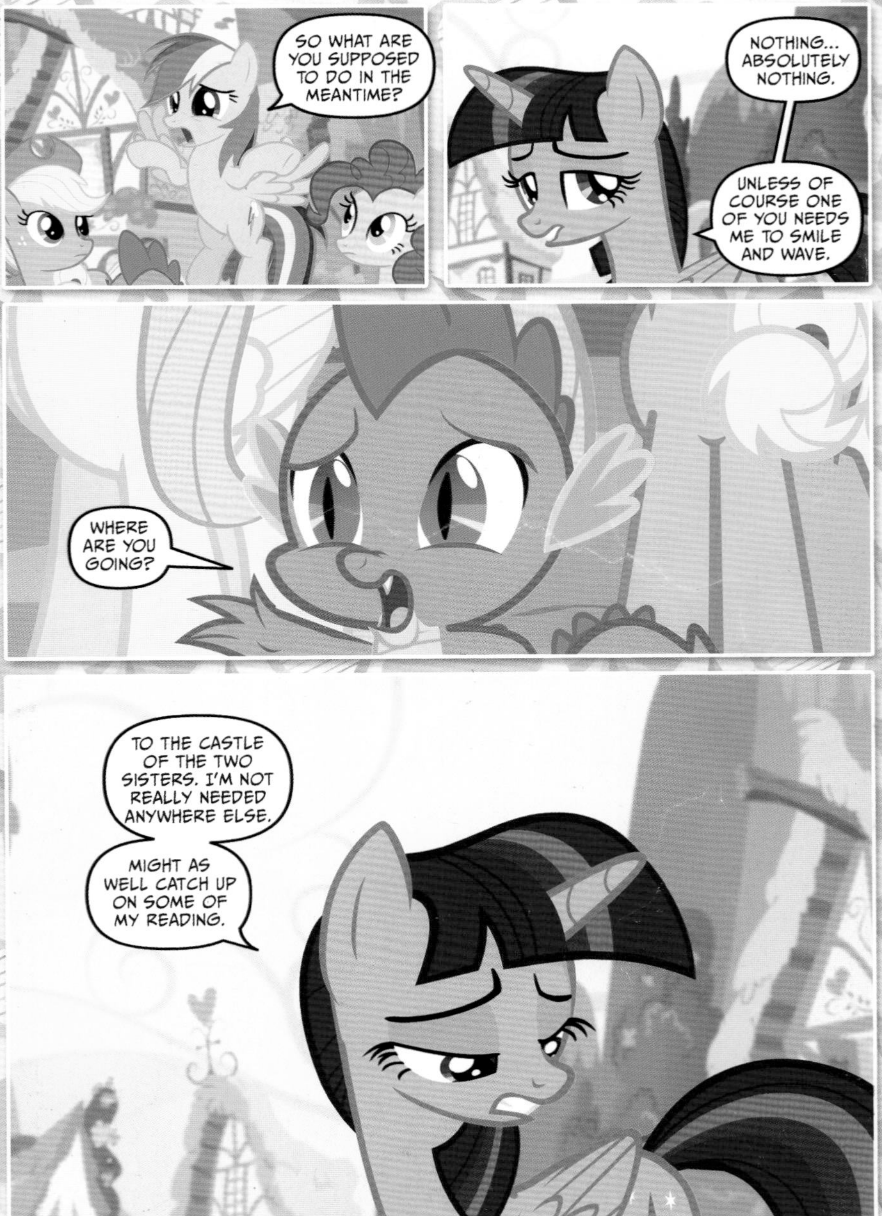
SO WHAT ARE YOU SUPPOSED TO DO IN THE MEANTIME?
NOTHING... ABSOLUTELY NOTHING.
UNLESS OF COURSE ONE OF YOU NEEDS ME TO SMILE AND WAVE.
WHERE ARE YOU GOING?
TO THE CASTLE OF THE TWO SISTERS. I'M NOT REALLY NEEDED ANYWHERE ELSE.
MIGHT AS WELL CATCH UP ON SOME OF MY READING.

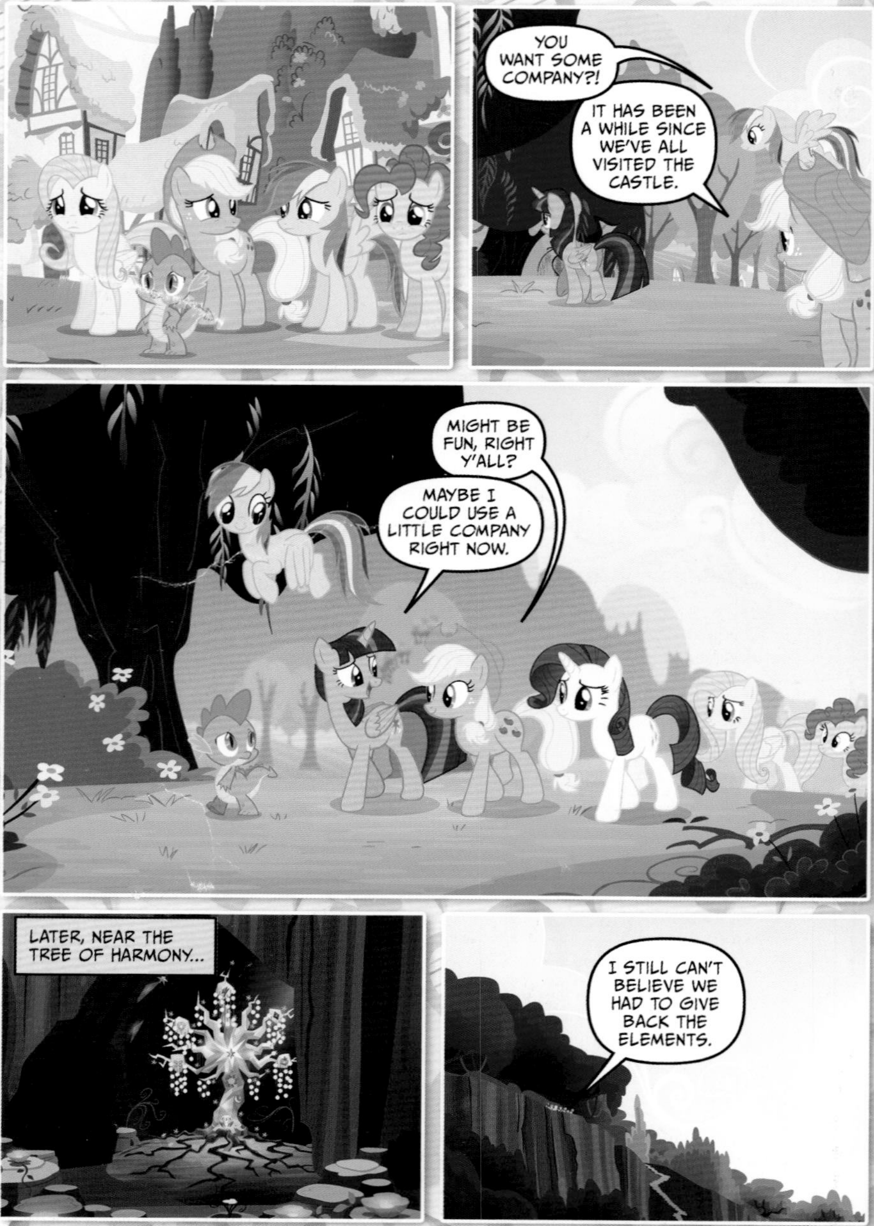
YOU WANT SOME COMPANY?!
IT HAS BEEN A WHILE SINCE WE'VE ALL VISITED THE CASTLE.
MIGHT BE FUN, RIGHT Y'ALL?
MAYBE I COULD USE A LITTLE COMPANY RIGHT NOW.
LATER, NEAR THE TREE OF HARMONY...
I STILL CAN'T BELIEVE WE HAD TO GIVE BACK THE ELEMENTS.

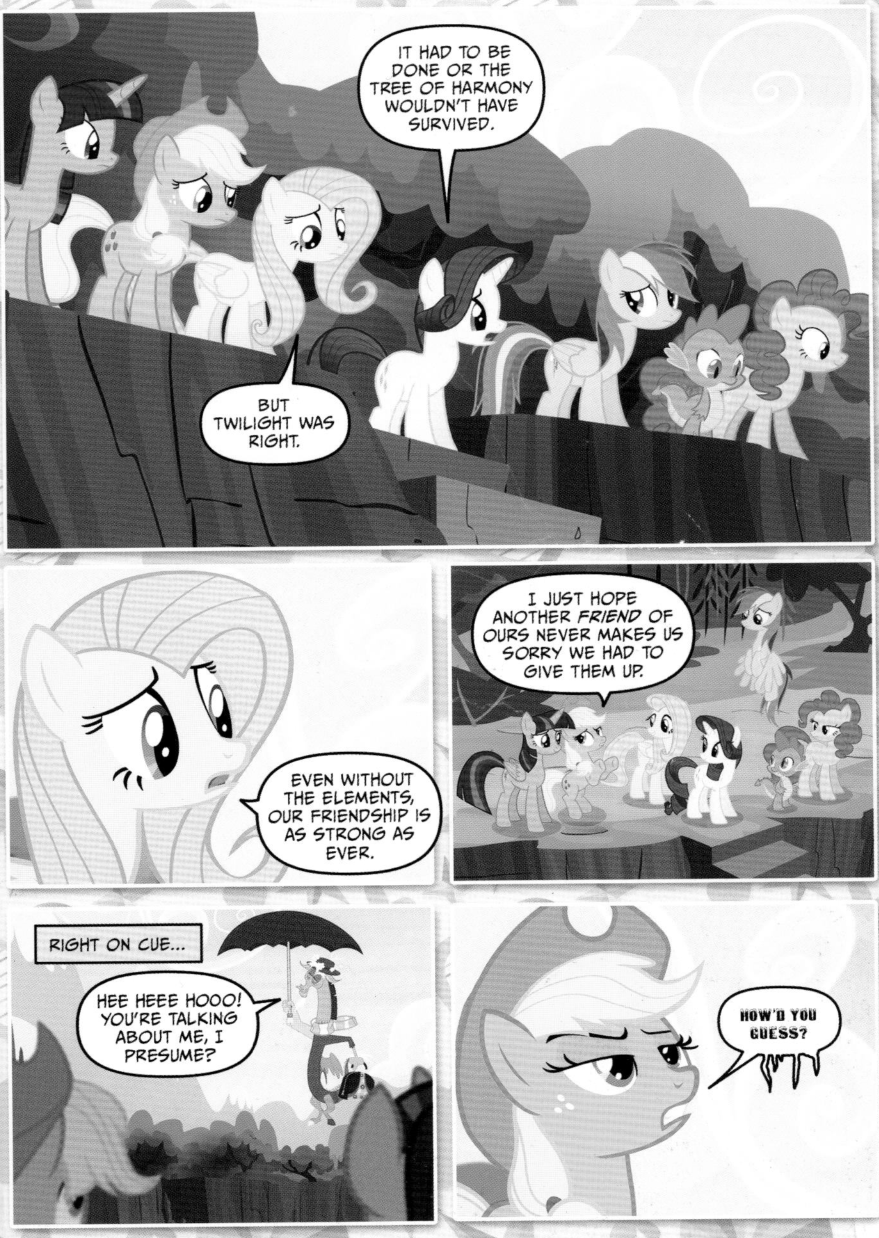
IT HAD TO BE DONE OR THE TREE OF HARMONY WOULDN'T HAVE SURVIVED.
BUT TWILIGHT WAS RIGHT.
EVEN WITHOUT THE ELEMENTS, OUR FRIENDSHIP IS AS STRONG AS EVER.
I JUST HOPE ANOTHER *FRIEND* OF OURS NEVER MAKES US SORRY WE HAD TO GIVE THEM UP.
RIGHT ON CUE...
HEE HEEE HOOO! YOU'RE TALKING ABOUT ME, I PRESUME?
HOW'D YOU GUESS?

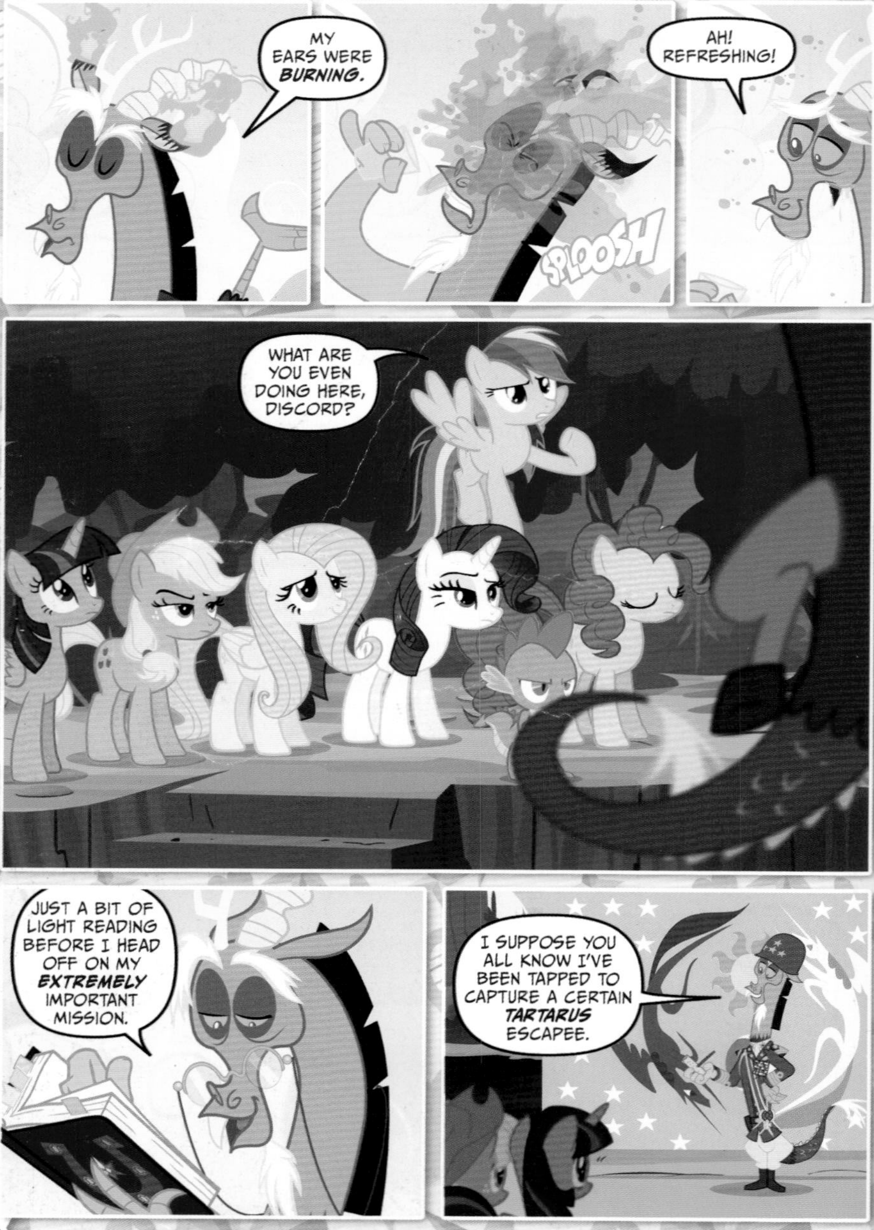
MY EARS WERE BURNING.
SPLOOSH
AH! REFRESHING!
WHAT ARE YOU EVEN DOING HERE, DISCORD?
JUST A BIT OF LIGHT READING BEFORE I HEAD OFF ON MY EXTREMELY IMPORTANT MISSION.
I SUPPOSE YOU ALL KNOW I'VE BEEN TAPPED TO CAPTURE A CERTAIN TARTARUS ESCAPEE.

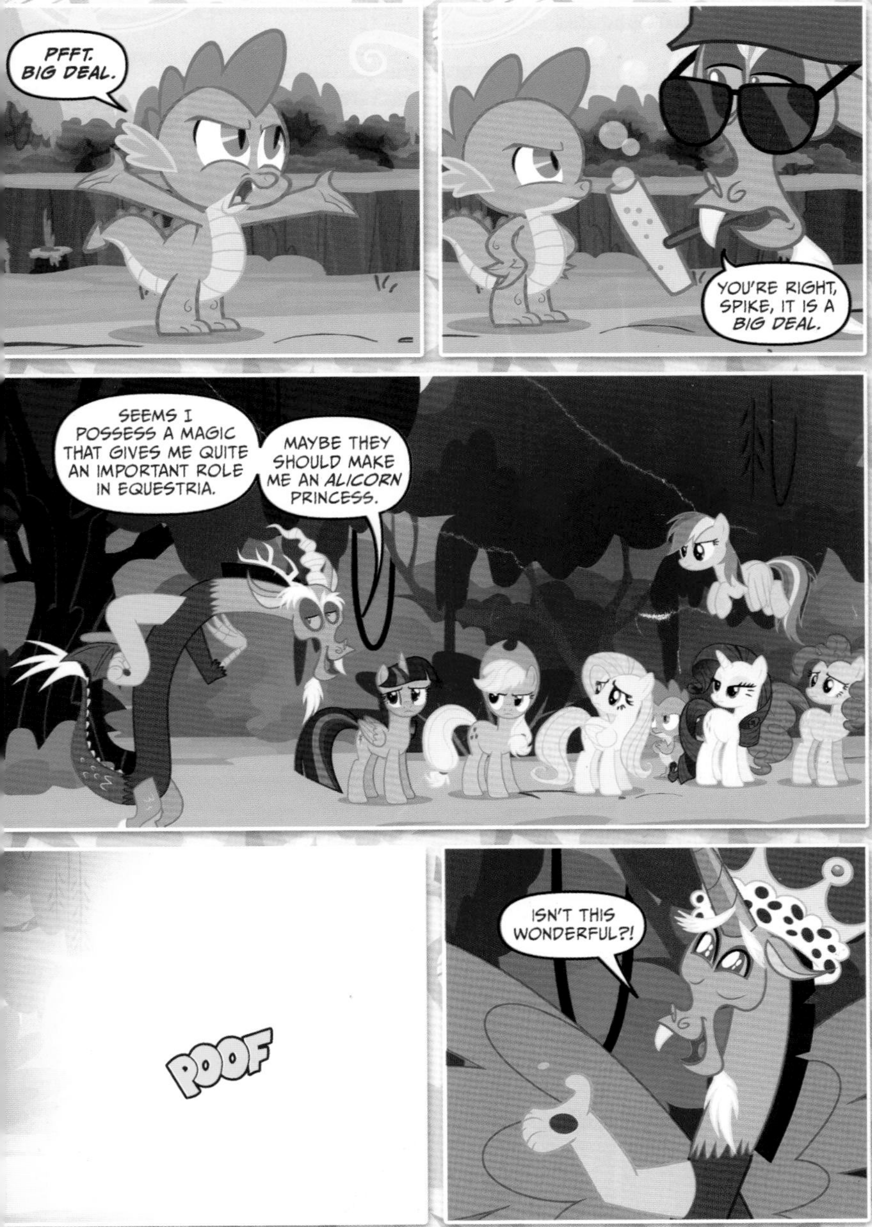
PFFT. BIG DEAL.
YOU'RE RIGHT, SPIKE, IT IS A BIG DEAL.
SEEMS I POSSESS A MAGIC THAT GIVES ME QUITE AN IMPORTANT ROLE IN EQUESTRIA.
MAYBE THEY SHOULD MAKE ME AN ALICORN PRINCESS.
POOF
ISN'T THIS WONDERFUL?!

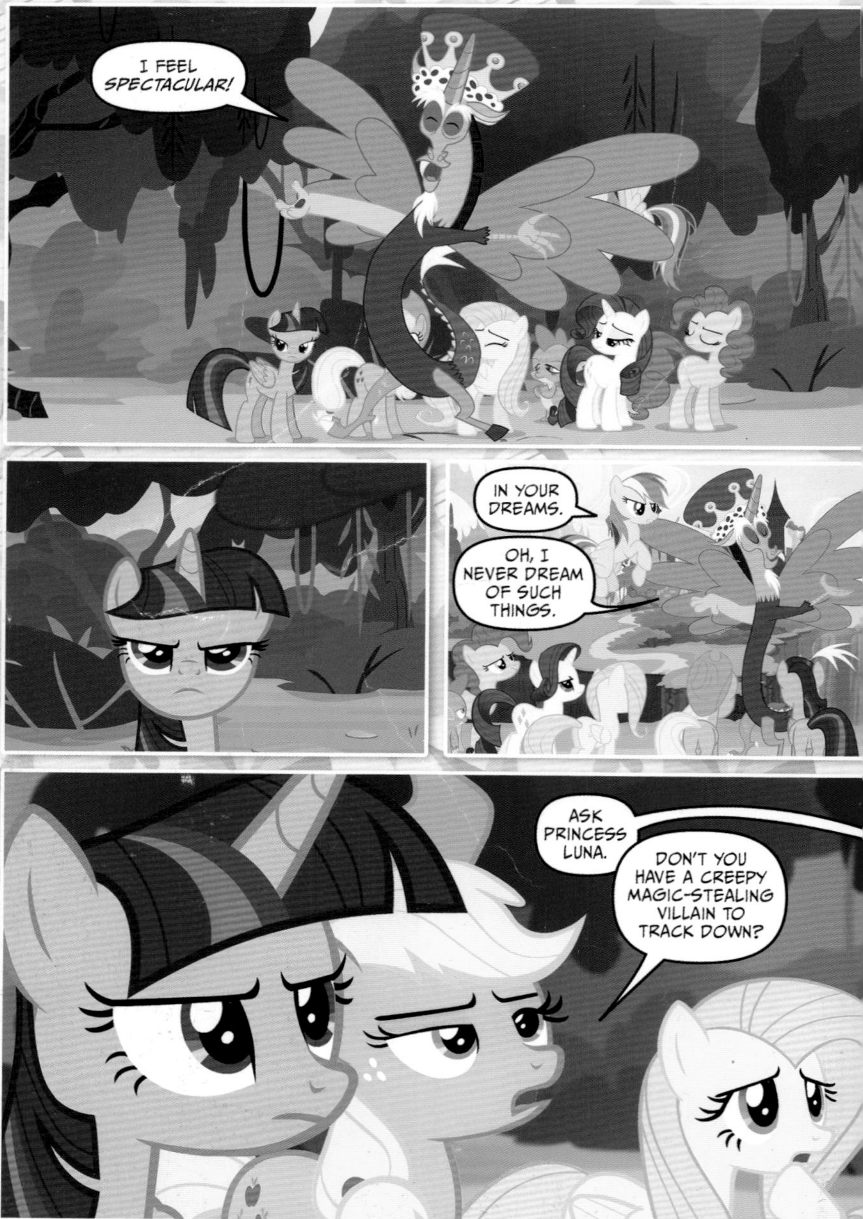
I FEEL SPECTACULAR!
IN YOUR DREAMS.
OH, I NEVER DREAM OF SUCH THINGS.
ASK PRINCESS LUNA.
DON'T YOU HAVE A CREEPY MAGIC-STEALING VILLAIN TO TRACK DOWN?

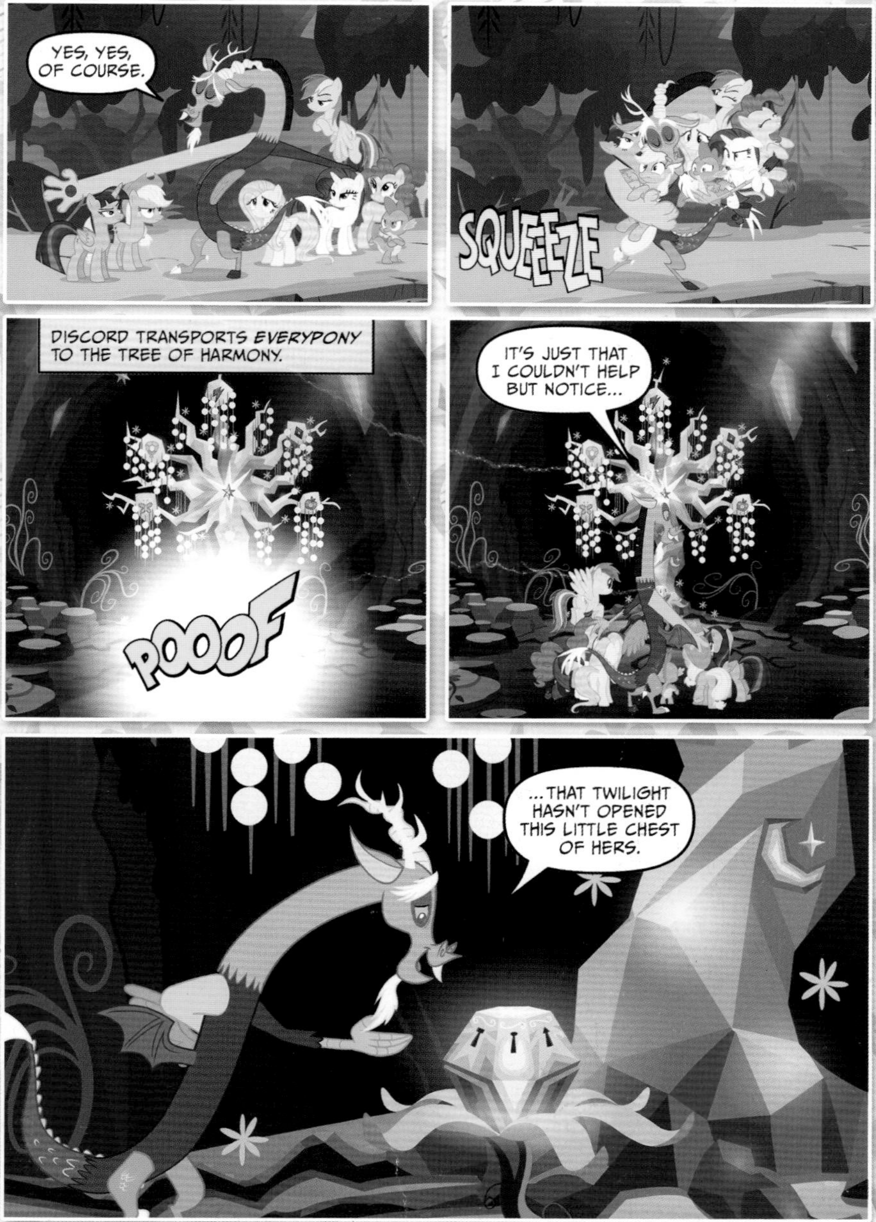
YES, YES, OF COURSE.
SQUEEEZE
DISCORD TRANSPORTS *EVERYPONY* TO THE TREE OF HARMONY.
POOOF
IT'S JUST THAT I COULDN'T HELP BUT NOTICE...
...THAT TWILIGHT HASN'T OPENED THIS LITTLE CHEST OF HERS.

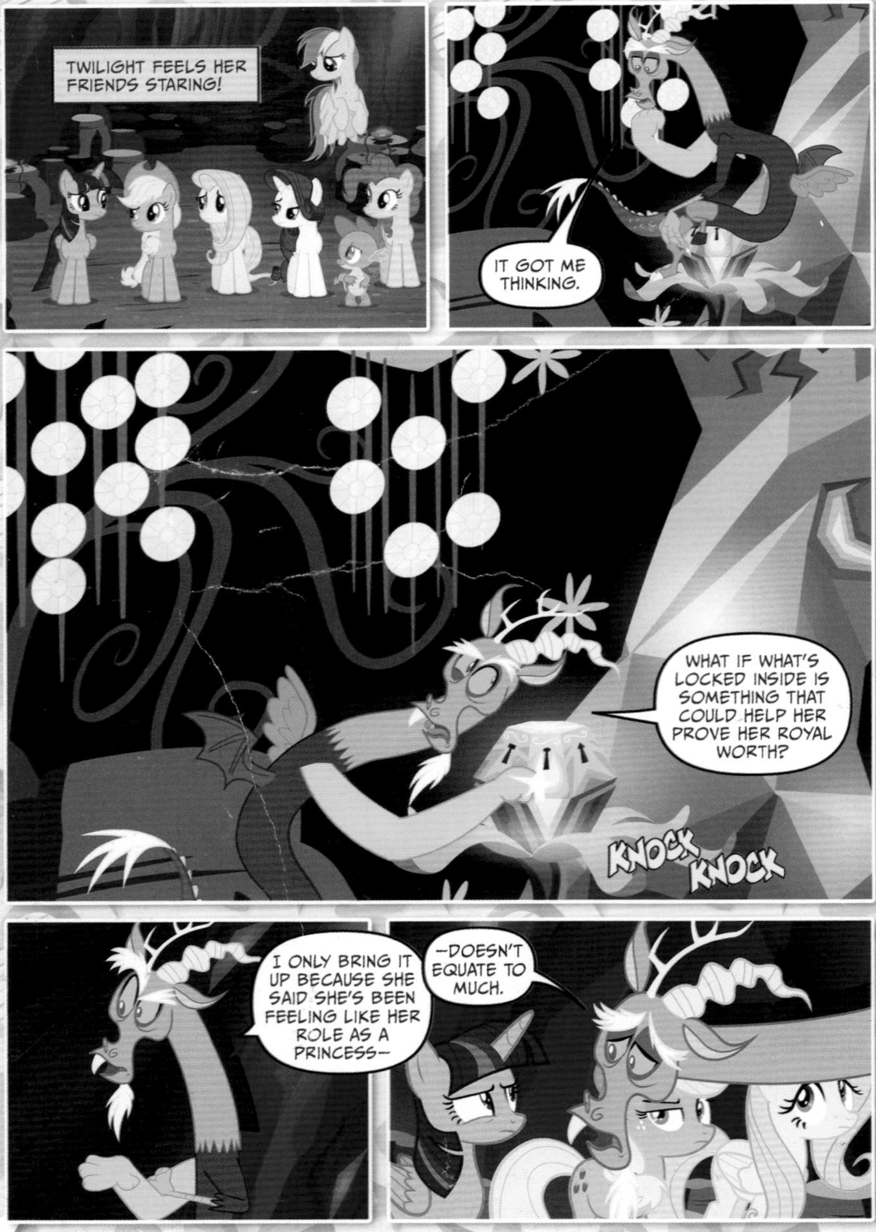

TWILIGHT FEELS HER FRIENDS STARING!
IT GOT ME THINKING.
WHAT IF WHAT'S LOCKED INSIDE IS SOMETHING THAT COULD HELP HER PROVE HER ROYAL WORTH?
KNOCK KNOCK
I ONLY BRING IT UP BECAUSE SHE SAID SHE'S BEEN FEELING LIKE HER ROLE AS A PRINCESS—
—DOESN'T EQUATE TO MUCH.

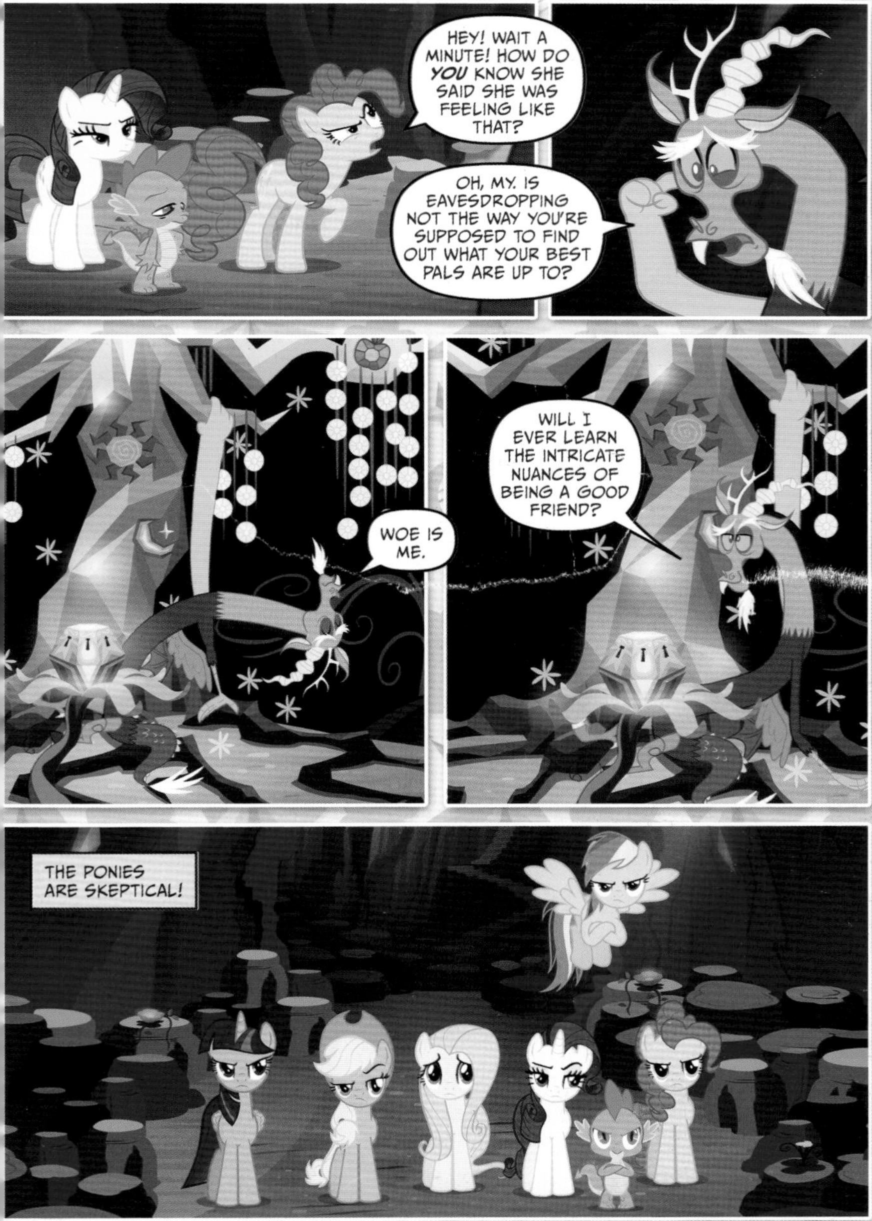
HEY! WAIT A MINUTE! HOW DO *YOU* KNOW SHE SAID SHE WAS FEELING LIKE THAT?
OH, MY. IS EAVESDROPPING NOT THE WAY YOU'RE SUPPOSED TO FIND OUT WHAT YOUR BEST PALS ARE UP TO?
WOE IS ME.
WILL I EVER LEARN THE INTRICATE NUANCES OF BEING A GOOD FRIEND?
THE PONIES ARE SKEPTICAL!

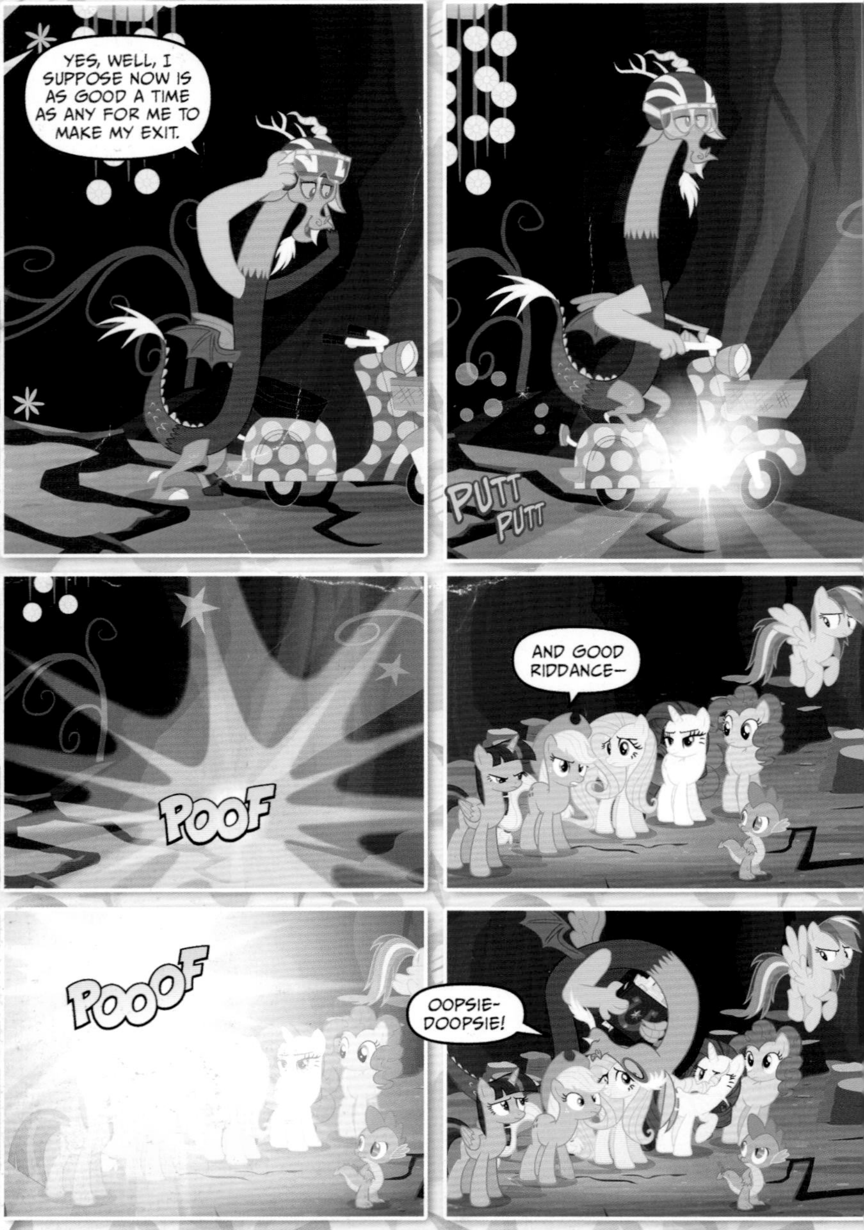
YES, WELL, I SUPPOSE NOW IS AS GOOD A TIME AS ANY FOR ME TO MAKE MY EXIT.
PUTT PUTT
POOF
AND GOOD RIDDANCE–
POOOF
OOPSIE-DOOPSIE!

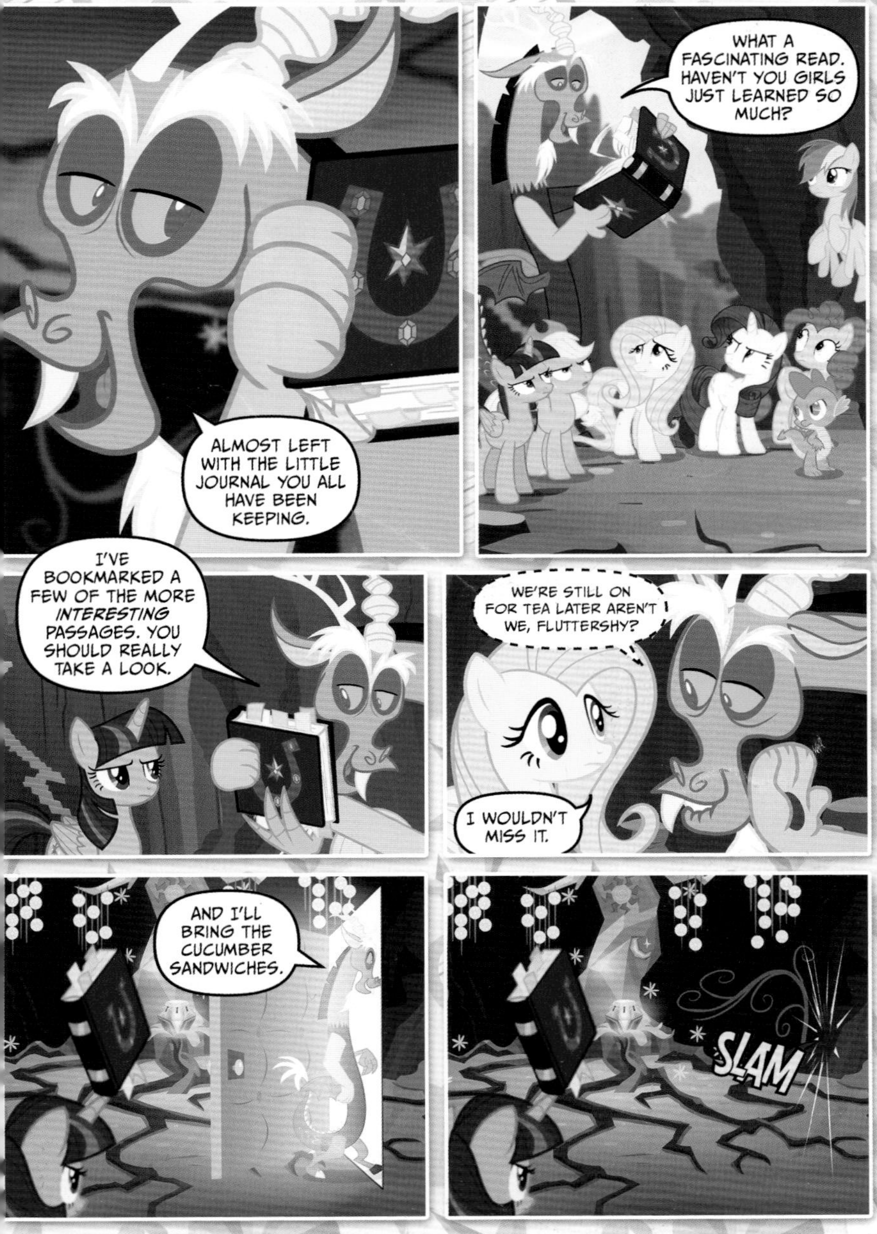
ALMOST LEFT WITH THE LITTLE JOURNAL YOU ALL HAVE BEEN KEEPING.
WHAT A FASCINATING READ. HAVEN'T YOU GIRLS JUST LEARNED SO MUCH?
I'VE BOOKMARKED A FEW OF THE MORE *INTERESTING* PASSAGES. YOU SHOULD REALLY TAKE A LOOK.
WE'RE STILL ON FOR TEA LATER AREN'T WE, FLUTTERSHY?
I WOULDN'T MISS IT.
AND I'LL BRING THE CUCUMBER SANDWICHES.
SLAM

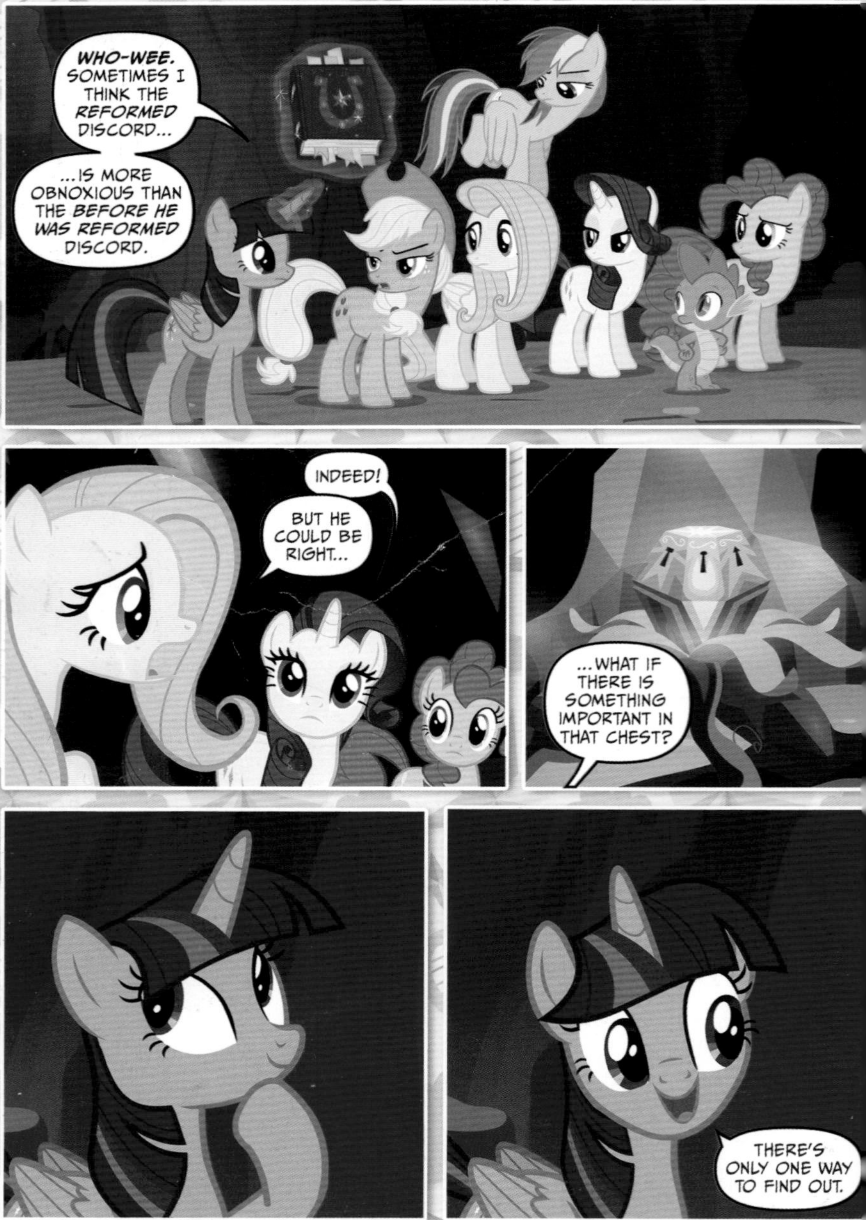

WHO-WEE. SOMETIMES I THINK THE *REFORMED* DISCORD...
...IS MORE OBNOXIOUS THAN THE *BEFORE HE WAS REFORMED* DISCORD.
INDEED!
BUT HE COULD BE RIGHT...
...WHAT IF THERE IS SOMETHING IMPORTANT IN THAT CHEST?
THERE'S ONLY ONE WAY TO FIND OUT.

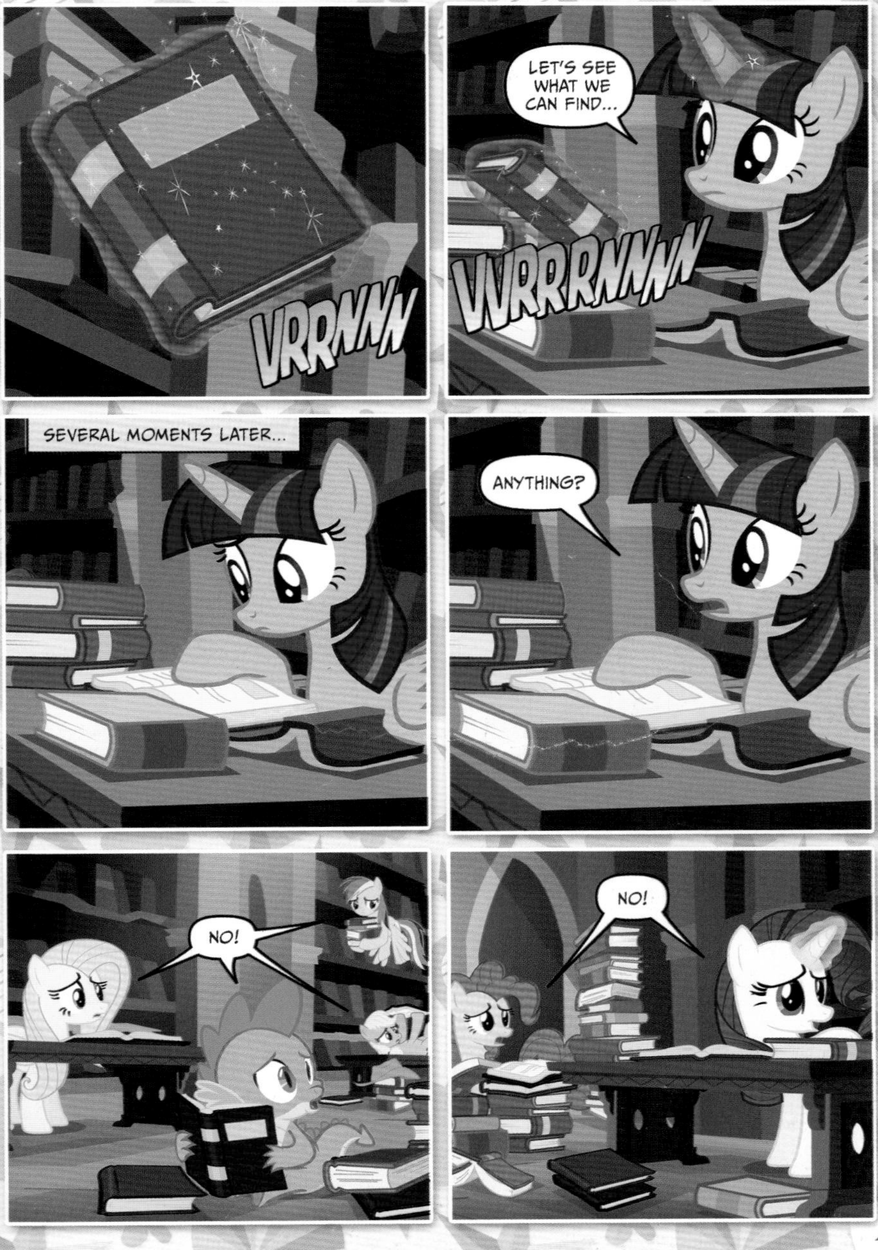
VRRNNN
LET'S SEE WHAT WE CAN FIND...
VVRRRNNNN
SEVERAL MOMENTS LATER...
ANYTHING?
NO!
NO!

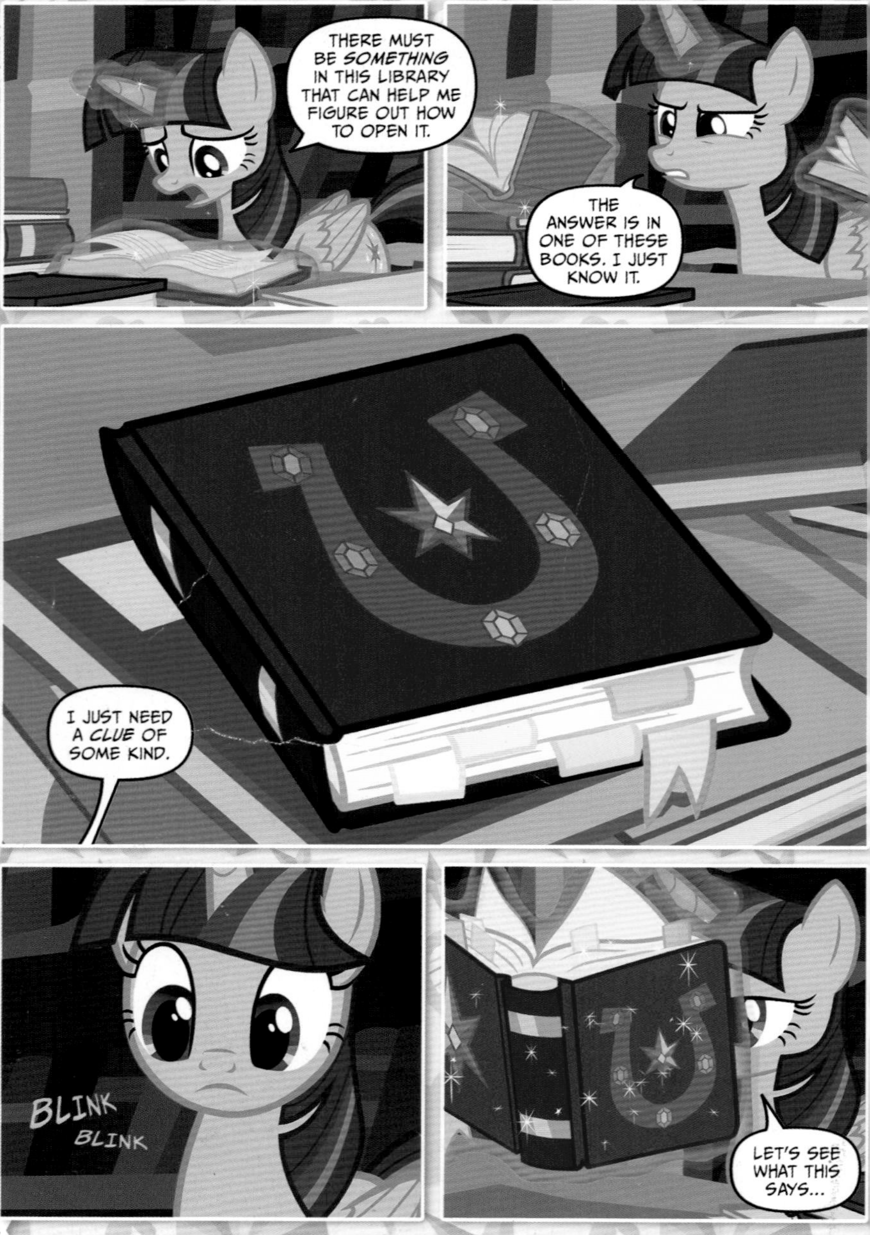
THERE MUST BE SOMETHING IN THIS LIBRARY THAT CAN HELP ME FIGURE OUT HOW TO OPEN IT.
THE ANSWER IS IN ONE OF THESE BOOKS. I JUST KNOW IT.
I JUST NEED A CLUE OF SOME KIND.
BLINK
BLINK
LET'S SEE WHAT THIS SAYS...

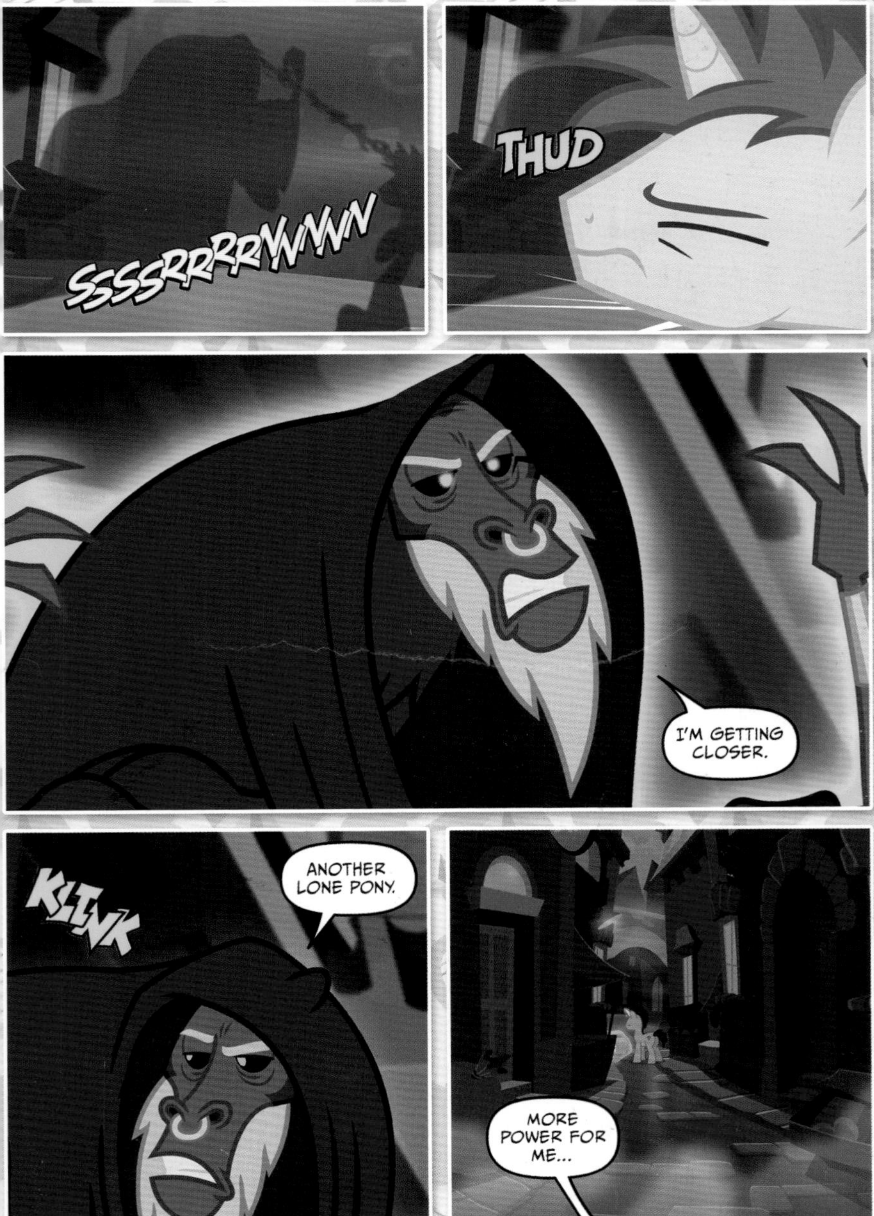

SSSSRRRRNNNN
THUD
I'M GETTING CLOSER.
KLINK
ANOTHER LONE PONY.
MORE POWER FOR ME...

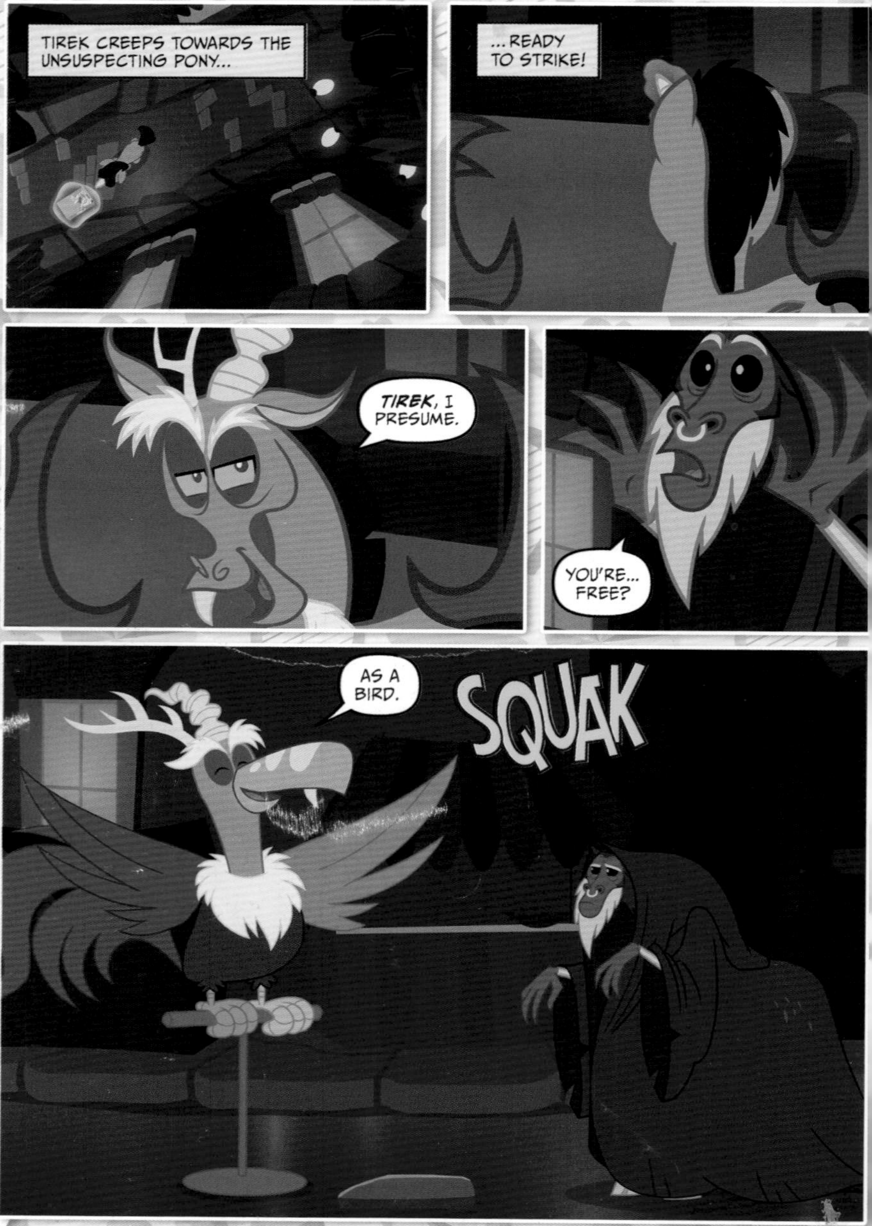

TIREK CREEPS TOWARDS THE UNSUSPECTING PONY...
...READY TO STRIKE!
TIREK, I PRESUME.
YOU'RE... FREE?
AS A BIRD.
SQUAK

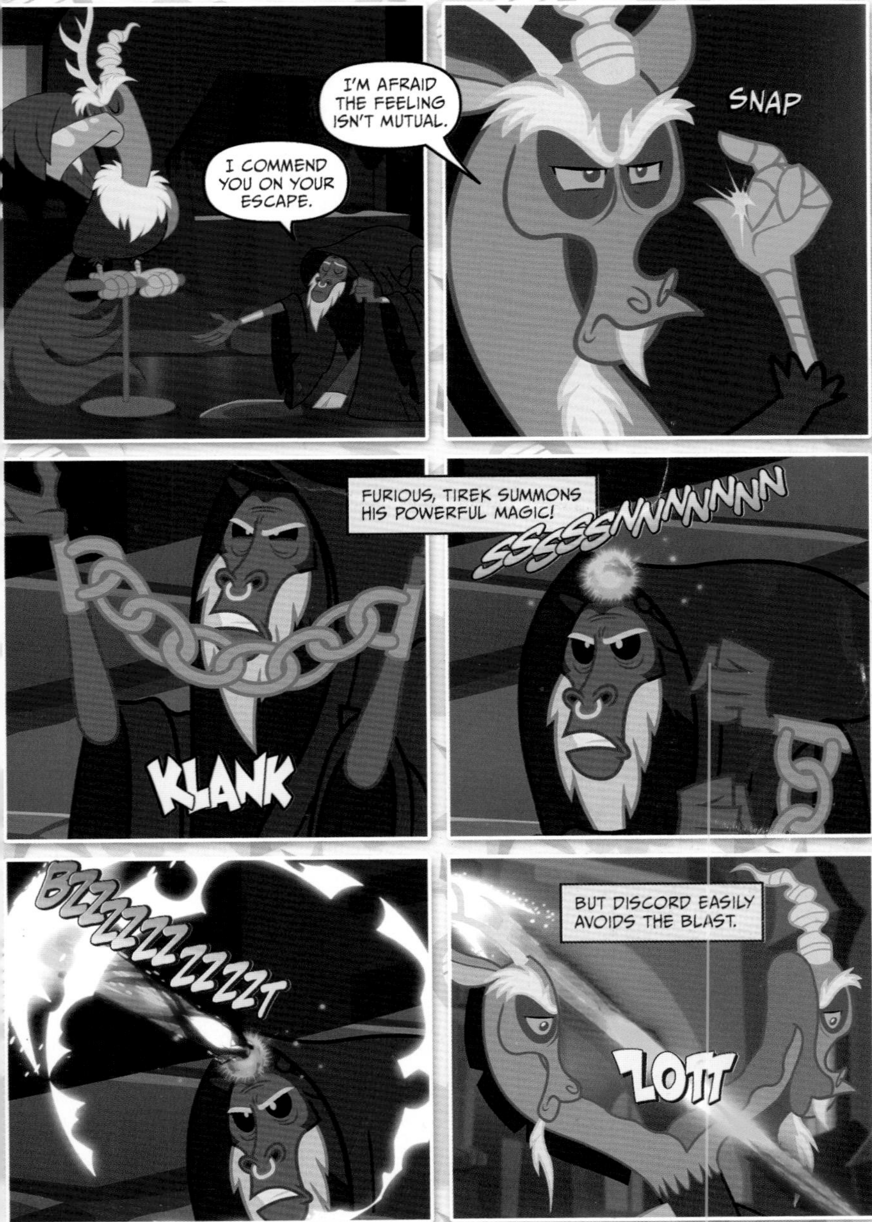
I COMMEND YOU ON YOUR ESCAPE.
I'M AFRAID THE FEELING ISN'T MUTUAL.
SNAP
FURIOUS, TIREK SUMMONS HIS POWERFUL MAGIC!
KLANK
SSSSSNNNNNNNN
BZZZZZZZZZZZT
BUT DISCORD EASILY AVOIDS THE BLAST.
ZOTT

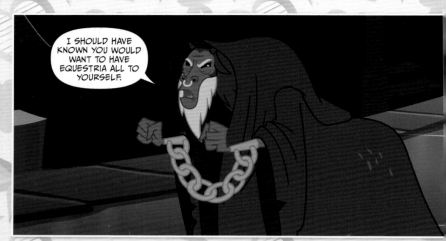

I SHOULD HAVE KNOWN YOU WOULD WANT TO HAVE EQUESTRIA ALL TO YOURSELF.

OH, I'M NOT DOING THIS FOR *ME*. I'M DOING IT FOR MY *FRIENDS*.

JUST BETWEEN THE TWO OF US, IT'S MOSTLY FOR FLUTTERSHY.

FLUTTERSHY?

YOU'RE NOT SAYING YOU'RE FRIENDS WITH... *PONIES?*

SURPRISE!

SPLORT

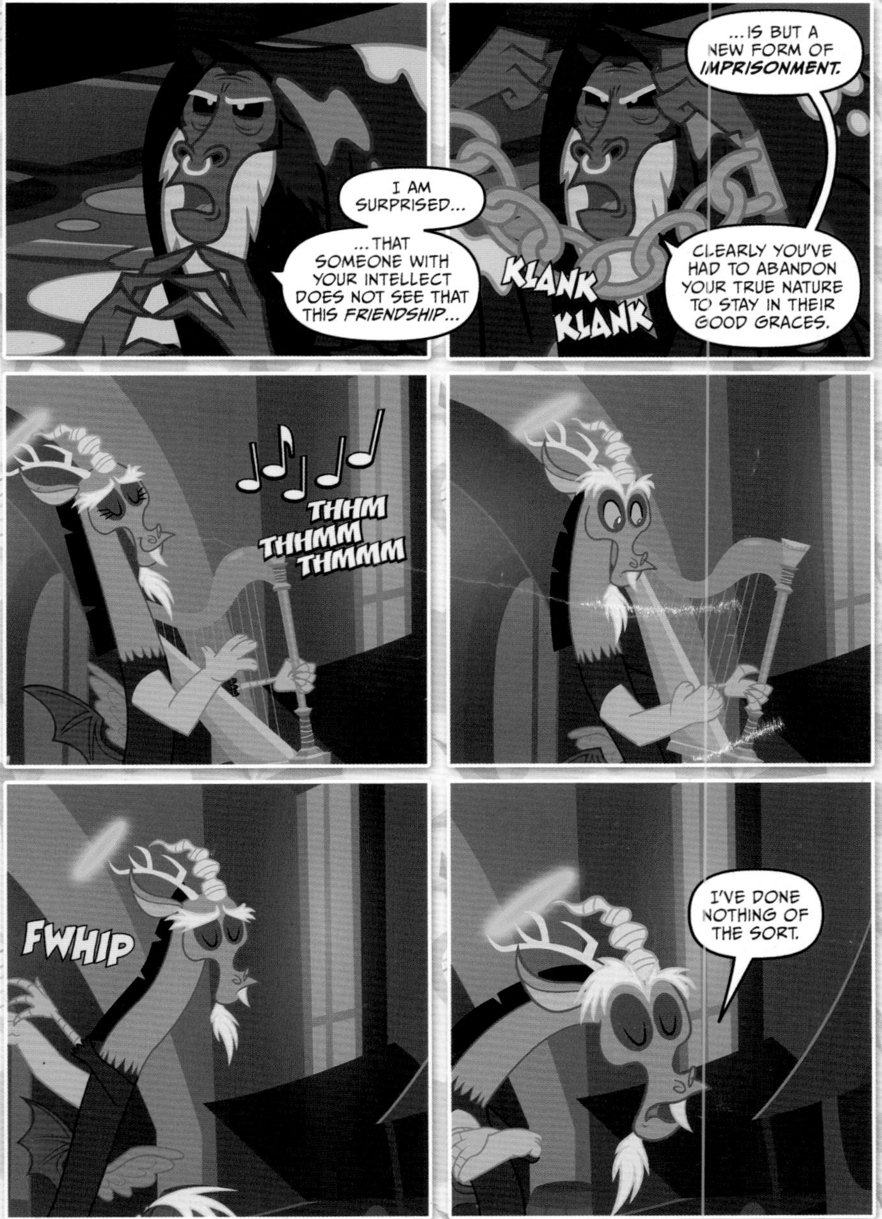
I AM SURPRISED...
...THAT SOMEONE WITH YOUR INTELLECT DOES NOT SEE THAT THIS *FRIENDSHIP*...
...IS BUT A NEW FORM OF *IMPRISONMENT.*
KLANK
KLANK
CLEARLY YOU'VE HAD TO ABANDON YOUR TRUE NATURE TO STAY IN THEIR GOOD GRACES.
THHM
THHMM
THMMM
FWHIP
I'VE DONE NOTHING OF THE SORT.

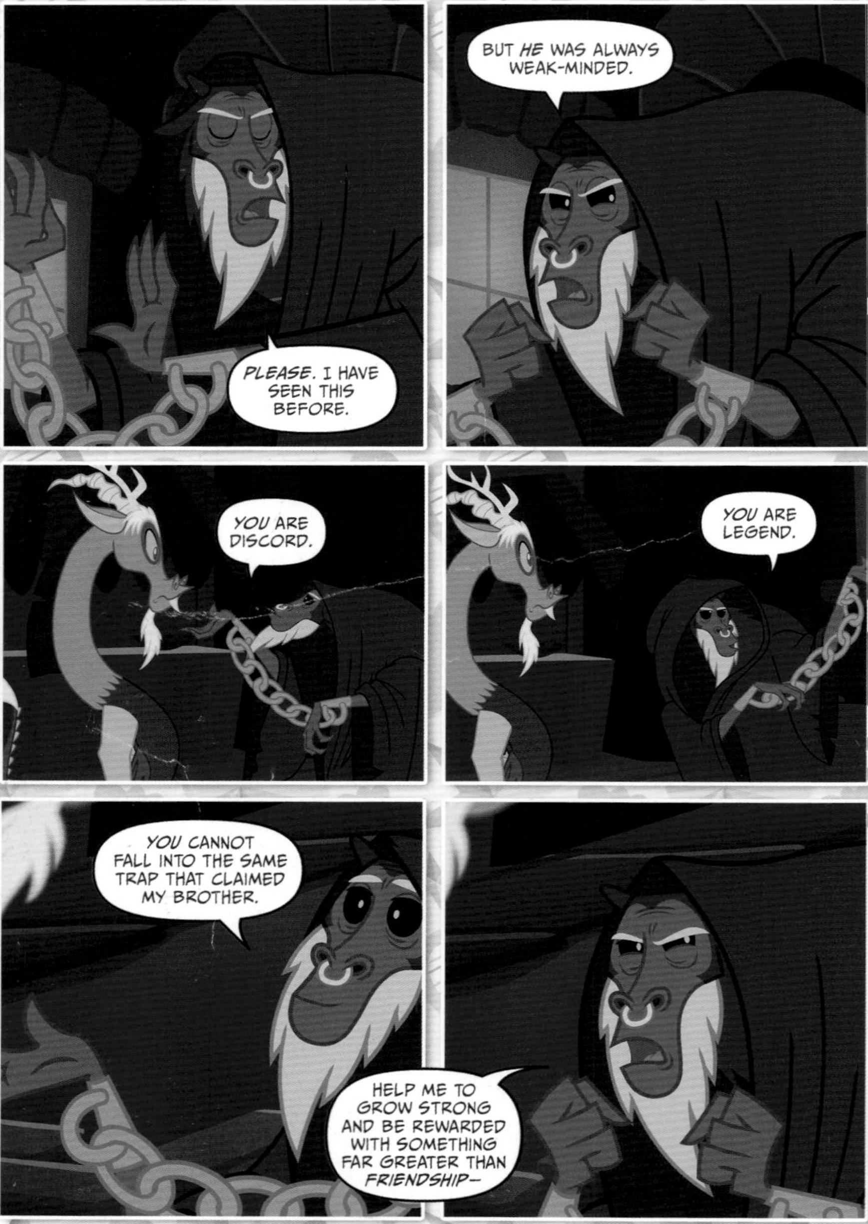
PLEASE. I HAVE SEEN THIS BEFORE.
BUT HE WAS ALWAYS WEAK-MINDED.
YOU ARE DISCORD.
YOU ARE LEGEND.
YOU CANNOT FALL INTO THE SAME TRAP THAT CLAIMED MY BROTHER.
HELP ME TO GROW STRONG AND BE REWARDED WITH SOMETHING FAR GREATER THAN FRIENDSHIP—

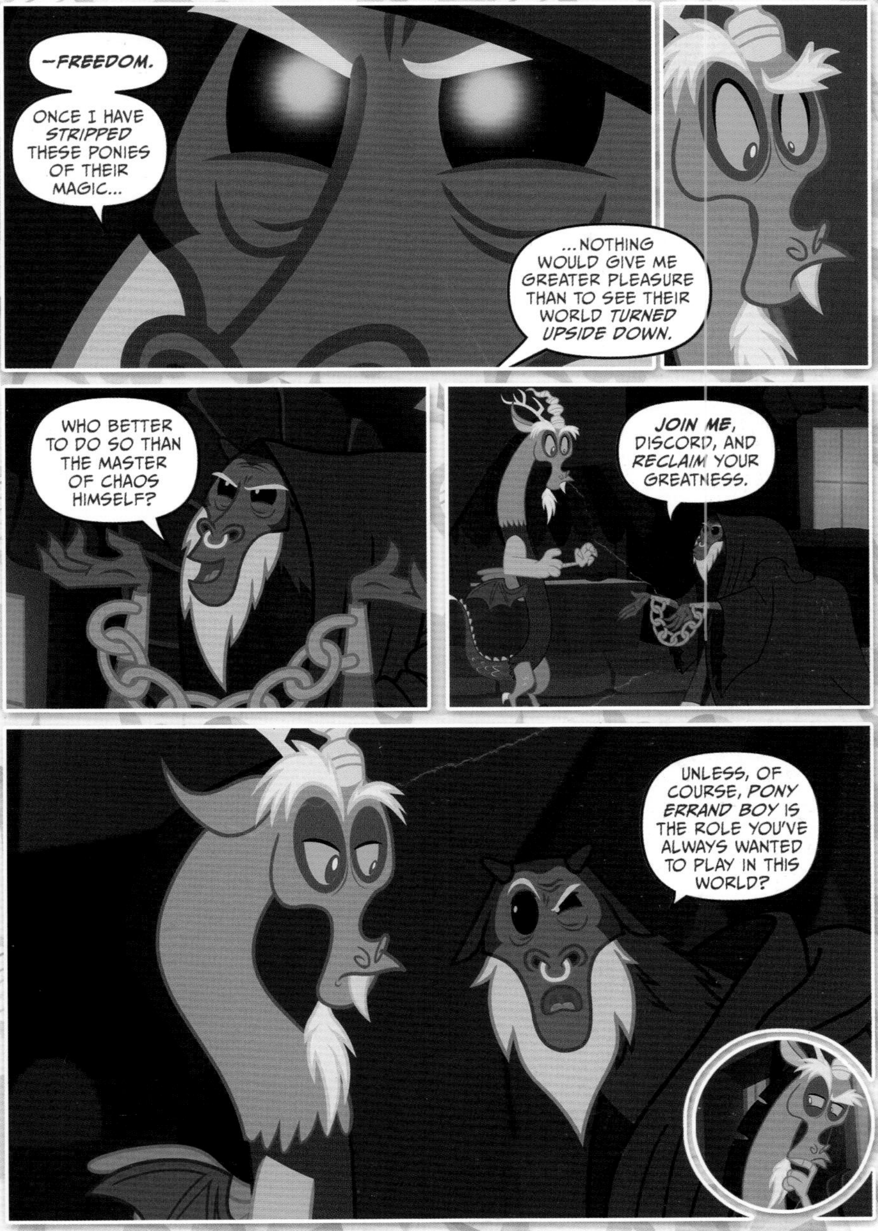
—FREEDOM.
ONCE I HAVE STRIPPED THESE PONIES OF THEIR MAGIC...
...NOTHING WOULD GIVE ME GREATER PLEASURE THAN TO SEE THEIR WORLD TURNED UPSIDE DOWN.
WHO BETTER TO DO SO THAN THE MASTER OF CHAOS HIMSELF?
JOIN ME, DISCORD, AND RECLAIM YOUR GREATNESS.
UNLESS, OF COURSE, PONY ERRAND BOY IS THE ROLE YOU'VE ALWAYS WANTED TO PLAY IN THIS WORLD?

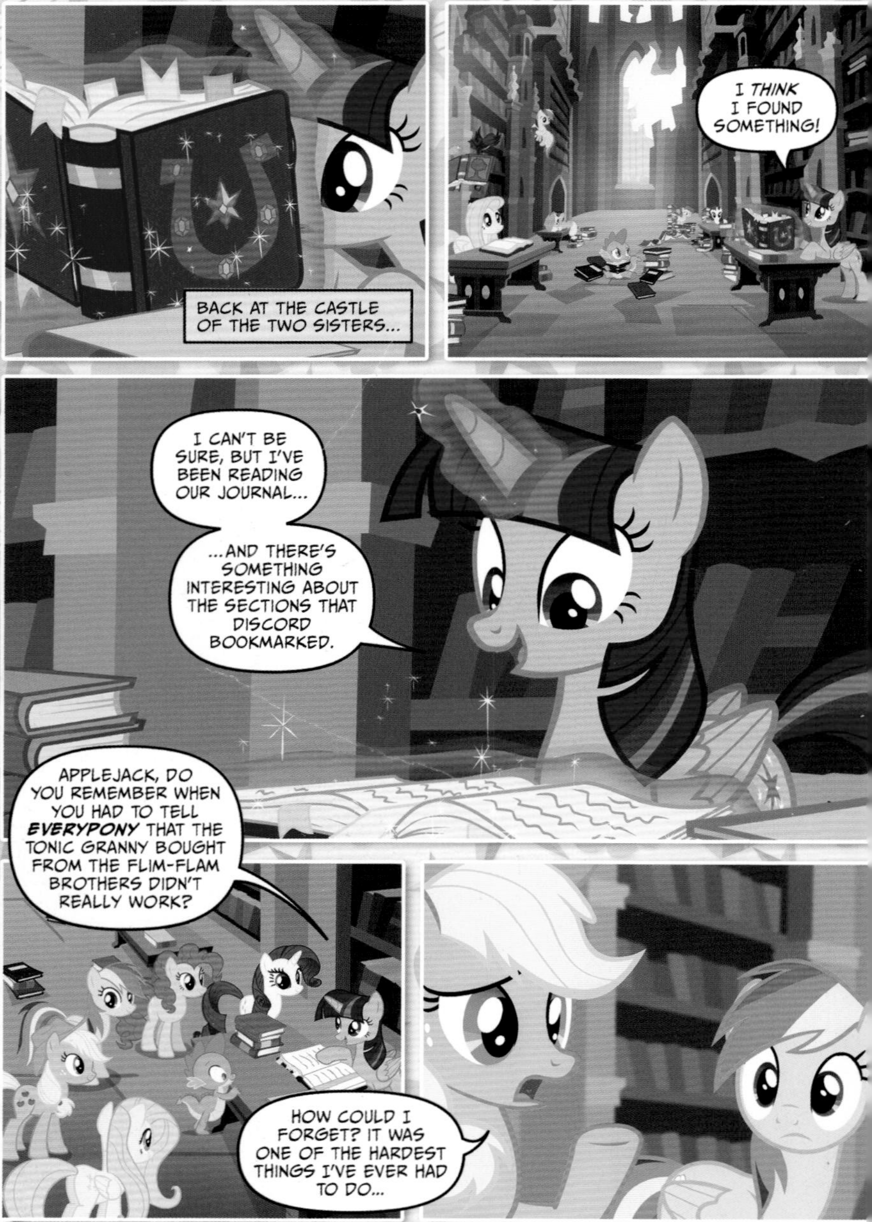
BACK AT THE CASTLE OF THE TWO SISTERS...
I THINK I FOUND SOMETHING!
I CAN'T BE SURE, BUT I'VE BEEN READING OUR JOURNAL...
...AND THERE'S SOMETHING INTERESTING ABOUT THE SECTIONS THAT DISCORD BOOKMARKED.
APPLEJACK, DO YOU REMEMBER WHEN YOU HAD TO TELL EVERYPONY THAT THE TONIC GRANNY BOUGHT FROM THE FLIM-FLAM BROTHERS DIDN'T REALLY WORK?
HOW COULD I FORGET? IT WAS ONE OF THE HARDEST THINGS I'VE EVER HAD TO DO...

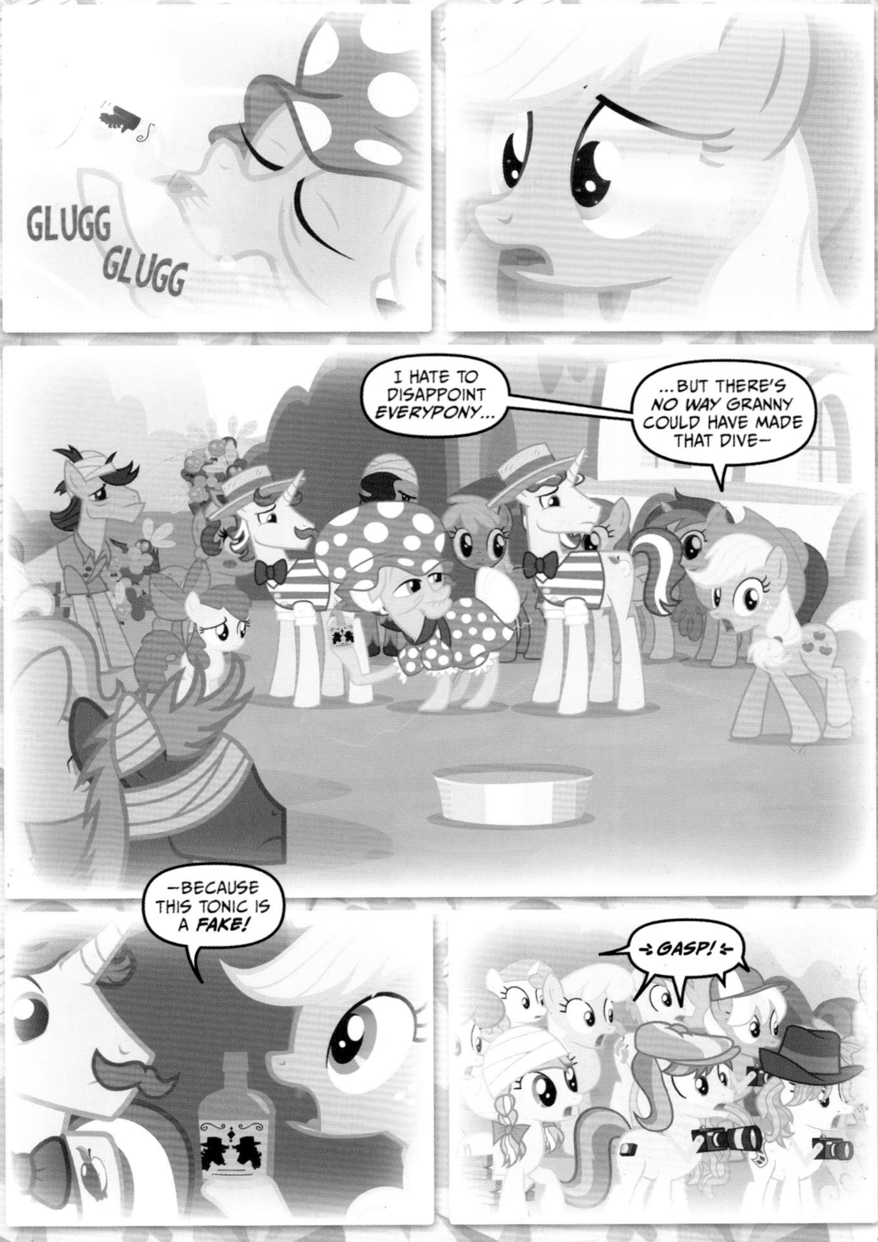
GLUGG
GLUGG
I HATE TO DISAPPOINT EVERYPONY...
...BUT THERE'S NO WAY GRANNY COULD HAVE MADE THAT DIVE–
–BECAUSE THIS TONIC IS A FAKE!
GASP!

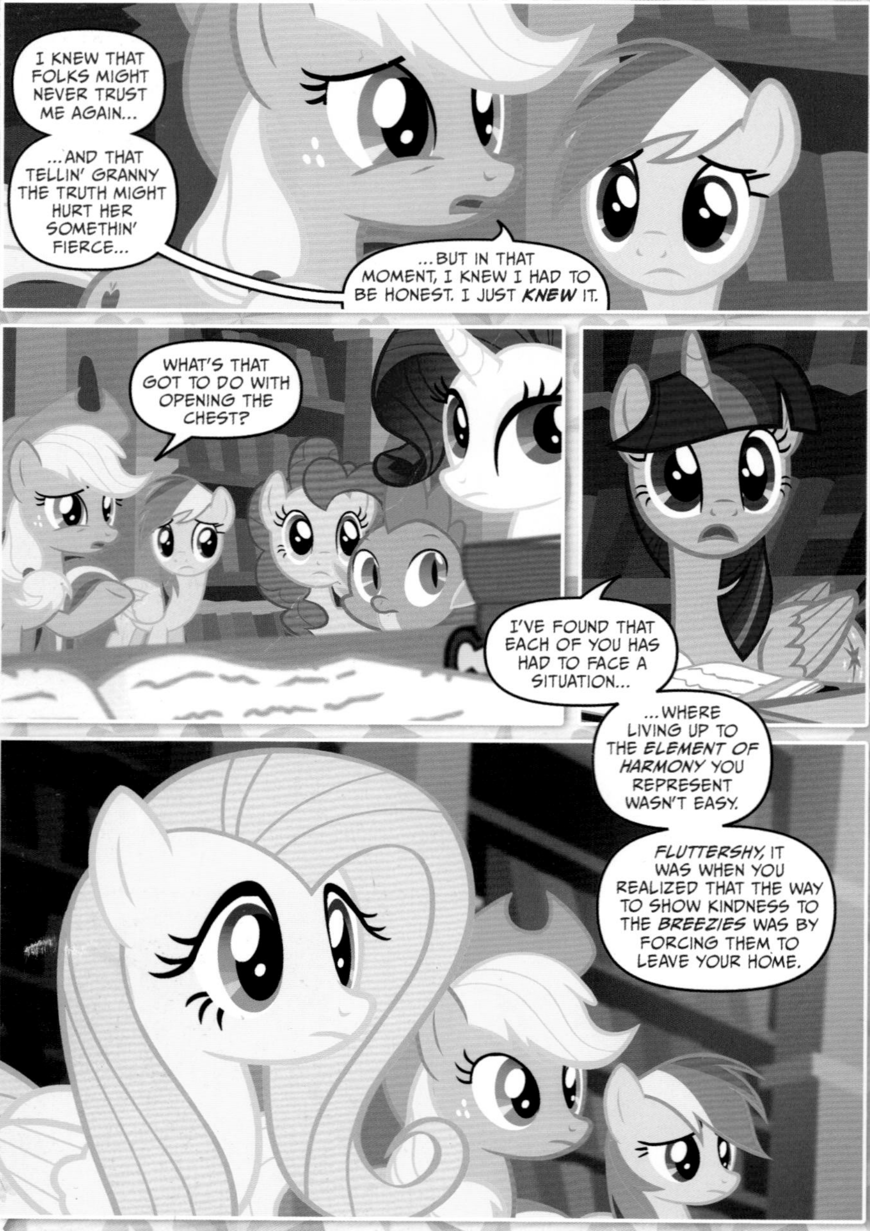
I KNEW THAT FOLKS MIGHT NEVER TRUST ME AGAIN...
...AND THAT TELLIN' GRANNY THE TRUTH MIGHT HURT HER SOMETHIN' FIERCE...
...BUT IN THAT MOMENT, I KNEW I HAD TO BE HONEST. I JUST *KNEW* IT.
WHAT'S THAT GOT TO DO WITH OPENING THE CHEST?
I'VE FOUND THAT EACH OF YOU HAS HAD TO FACE A SITUATION...
...WHERE LIVING UP TO THE *ELEMENT OF HARMONY* YOU REPRESENT WASN'T EASY.
FLUTTERSHY, IT WAS WHEN YOU REALIZED THAT THE WAY TO SHOW KINDNESS TO THE *BREEZIES* WAS BY FORCING THEM TO LEAVE YOUR HOME.

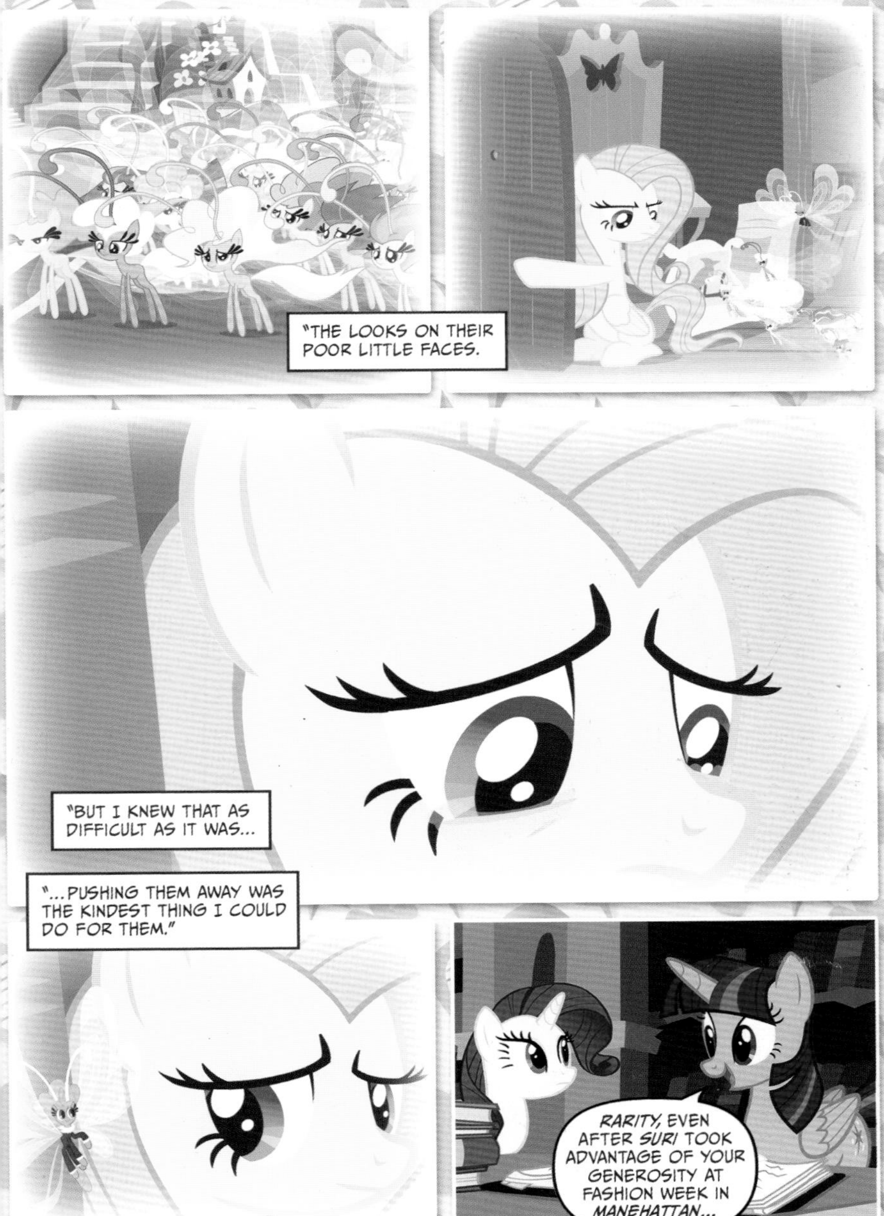
"THE LOOKS ON THEIR POOR LITTLE FACES.
"BUT I KNEW THAT AS DIFFICULT AS IT WAS...
"...PUSHING THEM AWAY WAS THE KINDEST THING I COULD DO FOR THEM."
RARITY, EVEN AFTER SURI TOOK ADVANTAGE OF YOUR GENEROSITY AT FASHION WEEK IN MANEHATTAN...

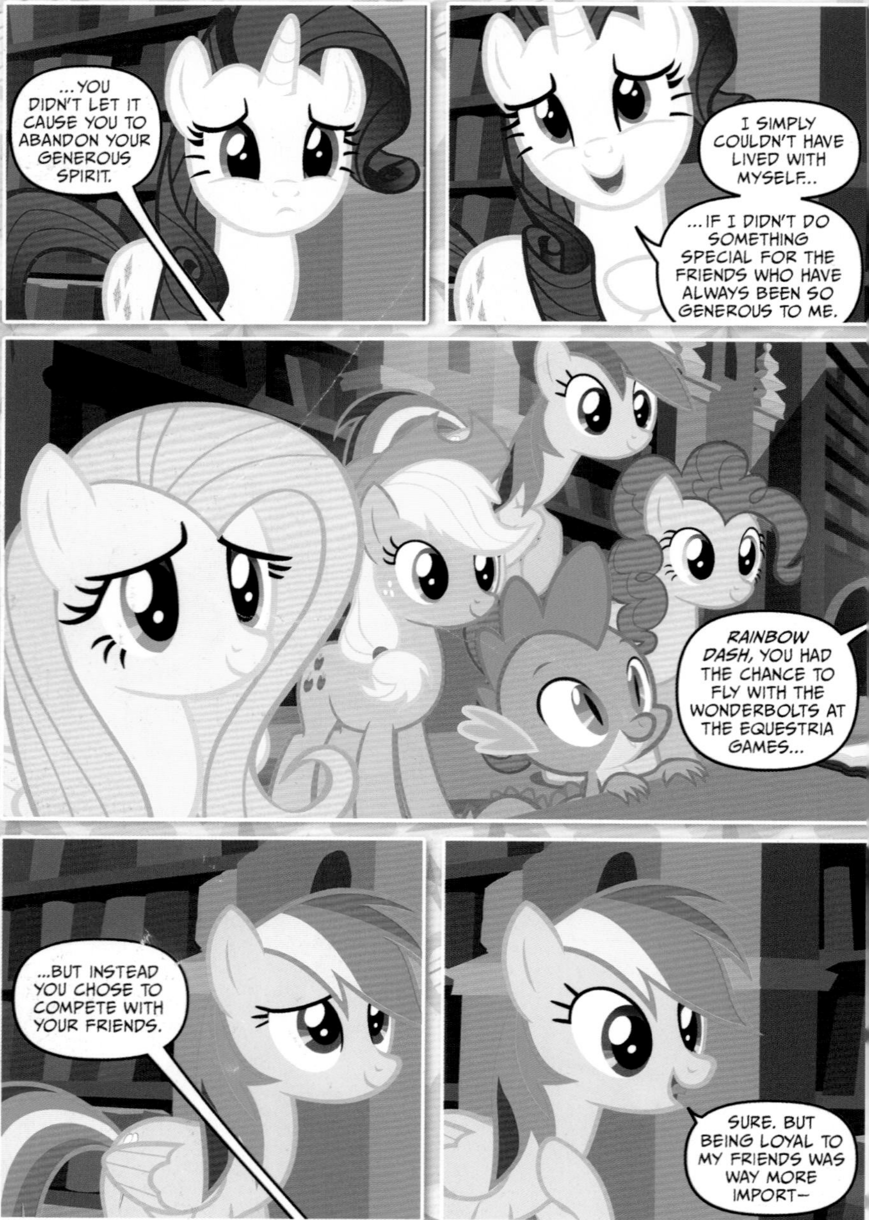
...YOU DIDN'T LET IT CAUSE YOU TO ABANDON YOUR GENEROUS SPIRIT.
I SIMPLY COULDN'T HAVE LIVED WITH MYSELF...
...IF I DIDN'T DO SOMETHING SPECIAL FOR THE FRIENDS WHO HAVE ALWAYS BEEN SO GENEROUS TO ME.
RAINBOW DASH, YOU HAD THE CHANCE TO FLY WITH THE WONDERBOLTS AT THE EQUESTRIA GAMES...
...BUT INSTEAD YOU CHOSE TO COMPETE WITH YOUR FRIENDS.
SURE. BUT BEING LOYAL TO MY FRIENDS WAS WAY MORE IMPORT–

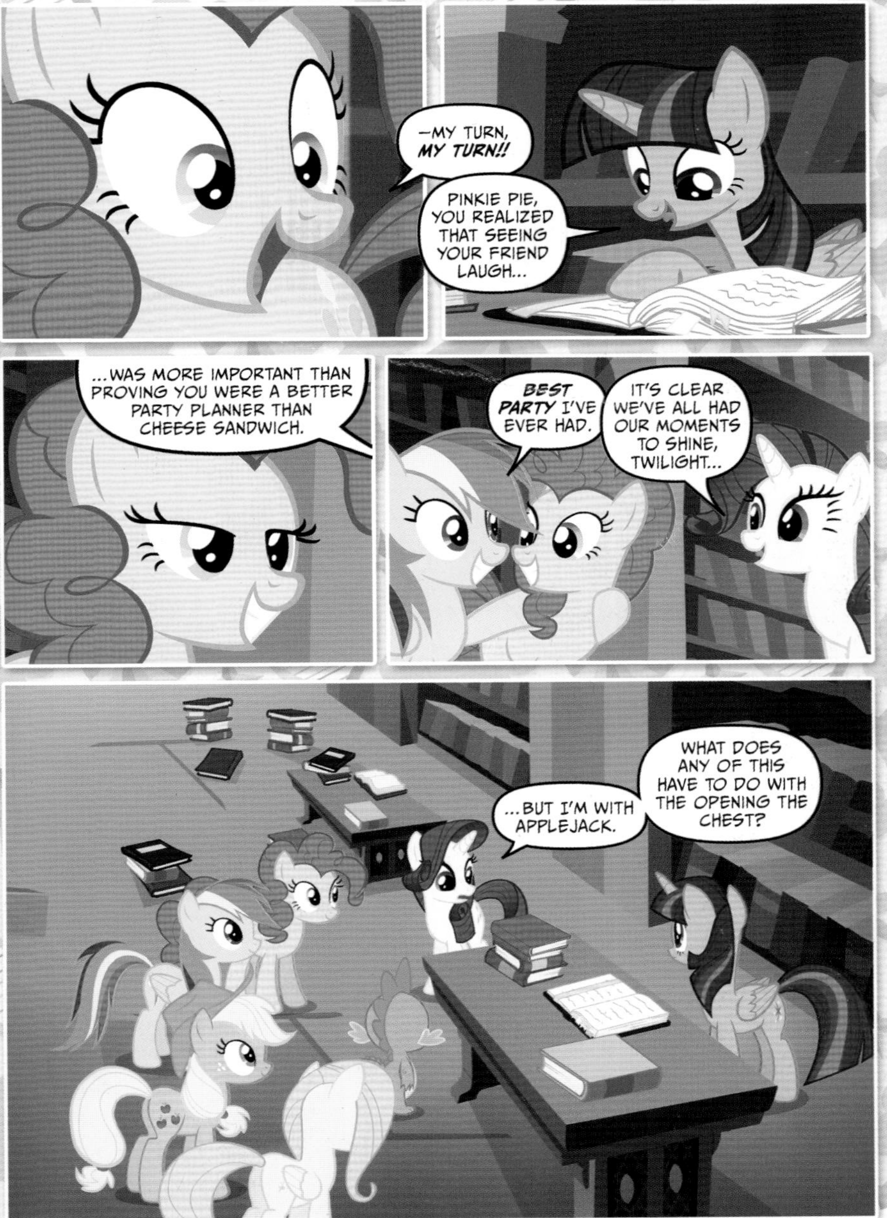

—MY TURN, *MY TURN!!*
PINKIE PIE, YOU REALIZED THAT SEEING YOUR FRIEND LAUGH...
...WAS MORE IMPORTANT THAN PROVING YOU WERE A BETTER PARTY PLANNER THAN CHEESE SANDWICH.
BEST PARTY I'VE EVER HAD.
IT'S CLEAR WE'VE ALL HAD OUR MOMENTS TO SHINE, TWILIGHT...
...BUT I'M WITH APPLEJACK.
WHAT DOES ANY OF THIS HAVE TO DO WITH THE OPENING THE CHEST?

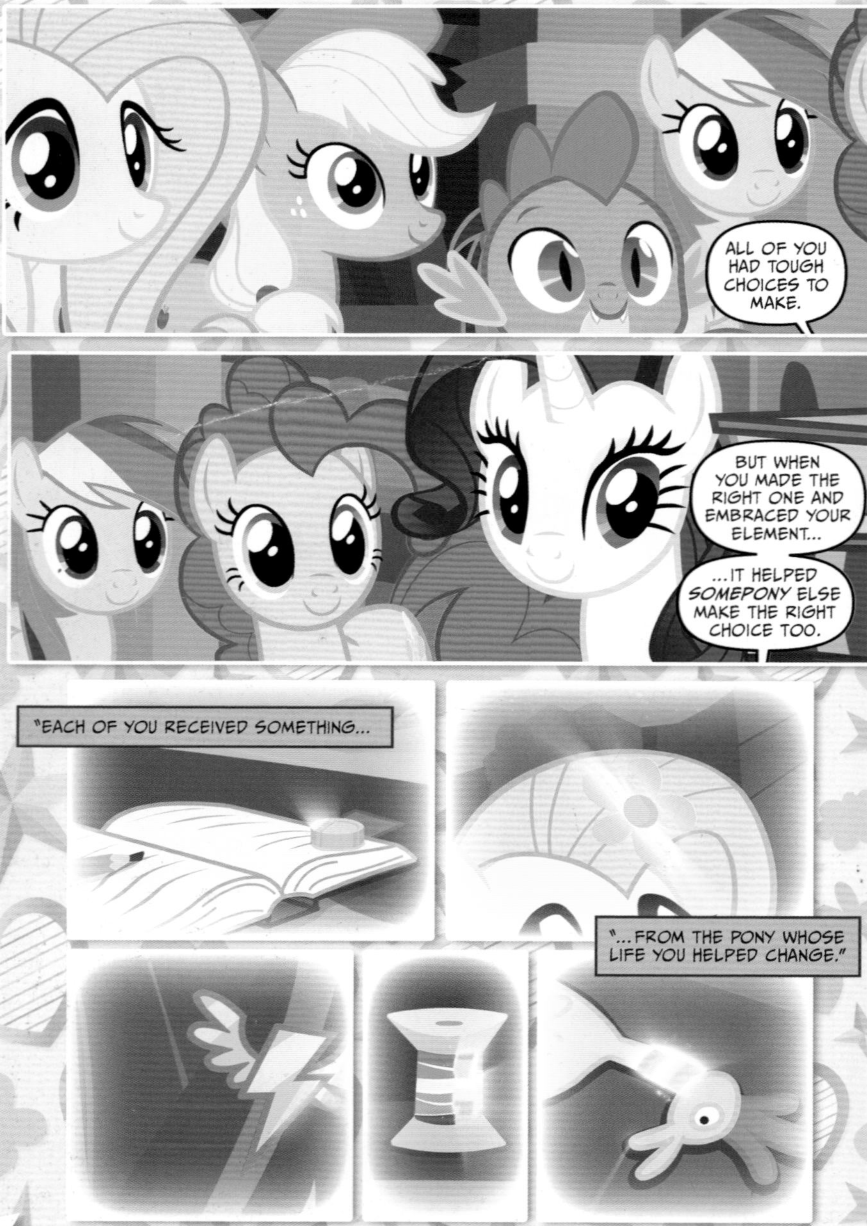
ALL OF YOU HAD TOUGH CHOICES TO MAKE.
BUT WHEN YOU MADE THE RIGHT ONE AND EMBRACED YOUR ELEMENT...
...IT HELPED SOMEPONY ELSE MAKE THE RIGHT CHOICE TOO.
"EACH OF YOU RECEIVED SOMETHING...
"...FROM THE PONY WHOSE LIFE YOU HELPED CHANGE."

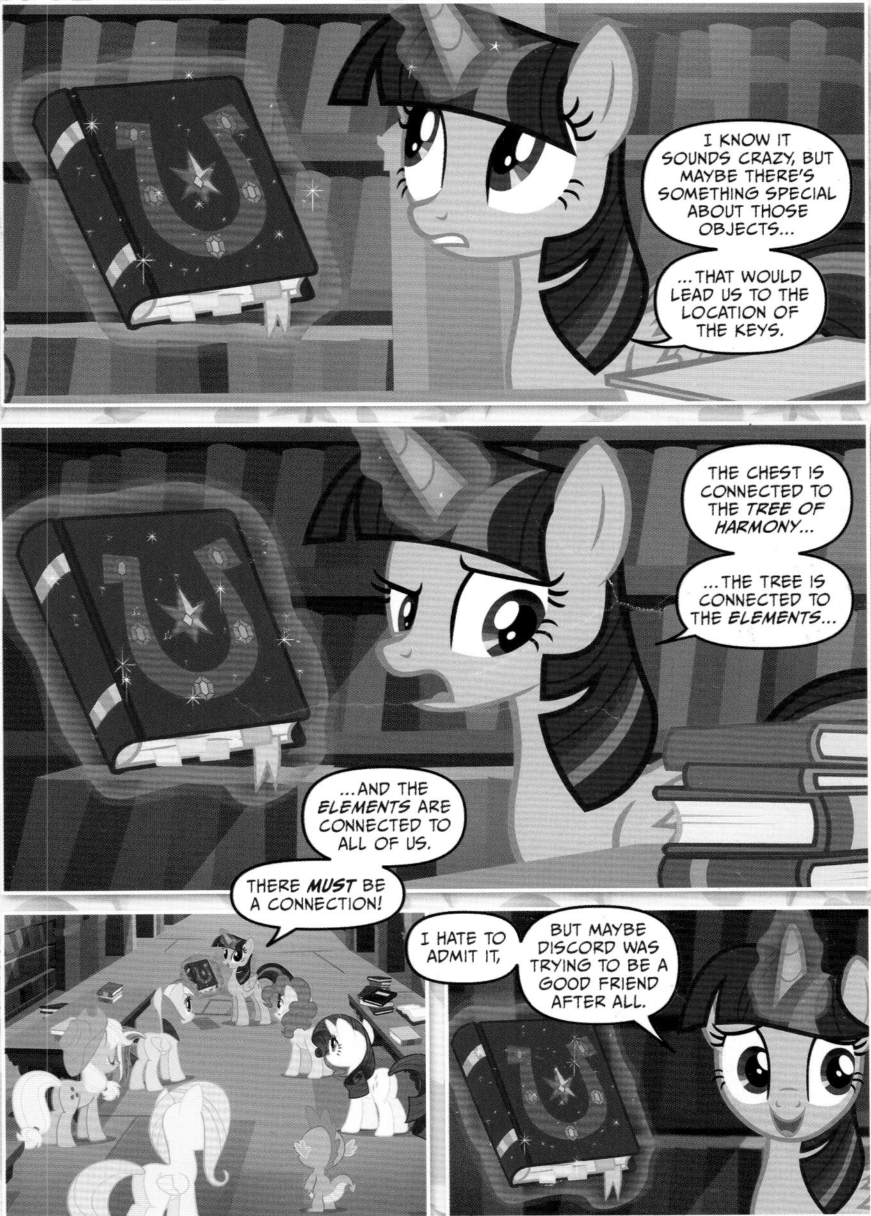
I KNOW IT SOUNDS CRAZY, BUT MAYBE THERE'S SOMETHING SPECIAL ABOUT THOSE OBJECTS...
...THAT WOULD LEAD US TO THE LOCATION OF THE KEYS.
THE CHEST IS CONNECTED TO THE *TREE OF HARMONY*...
...THE TREE IS CONNECTED TO THE *ELEMENTS*...
...AND THE *ELEMENTS* ARE CONNECTED TO ALL OF US.
THERE ***MUST*** BE A CONNECTION!
I HATE TO ADMIT IT,
BUT MAYBE DISCORD WAS TRYING TO BE A GOOD FRIEND AFTER ALL.

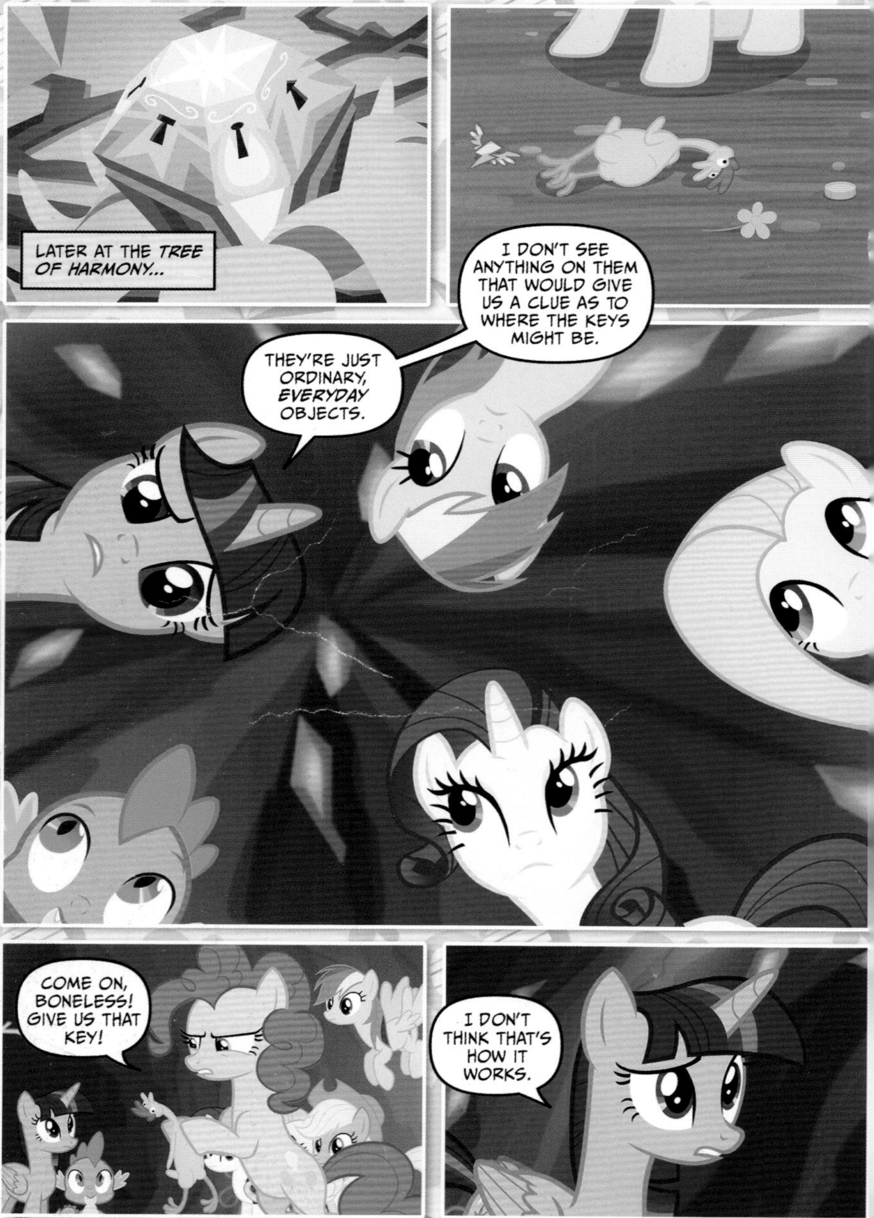

LATER AT THE *TREE OF HARMONY*...
I DON'T SEE ANYTHING ON THEM THAT WOULD GIVE US A CLUE AS TO WHERE THE KEYS MIGHT BE.
THEY'RE JUST ORDINARY, *EVERYDAY* OBJECTS.
COME ON, BONELESS! GIVE US THAT KEY!
I DON'T THINK THAT'S HOW IT WORKS.

FWIFFFT

SPLURCH

VVVVVRRRRNNNN

BUT THE RUBBER CHICKEN ACTIVATES A HIDDEN MAGIC...

-:GASP!:-

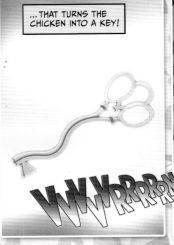

...THAT TURNS THE CHICKEN INTO A KEY!

VVVVVRRRRRNNNN

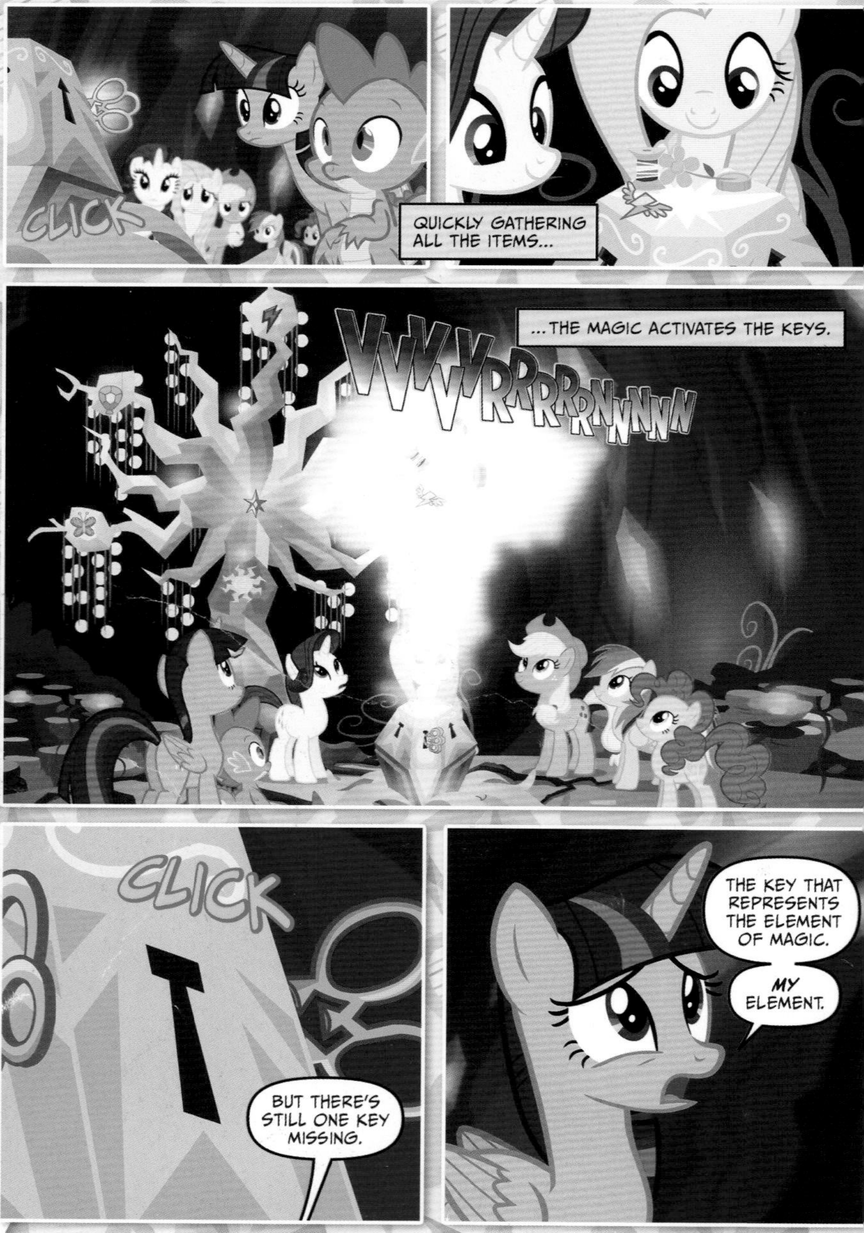
CLICK
QUICKLY GATHERING ALL THE ITEMS...
...THE MAGIC ACTIVATES THE KEYS.
VVVVVRRRRRNNNNN
CLICK
BUT THERE'S STILL ONE KEY MISSING.
THE KEY THAT REPRESENTS THE ELEMENT OF MAGIC.
MY ELEMENT.

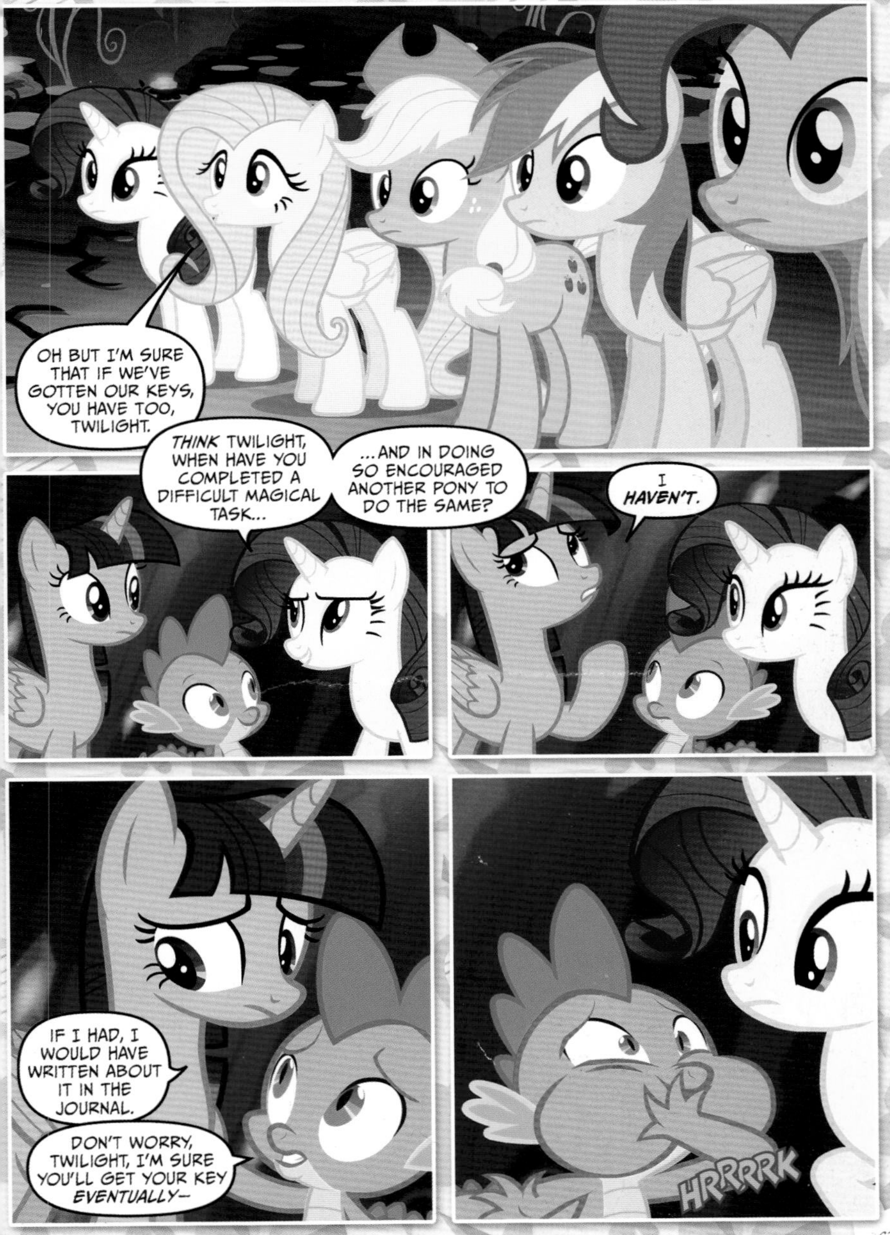
OH BUT I'M SURE THAT IF WE'VE GOTTEN OUR KEYS, YOU HAVE TOO, TWILIGHT.
THINK TWILIGHT, WHEN HAVE YOU COMPLETED A DIFFICULT MAGICAL TASK...
...AND IN DOING SO ENCOURAGED ANOTHER PONY TO DO THE SAME?
I *HAVEN'T.*
IF I HAD, I WOULD HAVE WRITTEN ABOUT IT IN THE JOURNAL.
DON'T WORRY, TWILIGHT, I'M SURE YOU'LL GET YOUR KEY *EVENTUALLY*—
HRRRRK

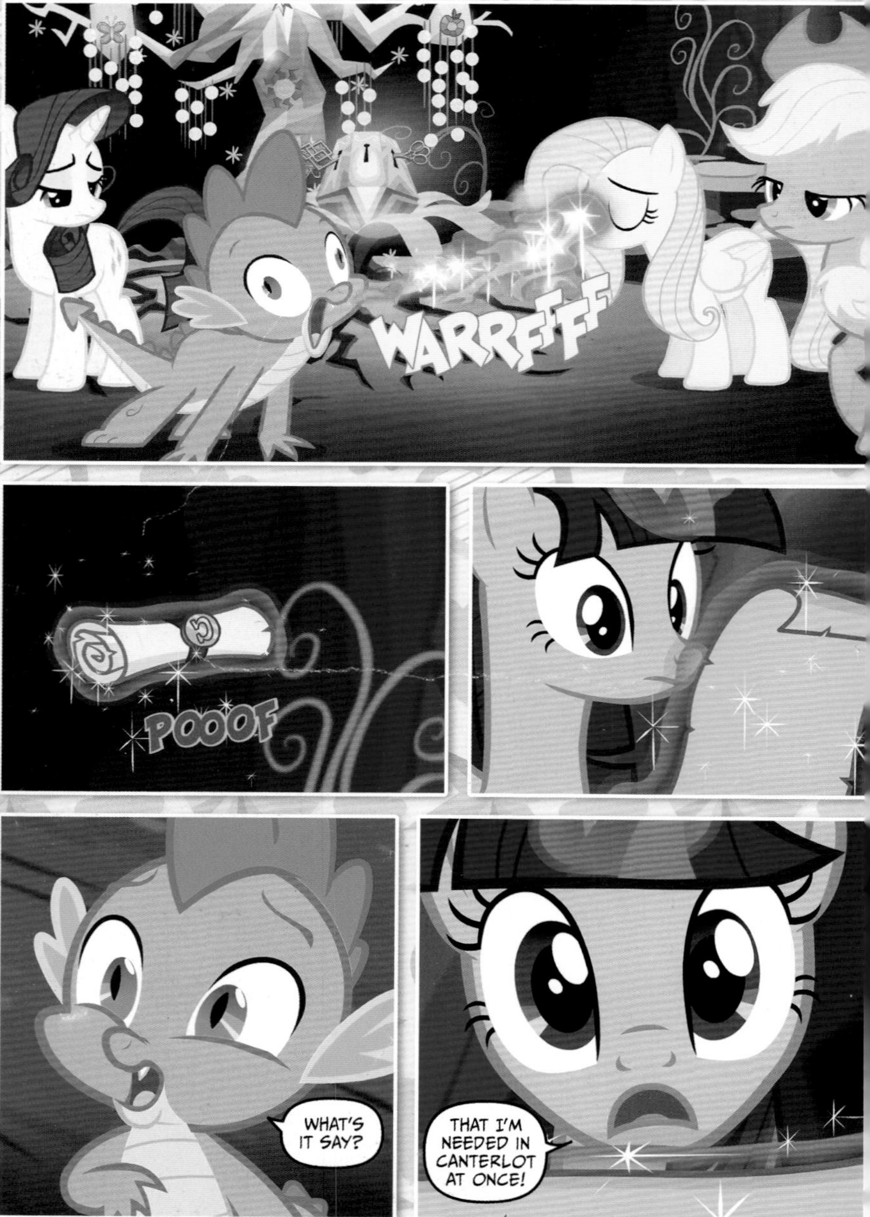

WARRFFFF
POOOF
WHAT'S IT SAY?
THAT I'M NEEDED IN CANTERLOT AT ONCE!

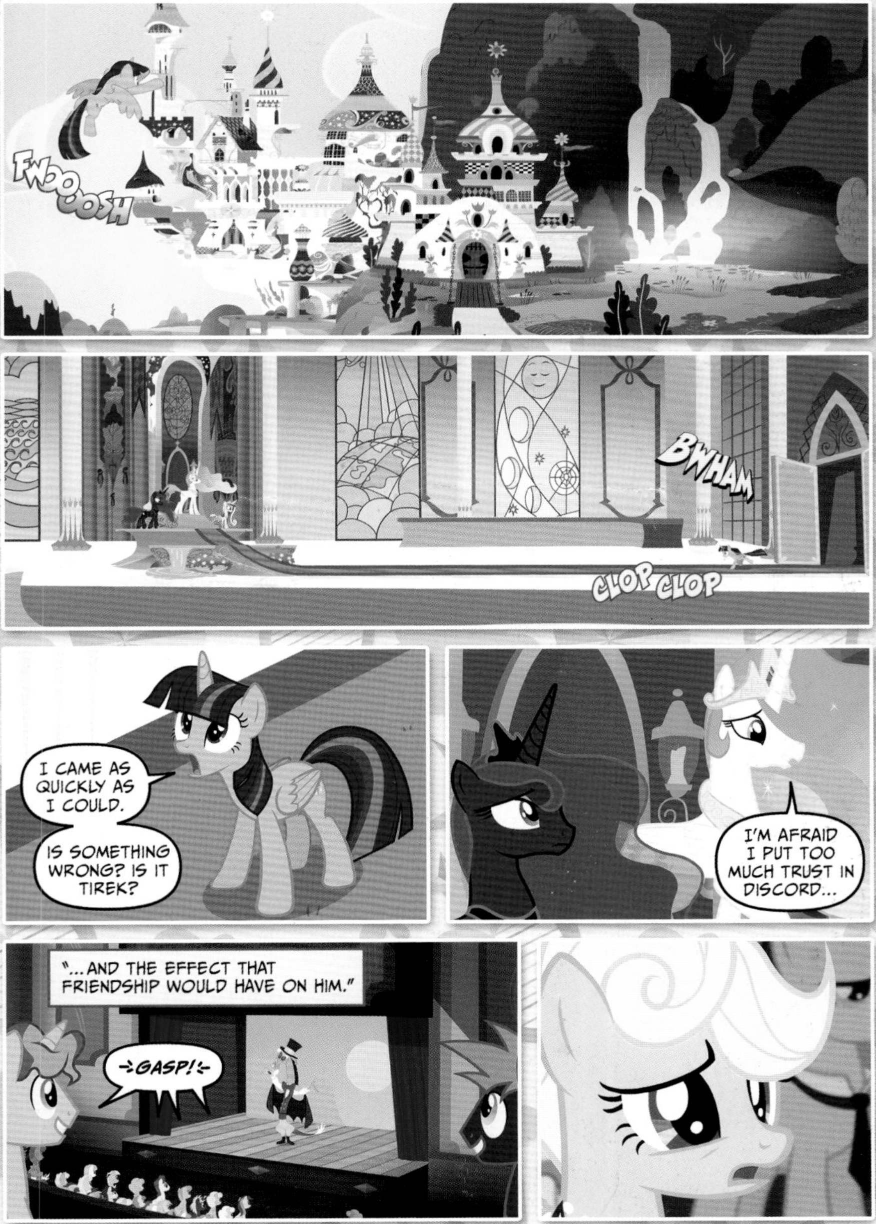
FWOOOOSH
BWHAM
CLOP CLOP
I CAME AS QUICKLY AS I COULD.
IS SOMETHING WRONG? IS IT TIREK?
I'M AFRAID I PUT TOO MUCH TRUST IN DISCORD...
"...AND THE EFFECT THAT FRIENDSHIP WOULD HAVE ON HIM."
GASP!

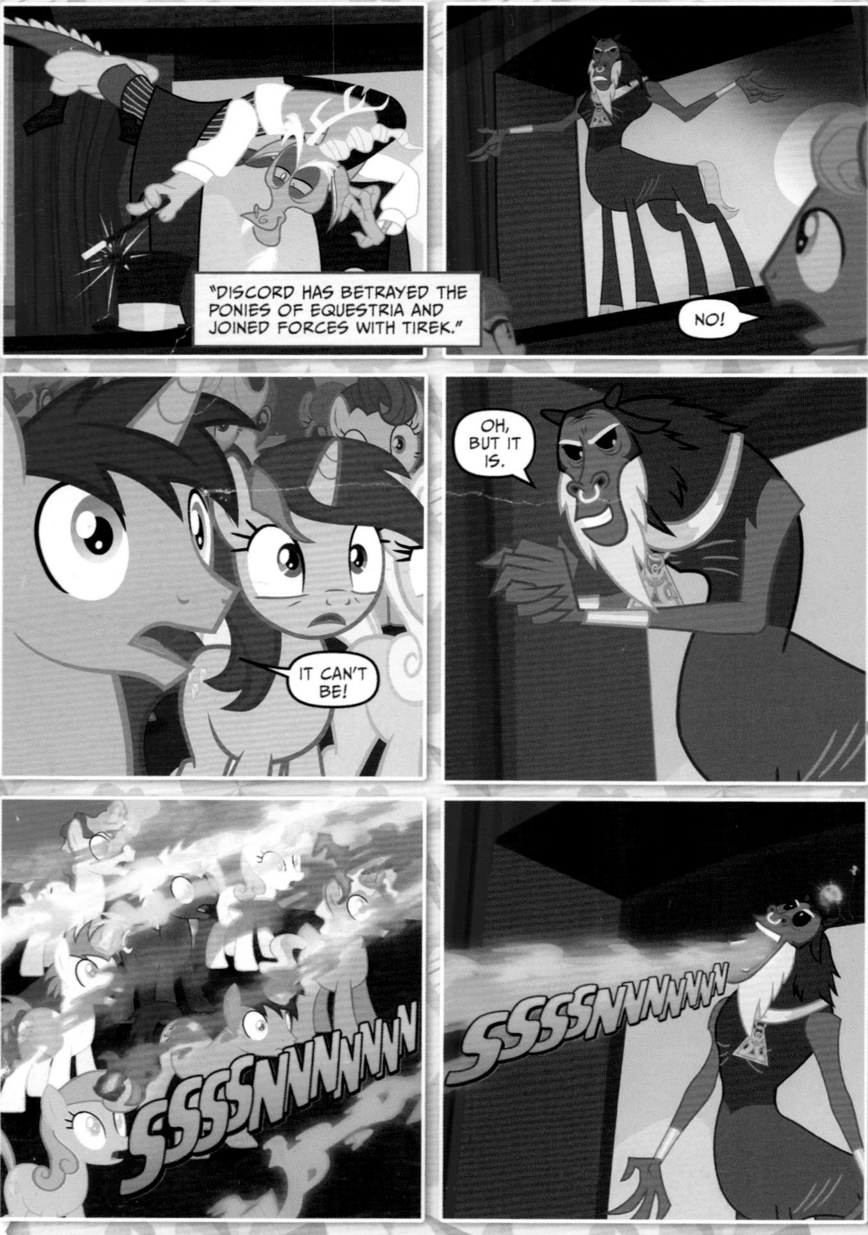
"DISCORD HAS BETRAYED THE PONIES OF EQUESTRIA AND JOINED FORCES WITH TIREK."
NO!
OH, BUT IT IS.
IT CAN'T BE!
SSSSNNNNNNN
SSSSNNNNNNN

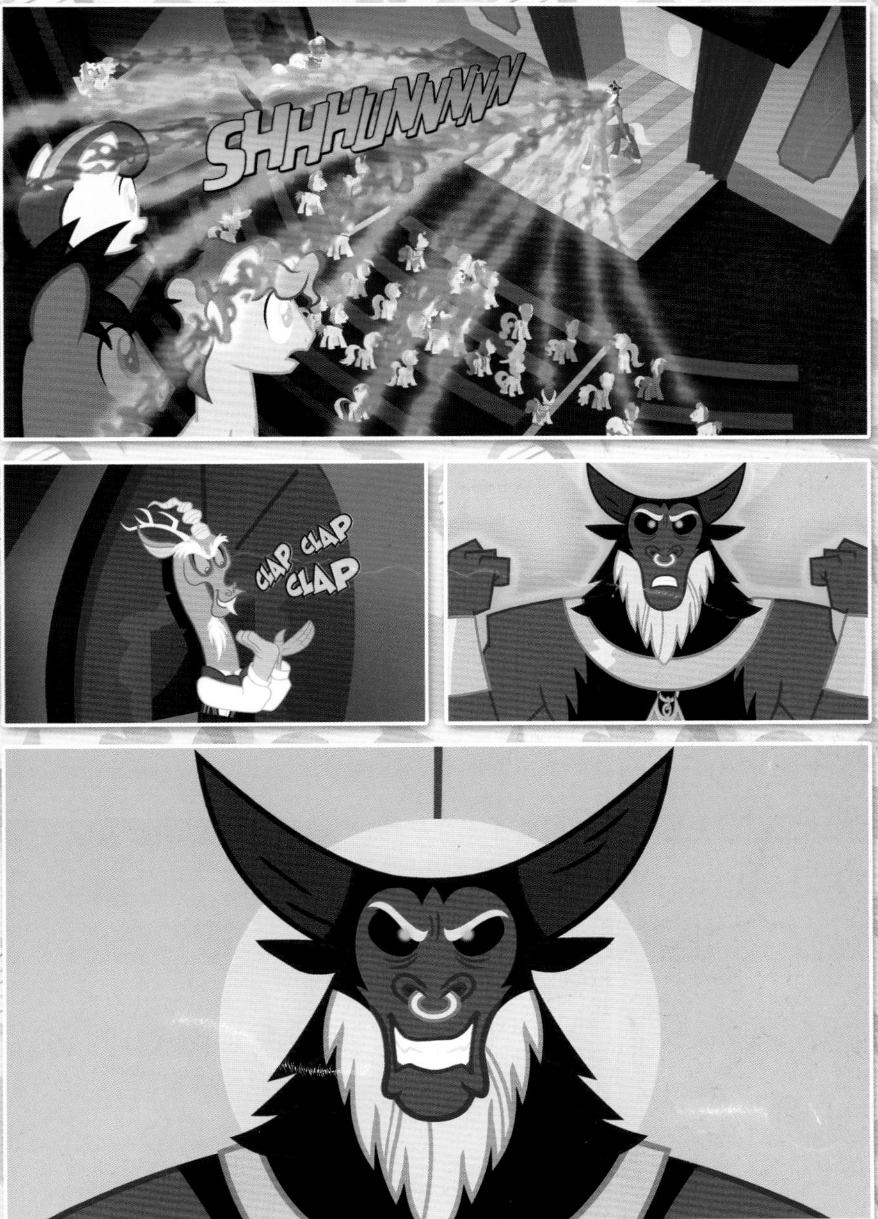
SHHHUNNNNN
CLAP CLAP
CLAP

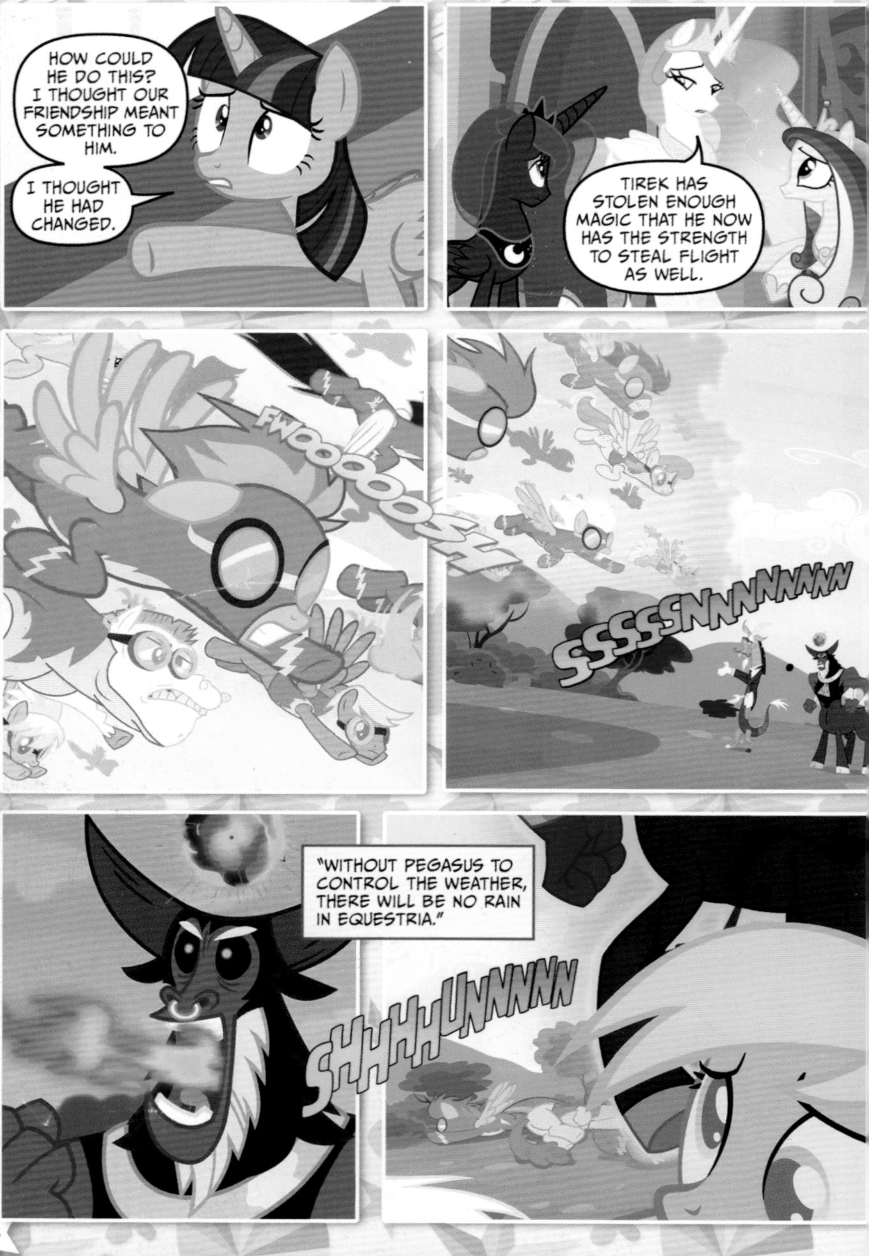
HOW COULD HE DO THIS? I THOUGHT OUR FRIENDSHIP MEANT SOMETHING TO HIM.
I THOUGHT HE HAD CHANGED.
TIREK HAS STOLEN ENOUGH MAGIC THAT HE NOW HAS THE STRENGTH TO STEAL FLIGHT AS WELL.
FWOOOOOOSH
SSSSSNNNNNNNN
"WITHOUT PEGASUS TO CONTROL THE WEATHER, THERE WILL BE NO RAIN IN EQUESTRIA."
SHHHHUNNNNNN

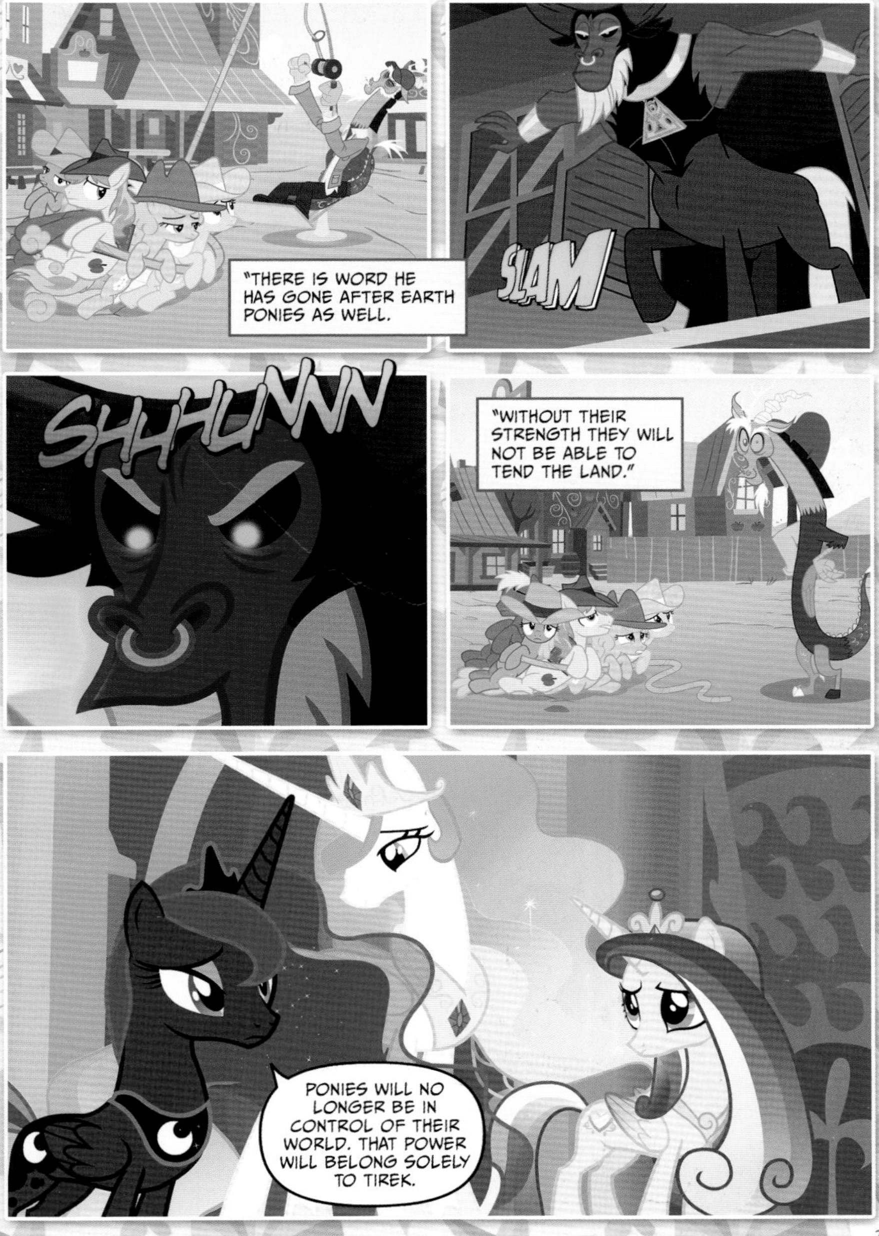
"THERE IS WORD HE HAS GONE AFTER EARTH PONIES AS WELL.
SLAM
SHHHUNNNN
"WITHOUT THEIR STRENGTH THEY WILL NOT BE ABLE TO TEND THE LAND."
PONIES WILL NO LONGER BE IN CONTROL OF THEIR WORLD. THAT POWER WILL BELONG SOLELY TO TIREK.

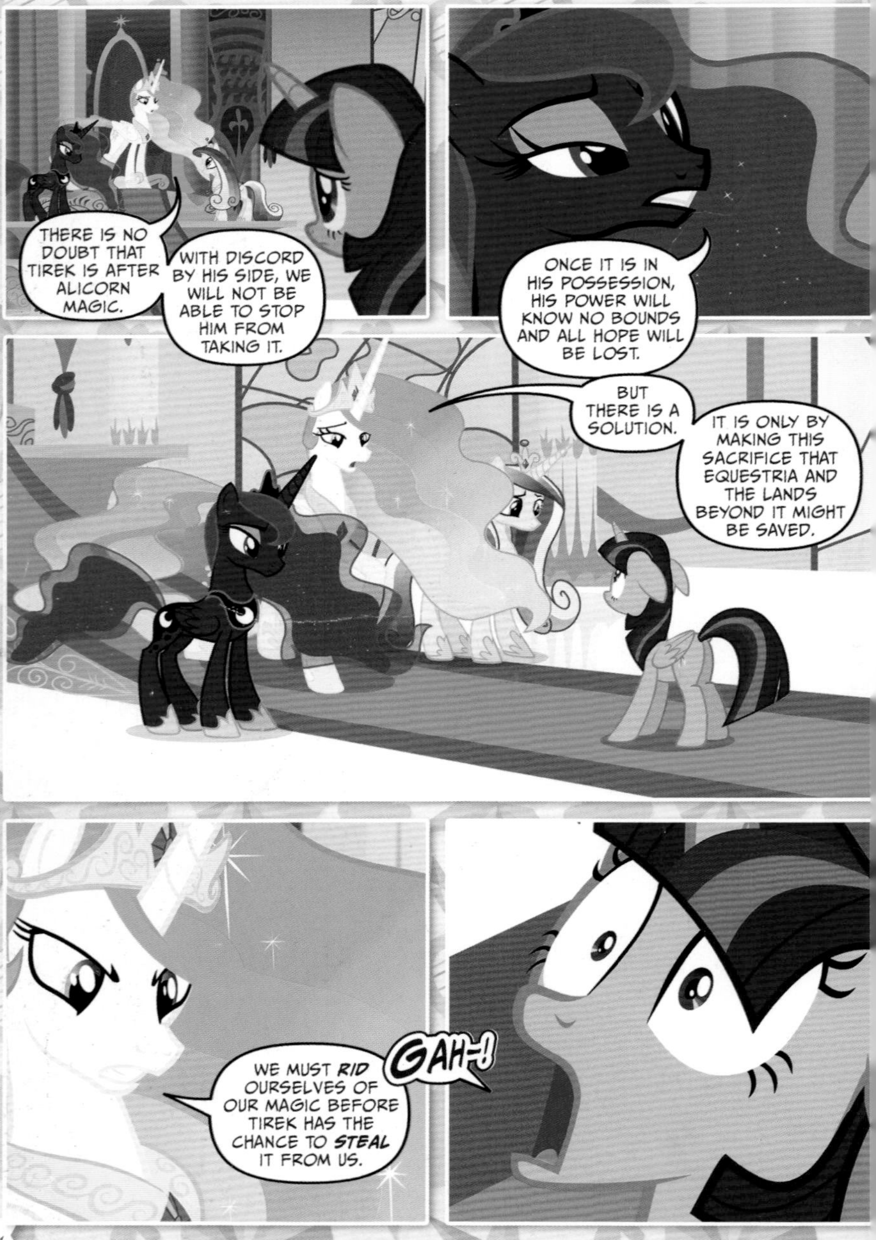

THERE IS NO DOUBT THAT TIREK IS AFTER ALICORN MAGIC.
WITH DISCORD BY HIS SIDE, WE WILL NOT BE ABLE TO STOP HIM FROM TAKING IT.
ONCE IT IS IN HIS POSSESSION, HIS POWER WILL KNOW NO BOUNDS AND ALL HOPE WILL BE LOST.
BUT THERE IS A SOLUTION.
IT IS ONLY BY MAKING THIS SACRIFICE THAT EQUESTRIA AND THE LANDS BEYOND IT MIGHT BE SAVED.
WE MUST *RID* OURSELVES OF OUR MAGIC BEFORE TIREK HAS THE CHANCE TO *STEAL* IT FROM US.
GAH-!

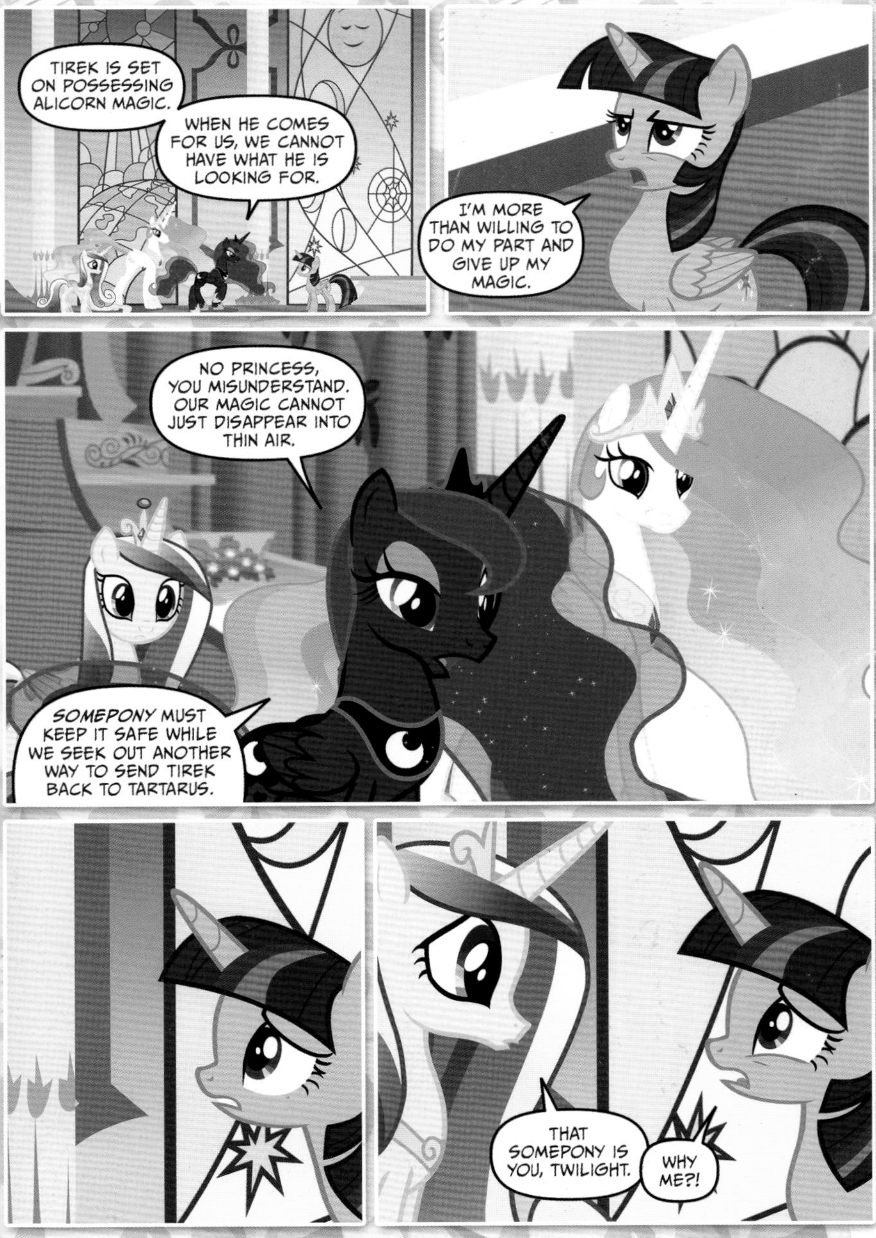
TIREK IS SET ON POSSESSING ALICORN MAGIC.
WHEN HE COMES FOR US, WE CANNOT HAVE WHAT HE IS LOOKING FOR.
I'M MORE THAN WILLING TO DO MY PART AND GIVE UP MY MAGIC.
NO PRINCESS, YOU MISUNDERSTAND. OUR MAGIC CANNOT JUST DISAPPEAR INTO THIN AIR.
SOMEPONY MUST KEEP IT SAFE WHILE WE SEEK OUT ANOTHER WAY TO SEND TIREK BACK TO TARTARUS.
THAT SOMEPONY IS YOU, TWILIGHT.
WHY ME?!

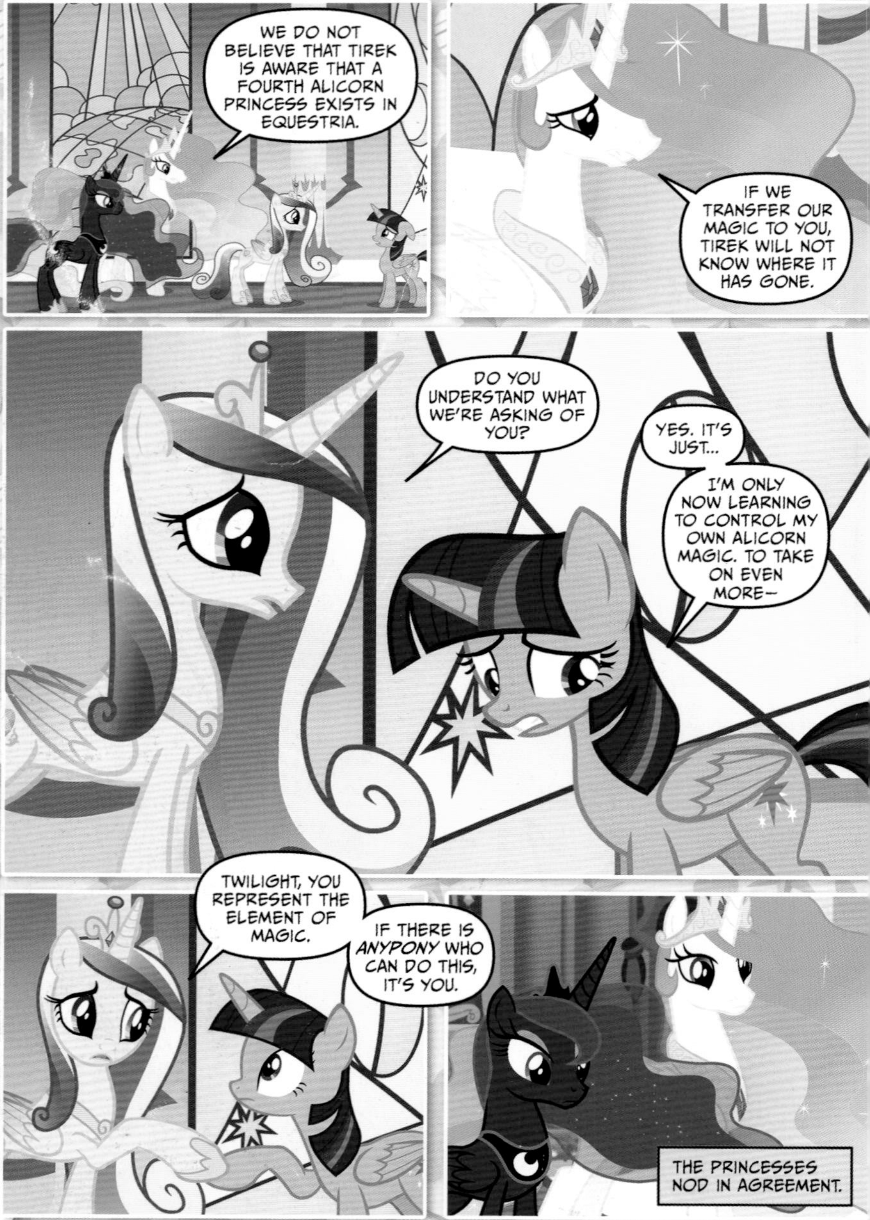

WE DO NOT BELIEVE THAT TIREK IS AWARE THAT A FOURTH ALICORN PRINCESS EXISTS IN EQUESTRIA.
IF WE TRANSFER OUR MAGIC TO YOU, TIREK WILL NOT KNOW WHERE IT HAS GONE.
DO YOU UNDERSTAND WHAT WE'RE ASKING OF YOU?
YES. IT'S JUST...
I'M ONLY NOW LEARNING TO CONTROL MY OWN ALICORN MAGIC. TO TAKE ON EVEN MORE–
TWILIGHT, YOU REPRESENT THE ELEMENT OF MAGIC.
IF THERE IS *ANYPONY* WHO CAN DO THIS, IT'S YOU.
THE PRINCESSES NOD IN AGREEMENT.

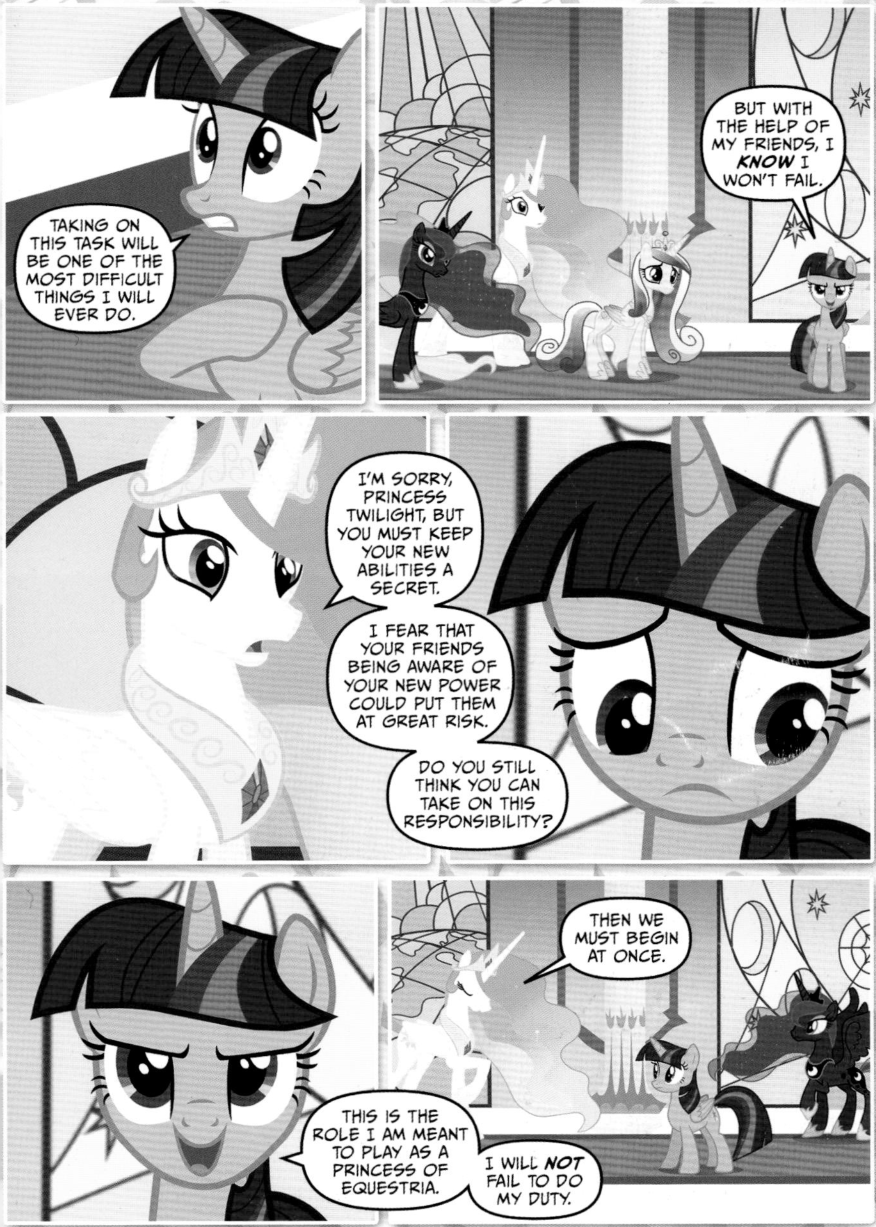
TAKING ON THIS TASK WILL BE ONE OF THE MOST DIFFICULT THINGS I WILL EVER DO.
BUT WITH THE HELP OF MY FRIENDS, I ***KNOW*** I WON'T FAIL.
I'M SORRY, PRINCESS TWILIGHT, BUT YOU MUST KEEP YOUR NEW ABILITIES A SECRET.
I FEAR THAT YOUR FRIENDS BEING AWARE OF YOUR NEW POWER COULD PUT THEM AT GREAT RISK.
DO YOU STILL THINK YOU CAN TAKE ON THIS RESPONSIBILITY?
THIS IS THE ROLE I AM MEANT TO PLAY AS A PRINCESS OF EQUESTRIA.
I WILL ***NOT*** FAIL TO DO MY DUTY.
THEN WE MUST BEGIN AT ONCE.

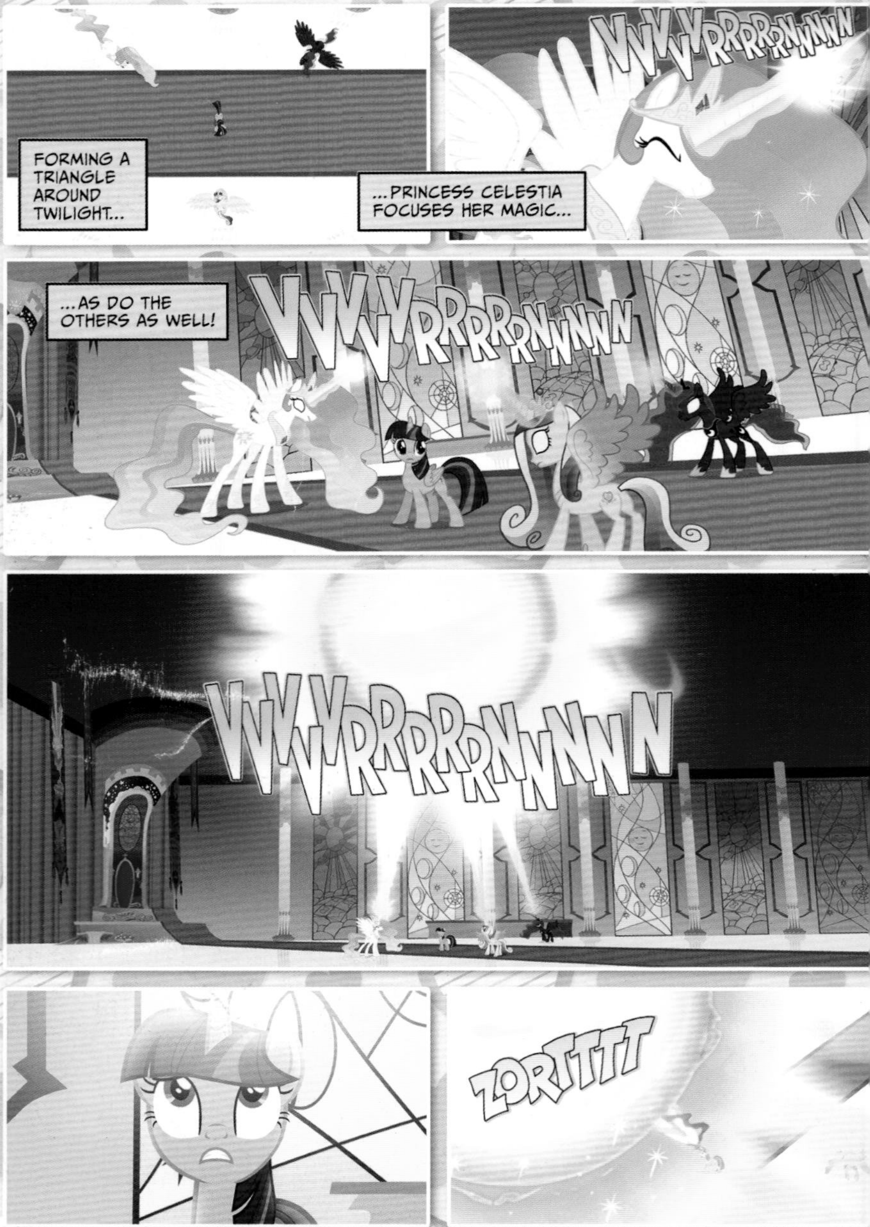
FORMING A TRIANGLE AROUND TWILIGHT...
...PRINCESS CELESTIA FOCUSES HER MAGIC...
VVVVVRRRRRNNNNN
...AS DO THE OTHERS AS WELL!
VVVVVRRRRRNNNNN
VVVVVRRRRRNNNNN
ZORTTTT

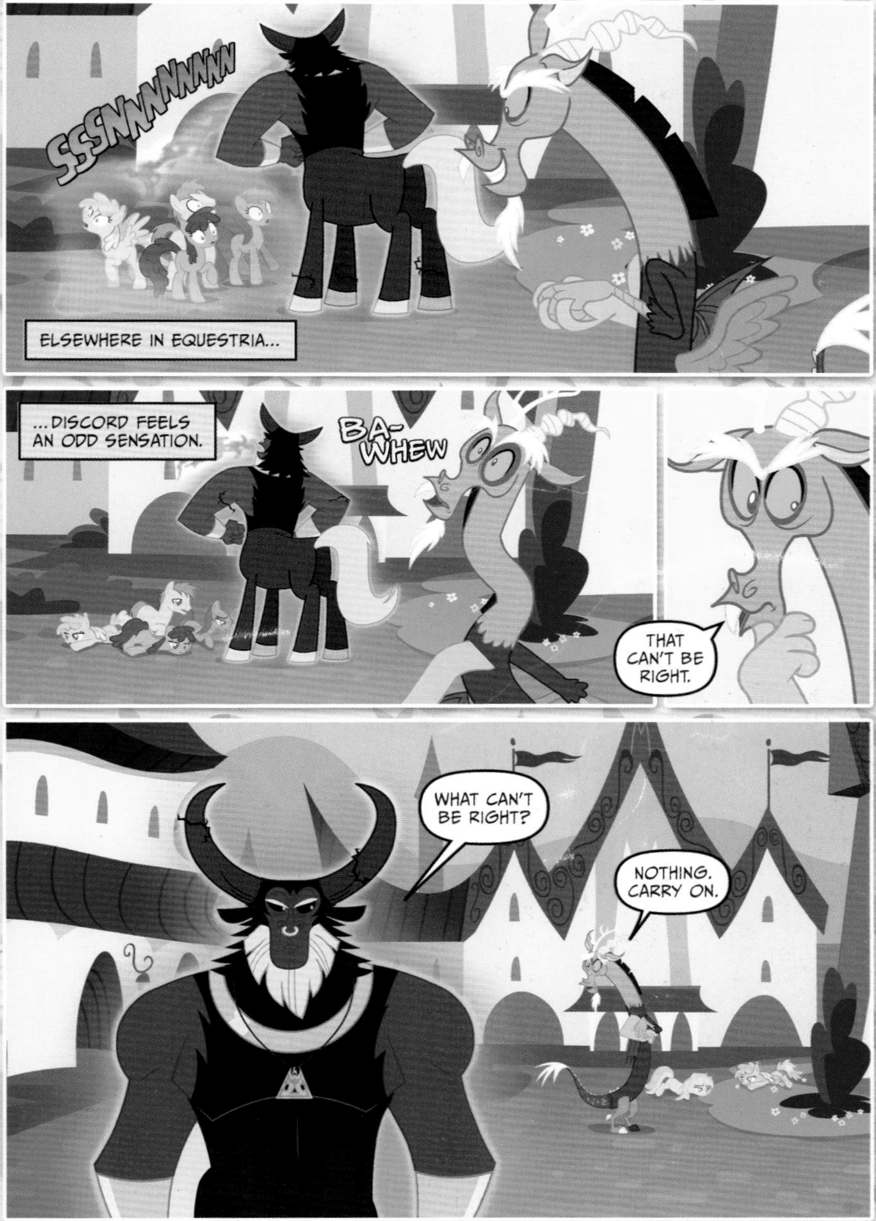
SSSNNNNNNNNN
ELSEWHERE IN EQUESTRIA...
...DISCORD FEELS AN ODD SENSATION.
BA-WHEW
THAT CAN'T BE RIGHT.
WHAT CAN'T BE RIGHT?
NOTHING. CARRY ON.

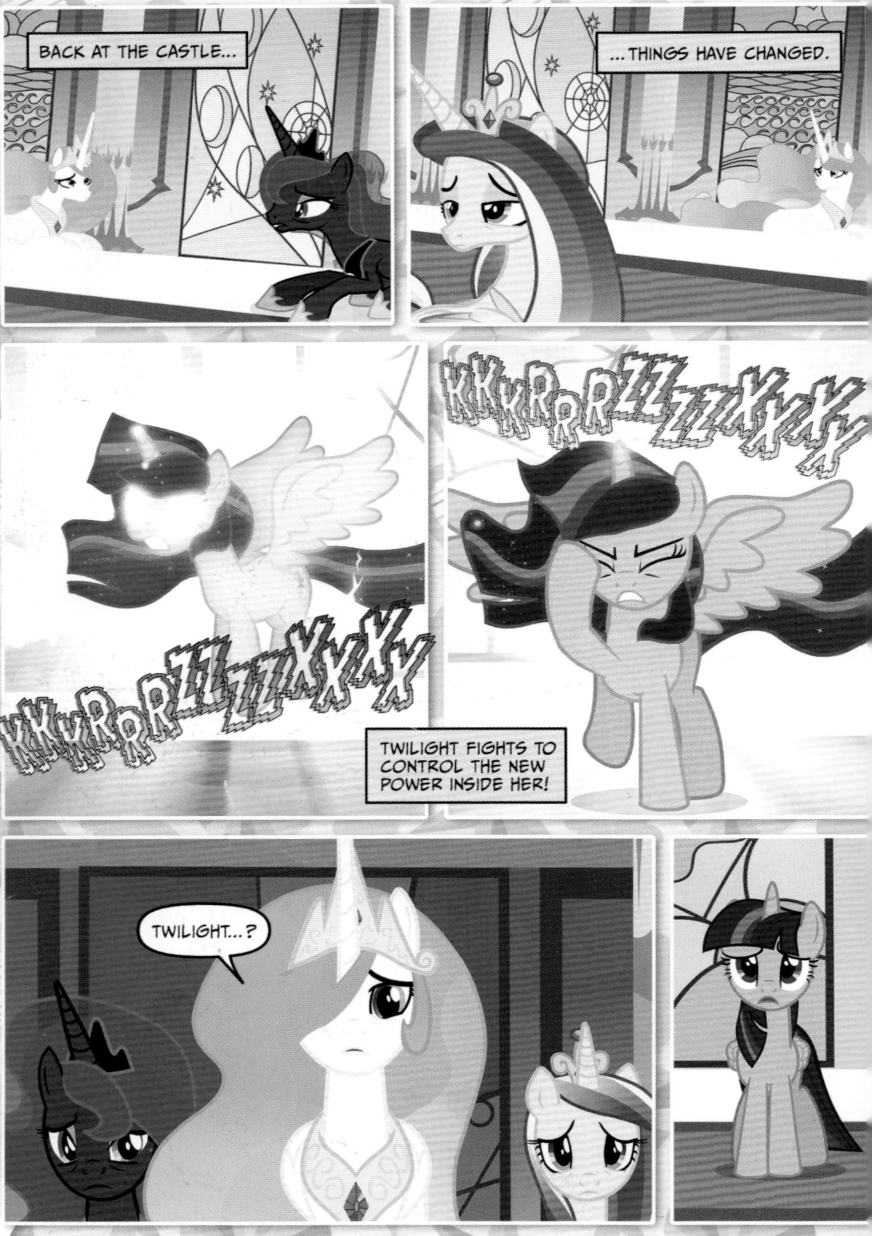

BACK AT THE CASTLE...
...THINGS HAVE CHANGED.
KKKRRRZZZZZXXXX
KKKRRRZZZZZXXXX
TWILIGHT FIGHTS TO CONTROL THE NEW POWER INSIDE HER!
TWILIGHT...?

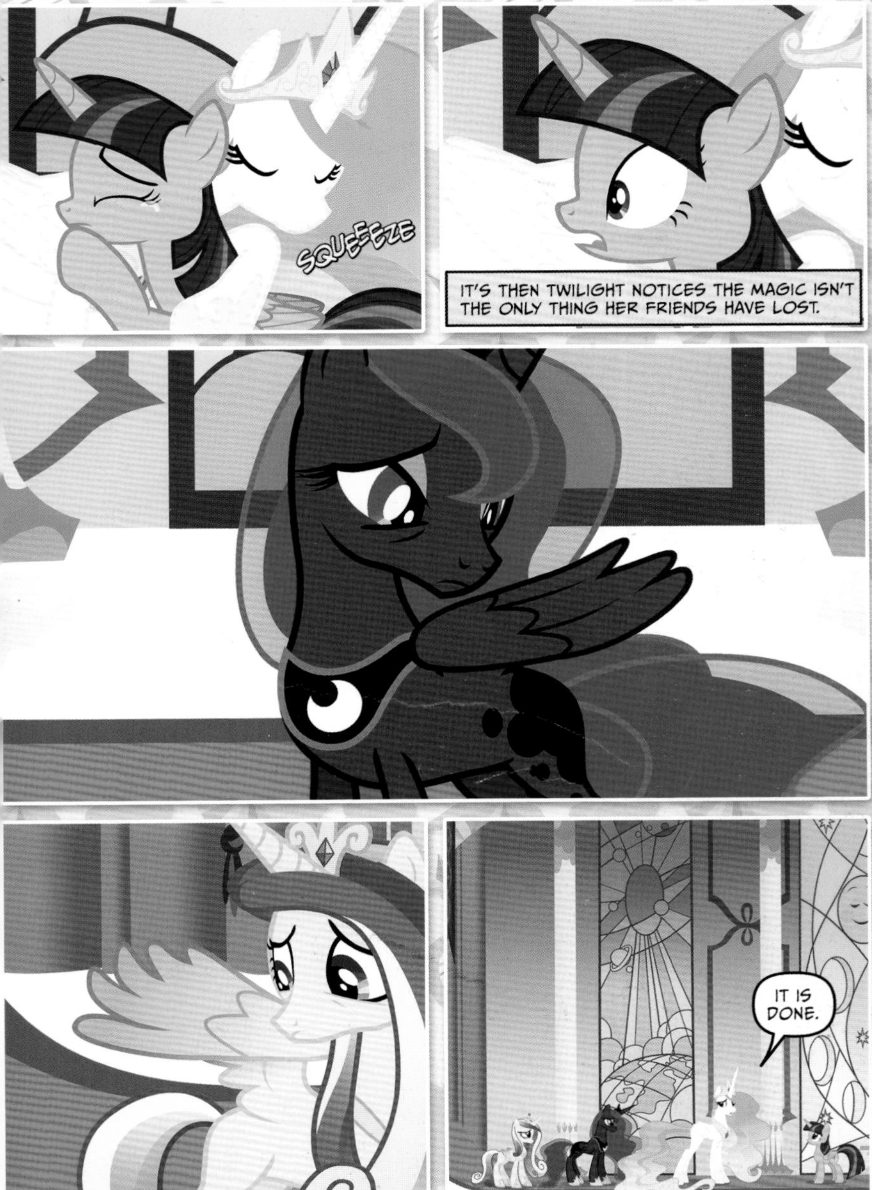
SQUEEEEZE
IT'S THEN TWILIGHT NOTICES THE MAGIC ISN'T THE ONLY THING HER FRIENDS HAVE LOST.
IT IS DONE.

BACK AT TWILIGHT'S...

SSSSZZ-ZZZ-ZIT!

YOU WEREN'T GONE VERY LONG.

DOES THAT MEAN EVERYTHING IS OKAY?

BUT TWILIGHT CAN BARELY CONTAIN HER NEW POWERS!

YES. EVERYTHING'S FINE.

KKKRRAAZZXXX

IN THAT CASE, I'M GOING BACK TO BED.

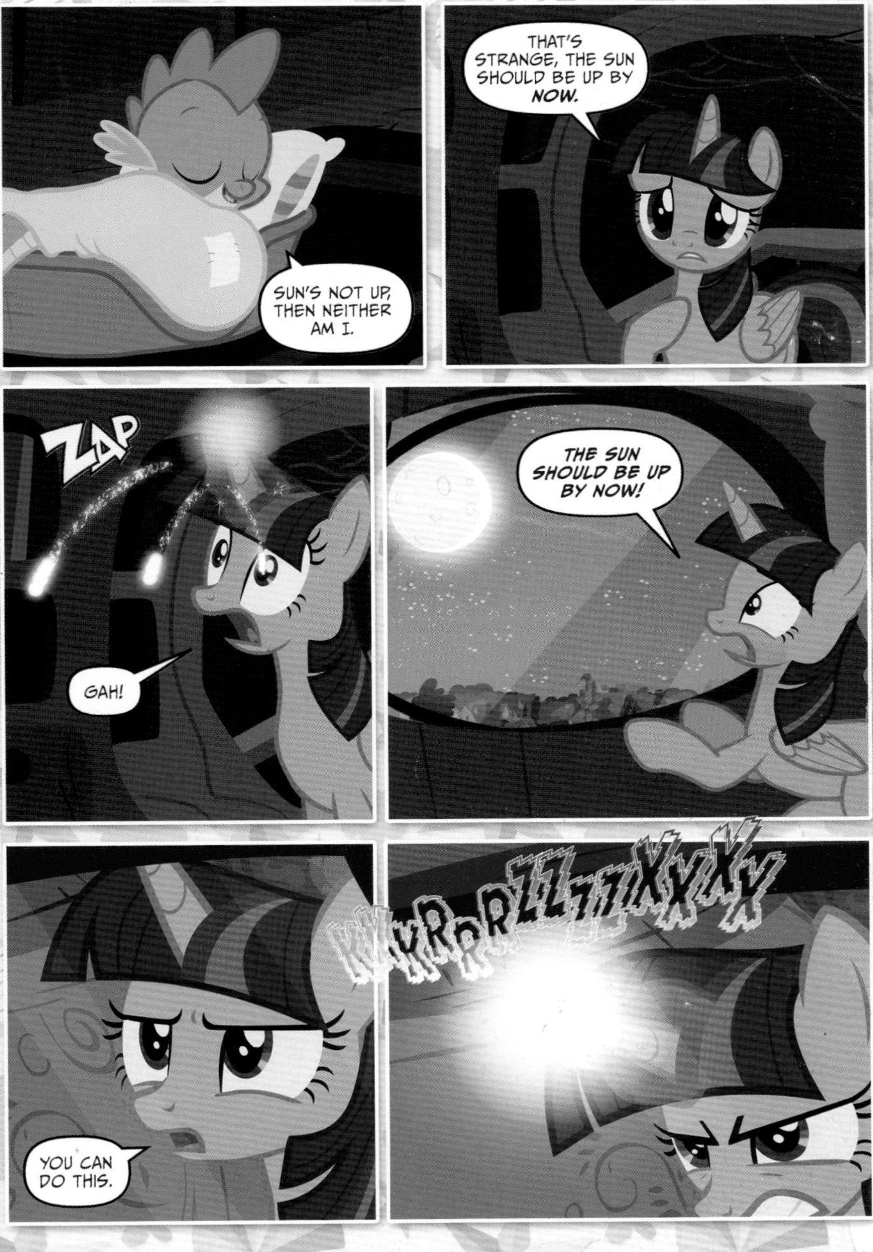
SUN'S NOT UP, THEN NEITHER AM I.
THAT'S STRANGE, THE SUN SHOULD BE UP BY **NOW.**
ZAP
GAH!
THE SUN SHOULD BE UP BY NOW!
YOU CAN DO THIS.
KKKRRRZZZZZZXXXX

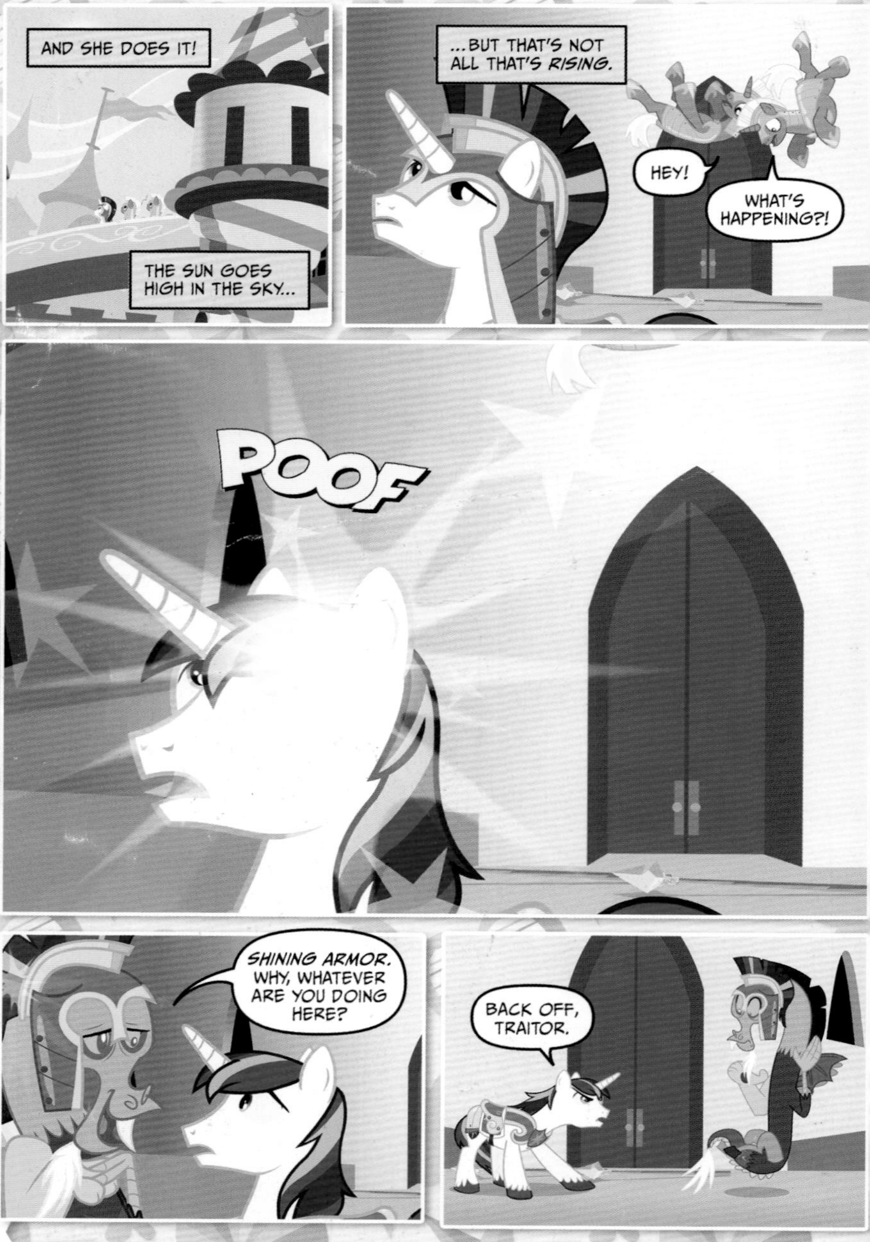
AND SHE DOES IT!
THE SUN GOES HIGH IN THE SKY...
...BUT THAT'S NOT ALL THAT'S *RISING.*
HEY!
WHAT'S HAPPENING?!
POOF
SHINING ARMOR. WHY, WHATEVER ARE YOU DOING HERE?
BACK OFF, TRAITOR.

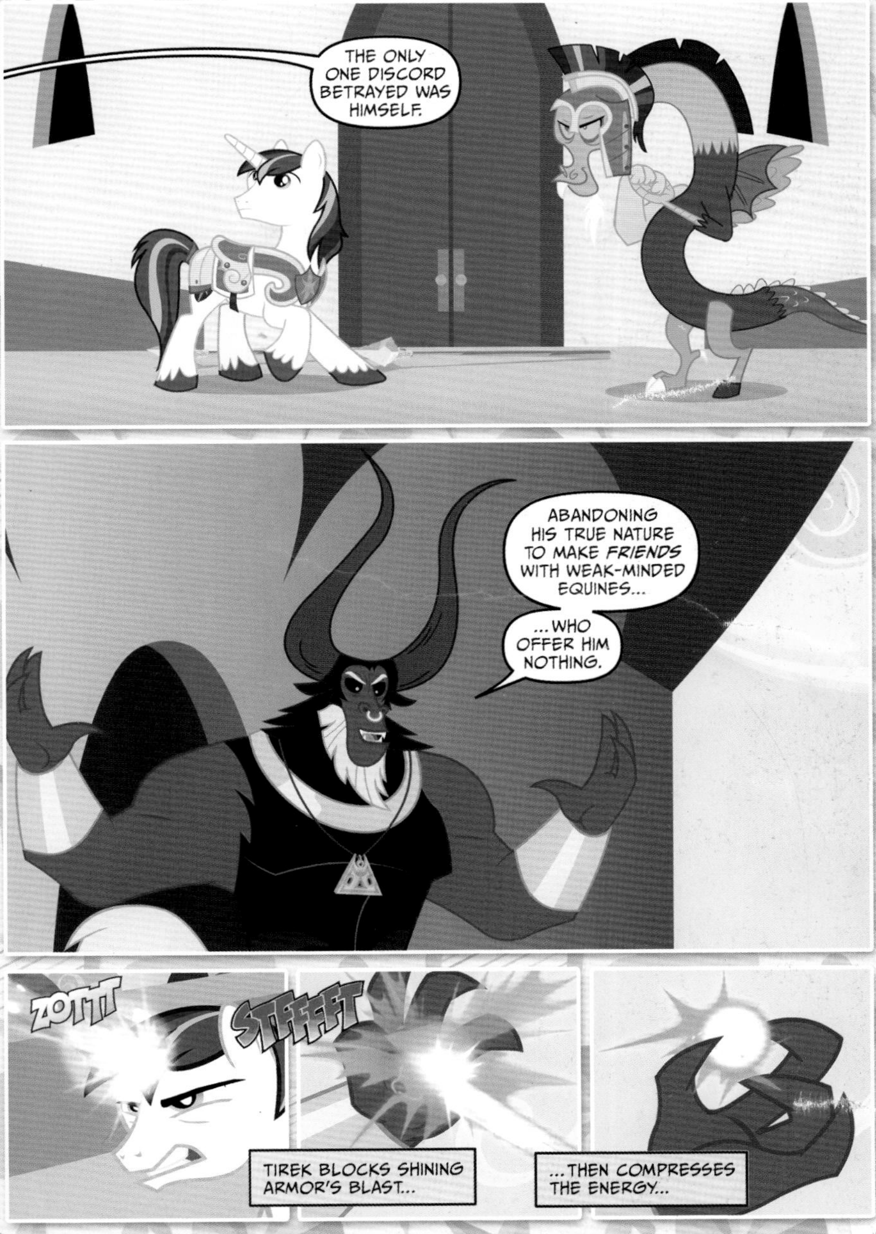
THE ONLY ONE DISCORD BETRAYED WAS HIMSELF.
ABANDONING HIS TRUE NATURE TO MAKE *FRIENDS* WITH WEAK-MINDED EQUINES...
...WHO OFFER HIM NOTHING.
ZOTTT
STFFFFT
TIREK BLOCKS SHINING ARMOR'S BLAST...
...THEN COMPRESSES THE ENERGY...

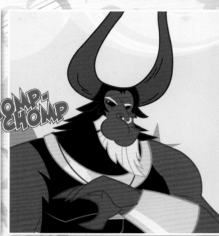

...BEFORE EATING IT!

CHOMP-CHOMP

SSSRRRRNNNN

CHUK

WHAM

HOW COULD YOU... DO THIS?

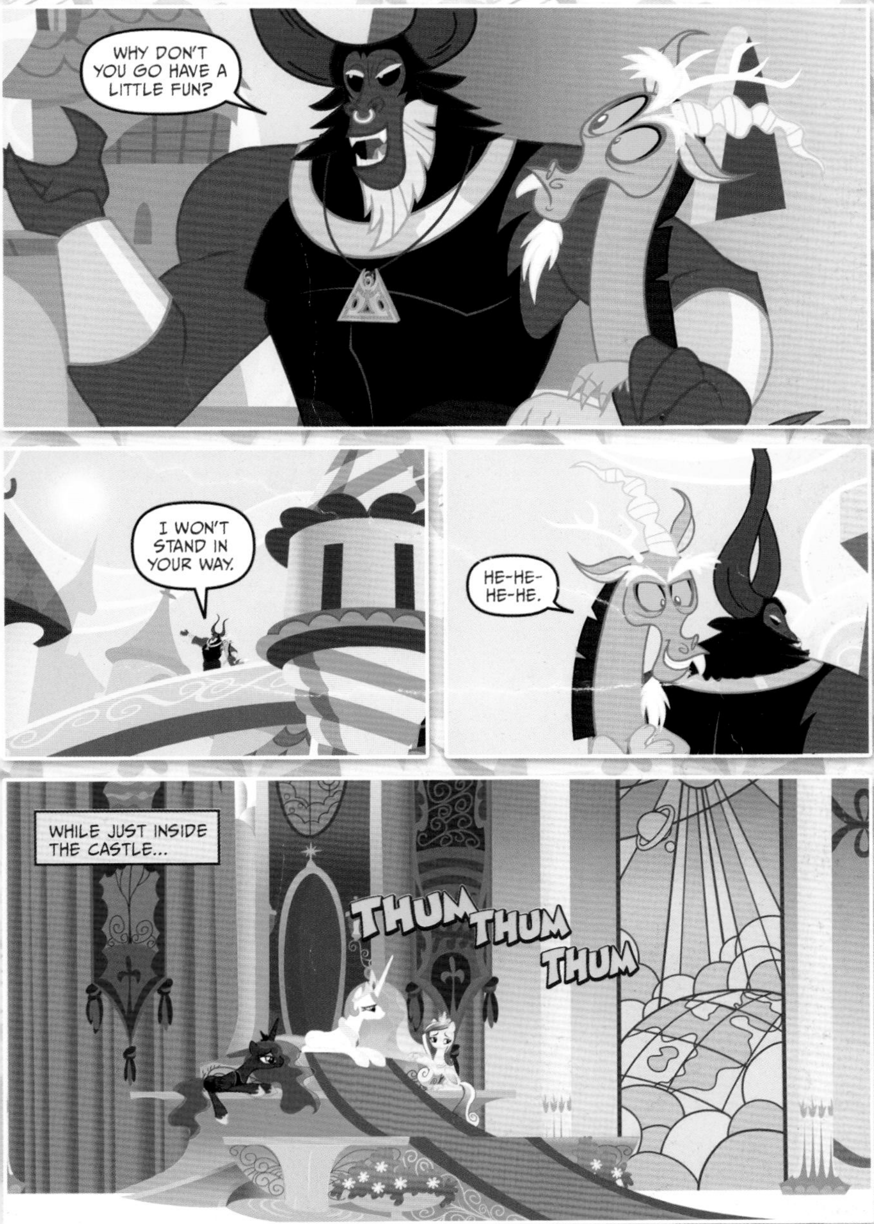
WHY DON'T YOU GO HAVE A LITTLE FUN?
I WON'T STAND IN YOUR WAY.
HE-HE-HE-HE.
WHILE JUST INSIDE THE CASTLE...
THUM THUM THUM

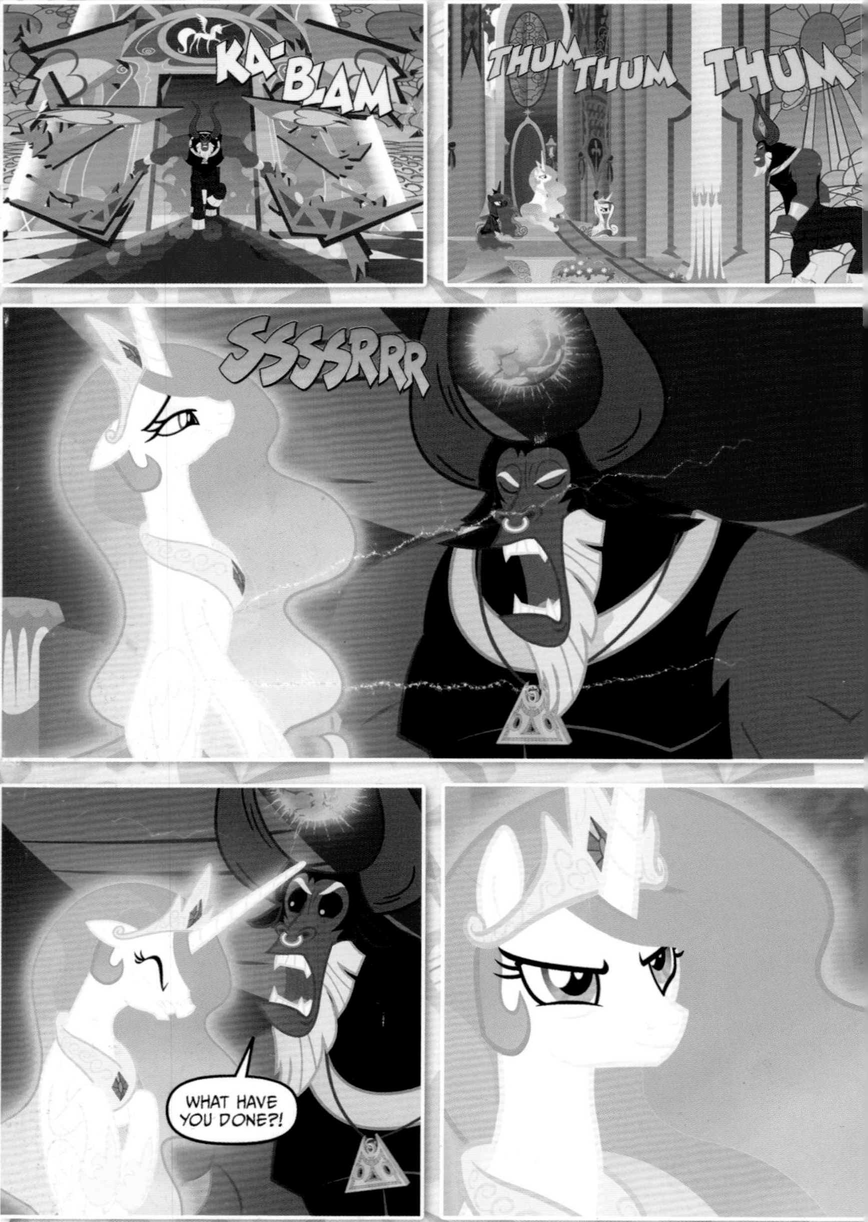
KA-BLAM
THUM THUM THUM
SSSSRRR
WHAT HAVE YOU DONE?!

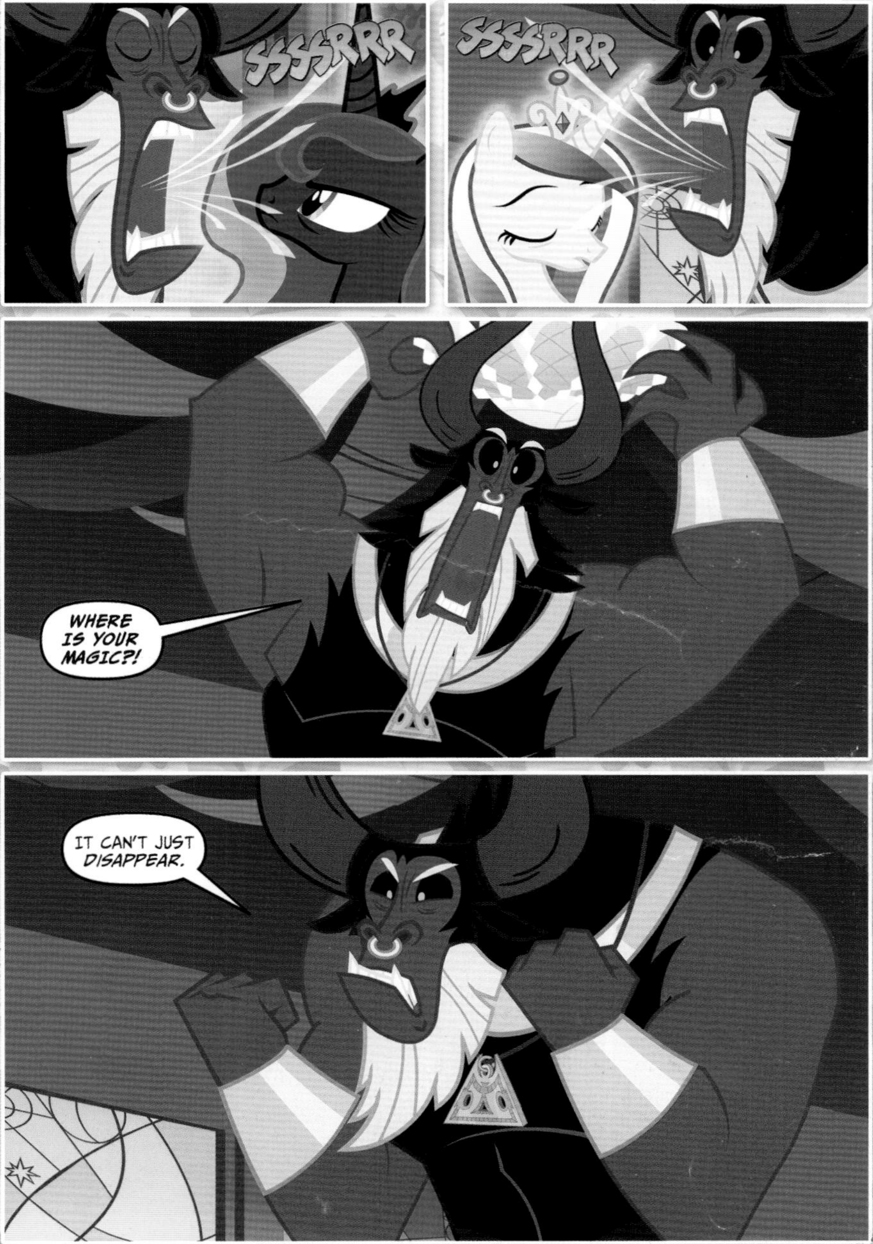
SSSSRRR
SSSSRRR
WHERE IS YOUR MAGIC?!
IT CAN'T JUST DISAPPEAR.

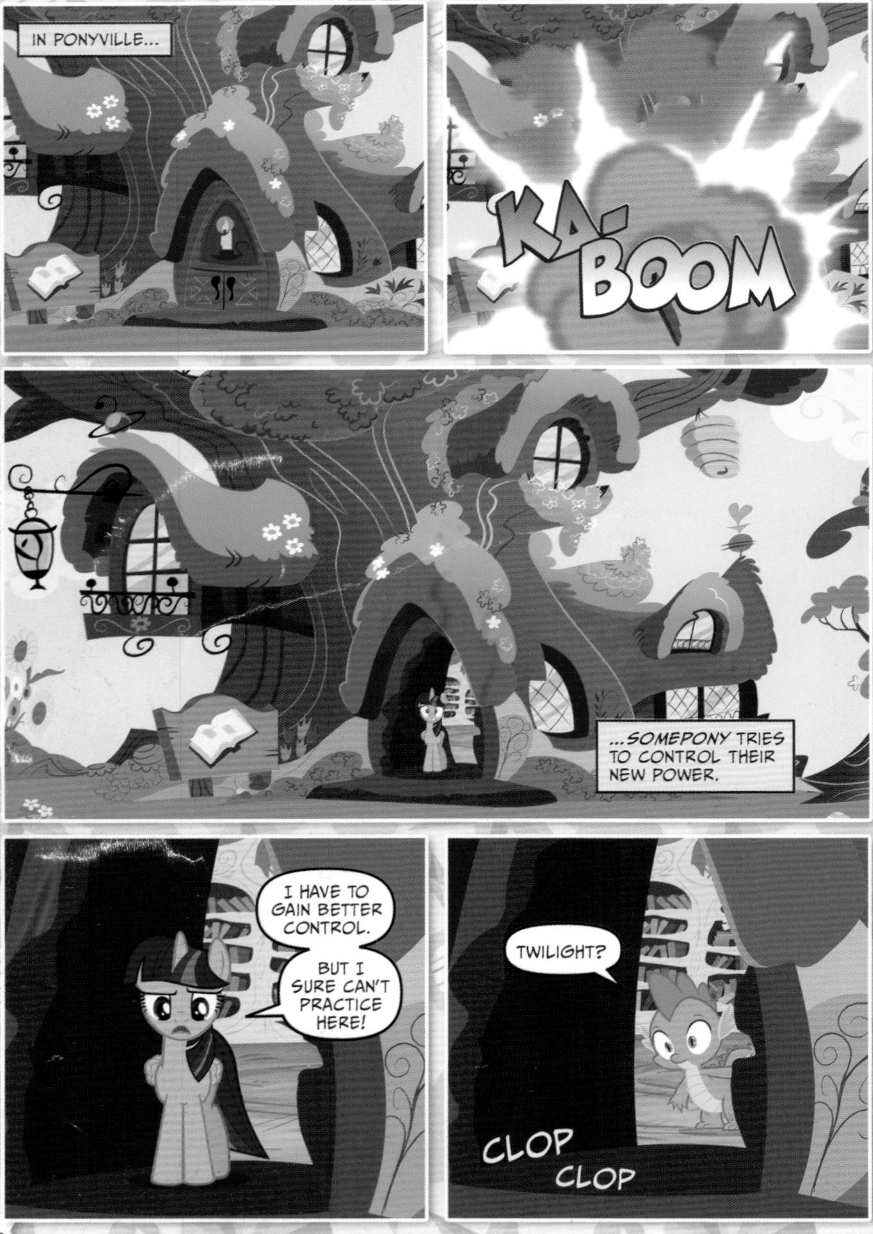
IN PONYVILLE...
KA-BOOM
...SOMEPONY TRIES TO CONTROL THEIR NEW POWER.
I HAVE TO GAIN BETTER CONTROL.
BUT I SURE CAN'T PRACTICE HERE!
TWILIGHT?
CLOP
CLOP

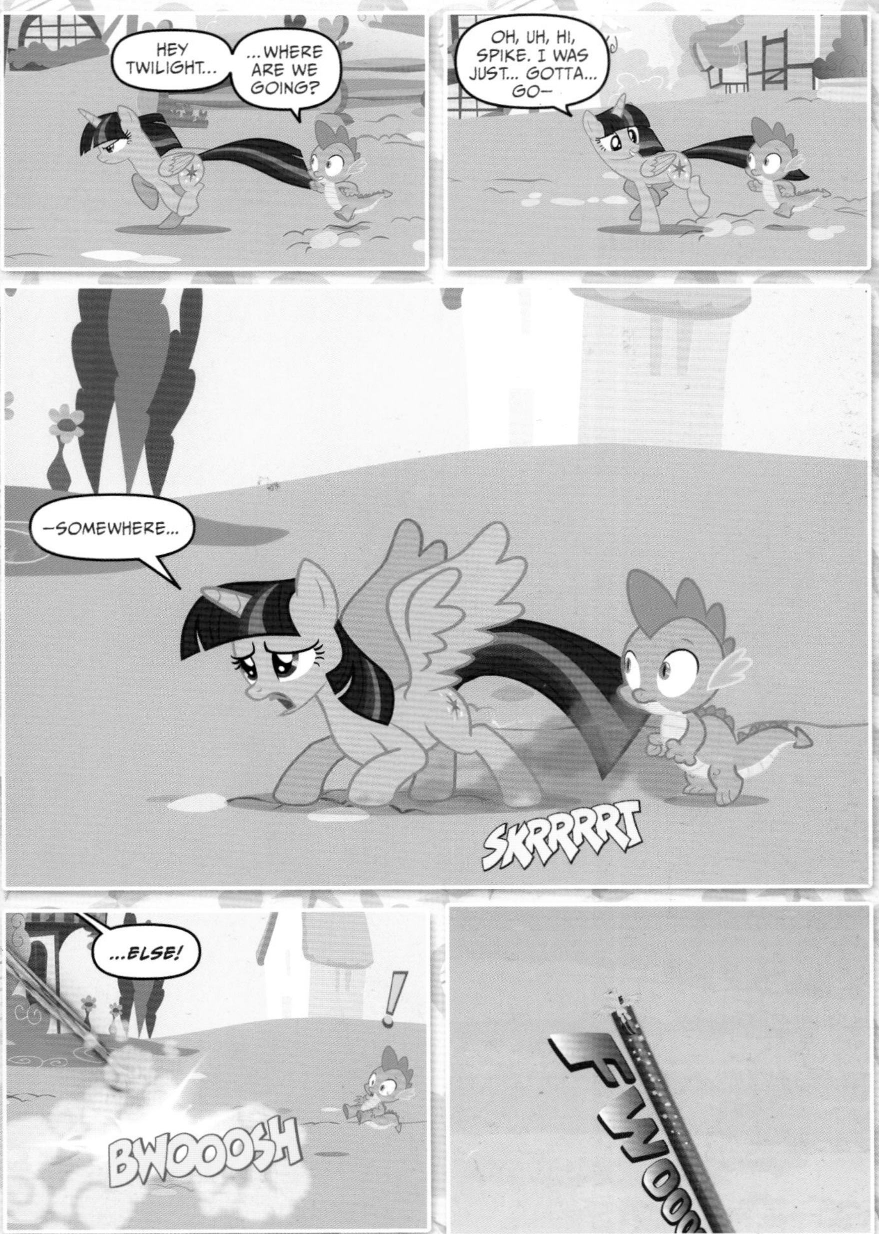
HEY TWILIGHT...
...WHERE ARE WE GOING?
OH, UH, HI, SPIKE. I WAS JUST... GOTTA... GO–
–SOMEWHERE...
SKRRRRT
...ELSE!
!
BWOOOSH
FWOOO

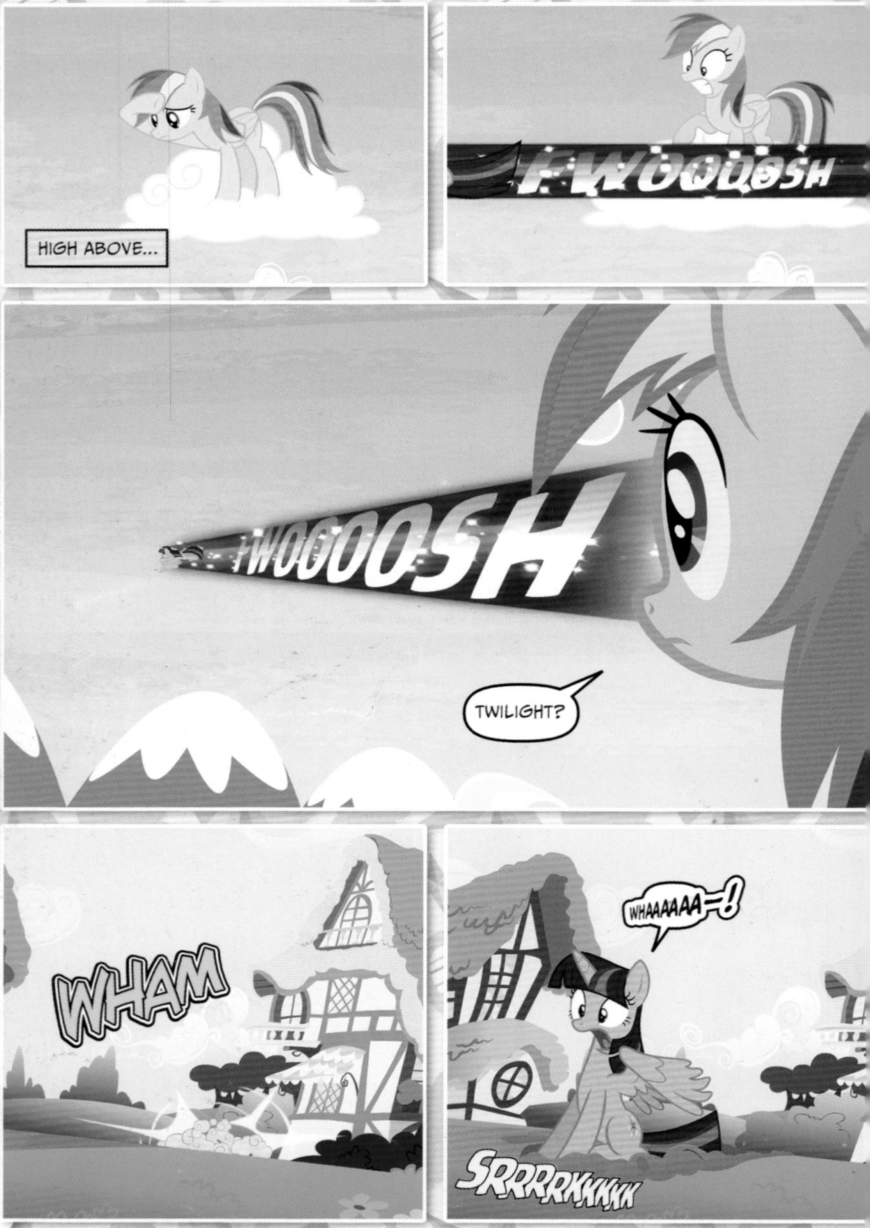
HIGH ABOVE...
FWOOOOSH
FWOOOOSH
TWILIGHT?
WHAM
WHAAAAAA—!
SRRRRKKKKK

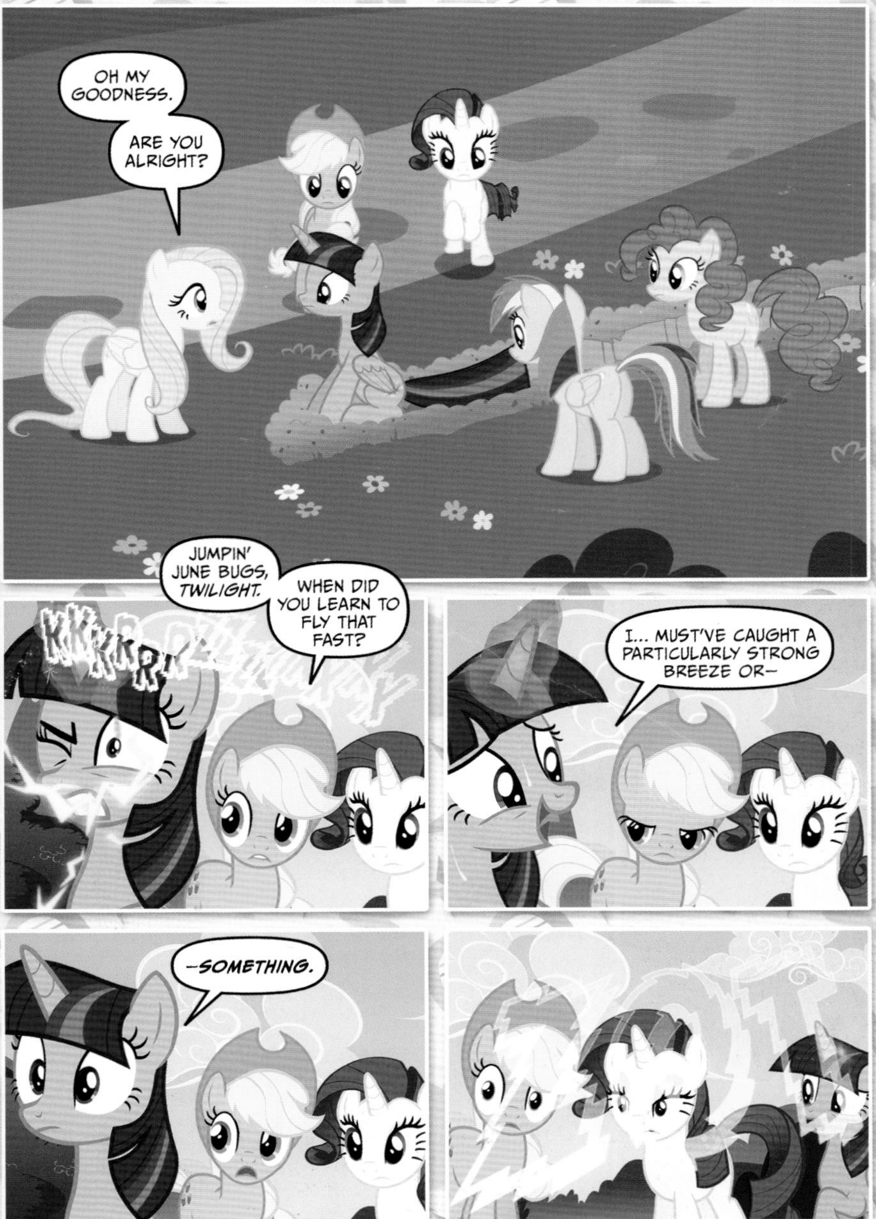
OH MY GOODNESS.
ARE YOU ALRIGHT?
JUMPIN' JUNE BUGS, *TWILIGHT.*
WHEN DID YOU LEARN TO FLY THAT FAST?
I... MUST'VE CAUGHT A PARTICULARLY STRONG BREEZE OR–
–SOMETHING.

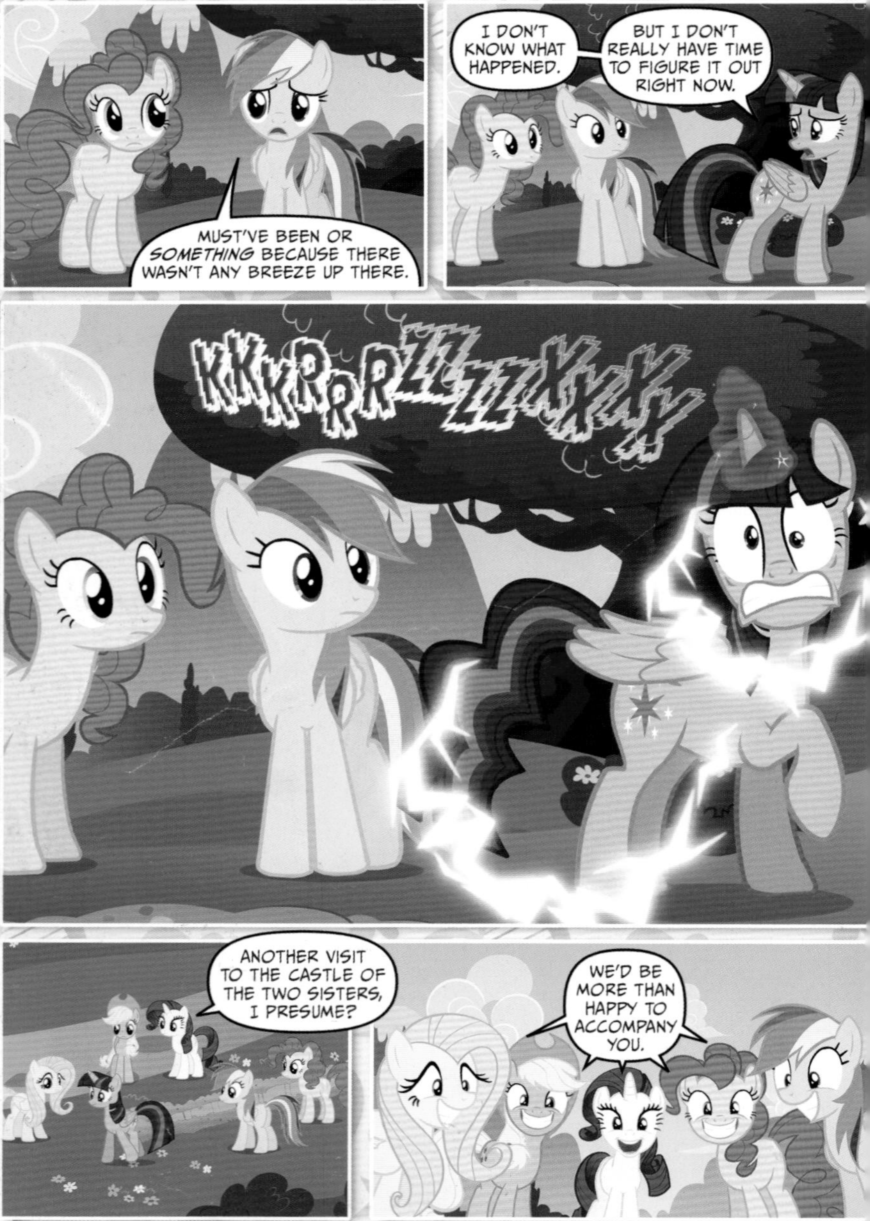
MUST'VE BEEN OR *SOMETHING* BECAUSE THERE WASN'T ANY BREEZE UP THERE.
I DON'T KNOW WHAT HAPPENED.
BUT I DON'T REALLY HAVE TIME TO FIGURE IT OUT RIGHT NOW.
KKKRRRZZZZZXXXX
ANOTHER VISIT TO THE CASTLE OF THE TWO SISTERS, I PRESUME?
WE'D BE MORE THAN HAPPY TO ACCOMPANY YOU.

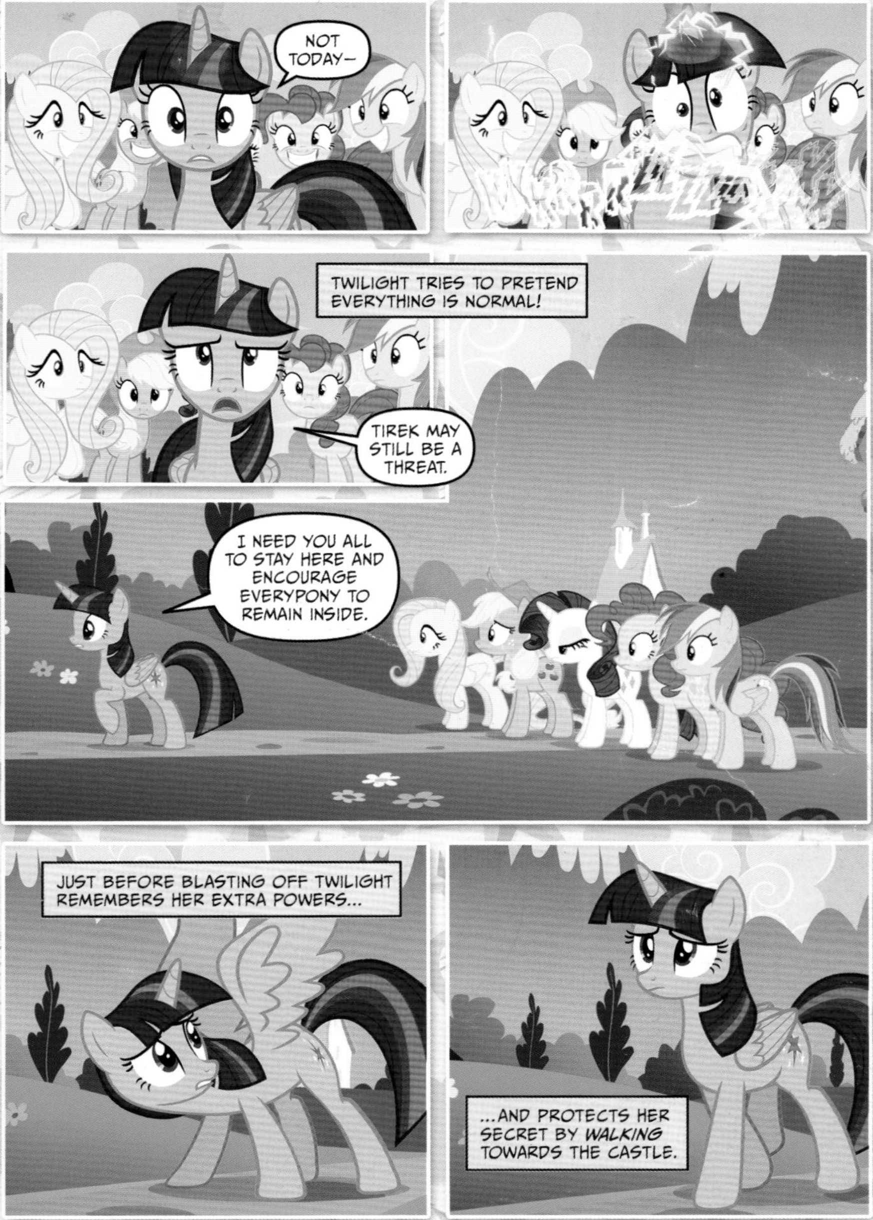

NOT TODAY—
TWILIGHT TRIES TO PRETEND EVERYTHING IS NORMAL!
TIREK MAY STILL BE A THREAT.
I NEED YOU ALL TO STAY HERE AND ENCOURAGE EVERYPONY TO REMAIN INSIDE.
JUST BEFORE BLASTING OFF TWILIGHT REMEMBERS HER EXTRA POWERS...
...AND PROTECTS HER SECRET BY *WALKING* TOWARDS THE CASTLE.

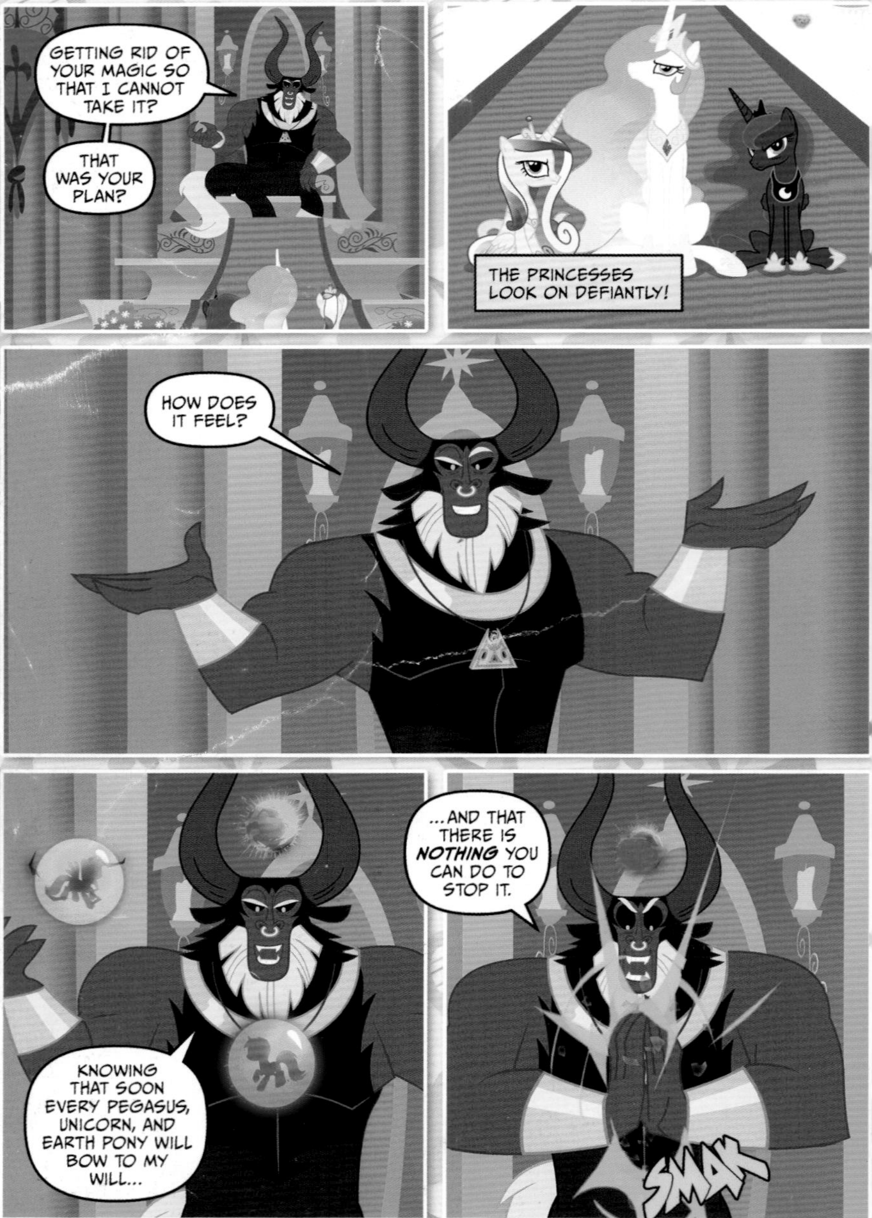
GETTING RID OF YOUR MAGIC SO THAT I CANNOT TAKE IT?
THAT WAS YOUR PLAN?
THE PRINCESSES LOOK ON DEFIANTLY!
HOW DOES IT FEEL?
KNOWING THAT SOON EVERY PEGASUS, UNICORN, AND EARTH PONY WILL BOW TO MY WILL...
...AND THAT THERE IS ***NOTHING*** YOU CAN DO TO STOP IT.
SMAK

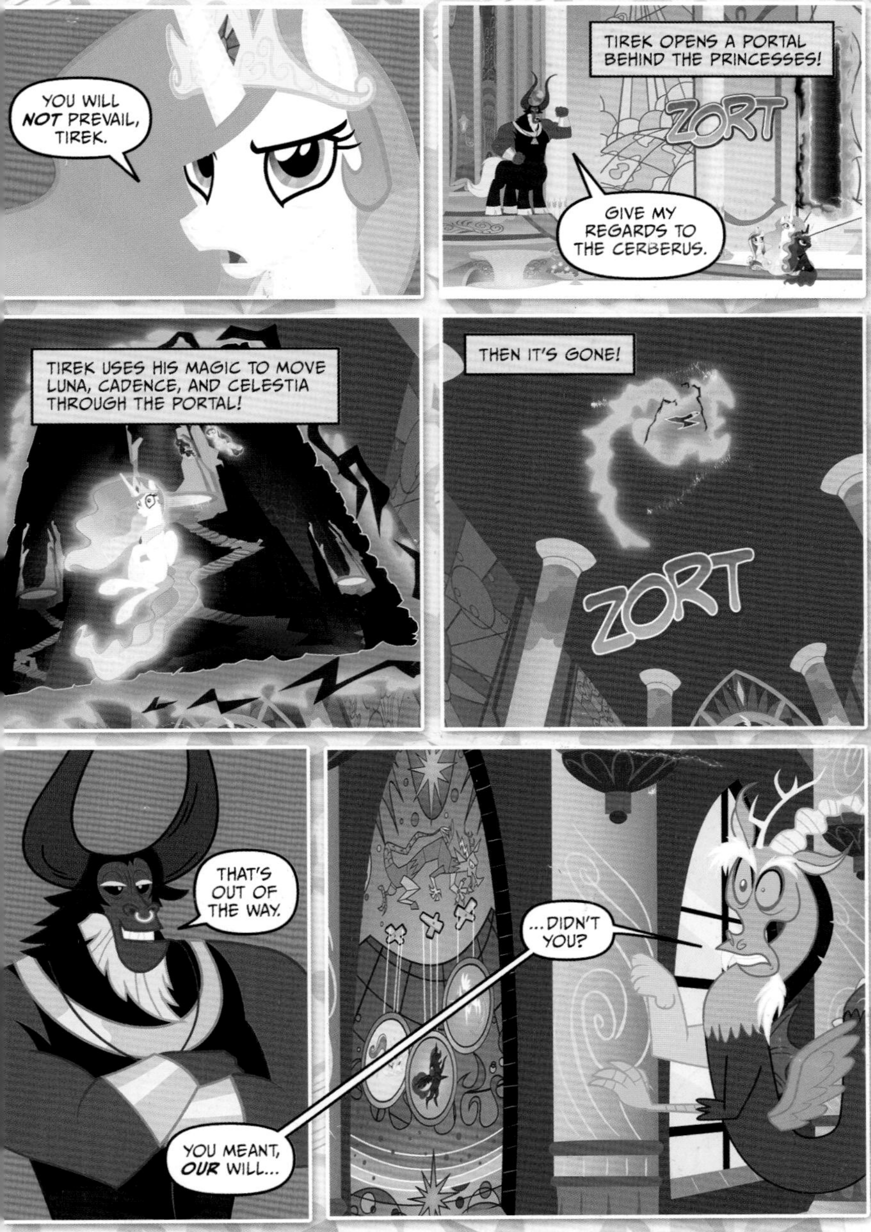
YOU WILL **NOT** PREVAIL, TIREK.
TIREK OPENS A PORTAL BEHIND THE PRINCESSES!
ZORT
GIVE MY REGARDS TO THE CERBERUS.
TIREK USES HIS MAGIC TO MOVE LUNA, CADENCE, AND CELESTIA THROUGH THE PORTAL!
THEN IT'S GONE!
ZORT
THAT'S OUT OF THE WAY.
YOU MEANT, **OUR** WILL...
...DIDN'T YOU?

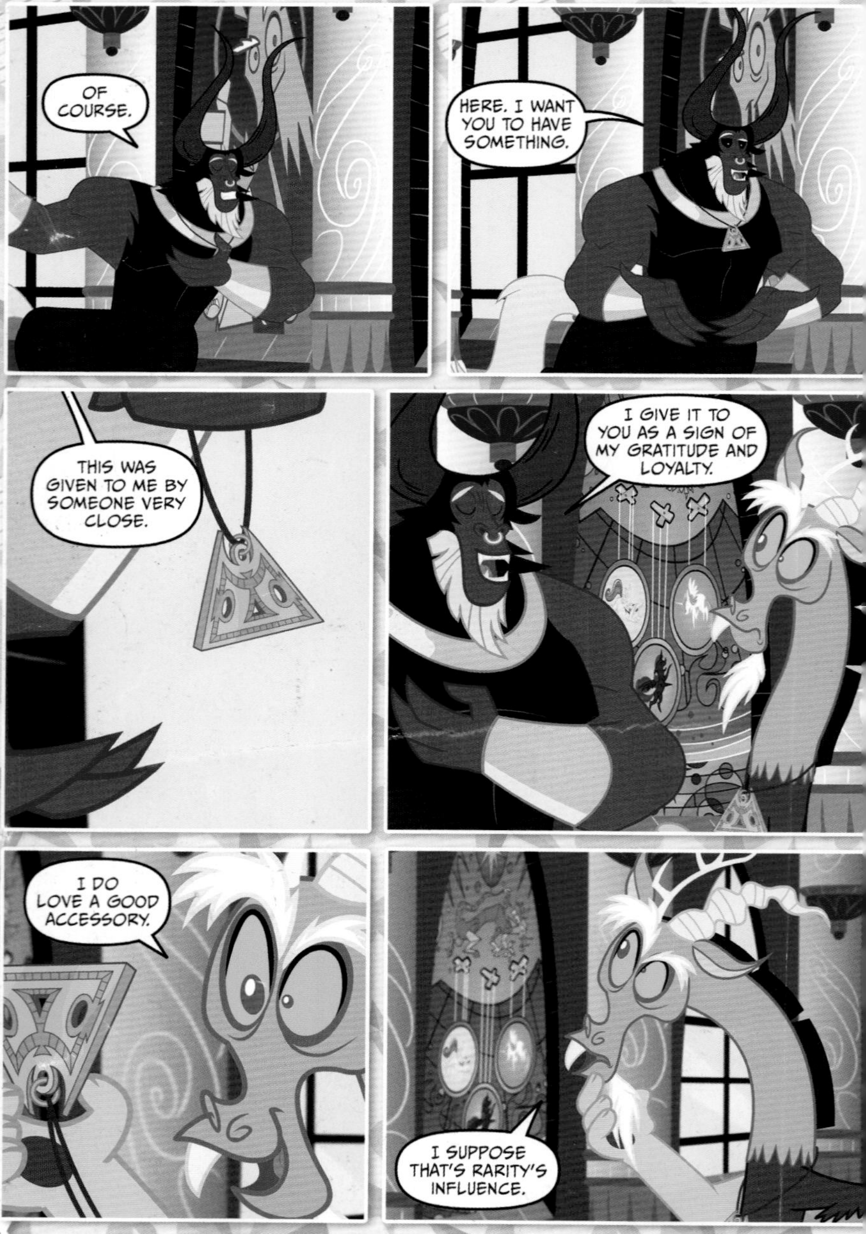
OF COURSE.
HERE. I WANT YOU TO HAVE SOMETHING.
THIS WAS GIVEN TO ME BY SOMEONE VERY CLOSE.
I GIVE IT TO YOU AS A SIGN OF MY GRATITUDE AND LOYALTY.
I DO LOVE A GOOD ACCESSORY.
I SUPPOSE THAT'S RARITY'S INFLUENCE.

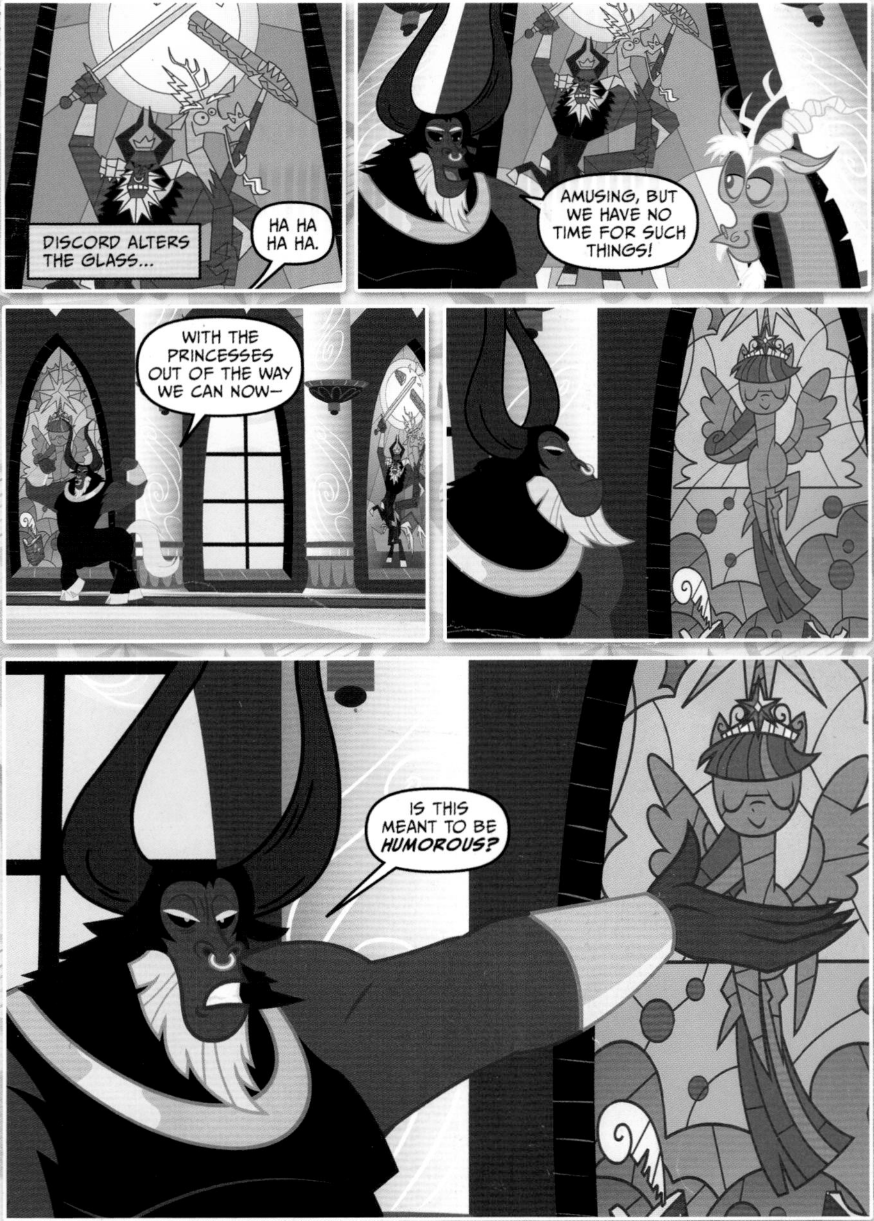
DISCORD ALTERS THE GLASS...
HA HA HA HA.
AMUSING, BUT WE HAVE NO TIME FOR SUCH THINGS!
WITH THE PRINCESSES OUT OF THE WAY WE CAN NOW—
IS THIS MEANT TO BE *HUMOROUS?*

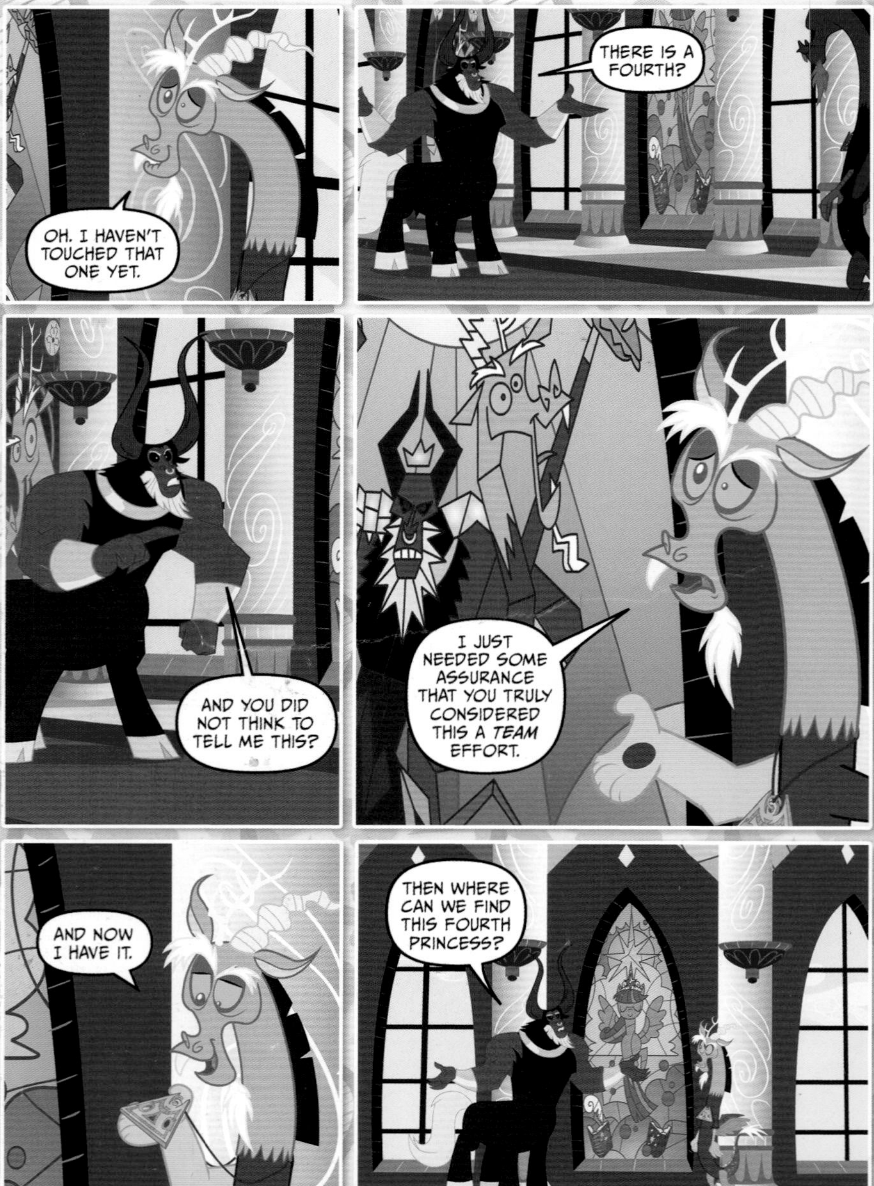
OH. I HAVEN'T TOUCHED THAT ONE YET.
THERE IS A FOURTH?
AND YOU DID NOT THINK TO TELL ME THIS?
I JUST NEEDED SOME ASSURANCE THAT YOU TRULY CONSIDERED THIS A *TEAM* EFFORT.
AND NOW I HAVE IT.
THEN WHERE CAN WE FIND THIS FOURTH PRINCESS?

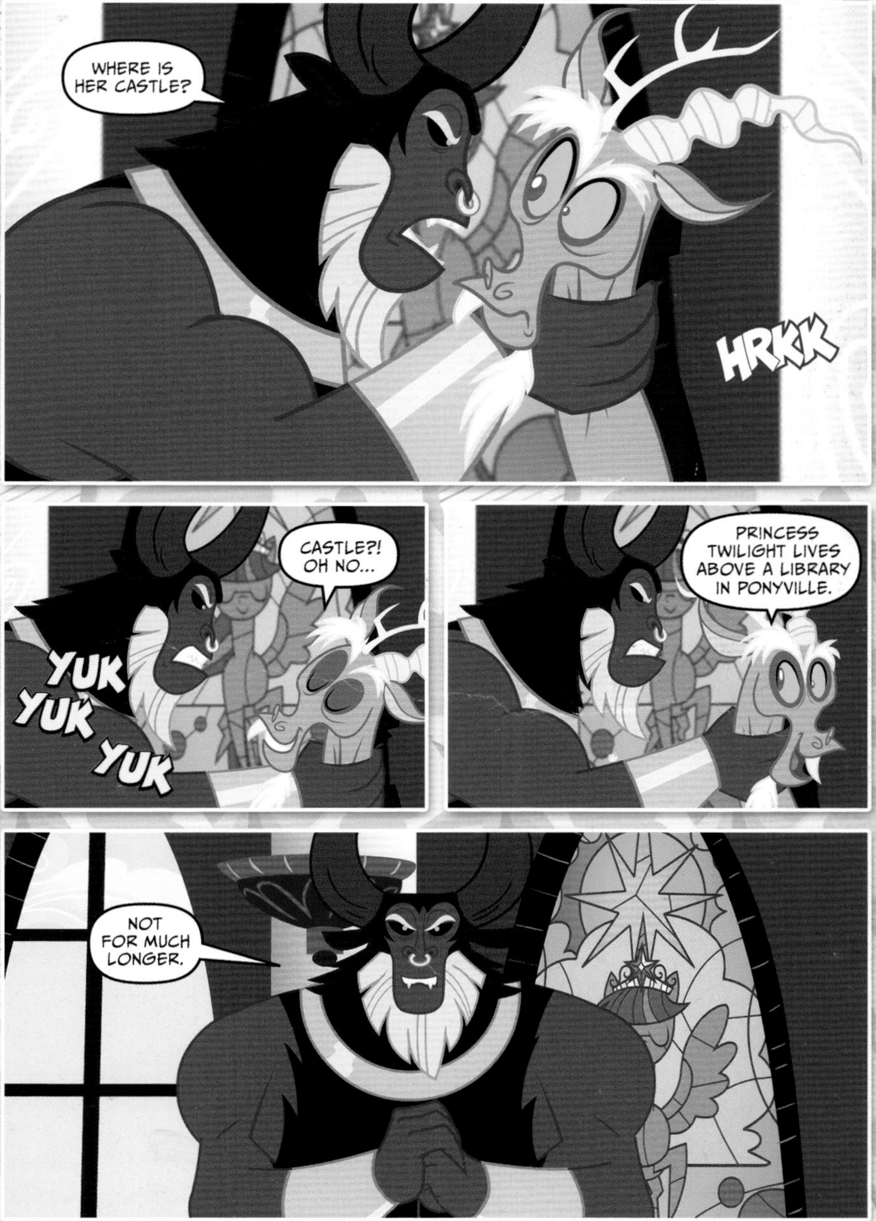

WHERE IS HER CASTLE?
HRKK
CASTLE?! OH NO...
YUK YUK YUK
PRINCESS TWILIGHT LIVES ABOVE A LIBRARY IN PONYVILLE.
NOT FOR MUCH LONGER.

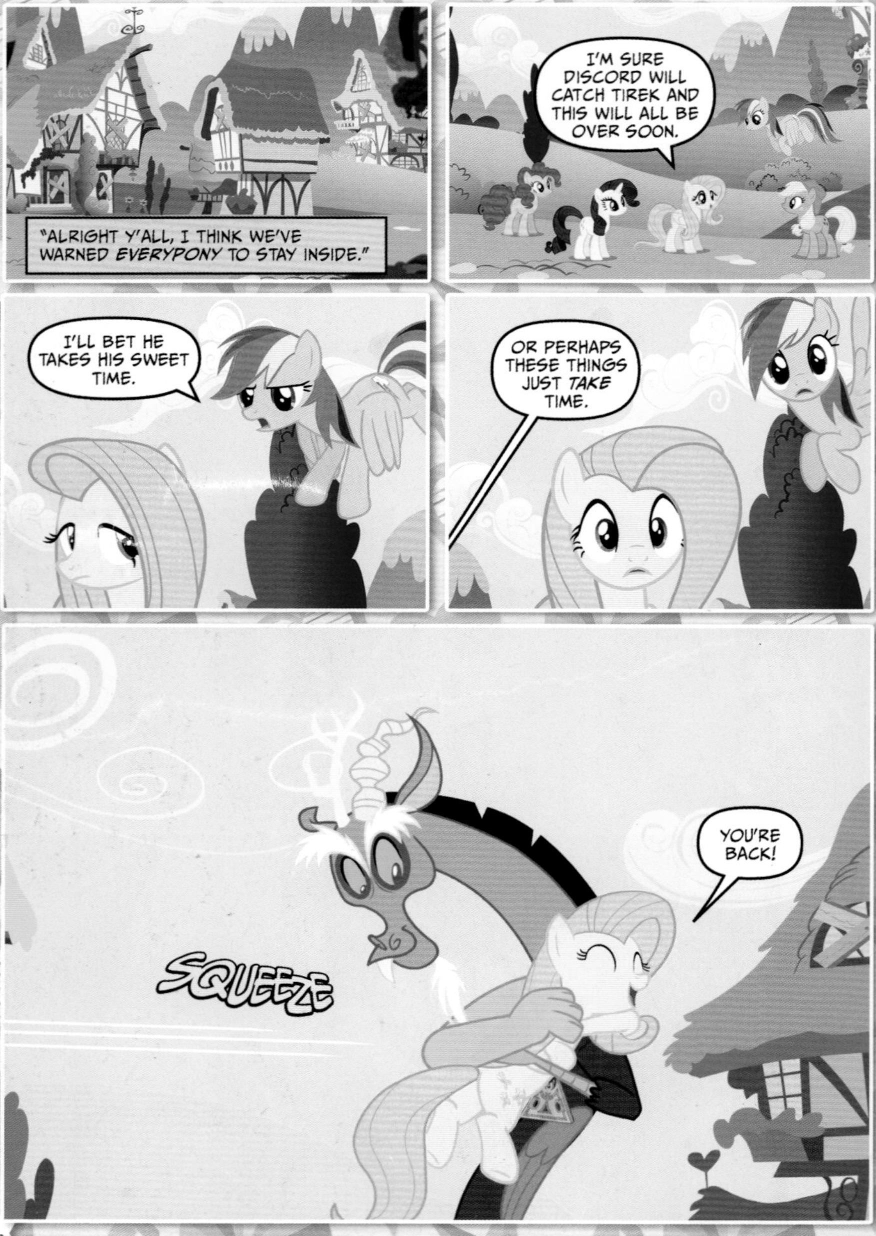

"ALRIGHT Y'ALL, I THINK WE'VE WARNED *EVERYPONY* TO STAY INSIDE."
I'M SURE DISCORD WILL CATCH TIREK AND THIS WILL ALL BE OVER SOON.
I'LL BET HE TAKES HIS SWEET TIME.
OR PERHAPS THESE THINGS JUST *TAKE* TIME.
SQUEEZE
YOU'RE BACK!

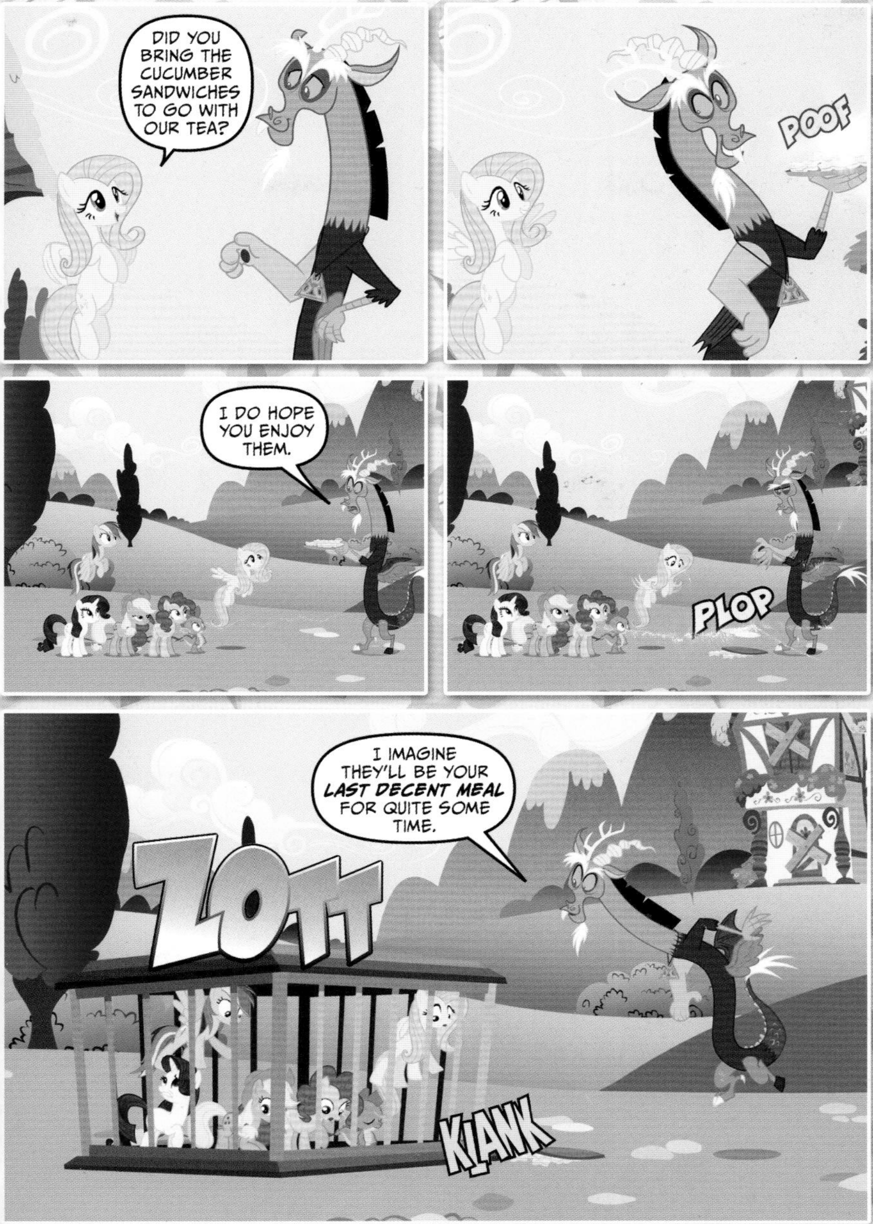
DID YOU BRING THE CUCUMBER SANDWICHES TO GO WITH OUR TEA?
POOF
I DO HOPE YOU ENJOY THEM.
PLOP
I IMAGINE THEY'LL BE YOUR LAST DECENT MEAL FOR QUITE SOME TIME.
ZOTT
KLANK

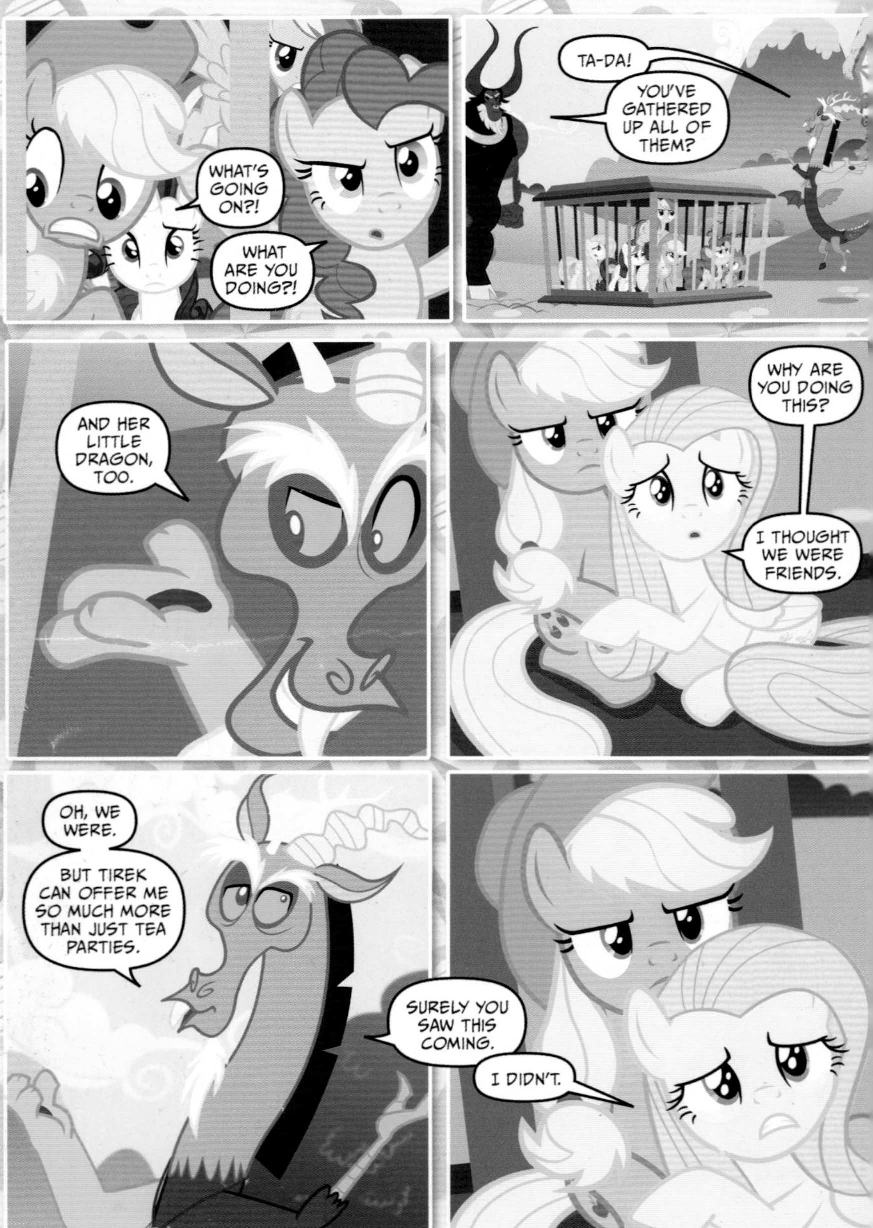
WHAT'S GOING ON?!
WHAT ARE YOU DOING?!
TA-DA!
YOU'VE GATHERED UP ALL OF THEM?
AND HER LITTLE DRAGON, TOO.
WHY ARE YOU DOING THIS?
I THOUGHT WE WERE FRIENDS.
OH, WE WERE.
BUT TIREK CAN OFFER ME SO MUCH MORE THAN JUST TEA PARTIES.
SURELY YOU SAW THIS COMING.
I DIDN'T.

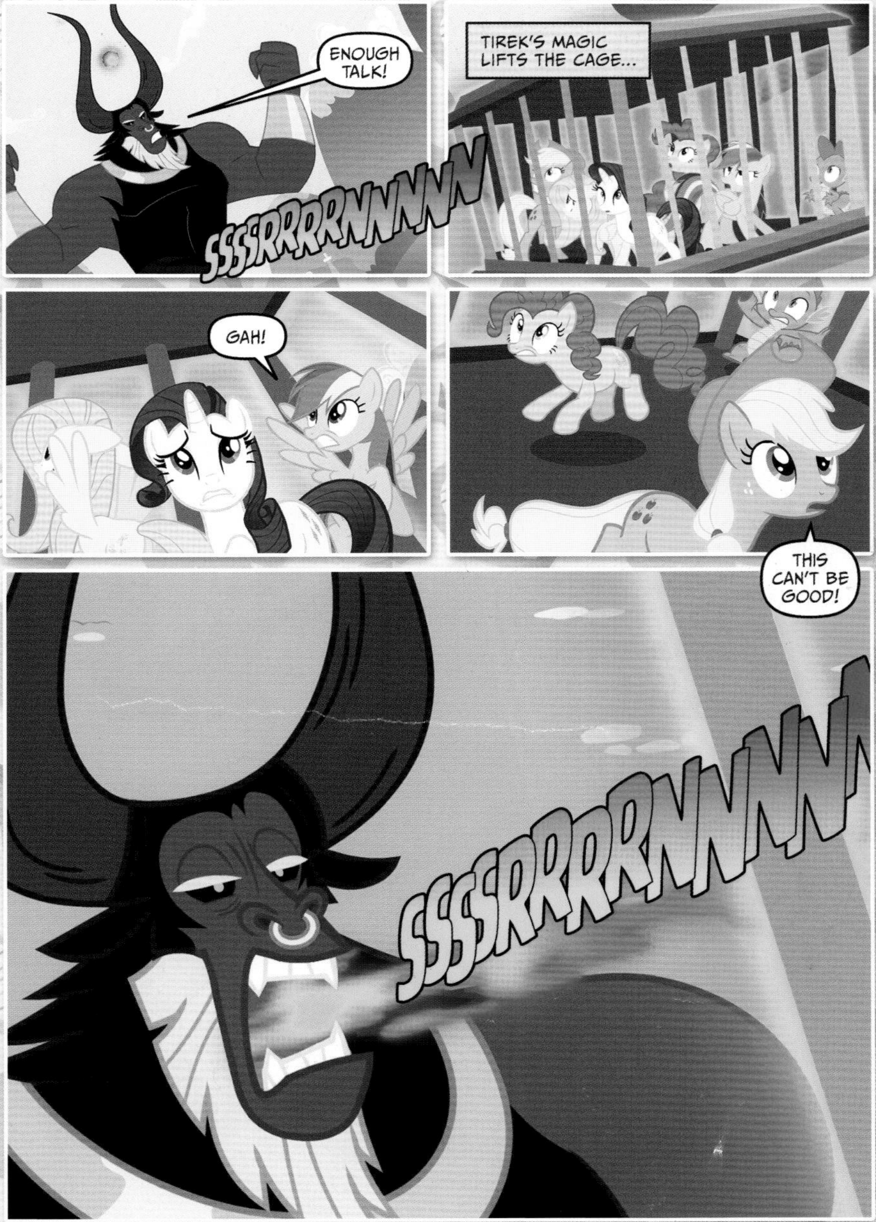
ENOUGH TALK!
SSSSRRRRNNNNNN
TIREK'S MAGIC LIFTS THE CAGE...
GAH!
THIS CAN'T BE GOOD!
SSSSRRRRNNNNNN

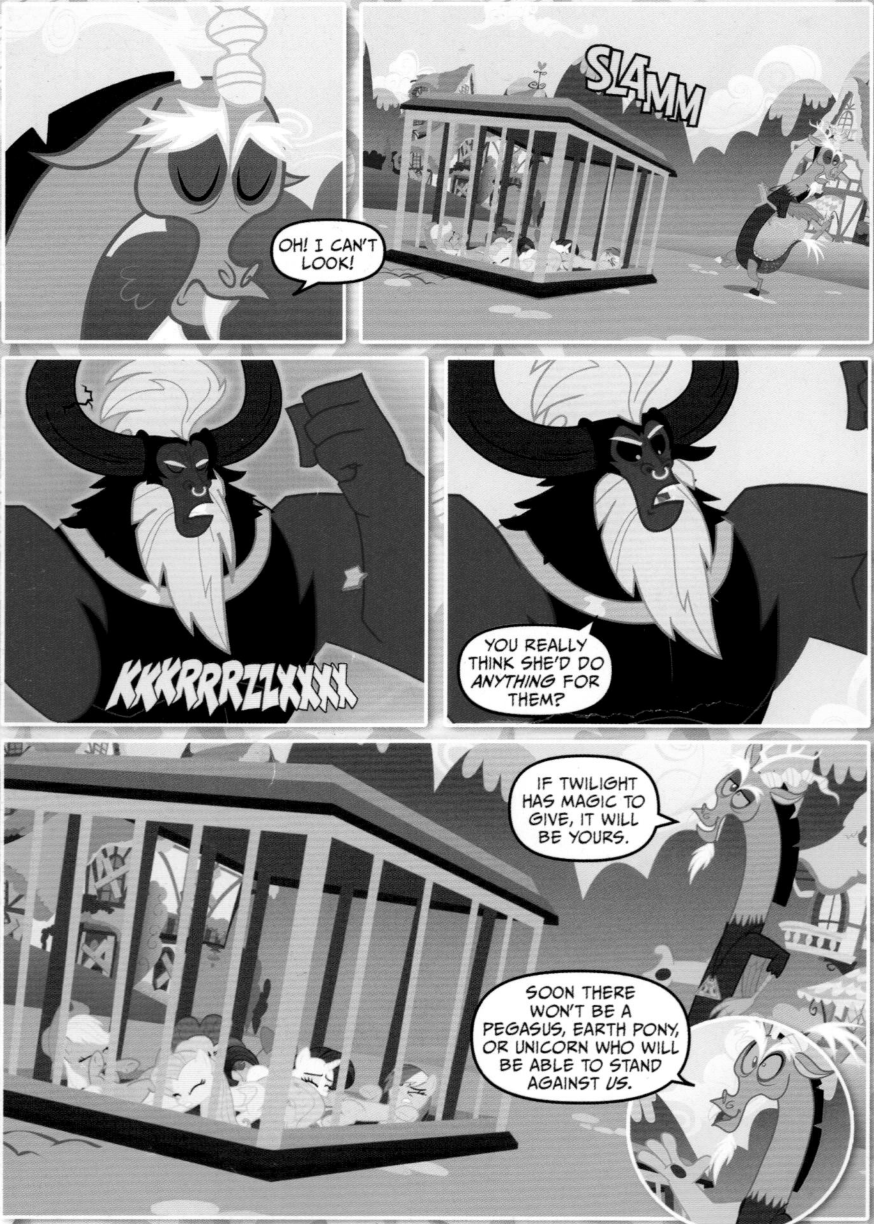
OH! I CAN'T LOOK!
SLAMM
KKKRRRZZLXXXX
YOU REALLY THINK SHE'D DO *ANYTHING* FOR THEM?
IF TWILIGHT HAS MAGIC TO GIVE, IT WILL BE YOURS.
SOON THERE WON'T BE A PEGASUS, EARTH PONY, OR UNICORN WHO WILL BE ABLE TO STAND AGAINST *US*.

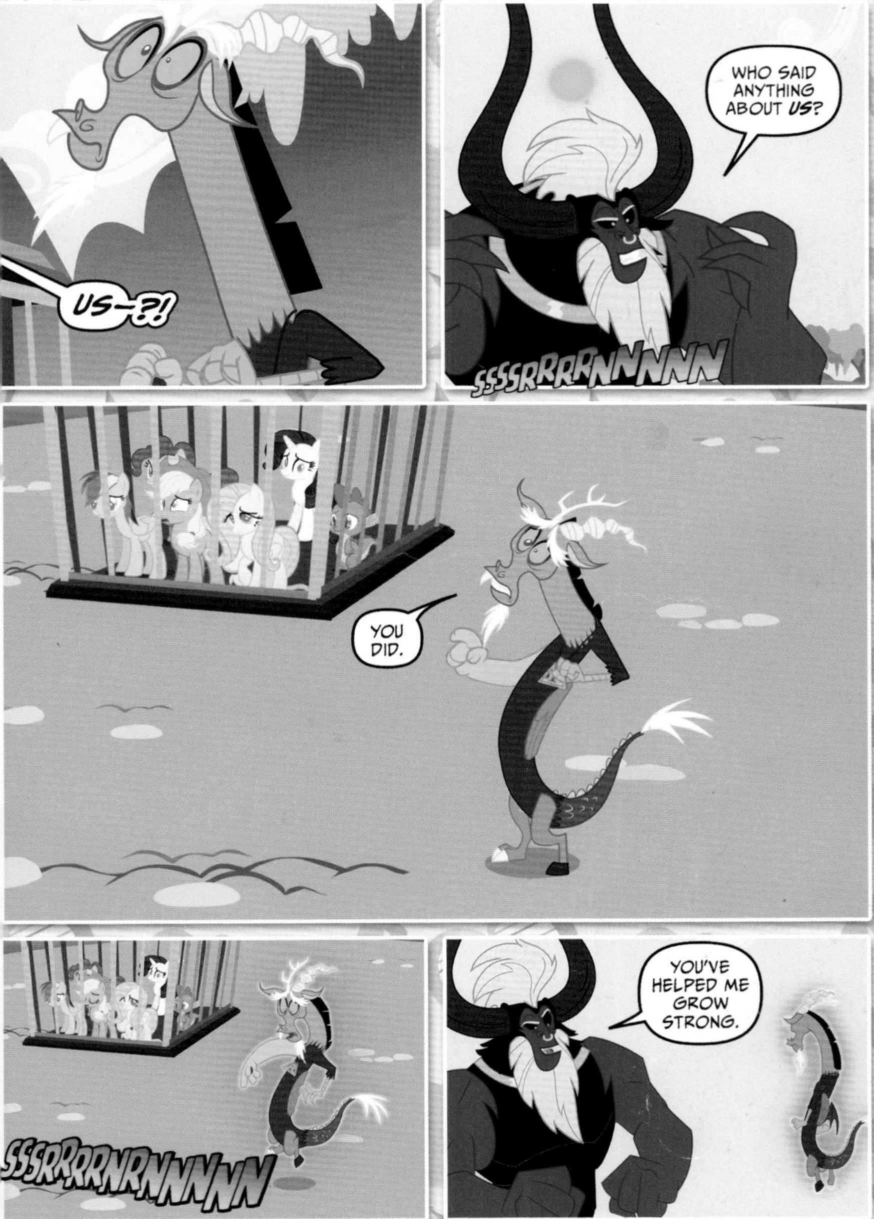
US--?!
WHO SAID ANYTHING ABOUT US?
SSSSRRRRNNNNNN
YOU DID.
SSSRRRRNRNNNNNN
YOU'VE HELPED ME GROW STRONG.

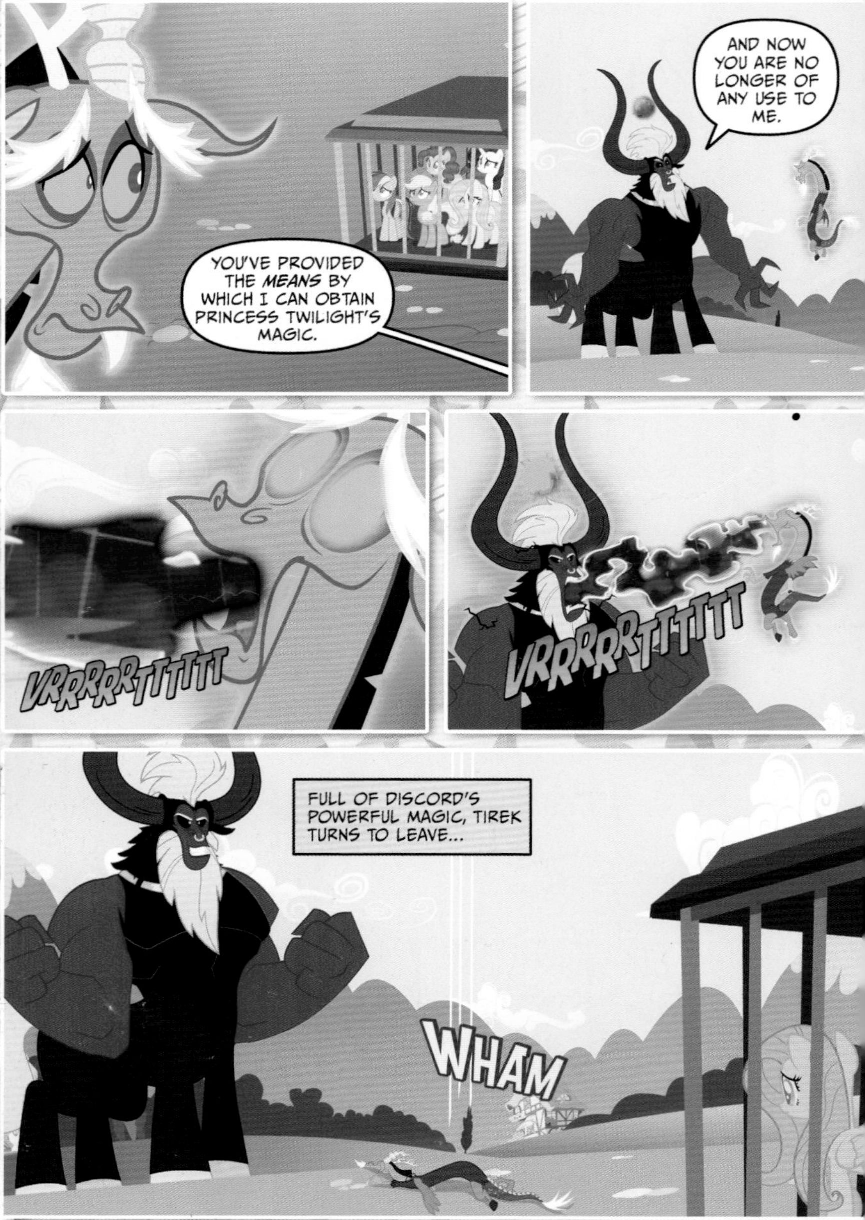
YOU'VE PROVIDED THE *MEANS* BY WHICH I CAN OBTAIN PRINCESS TWILIGHT'S MAGIC.
AND NOW YOU ARE NO LONGER OF ANY USE TO ME.
VRRRRRTTTTTT
VRRRRRTTTTTT
FULL OF DISCORD'S POWERFUL MAGIC, TIREK TURNS TO LEAVE...
WHAM

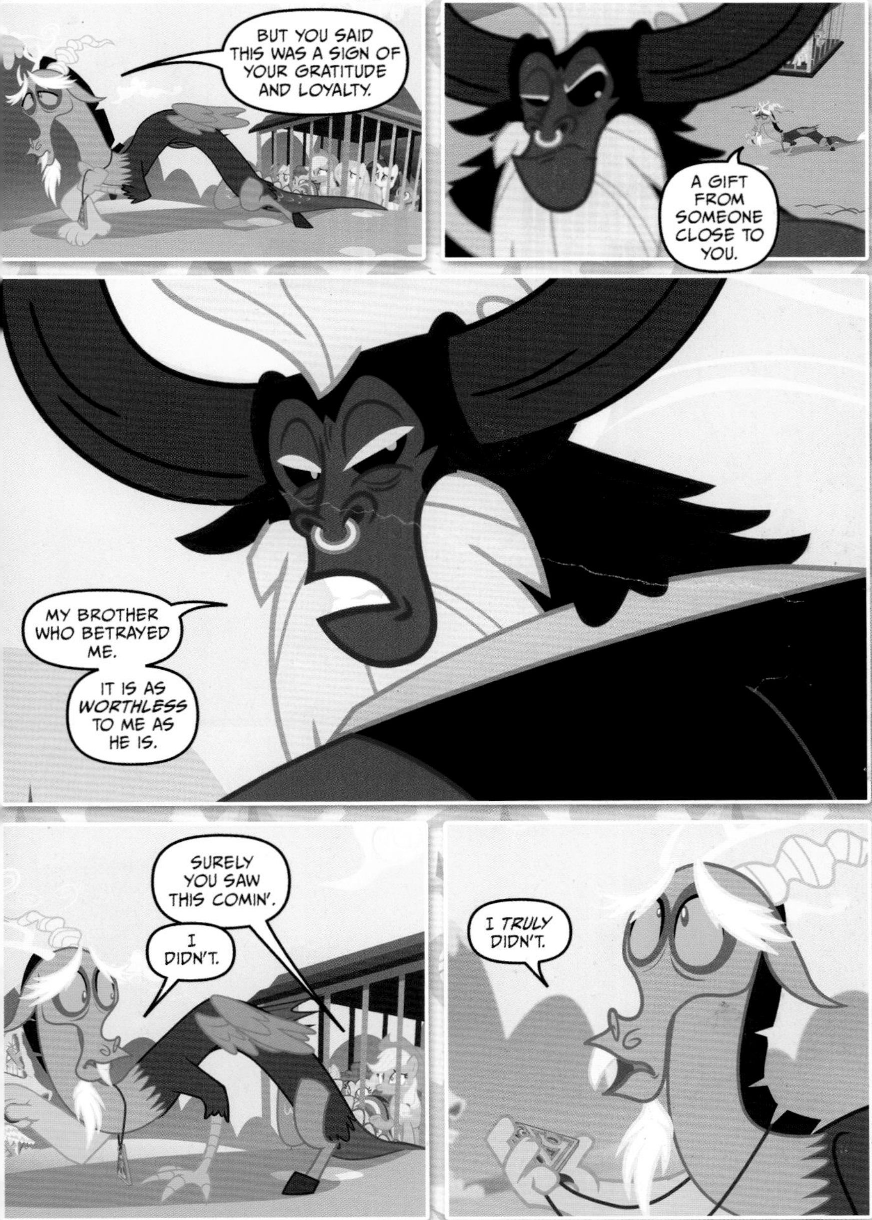
BUT YOU SAID THIS WAS A SIGN OF YOUR GRATITUDE AND LOYALTY.
A GIFT FROM SOMEONE CLOSE TO YOU.
MY BROTHER WHO BETRAYED ME.
IT IS AS WORTHLESS TO ME AS HE IS.
SURELY YOU SAW THIS COMIN'.
I DIDN'T.
I TRULY DIDN'T.

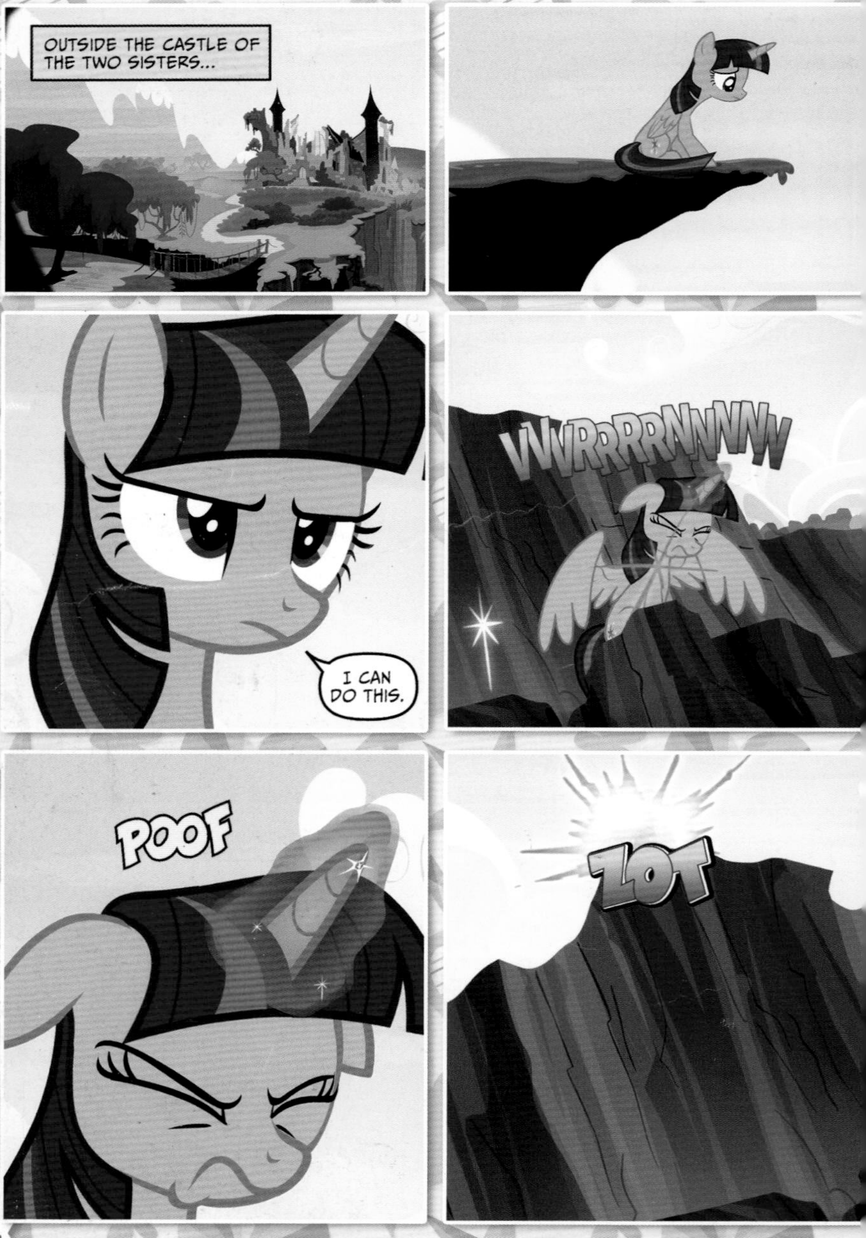

OUTSIDE THE CASTLE OF THE TWO SISTERS...
I CAN DO THIS.
VVVRRRRNNNNN
POOF
ZOT

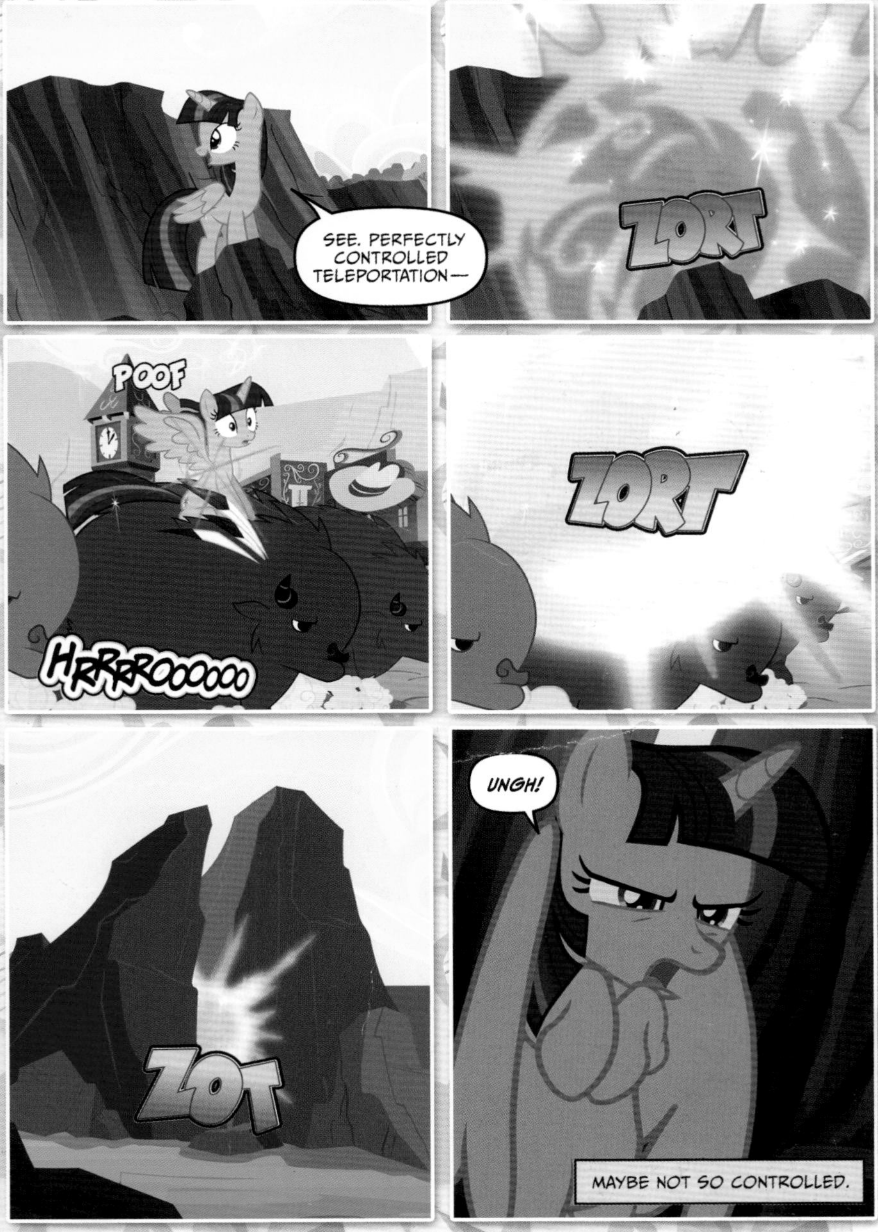
SEE. PERFECTLY CONTROLLED TELEPORTATION—
ZORT
POOF
HRRRROOOOOO
ZORT
ZOT
UNGH!
MAYBE NOT SO CONTROLLED.

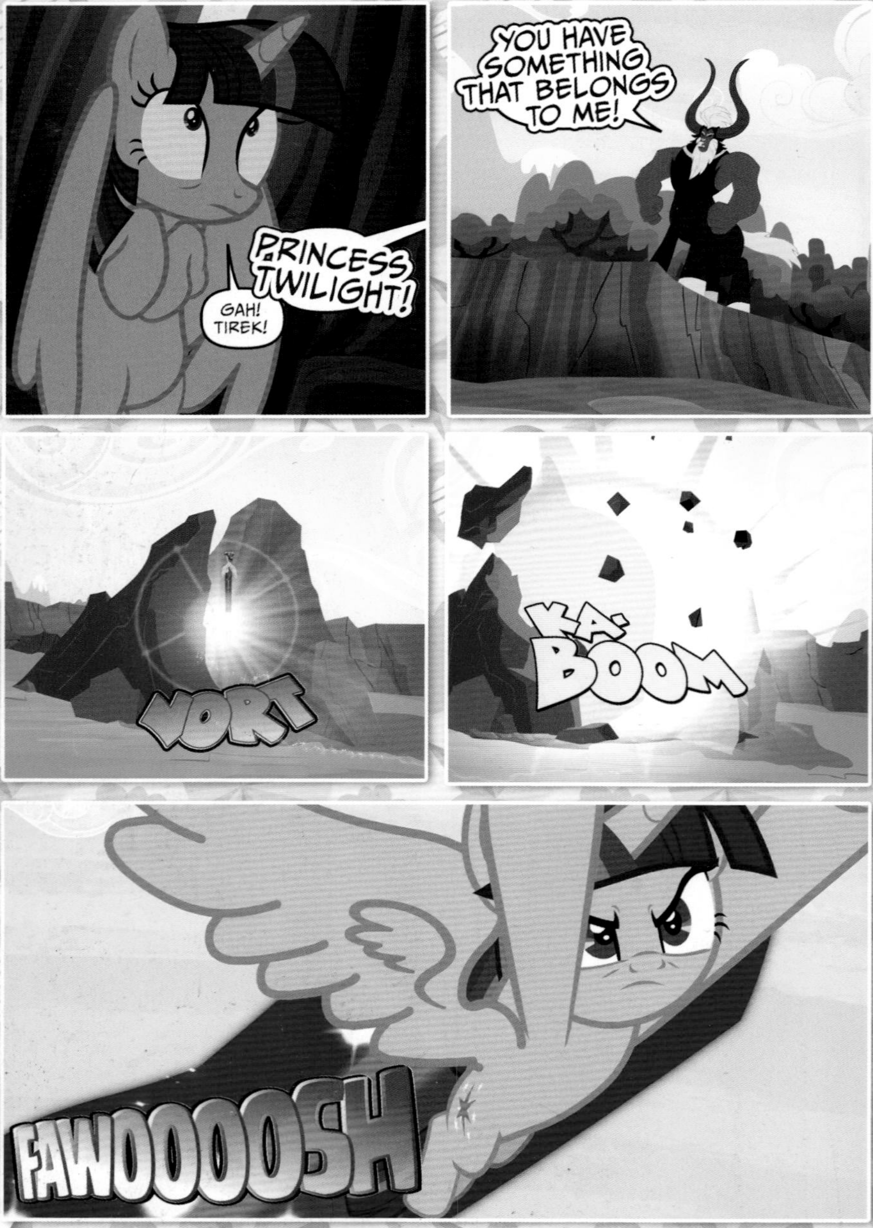
PRINCESS TWILIGHT!
GAH! TIREK!
YOU HAVE SOMETHING THAT BELONGS TO ME!
VORT
KA-BOOM
FAWOOOOSH

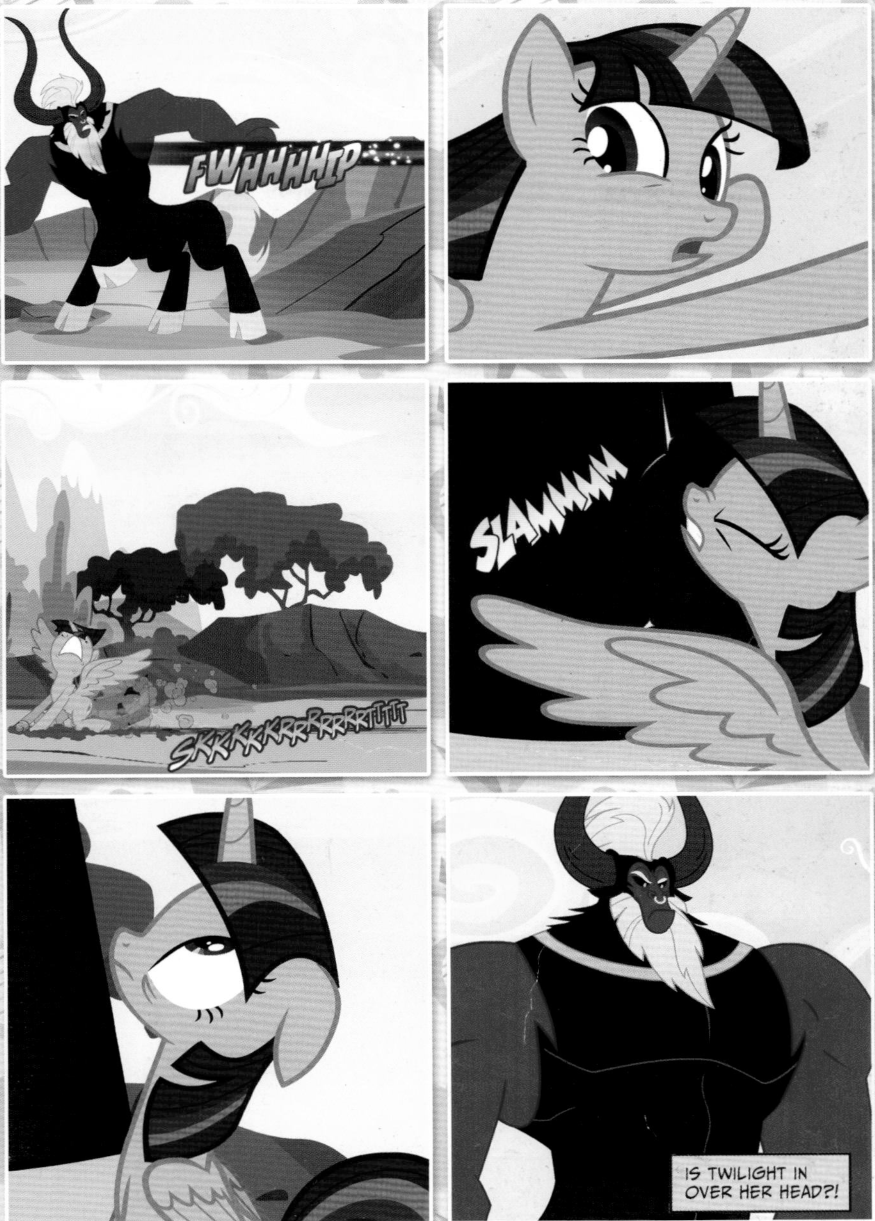
FWHHHHIP
SLAMMMM
SKKKKKRRRRRRRTTTT
IS TWILIGHT IN OVER HER HEAD?!

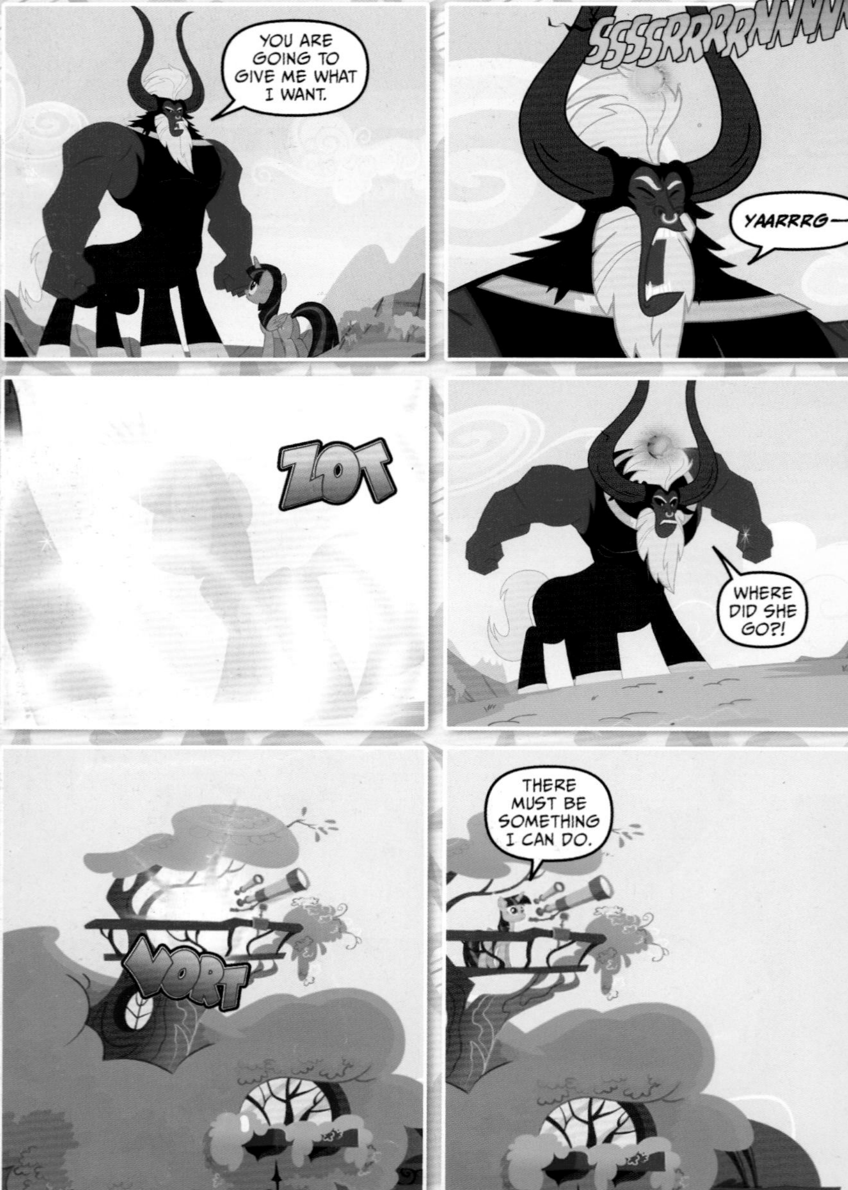
YOU ARE GOING TO GIVE ME WHAT I WANT.
SSSSRRRRRNNNNN
YAARRRG—
ZOT
WHERE DID SHE GO?!
VORT
THERE MUST BE SOMETHING I CAN DO.

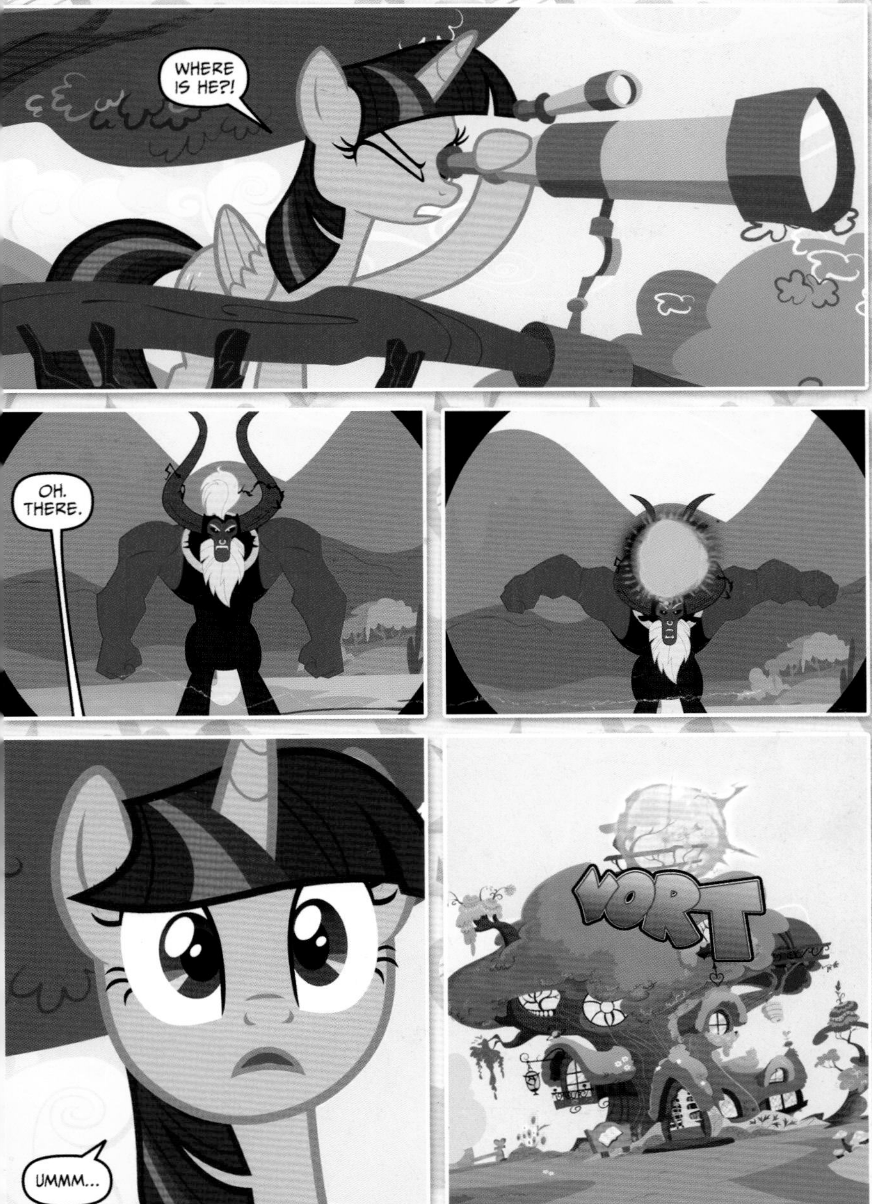
WHERE IS HE?!
OH. THERE.
VORT
UMMM...

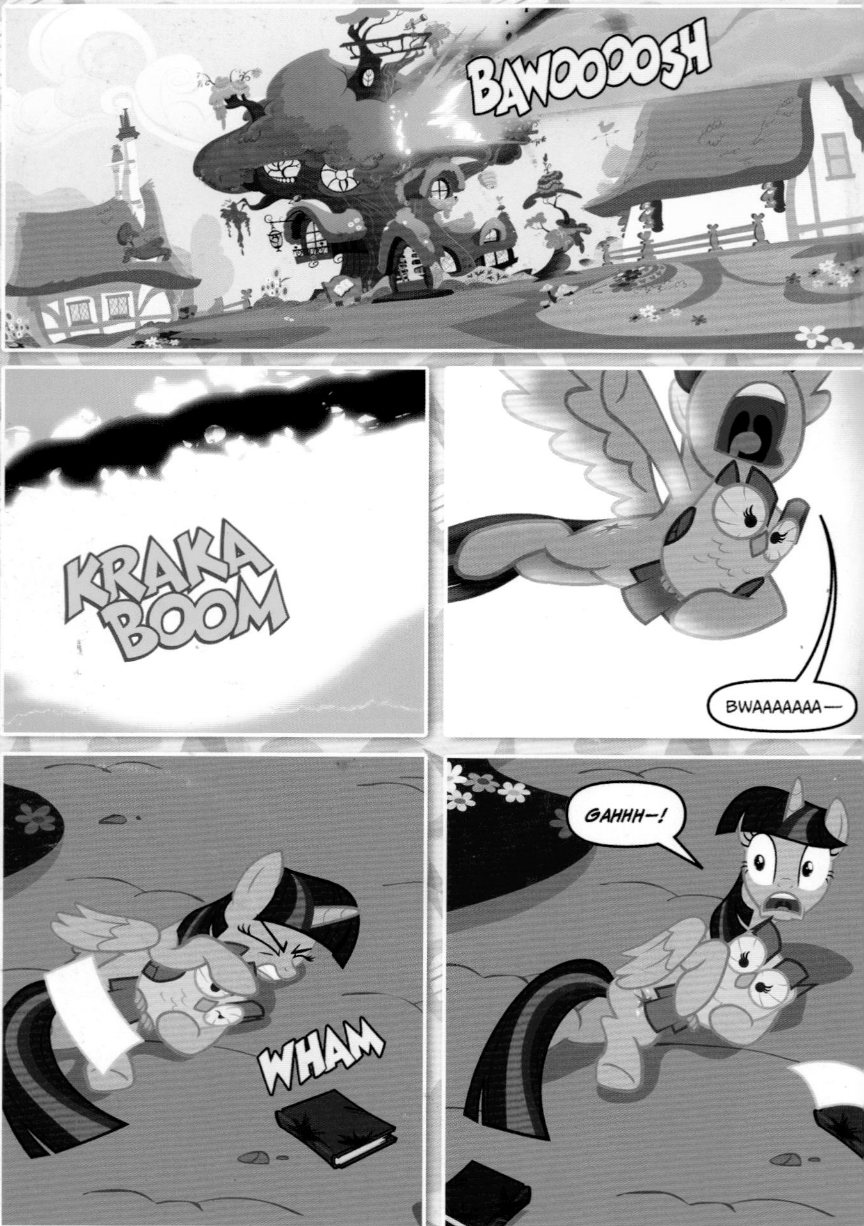
BAWOOOOSH
KRAKA BOOM
BWAAAAAAA—
WHAM
GAHHH—!

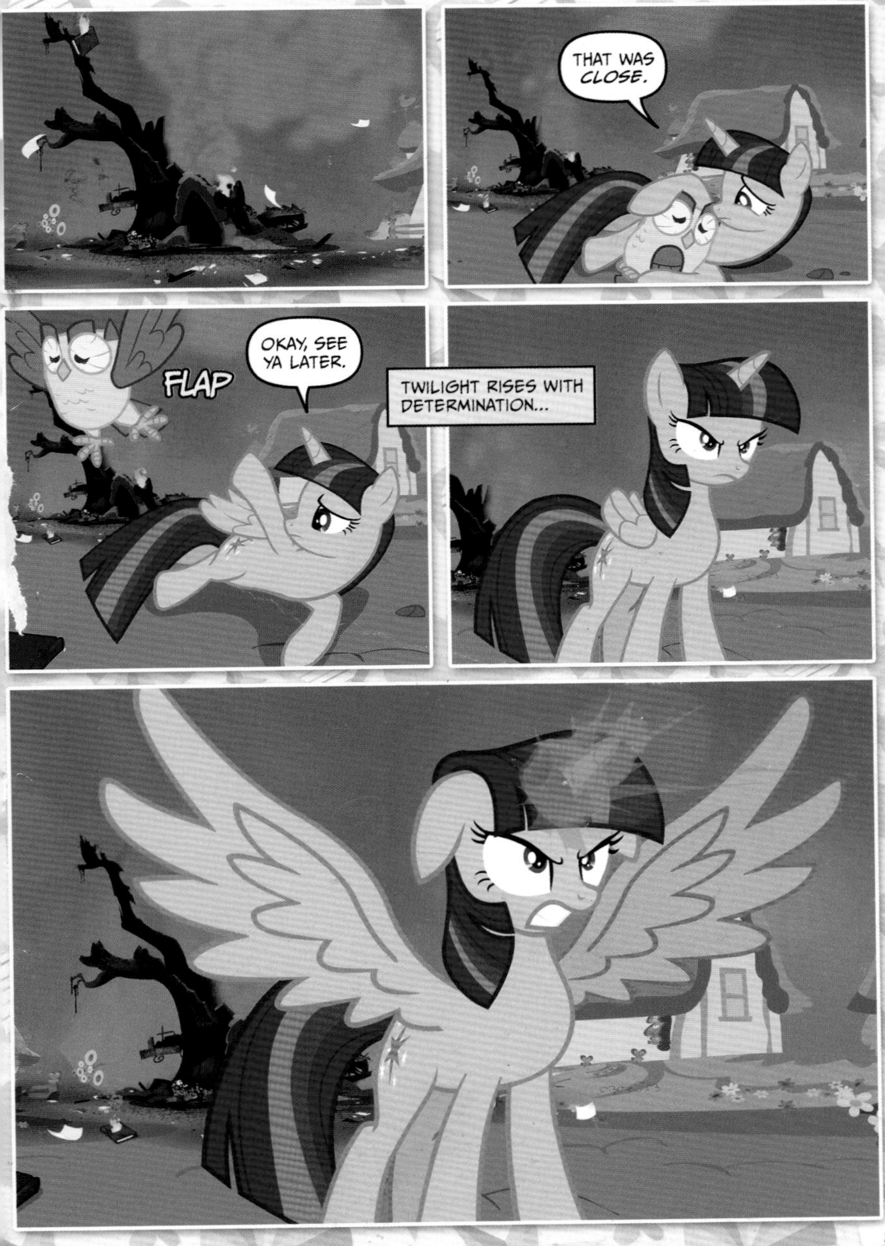
THAT WAS CLOSE.
FLAP
OKAY, SEE YA LATER.
TWILIGHT RISES WITH DETERMINATION...

...AND TAKES TO THE SKY!

BLORT

KRXXXTXXTXT

BUT TIREK IS POWERFUL!

KRXXXTXXXTTXXT

BA-DOOOOOM

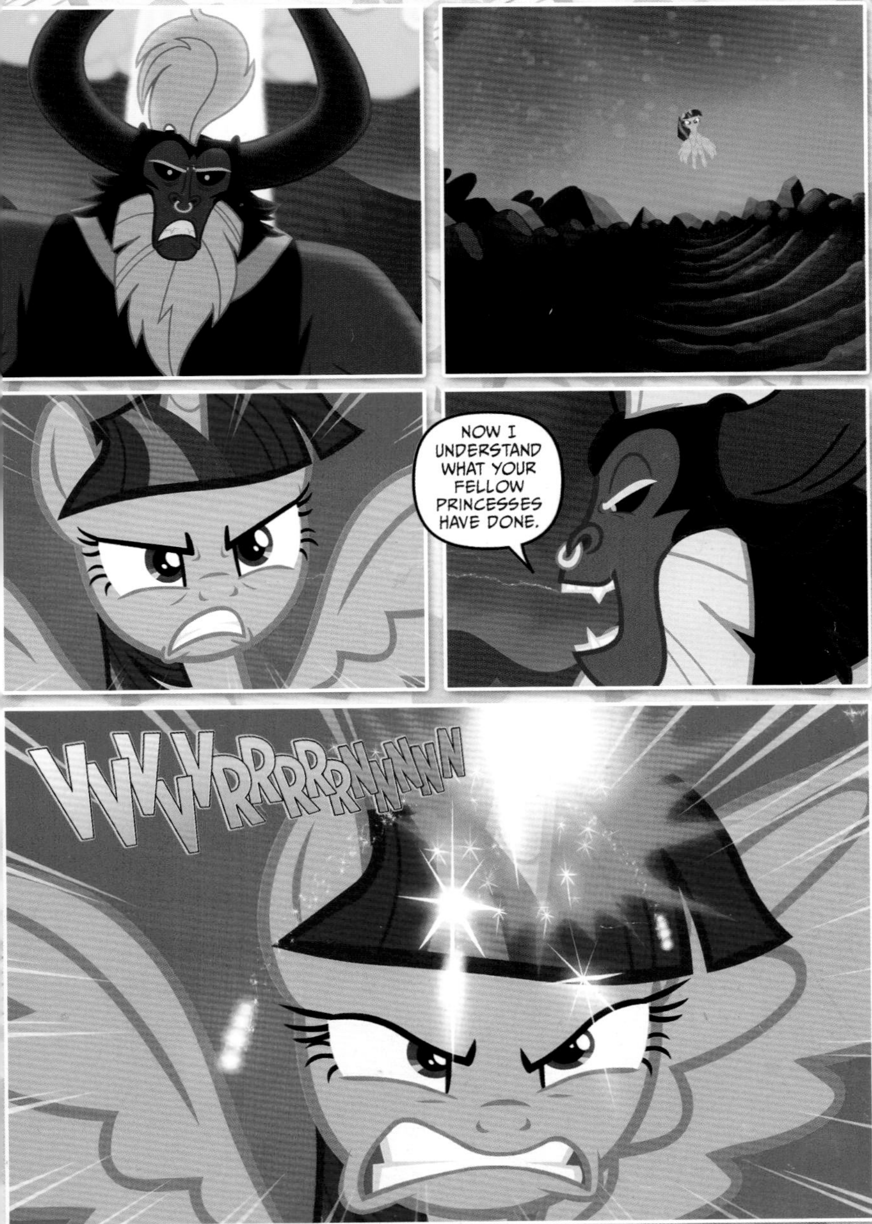
NOW I UNDERSTAND WHAT YOUR FELLOW PRINCESSES HAVE DONE.
VVVVVRRRRRNNNNN

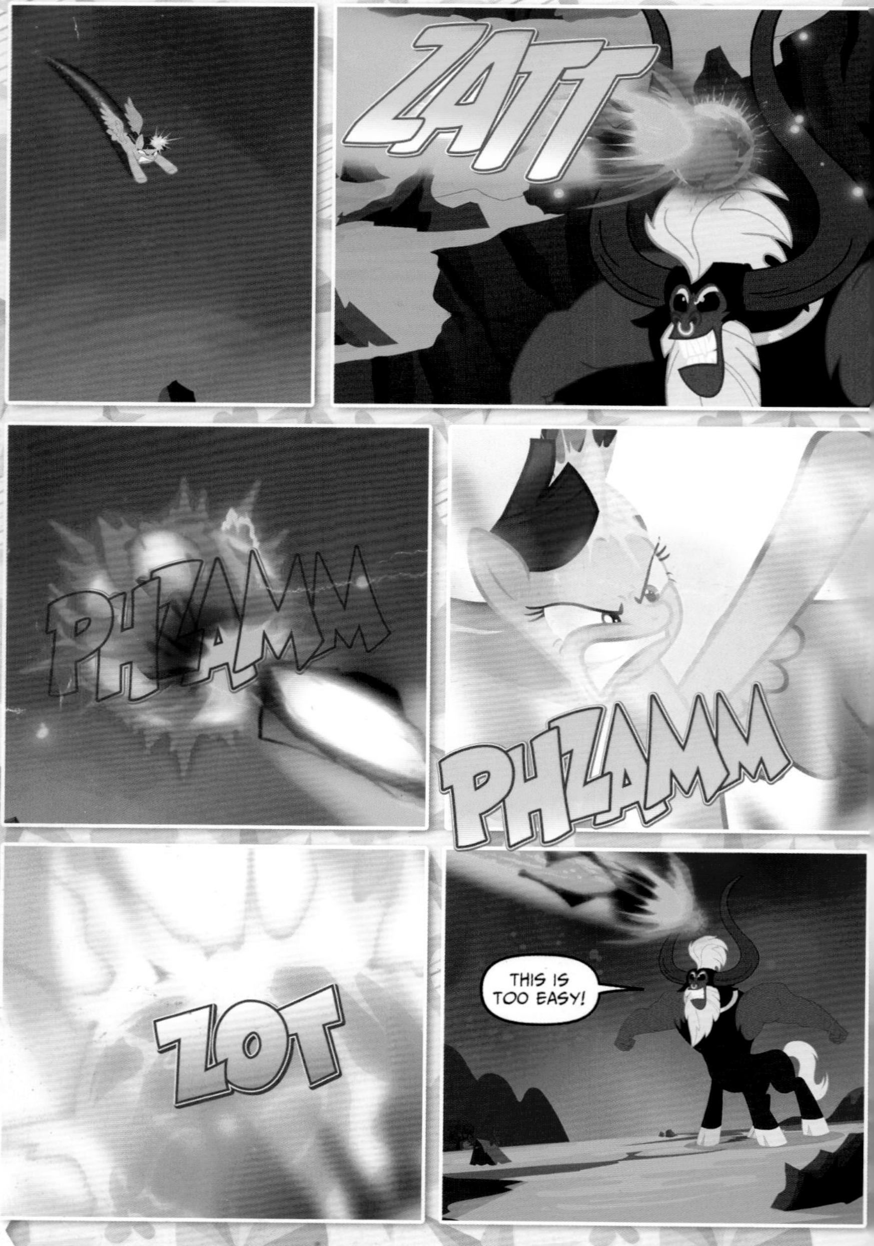
ZATT
PHZAMM
PHZAMM
ZOT
THIS IS TOO EASY!

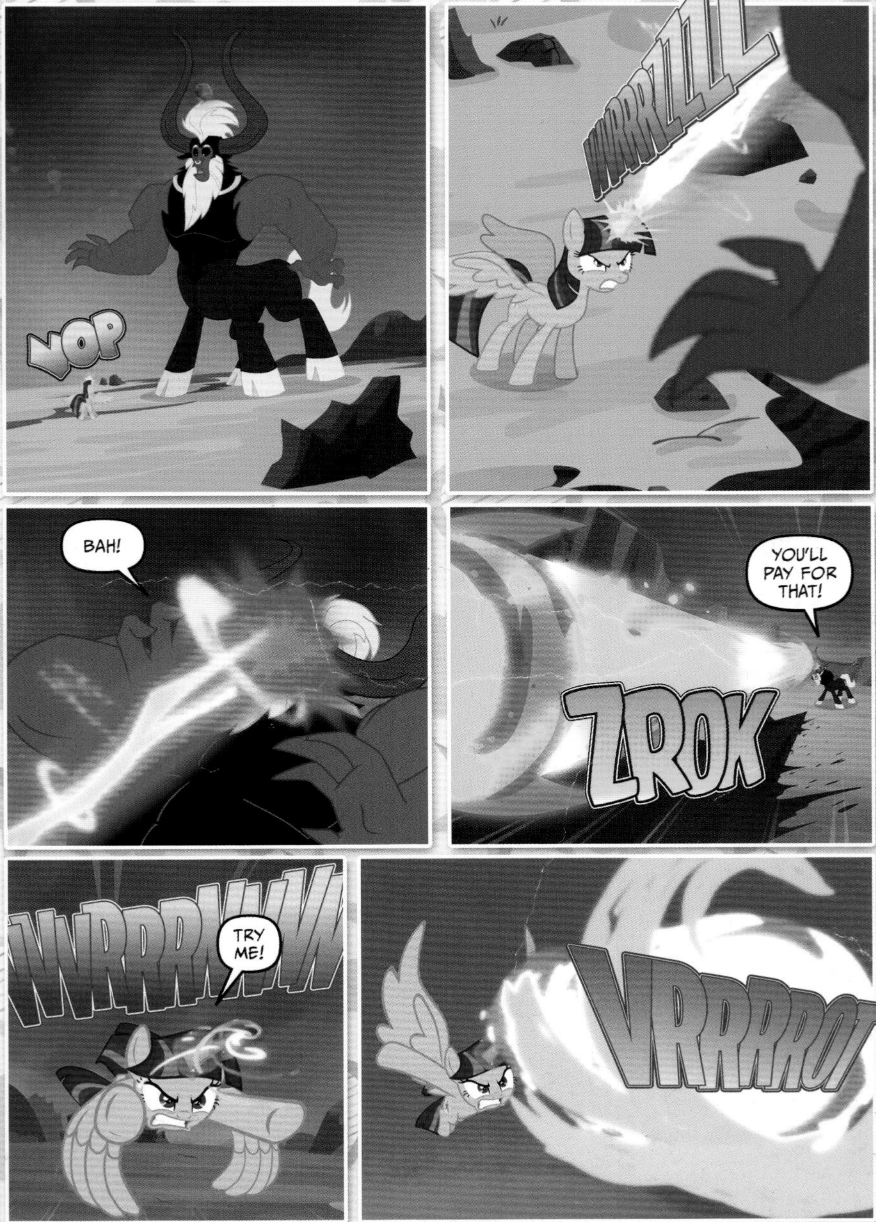
VOP
VVRRRZZZZZL
BAH!
YOU'LL PAY FOR THAT!
ZROK
VVVRRRNNNNN
TRY ME!
VRRRRROT

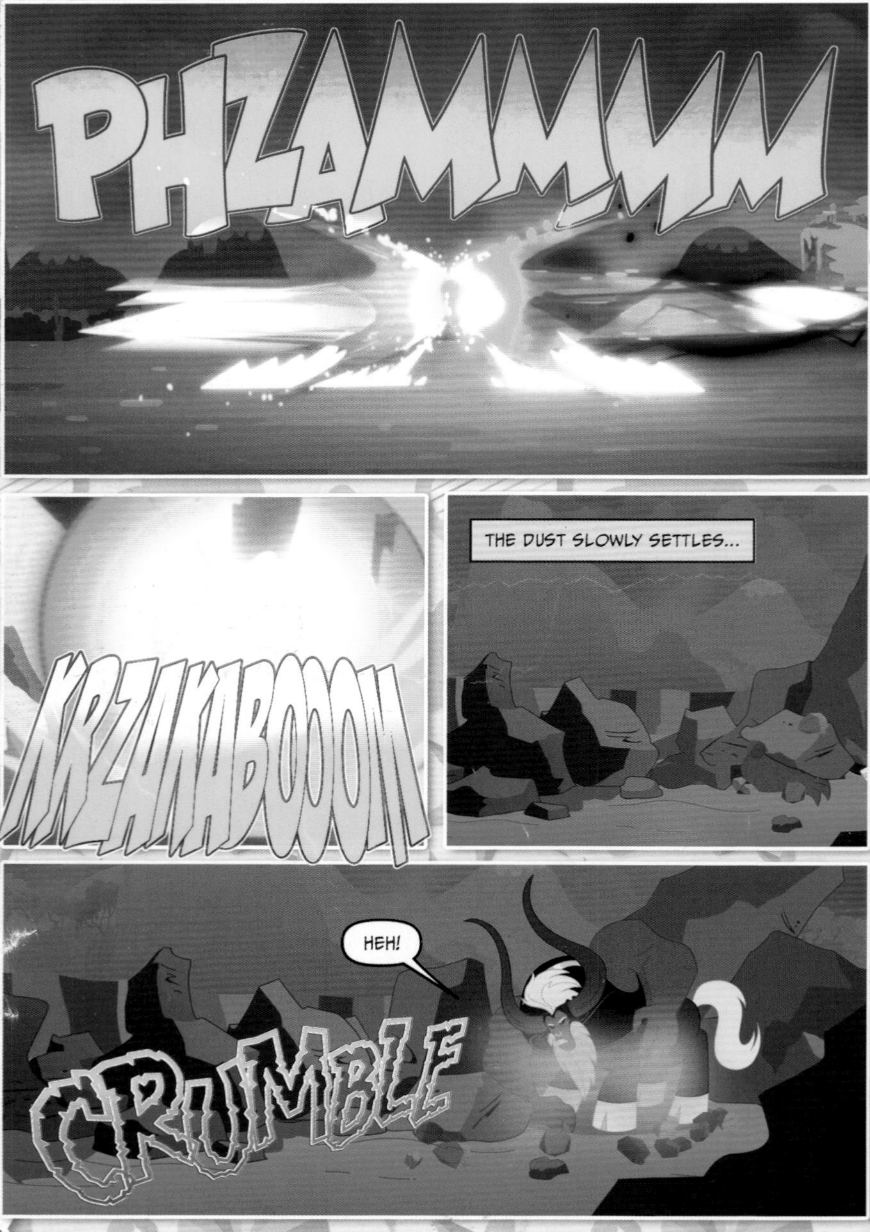
PHZAMMMM
KRZAKABOOOM
THE DUST SLOWLY SETTLES...
HEH!
CRUMBLE

BUT TIREK IS NOT ALONE...

HMPF.

IT APPEARS WE ARE AT AN IMPASSE.

HOW ABOUT A TRADE, PRINCESS TWILIGHT?

POP POP POP POP POP POP POP POP SNAP

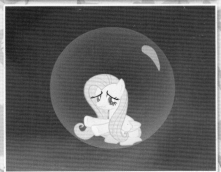

123

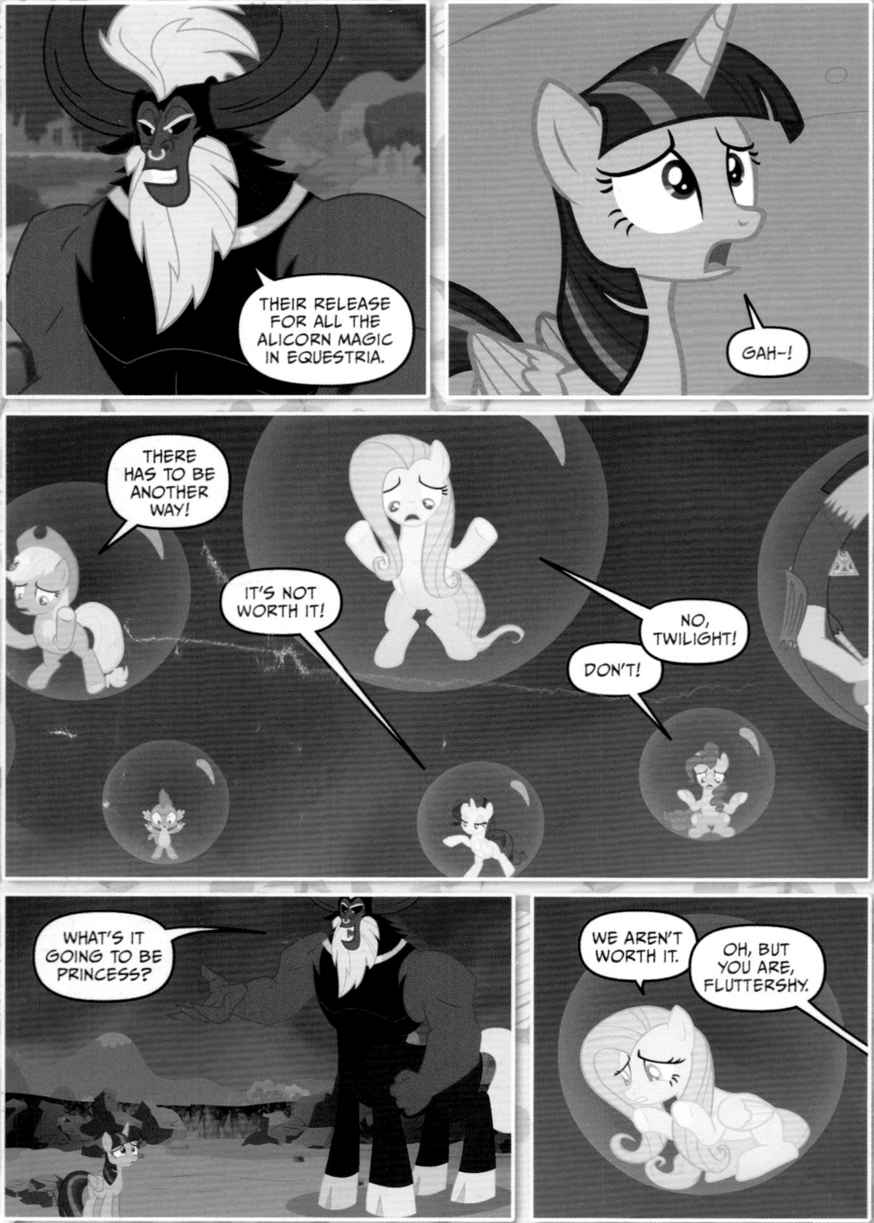
THEIR RELEASE FOR ALL THE ALICORN MAGIC IN EQUESTRIA.
GAH-!
THERE HAS TO BE ANOTHER WAY!
IT'S NOT WORTH IT!
NO, TWILIGHT!
DON'T!
WHAT'S IT GOING TO BE PRINCESS?
WE AREN'T WORTH IT.
OH, BUT YOU ARE, FLUTTERSHY.

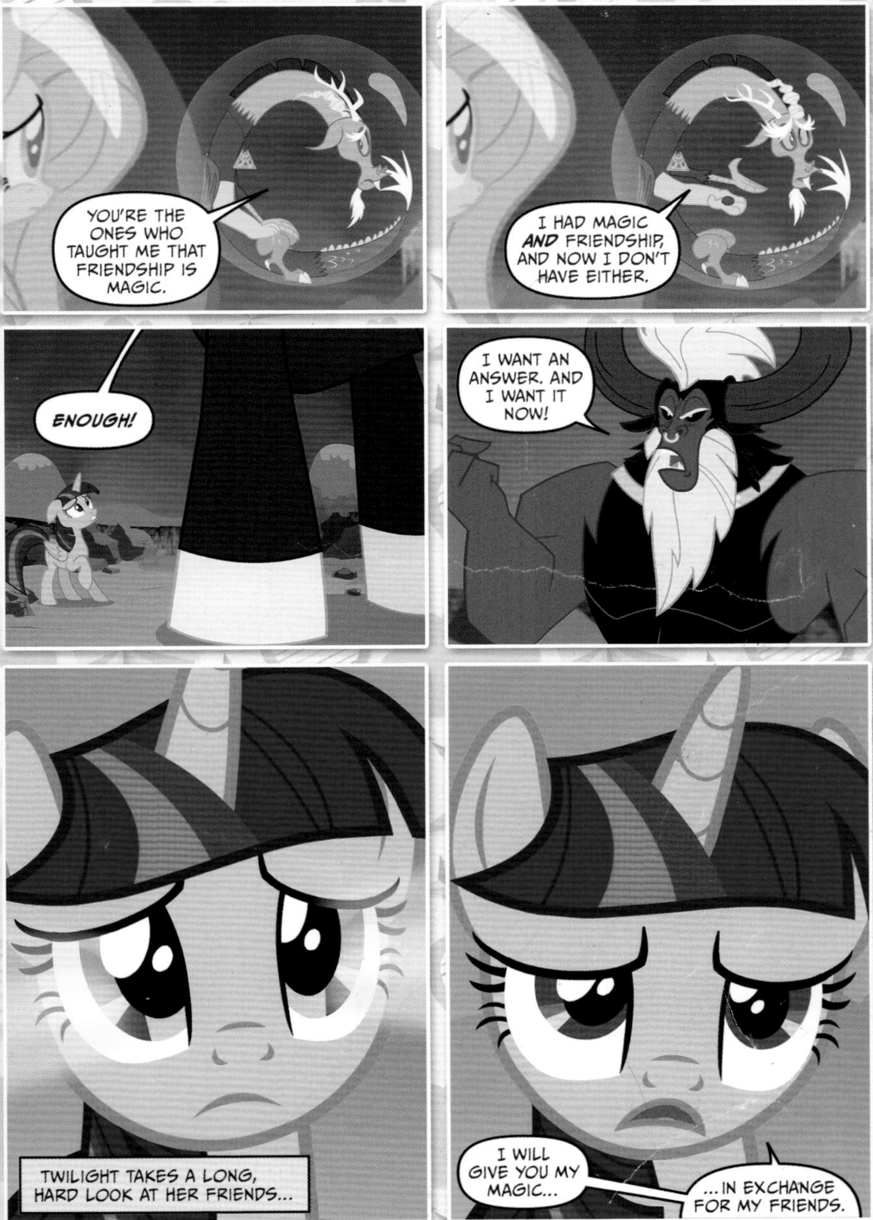
YOU'RE THE ONES WHO TAUGHT ME THAT FRIENDSHIP IS MAGIC.
I HAD MAGIC **AND** FRIENDSHIP, AND NOW I DON'T HAVE EITHER.
ENOUGH!
I WANT AN ANSWER. AND I WANT IT NOW!
TWILIGHT TAKES A LONG, HARD LOOK AT HER FRIENDS...
I WILL GIVE YOU MY MAGIC...
...IN EXCHANGE FOR MY FRIENDS.

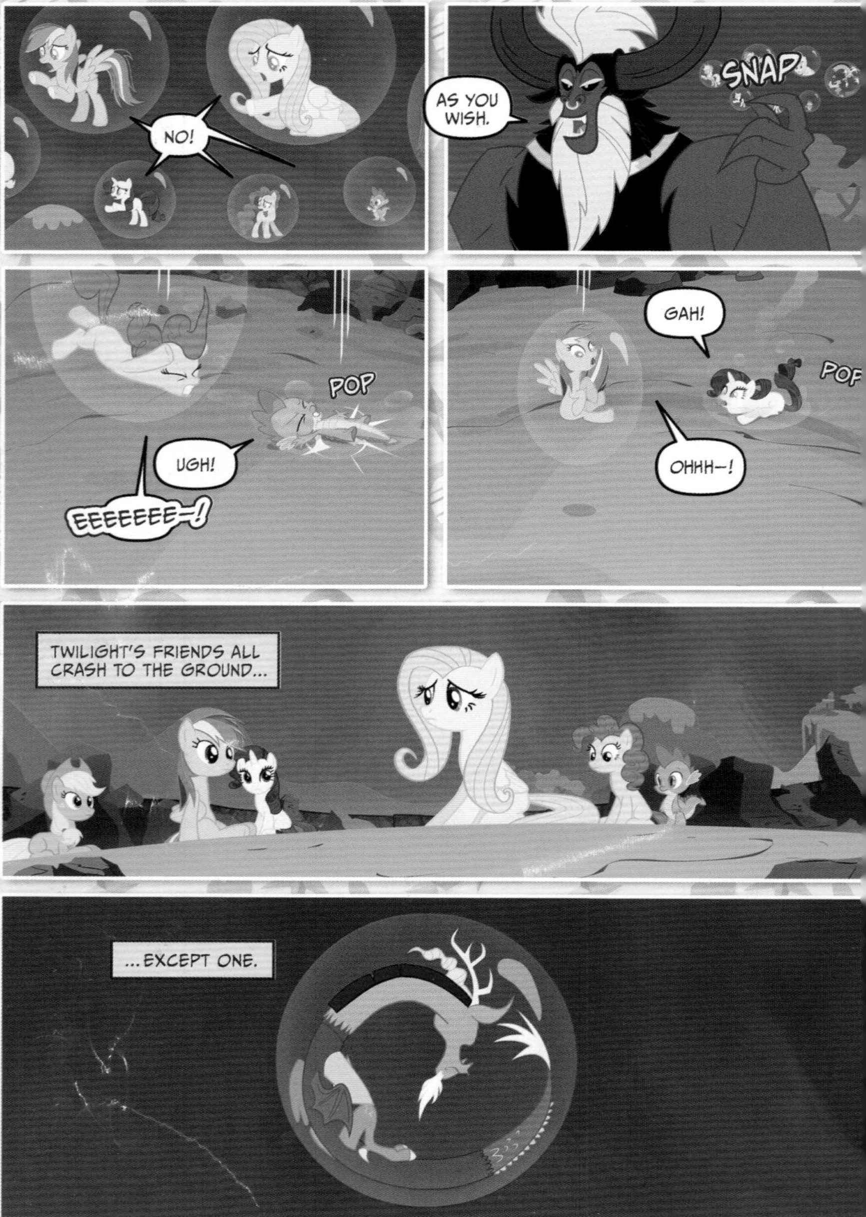
NO!
AS YOU WISH.
SNAP
POP
UGH!
EEEEEEE—!
GAH!
OHHH—!
POP
TWILIGHT'S FRIENDS ALL CRASH TO THE GROUND...
...EXCEPT ONE.

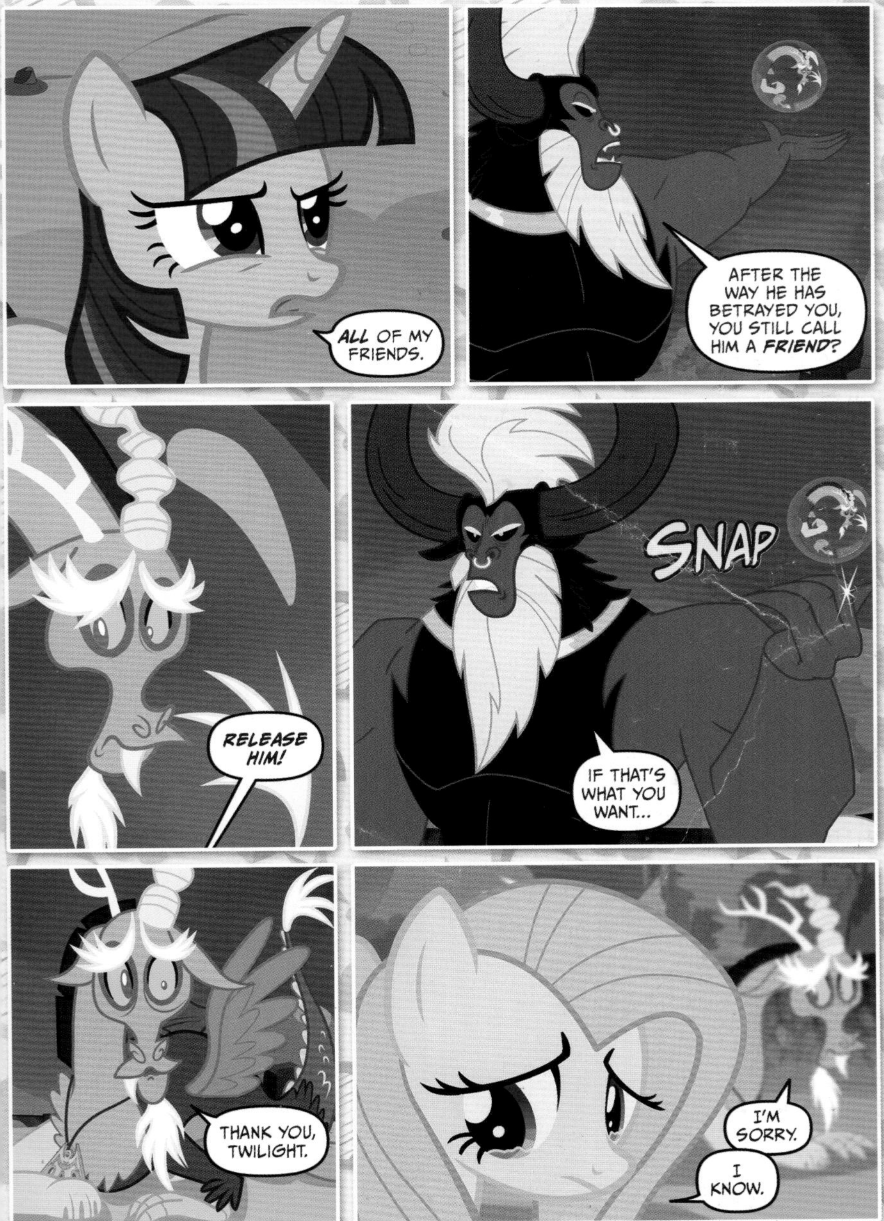
ALL OF MY FRIENDS.
AFTER THE WAY HE HAS BETRAYED YOU, YOU STILL CALL HIM A FRIEND?
RELEASE HIM!
SNAP
IF THAT'S WHAT YOU WANT...
THANK YOU, TWILIGHT.
I'M SORRY.
I KNOW.

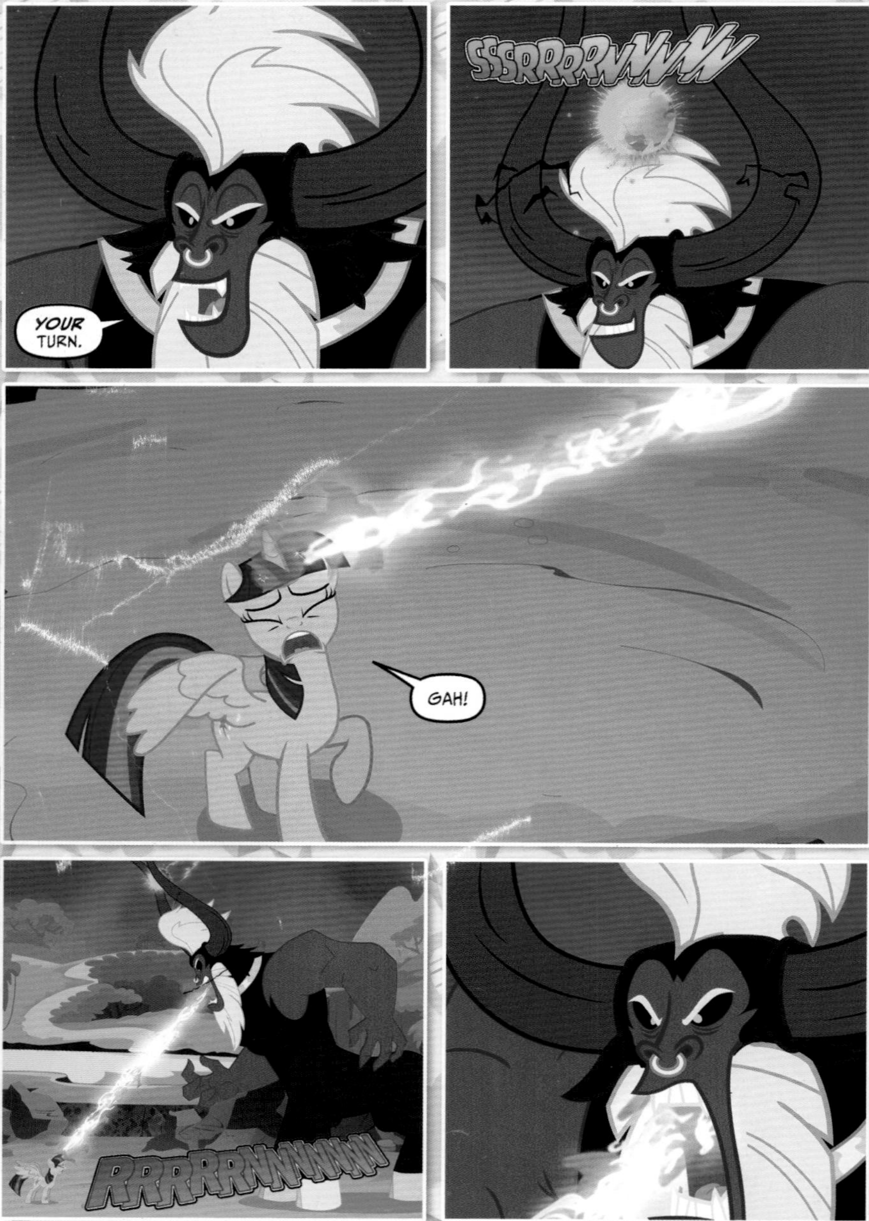
YOUR TURN.
SSSRRRRNNNN
GAH!
RRRRRNNNNNN

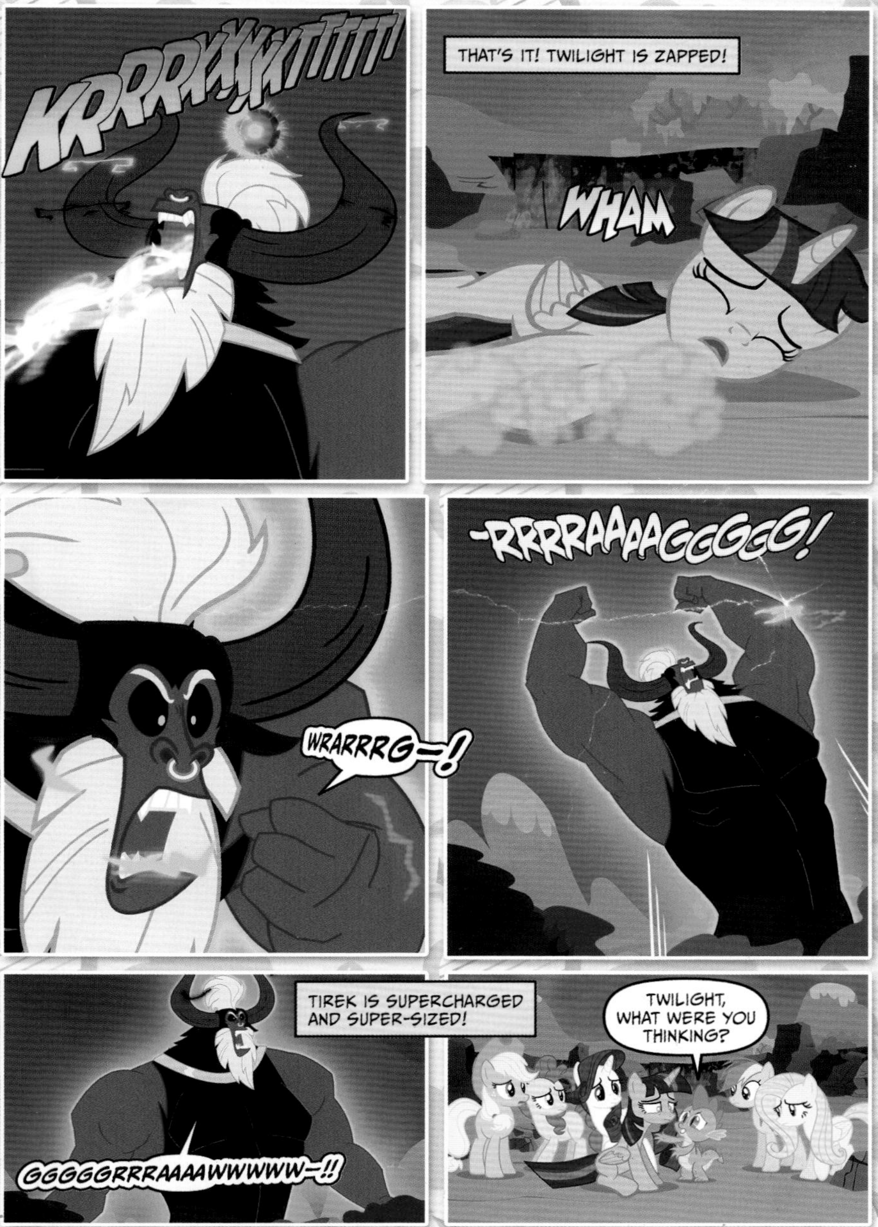
KRRRXXKTTTTT!
THAT'S IT! TWILIGHT IS ZAPPED!
WHAM
WRARRRG—!
-RRRRAAAAGGGGG!
TIREK IS SUPERCHARGED AND SUPER-SIZED!
GGGGGRRRAAAAWWWWW—!!
TWILIGHT, WHAT WERE YOU THINKING?

TIREK TRICKED ME INTO BELIEVING HE COULD OFFER ME SOMETHING MORE VALUABLE THAN FRIENDSHIP.

BUT THERE IS NOTHING WORTH MORE.

I SEE THAT NOW.

HE LIED WHEN HE SAID THIS WAS GIVEN AS A SIGN OF GRATITUDE AND LOYALTY.

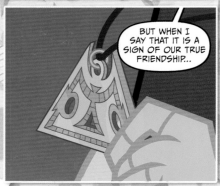

BUT WHEN I SAY THAT IT IS A SIGN OF OUR TRUE FRIENDSHIP...

...I AM TELLING THE TRUTH.

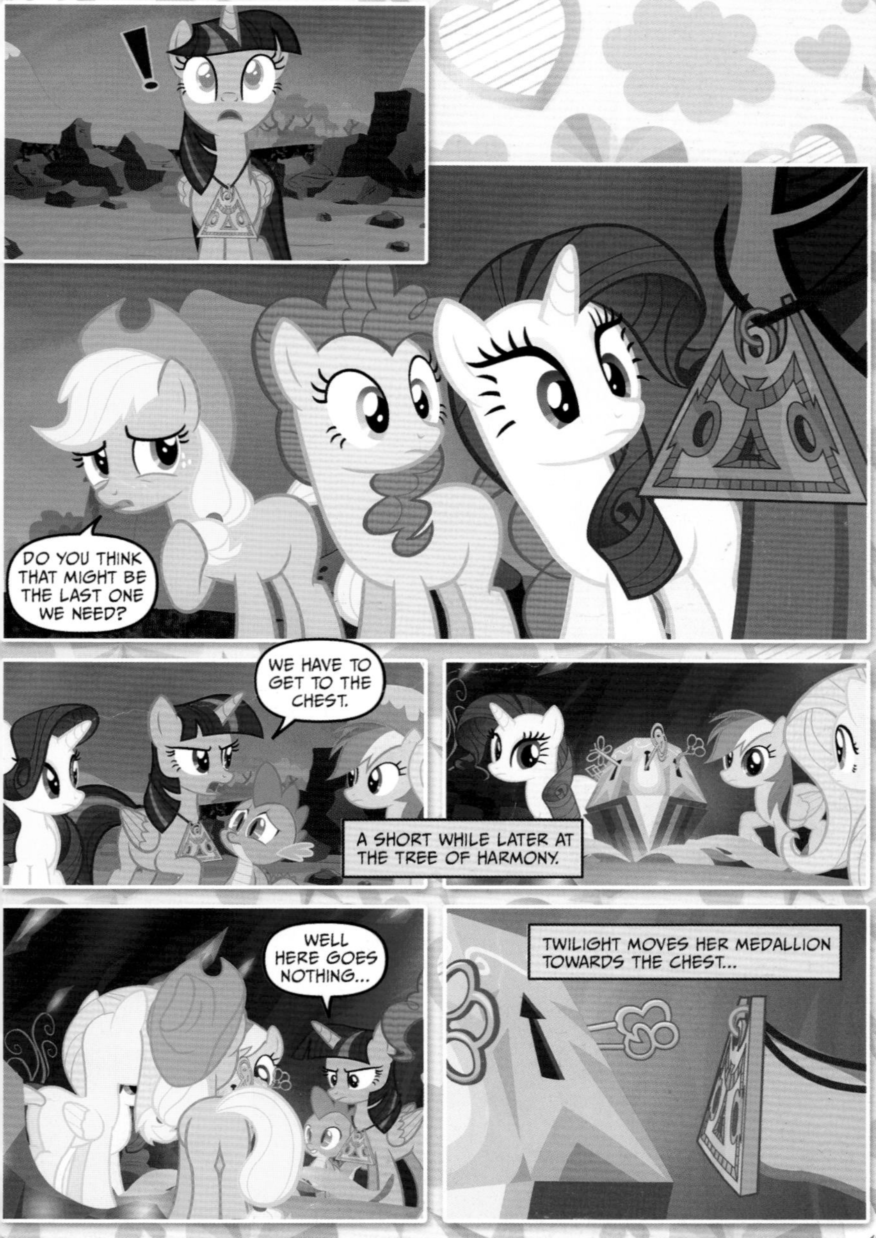
DO YOU THINK THAT MIGHT BE THE LAST ONE WE NEED?
WE HAVE TO GET TO THE CHEST.
A SHORT WHILE LATER AT THE TREE OF HARMONY.
WELL HERE GOES NOTHING...
TWILIGHT MOVES HER MEDALLION TOWARDS THE CHEST...

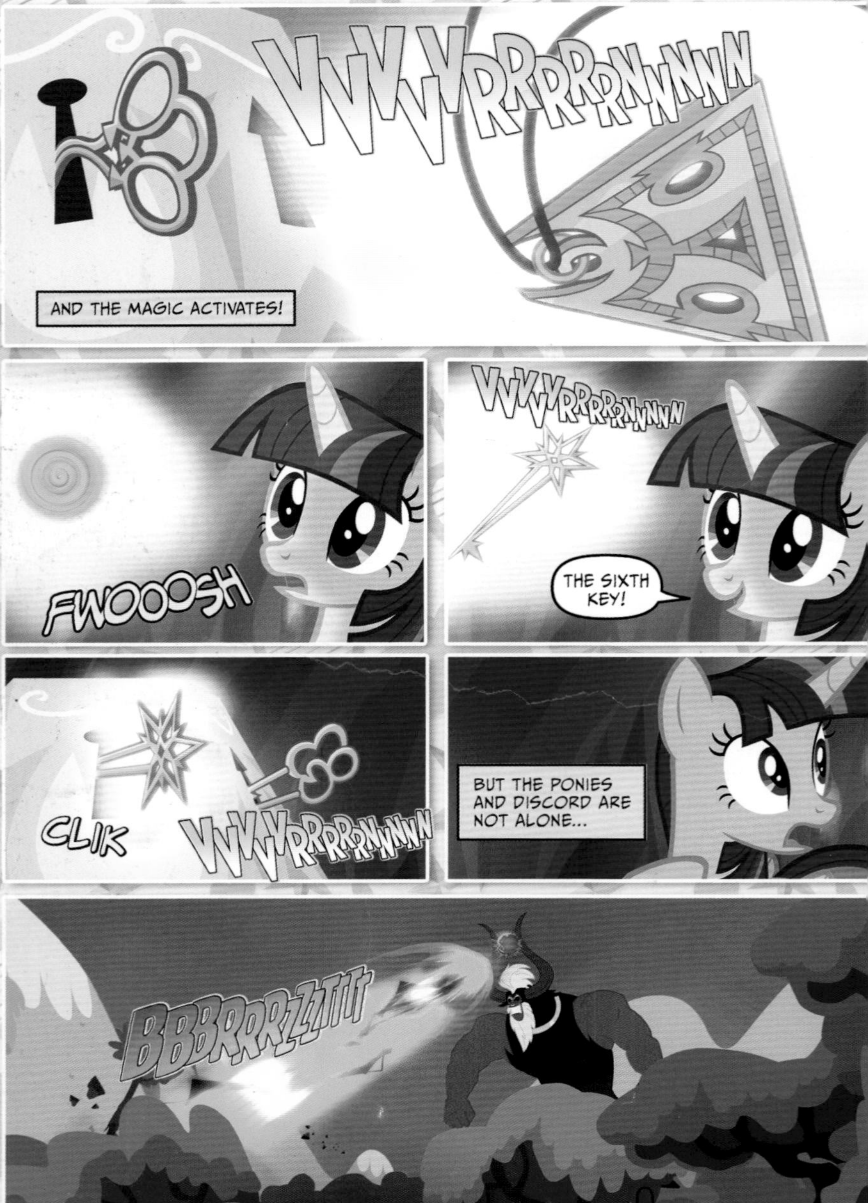
VVVVVRRRRRNNNNN
AND THE MAGIC ACTIVATES!
FWOOOSH
VVVVVRRRRRNNNNN
THE SIXTH KEY!
CLIK
VVVVVRRRRRNNNNN
BUT THE PONIES AND DISCORD ARE NOT ALONE...
BBBRRRZZTTTT

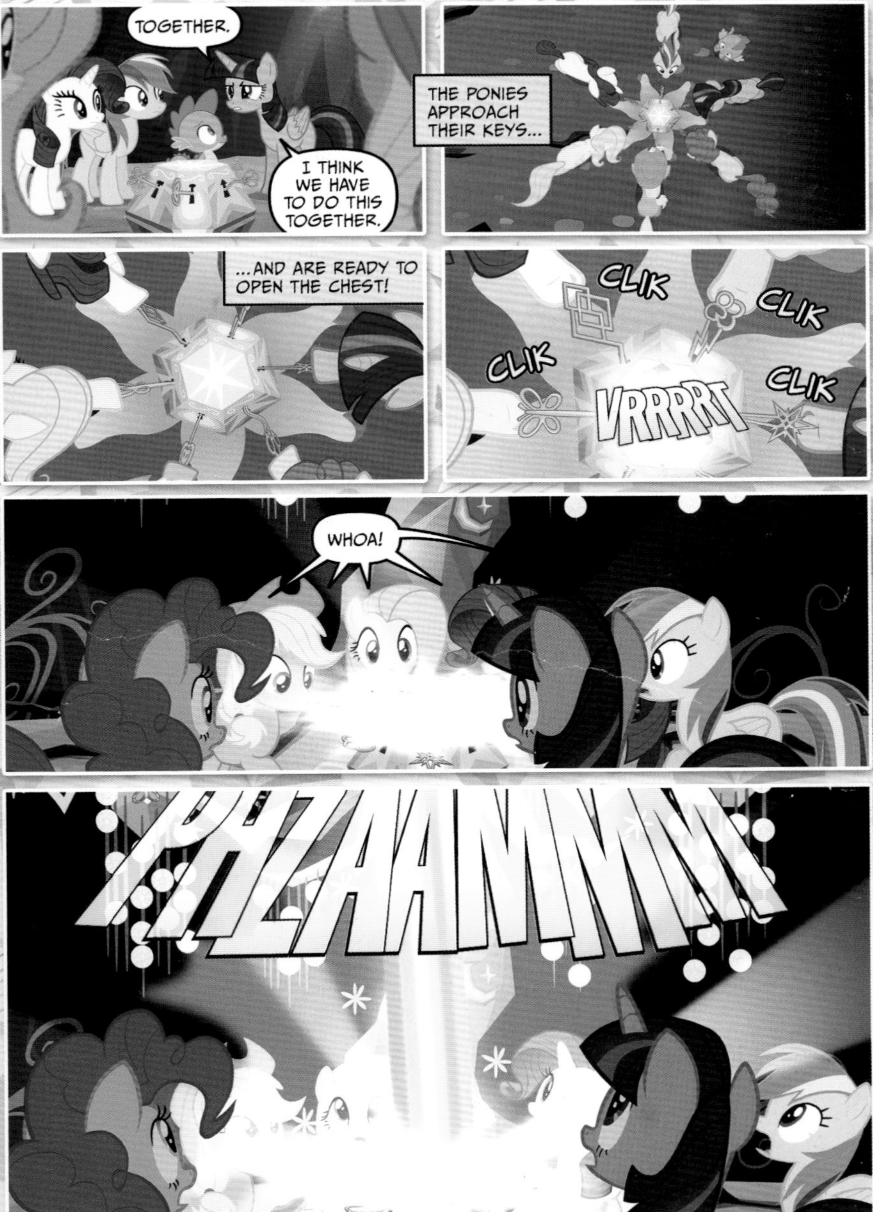
TOGETHER.
I THINK WE HAVE TO DO THIS TOGETHER.
THE PONIES APPROACH THEIR KEYS...
...AND ARE READY TO OPEN THE CHEST!
CLIK
CLIK
CLIK
CLIK
VRRRRT
WHOA!
PHZAAMMM!

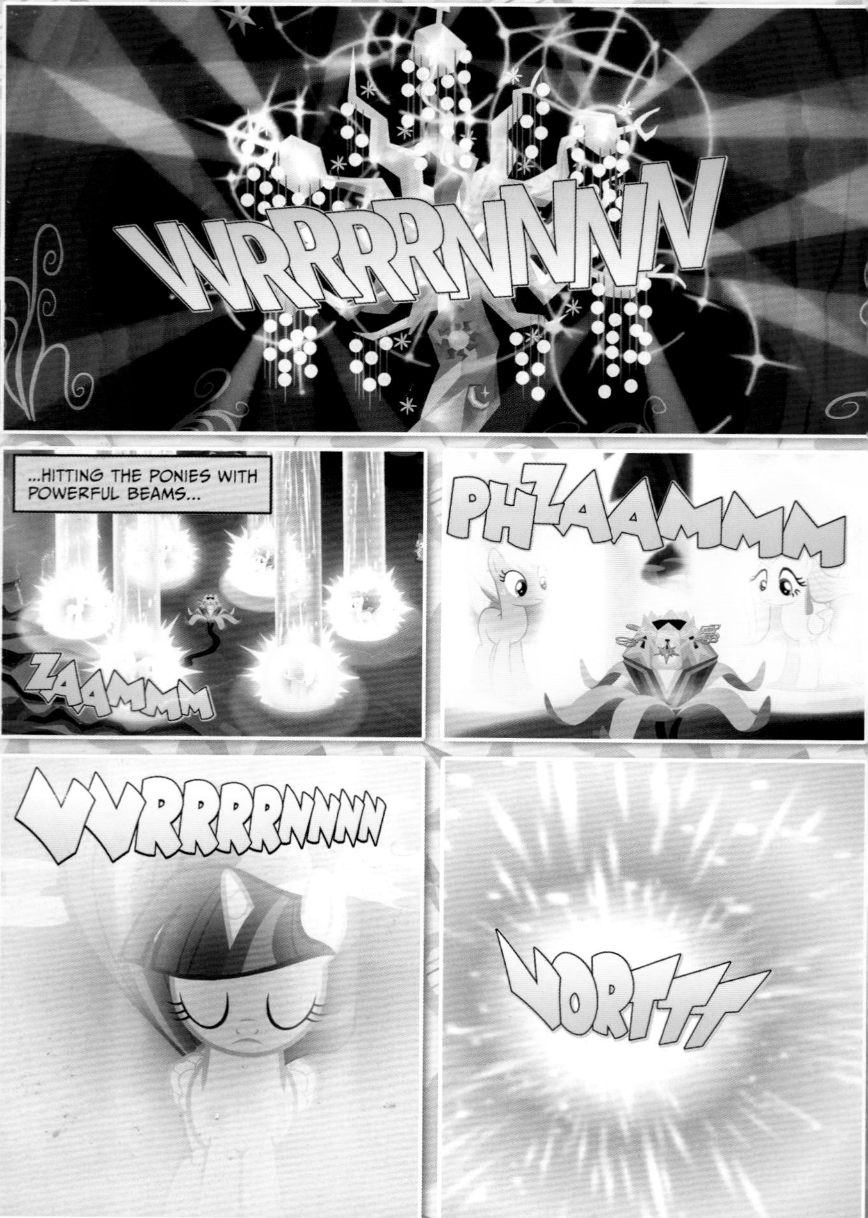
VVRRRRNNNNN
...HITTING THE PONIES WITH POWERFUL BEAMS...
ZAAMMM
PHZAAMMMM
VVRRRRNNNN
VORTTT

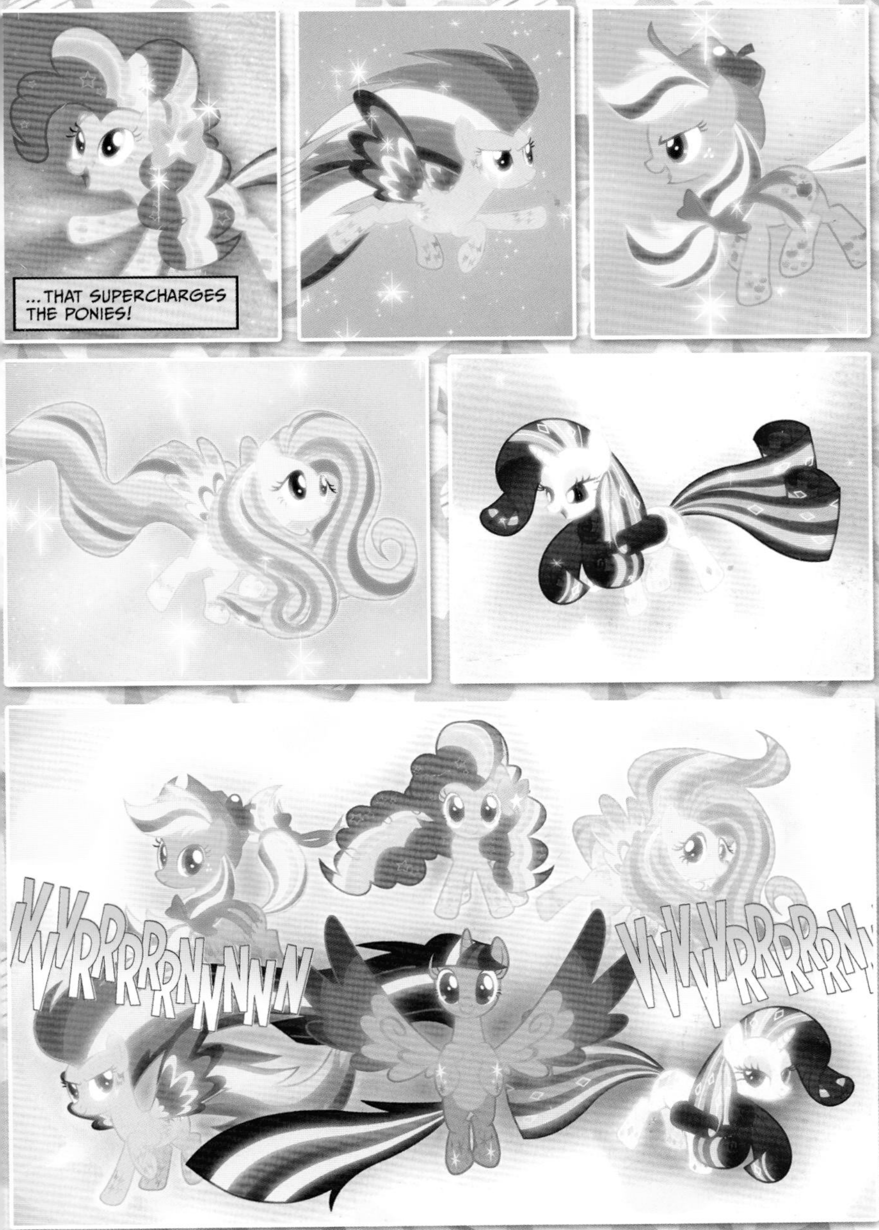
...THAT SUPERCHARGES THE PONIES!
VVVYRRRRRRNNNNNN
VVVVYRRRRRN

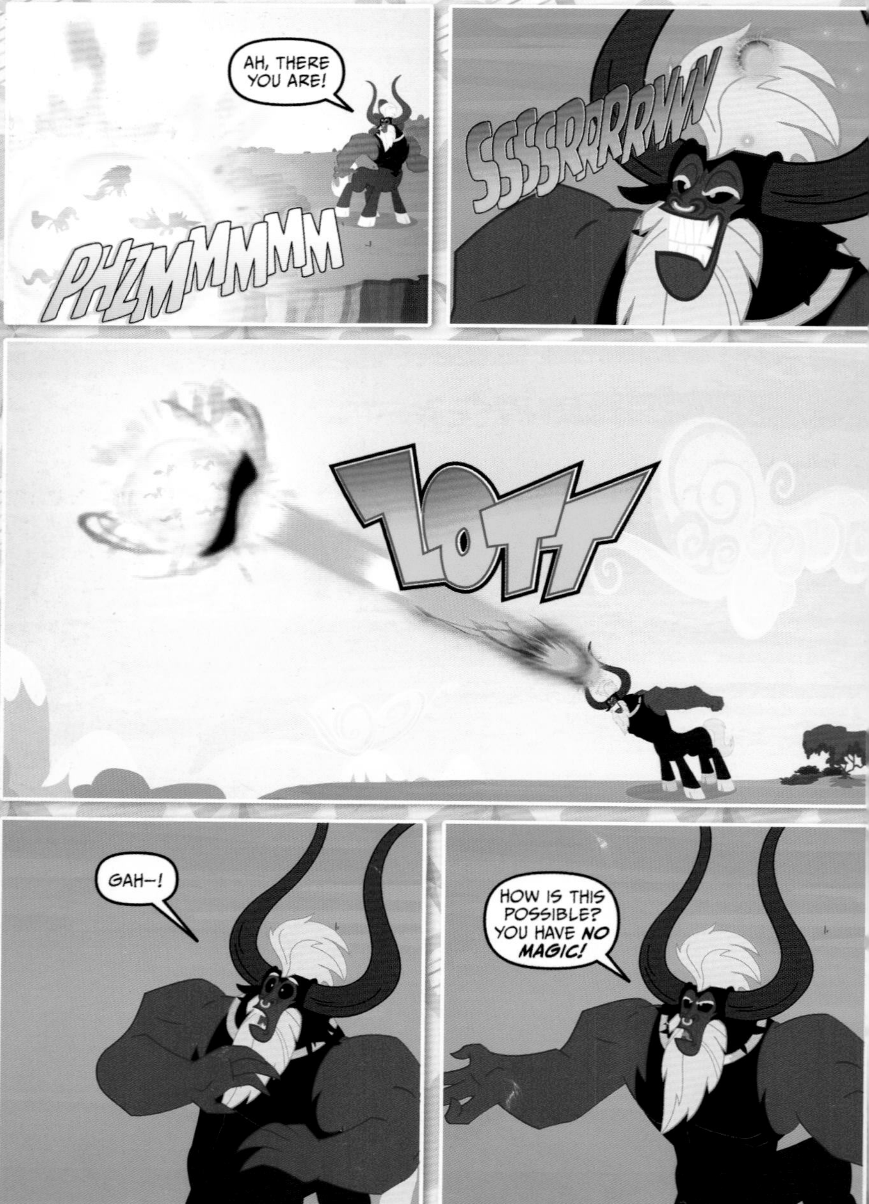
AH, THERE YOU ARE!
PHZMMMMMM
SSSSRRRRNNN
ZOTT
GAH--!
HOW IS THIS POSSIBLE? YOU HAVE **NO MAGIC!**

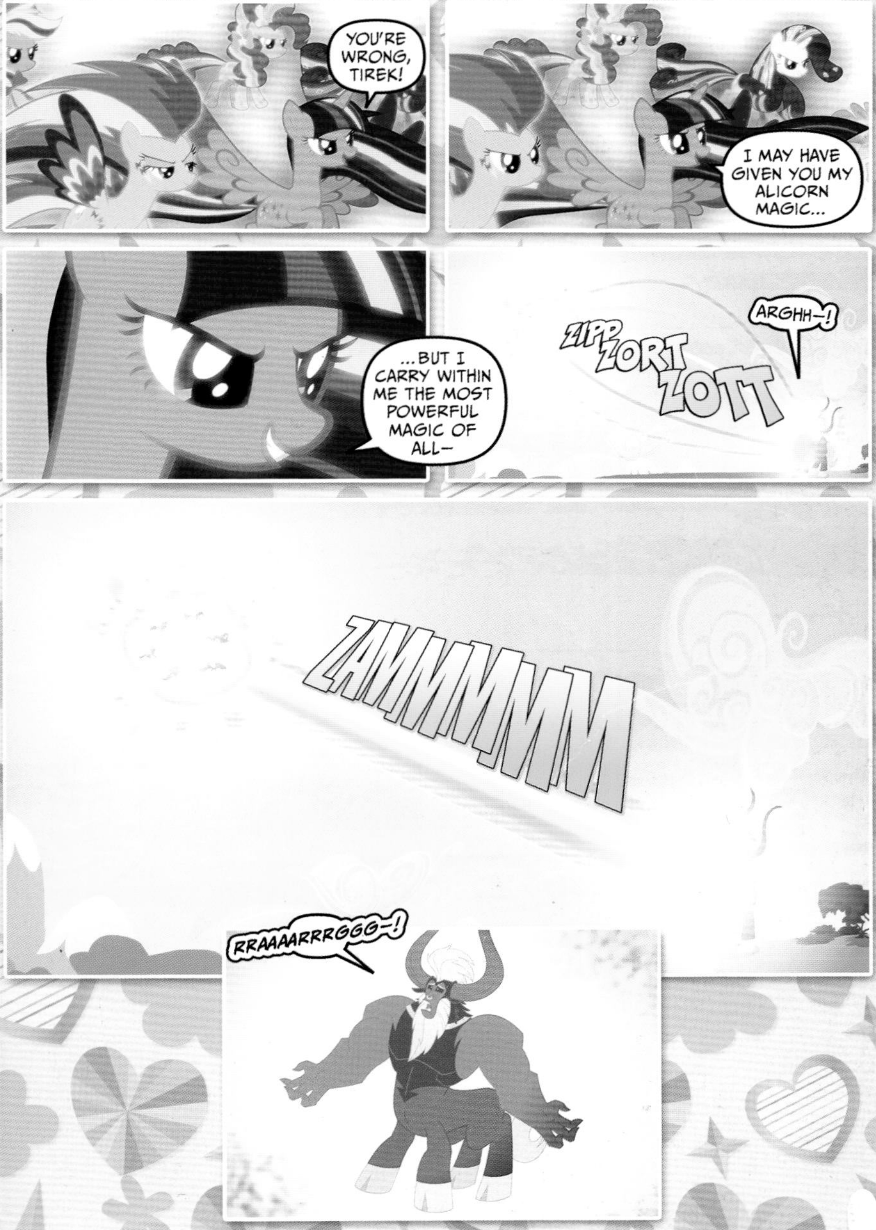
YOU'RE WRONG, TIREK!
I MAY HAVE GIVEN YOU MY ALICORN MAGIC...
...BUT I CARRY WITHIN ME THE MOST POWERFUL MAGIC OF ALL—
ARGHH—!
ZIPP ZORT ZOTT
ZAMMMMMM
RRAAAARRRGGG—!

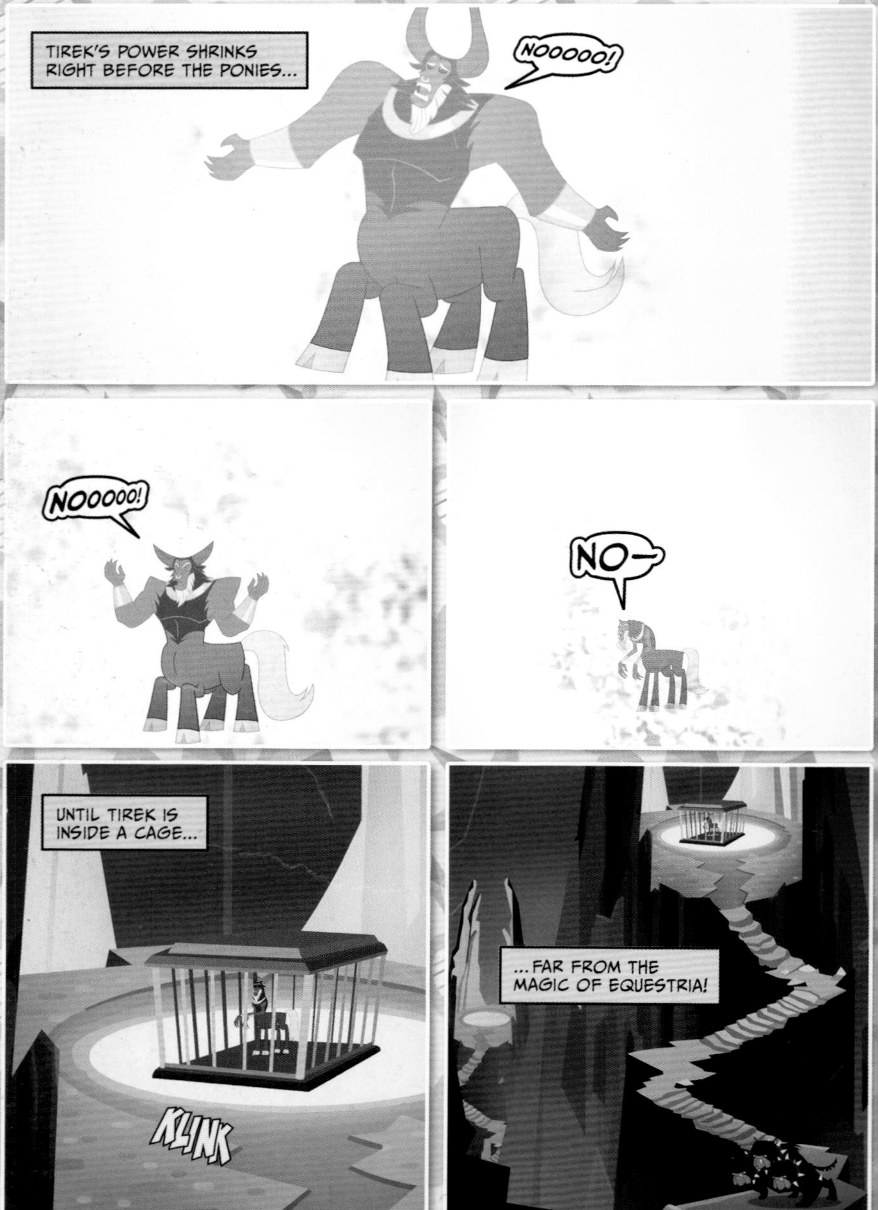
TIREK'S POWER SHRINKS RIGHT BEFORE THE PONIES...
NOOOOO!
NOOOOO!
NO–
UNTIL TIREK IS INSIDE A CAGE...
KLINK
...FAR FROM THE MAGIC OF EQUESTRIA!

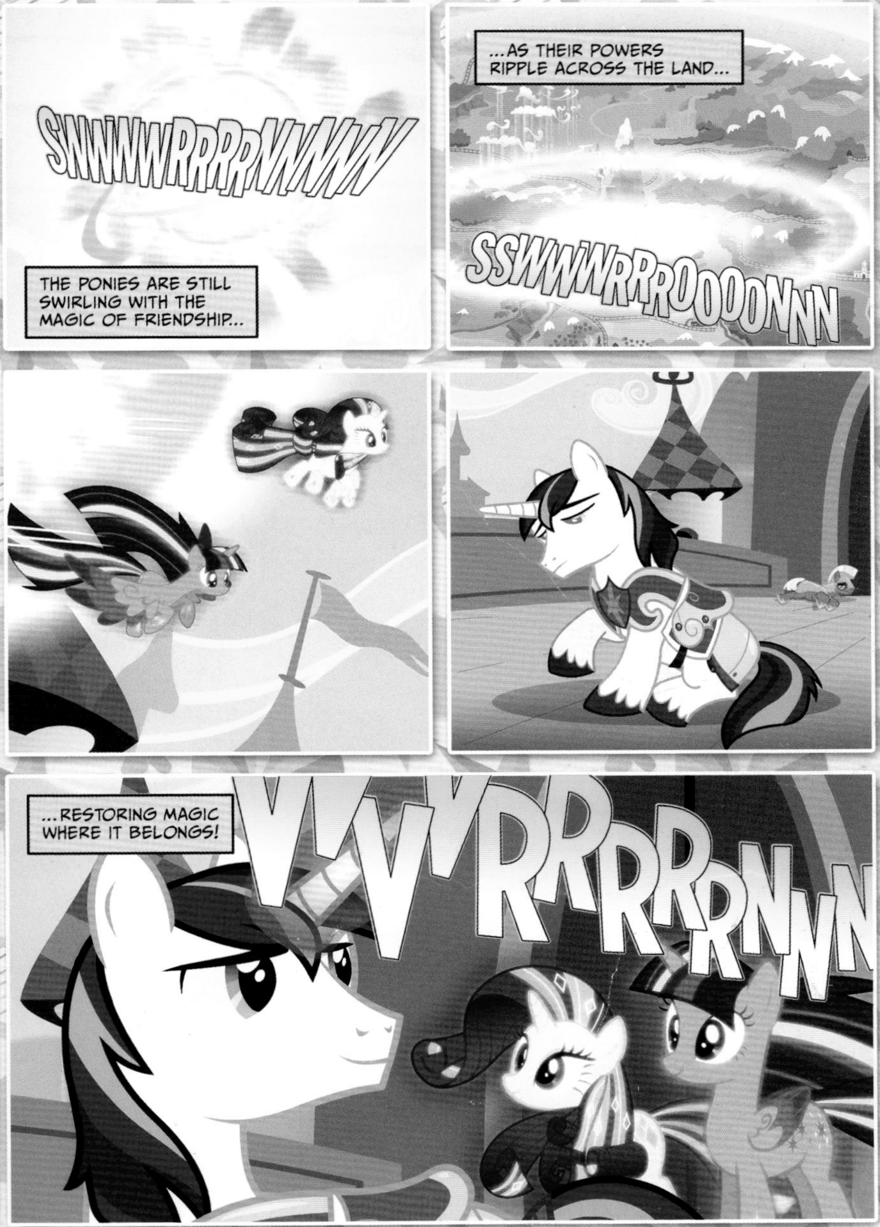
SNNNWWRRRRNNNNN
THE PONIES ARE STILL SWIRLING WITH THE MAGIC OF FRIENDSHIP...
...AS THEIR POWERS RIPPLE ACROSS THE LAND...
SSWWWRRROOOONNN
...RESTORING MAGIC WHERE IT BELONGS!
VVVRRRRRNNN

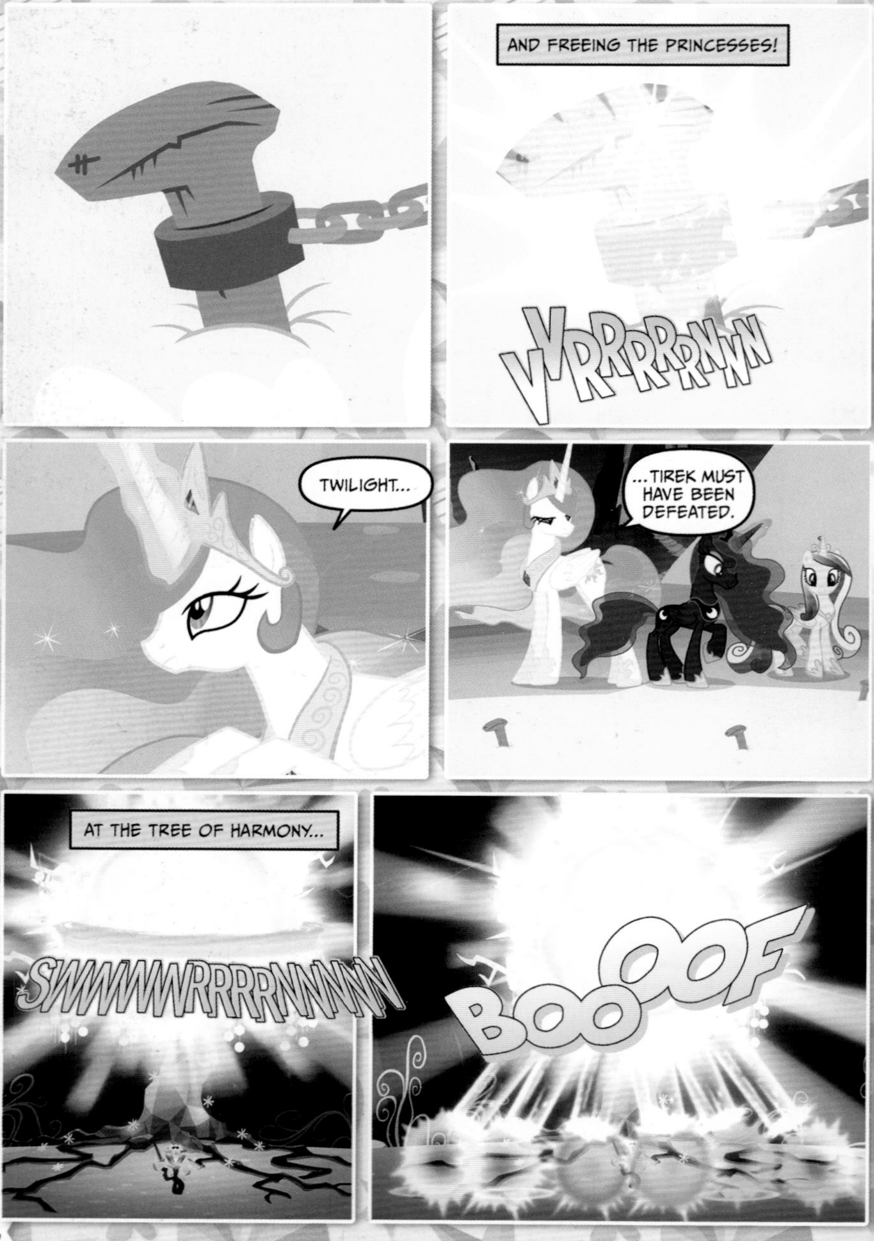
AND FREEING THE PRINCESSES!
VRRRRRNNN
TWILIGHT...
...TIREK MUST HAVE BEEN DEFEATED.
AT THE TREE OF HARMONY...
SWWWWRRRRNNNNN
BOOOOF

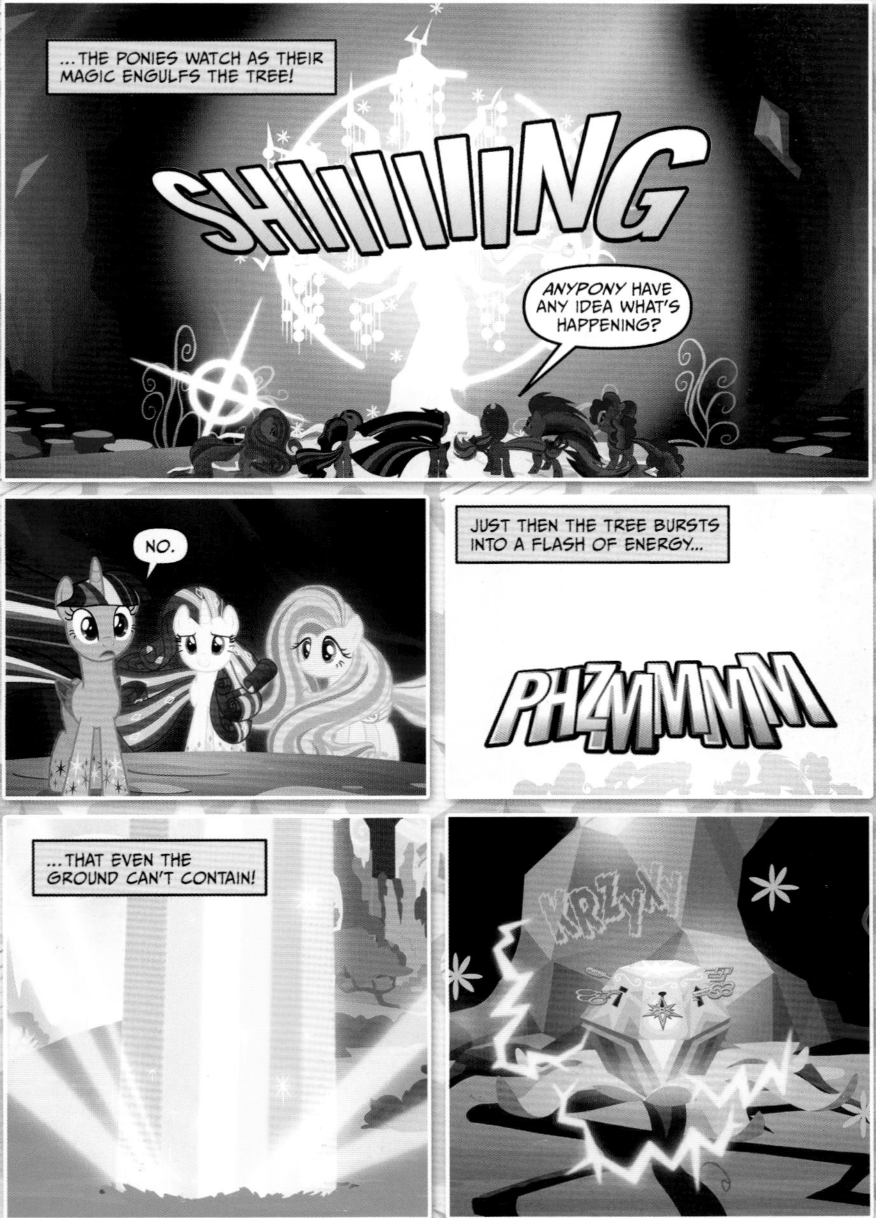
...THE PONIES WATCH AS THEIR MAGIC ENGULFS THE TREE!
SHIIIIIIING
ANYPONY HAVE ANY IDEA WHAT'S HAPPENING?
NO.
JUST THEN THE TREE BURSTS INTO A FLASH OF ENERGY...
PHZMMMMM
...THAT EVEN THE GROUND CAN'T CONTAIN!

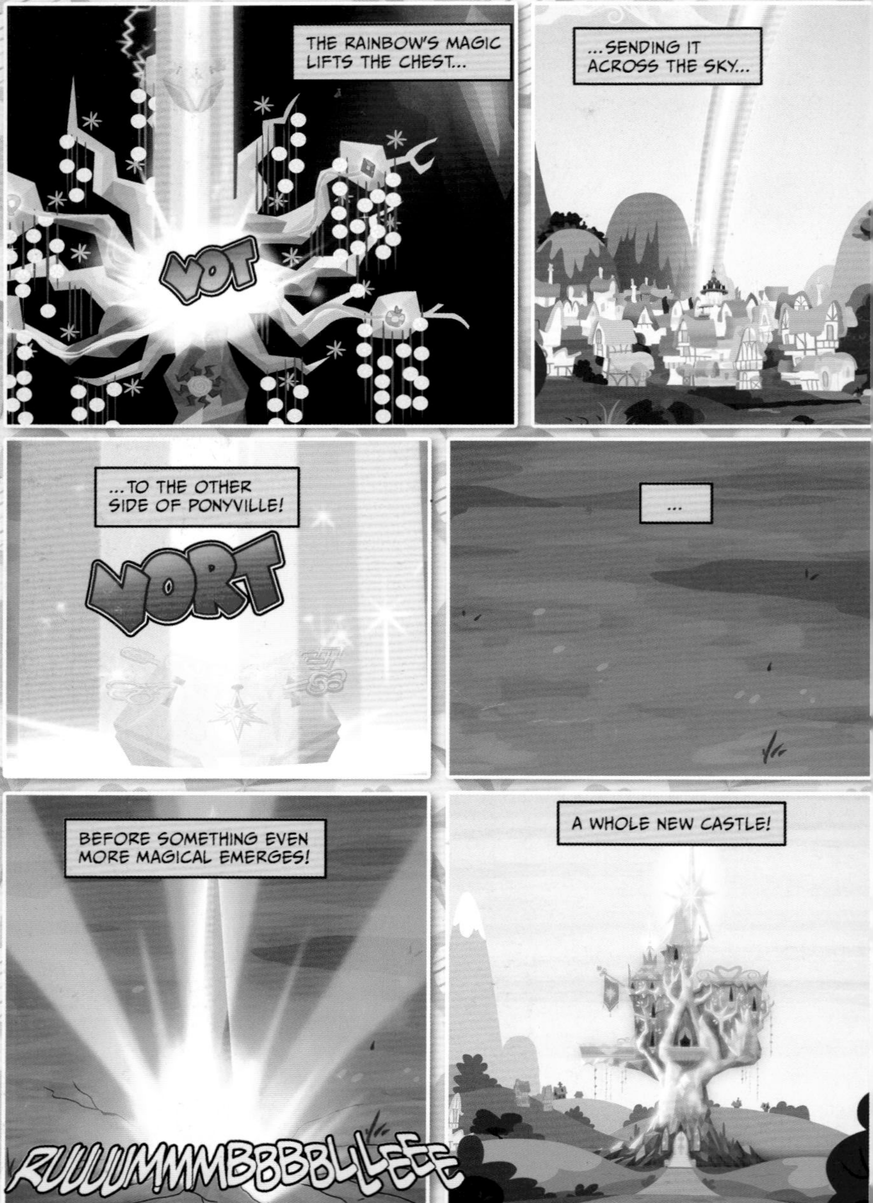
THE RAINBOW'S MAGIC LIFTS THE CHEST...
VOT
...SENDING IT ACROSS THE SKY...
...TO THE OTHER SIDE OF PONYVILLE!
VORT
...
BEFORE SOMETHING EVEN MORE MAGICAL EMERGES!
RUUUMMMBBBBLLLEEE
A WHOLE NEW CASTLE!

IN A FLASH THE PONIES ARE BEFORE THE NEW CASTLE...

PAWOOSH

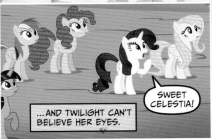

...AND TWILIGHT CAN'T BELIEVE HER EYES.

SWEET CELESTIA!

ARE YOU ALL SEEING WHAT I'M SEEING.

BUT WHO'S IS IT?

I BELIEVE IT IS YOURS...

143

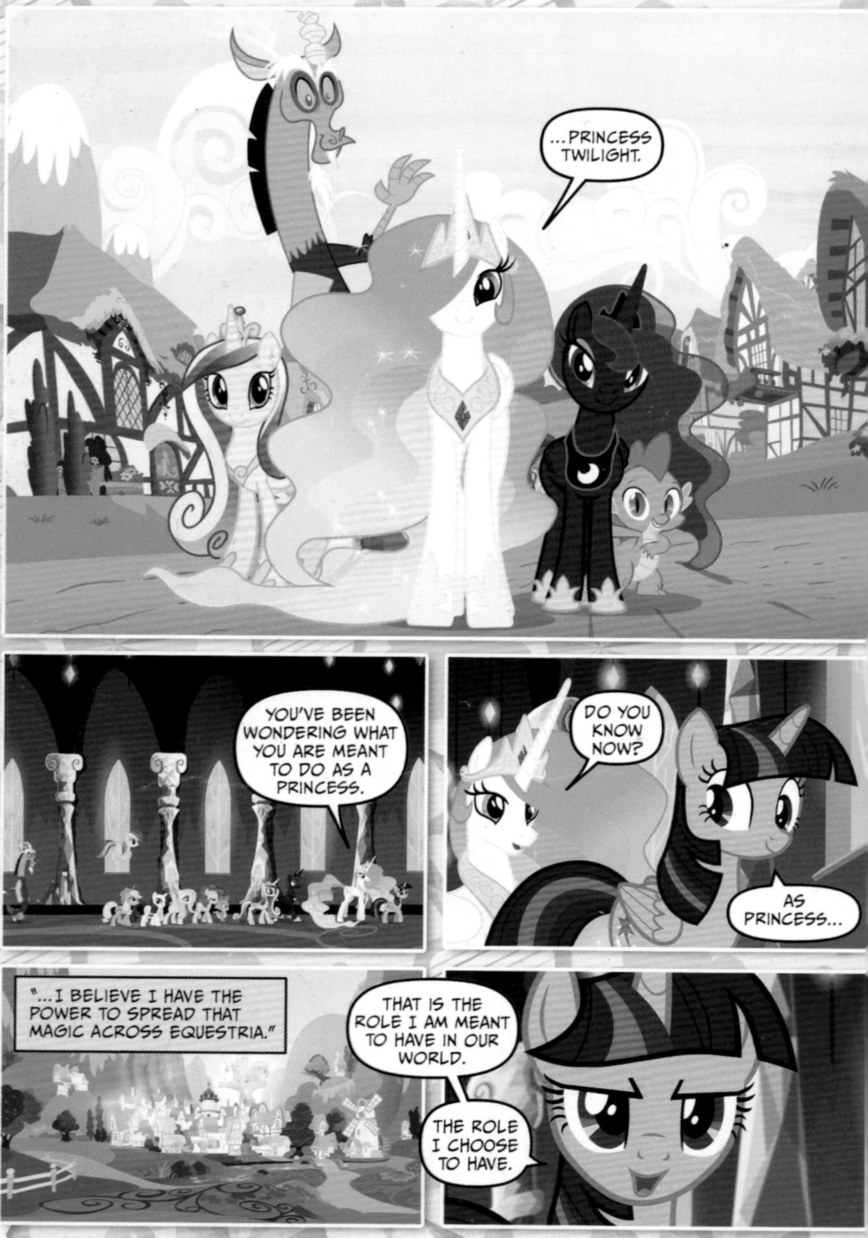
...PRINCESS TWILIGHT.
YOU'VE BEEN WONDERING WHAT YOU ARE MEANT TO DO AS A PRINCESS.
DO YOU KNOW NOW?
AS PRINCESS...
"...I BELIEVE I HAVE THE POWER TO SPREAD THAT MAGIC ACROSS EQUESTRIA."
THAT IS THE ROLE I AM MEANT TO HAVE IN OUR WORLD.
THE ROLE I CHOOSE TO HAVE.

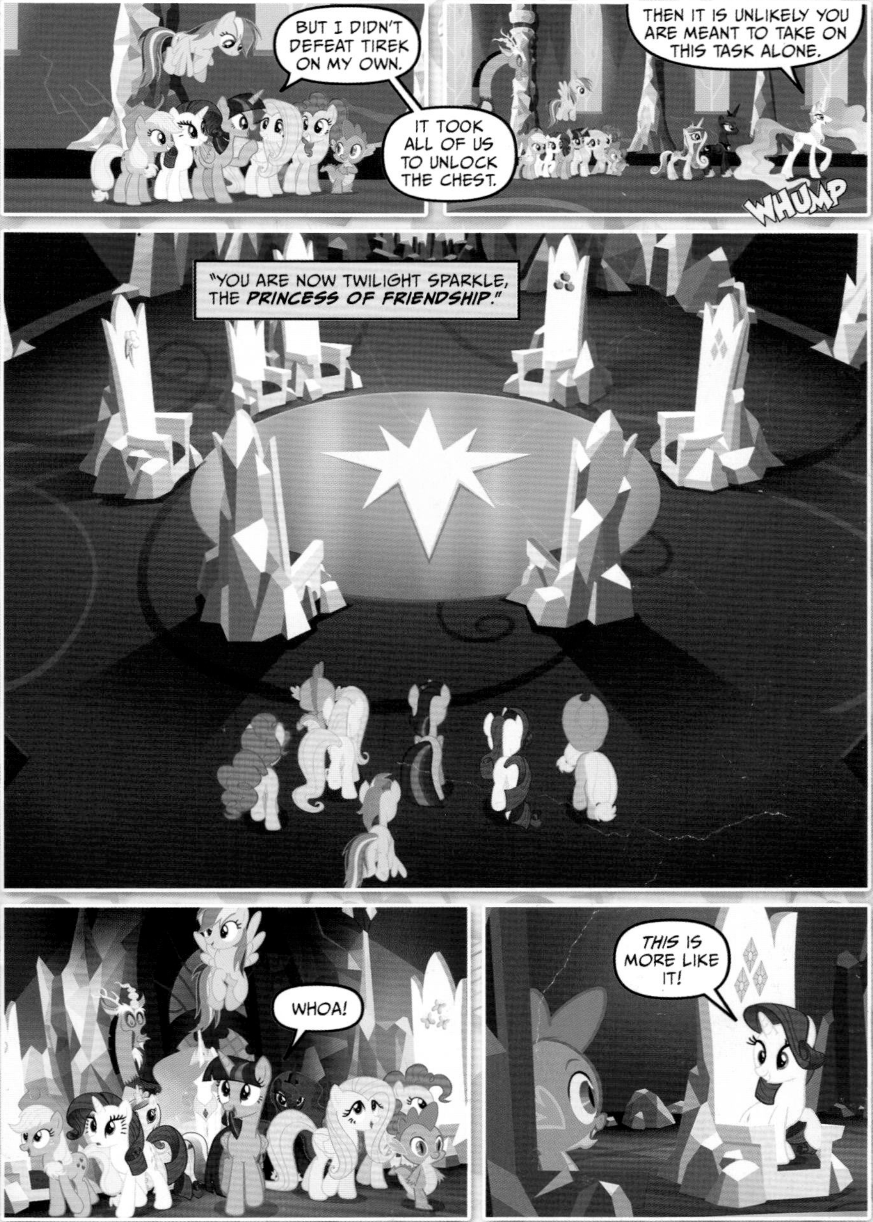
BUT I DIDN'T DEFEAT TIREK ON MY OWN.
IT TOOK ALL OF US TO UNLOCK THE CHEST.
THEN IT IS UNLIKELY YOU ARE MEANT TO TAKE ON THIS TASK ALONE.
WHUMP
"YOU ARE NOW TWILIGHT SPARKLE, THE *PRINCESS OF FRIENDSHIP.*"
WHOA!
THIS IS MORE LIKE IT!

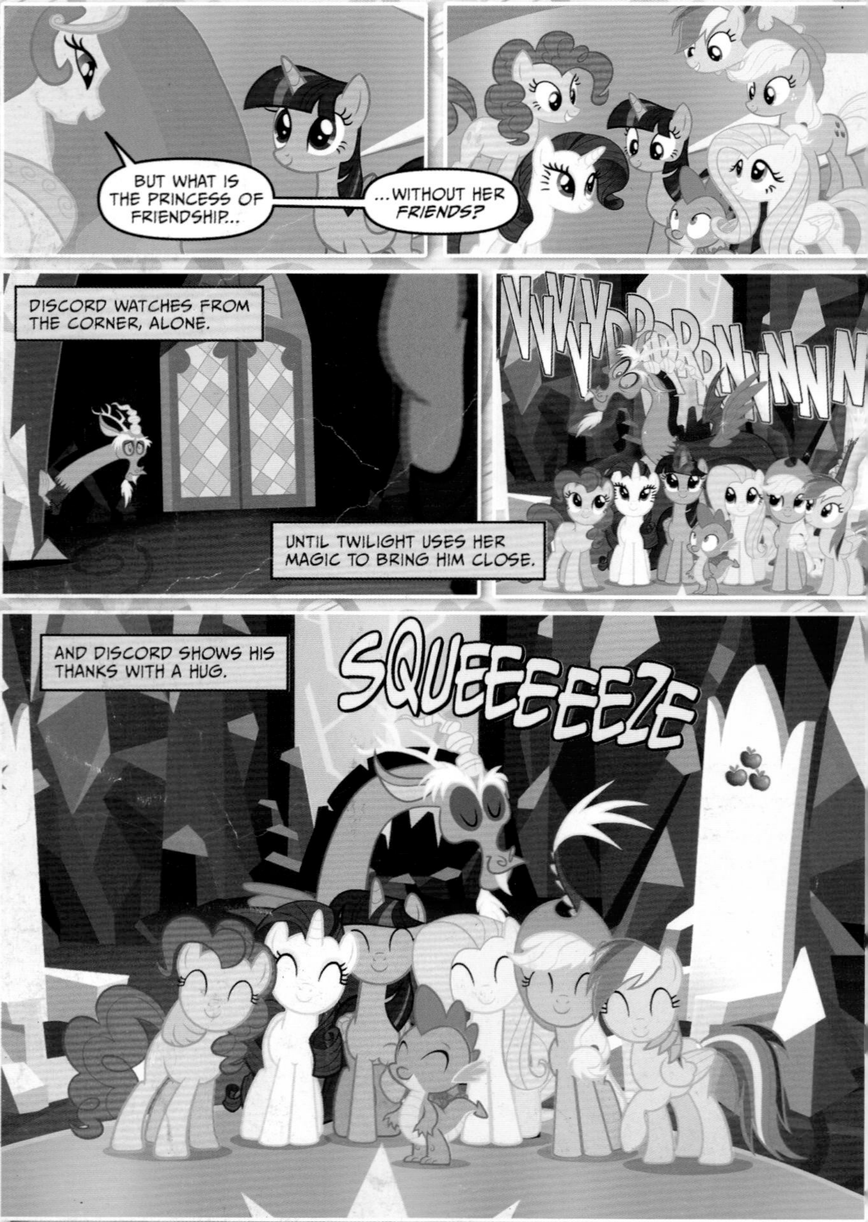
BUT WHAT IS THE PRINCESS OF FRIENDSHIP...
...WITHOUT HER FRIENDS?
DISCORD WATCHES FROM THE CORNER, ALONE.
VVVVVRRRRNNNNN
UNTIL TWILIGHT USES HER MAGIC TO BRING HIM CLOSE.
AND DISCORD SHOWS HIS THANKS WITH A HUG.
SQUEEEEEEZE

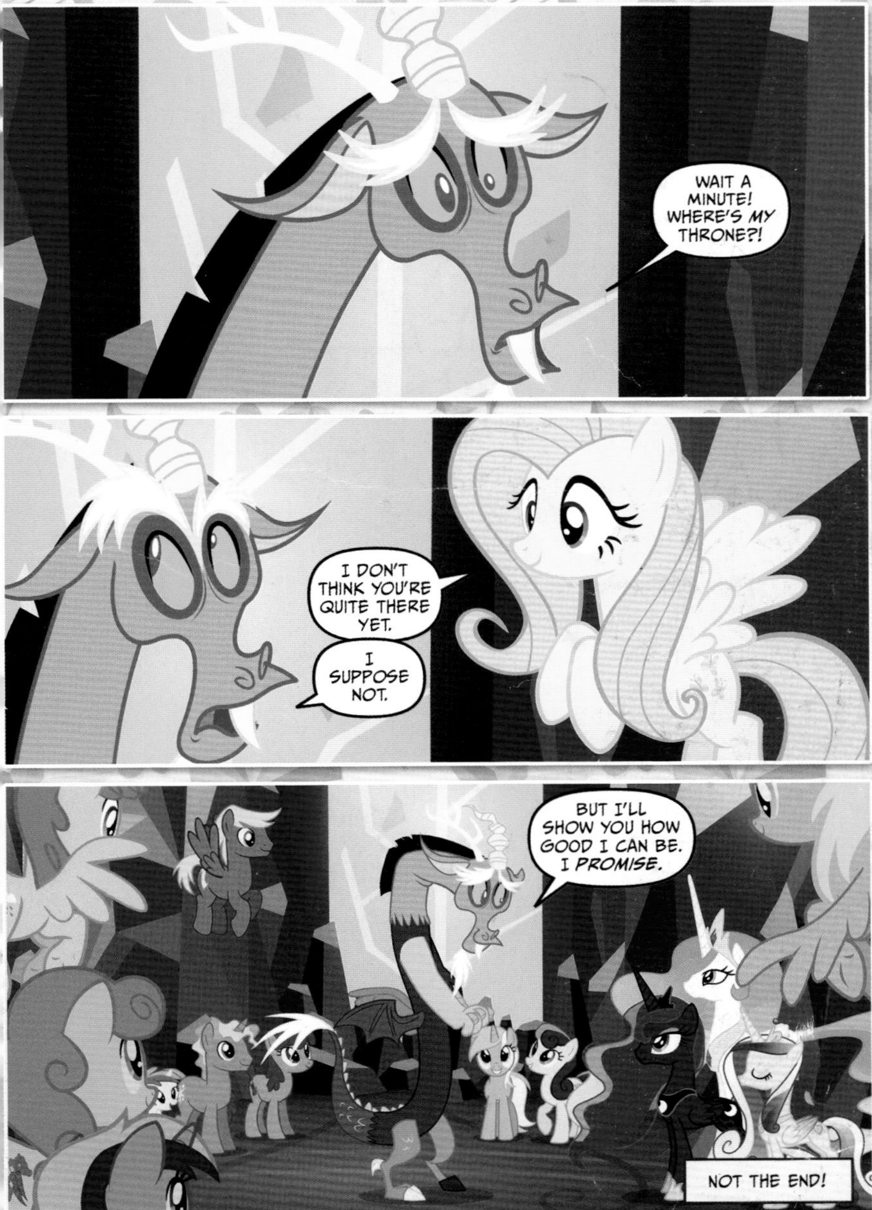
WAIT A MINUTE! WHERE'S *MY* THRONE?!
I DON'T THINK YOU'RE QUITE THERE YET.
I SUPPOSE NOT.
BUT I'LL SHOW YOU HOW GOOD I CAN BE. I *PROMISE.*
NOT THE END!

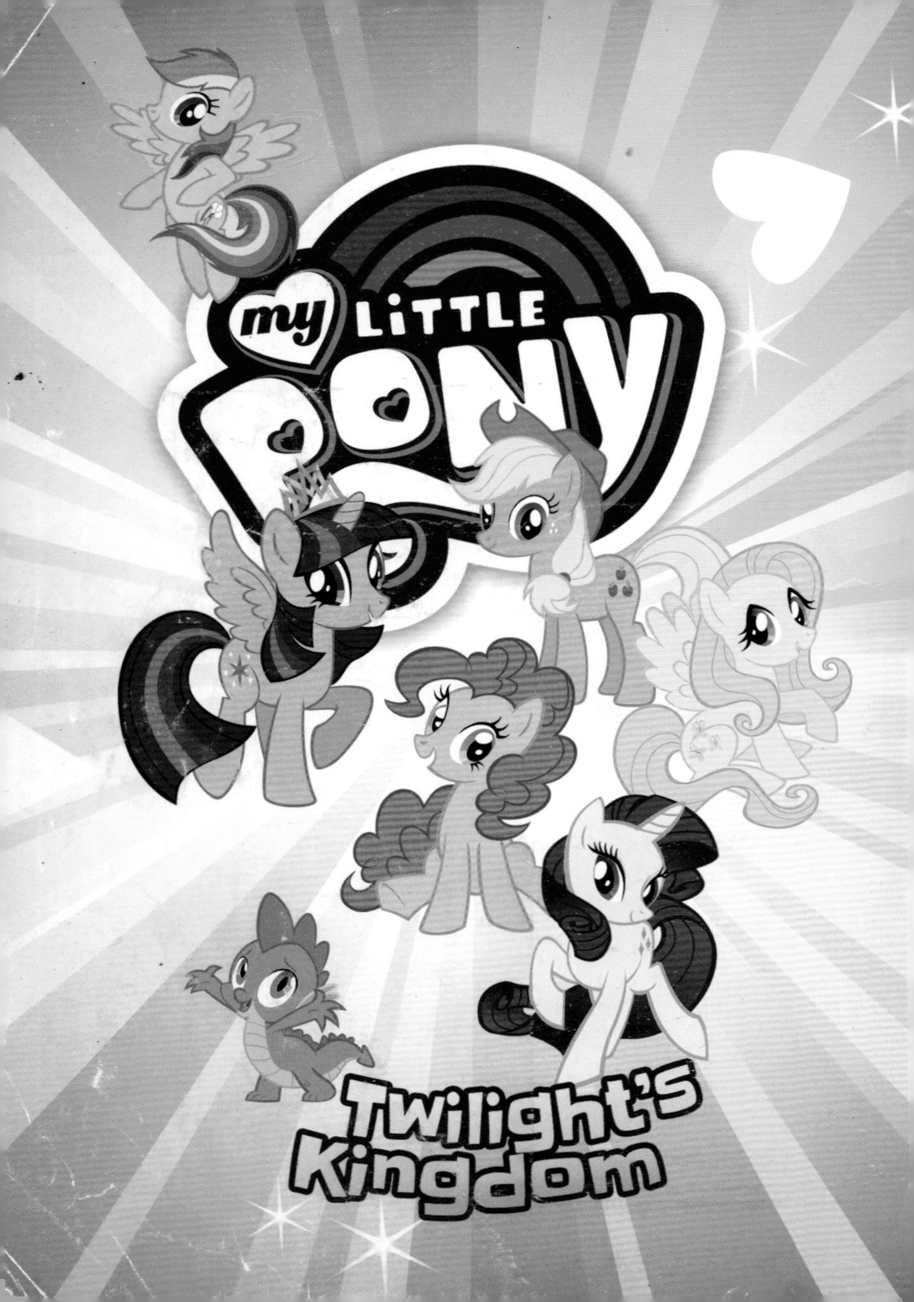
my LITTLE PONY
Twilight's Kingdom